EDWARD MARSTON was born and brought up in South Wales. A full-time writer for over thirty years, he has worked in radio, film, television and the theatre and is a former chairman of the Crime Writers' Association. Prolific and highly successful, he is equally at home writing children's books or literary criticism, plays or biographies. *The Repentant Rake* is the third book in the series featuring architect Christopher Redmayne and the Puritan Constable Jonathan Bale, set in Restoration London.

www.edwardmarston.com

By Edward Marston

a&b

The Repentant Rake

EDWARD MARSTON

This edition first published in 2010 by
Allison & Busby Limited
13 Charlotte Mews
London, W1T 4EJ
www.allisonandbusby.com

A CIP catalogue record for this book is available from
the British Library.

First published in the UK in 2001.

10 9 8 7 6 5 4 3 2 1

ISBN 978-0-7490-0808-6

Typeset in 10.5/15 pt Sabon by
Allison & Busby Ltd.

The paper used for this Allison & Busby publication
has been produced from trees that have been legally sourced
from well-managed and credibly certified forests.

Printed and bound in the UK by
CPI Bookmarque, Croydon, CR0 4TD

*In memory of
Arthur Heale, friend and historian,
who first took me down the long road into the past.*

*'The pleasure past, a threat'ning doubt remains,
That frights th'enjoyer with succeeding pains.'*

A Satyr Against Mankind: Lord Rochester

CHAPTER ONE

'London is a veritable cesspool!' he said, banging the table with a bunched fist. 'A swamp of corruption and crime.'

Christopher shrugged. 'It has its redeeming features, Sir Julius.'

'Does it?'

'I think so.'

'Well, I've never seen any of them. A capital city should be the jewel of the nation, not a running sewer. The place disgusts me, Mr Redmayne. It's full of arrogant fools and strutting fops. Babylon was a symbol of decency compared to it. Immorality runs riot in London. Whores and rogues people its streets. Drunkards and gamesters haunt it by night. Foul disease eats into its vitals. And the worst villains of all are those who sit in Parliament and allow this depravity to spread unchecked.'

The tirade continued. Christopher Redmayne listened

patiently while his host unburdened himself of his trenchant views. Sir Julius Cheever was not a man to be interrupted. He charged into a conversation like a bull at a gate and it was wise to offer him no further obstruction. Sir Julius was a wealthy farmer, big, brawny, opinionated and forthright. Now almost sixty, he bore the scars of war with honour on his rubicund face but it was his wounded soul that was now on display. The oak table was pounded once again. Eyes flashed.

'Why, in the bowels of Christ, did we let this happen?' he demanded. 'Did we spill all that blood to end up with something even worse than we had before? Has there been no progress at all? London is nothing but a monument to sin.'

'Then I am bound to wonder why you wish to build a house there, Sir Julius,' said Christopher gently. 'Given your low opinion of the capital, I would have thought you'd shun rather than seek to inhabit the place.'

'Necessity, Mr Redmayne. Necessity drives me there.'

'Against your will, by the sound of it.'

'My conscience has subdued my will.'

Christopher found it difficult to believe that anything could subdue Sir Julius Cheever's will. He positively exuded determination. Once set on a course of action, he would not be deflected from it. Evidently, his obstinacy and blunt manner would not make him an easy client but Christopher was prepared to make allowances. The commission appealed to him. In the interests of securing it, he was prepared to tolerate the old man's rasping tongue and uncompromising views.

'Let me explain,' said Sir Julius, legs apart and hands on

his hips. 'I'm an unrepentant Parliamentarian and I don't care who knows it. I fought at Naseby, Bristol, Preston, Dunbar and Worcester with the rank of colonel. You can see the results,' he added, indicating the livid scar on his cheek, the healed gash above one eye and the missing ear. 'The Lord Protector saw fit to reward me with a knighthood and I was grateful. Not that I agreed with everything he did, mark you, because I did not and he was left in no doubt about that. I favoured deposition of the king, not his execution. That was a cruel mistake. We are still paying for it.'

'You spoke of conscience, Sir Julius.'

'That is what is taking me to London.'

'For what reason?'

'To begin the process of cleansing it, of course. To root out vice before it takes too firm a hold. I'm not a man to stand back when there's important work to do, Mr Redmayne. I have a sense of duty.'

'I can see that.'

'Parliament needs people like me. Honest, upstanding, God-fearing men who will lead the fight against the creeping evil that has invaded our capital. I will shortly be elected as one of the members for the county of Northampton and look to knock a few heads together when I get to Westminster.'

Christopher smiled. 'I wish that I could see you in action, Sir Julius.'

'Fighting is in my blood. I'll not mince my words.'

'You'll cause quite a stir in the seat of government.'

'The seat of government deserves to be kicked hard and often.' Sir Julius gave a harsh laugh then stopped abruptly to pluck at his moustache.

They were in the parlour of the Cheever farmhouse in Northamptonshire. It was a big, sprawling, timber-framed structure, built with Tudor solidity but little architectural inspiration. The room was large, the oak floor gleaming and the bulky items of furniture suggesting money rather than taste. Christopher suspected that the place had looked identical for at least half a century. Sir Julius Cheever belonged there. He had the same generous dimensions, the same ignorance of fashion and the same hopelessly dated air. Yet there was something strangely engaging about him. Beneath the surface bluster, Christopher detected an essentially good man, given to introspection and animated by motives of altruism. He could see that Sir Julius would be a loyal friend but an extremely dangerous enemy.

Christopher was seated in a high-backed chair but his host remained on his feet. Stroking his moustache, Sir Julius studied his guest carefully before speaking.

'Thank you for coming so promptly, Mr Redmayne,' he said.

'Your letter implied urgency.'

'I make decisions quickly.'

'And are you firmly resolved to have a town house in London?'

'Now that I am to sit in Parliament, it is unavoidable.'

'There may be some delay, Sir Julius,' warned Christopher. 'Houses are not built overnight. When you first come to London, you will have to find other accommodation.'

Sir Julius waved a hand. 'That's all taken care of,' he said dismissively. 'My daughter, Brilliana, lives in Richmond with her dolt of a husband. I'll lodge with them until my own abode is complete. The sooner it's ready, the better.'

'I, too, can work quickly when required.'

'That's what I was told.'

'Does that mean you are engaging me to design your new house?'

'No, Mr Redmayne,' said the other. 'It means that I brought you here to gauge your fitness for the task. You are the third in line. It's only fair to tell you that your two predecessors were found seriously wanting.'

'You didn't care for their draughtsmanship?'

'It was their politics that I couldn't stomach.'

'I hope that I don't fall at the same hurdle, Sir Julius.' Christopher was puzzled. 'Before you put me to the test,' he said, 'may I please ask a question?'

'Of course.'

'How did you first become aware of my work?'

'Through the agency of a friend – Elijah Pembridge.'

Christopher was surprised. 'The bookseller?'

'I can read, you know,' said Sir Julius with a twinkle in his eye.

'Yes, yes, naturally. What surprises me is that someone so decidedly urban and bookish as Elijah Pembridge should number a country gentleman among his acquaintances.'

'I'm rather more than that, sir.'

'So I see.'

'Elijah tells me that you designed his new premises in Paternoster Row.'

'That's right, Sir Julius. The original shop was burnt to the ground in the Great Fire. It was a pleasing commission. He was a most obliging client.'

'And you, I understand, were an equally obliging architect. He found you polite and efficient, able to give sound advice yet willing to obey his wishes. Thanks to you, the place was built a month ahead of schedule.'

'Only because I chose a reliable builder.'

'Such men, I gather, are few in number.'

Christopher was circumspect. 'That's an exaggeration, Sir Julius. There are plenty of excellent builders in London but they are, for the most part, already engaged on the major projects that were necessitated by the Great Fire. Others, less scrupulous, have flocked to the capital. Speculators are the real problem,' he went on, a slight edge in his voice. 'Ruthless men who put commercial gain before architectural considerations. They throw up whole streets of houses in no time at all, augmenting their number by giving them narrow frontages and small gardens. Simplicity is their watchword, Sir Julius. They erect identical brick boxes for their clients. Whereas a true craftsman will build an individual dwelling.'

'That's what I require, Mr Redmayne.'

'Then I'll be happy to discuss the matter with you.'

'The plot of land is already secured.'

Christopher nodded. 'So you said in your letter, Sir Julius. I took the liberty of visiting the site. It's well chosen. You invested wisely.'

'Not for the first time, my young friend.'

'Oh?'

'I have an instinct that rarely lets me down.'

'You've bought property elsewhere?'

'From time to time, but I was not thinking of the purchase of land.' He took a step closer. 'The name of

Colonel Pride is not, I dare say, unknown to you.'

'Everyone has heard of Pride's Purge,' replied Christopher. 'His hostility to the House of Commons was given full vent when he expelled all those members from their seats. I fancy that he gained much satisfaction from that day's work.'

'Tom Pride and I fought together,' said Sir Julius, 'but our friendship did not end there. We went into business together. Colonel Pride was head of a syndicate that secured a contract to victual the Navy. I was one of his partners.' He gave a complacent smile. 'As I told you, farming is only one string to my bow.'

Christopher was grateful for the information. He had known that he had heard of Sir Julius Cheever before but could not recall when and in what context. His memory was now jogged. Sir Julius had been mentioned in connection with the Navy.

'My brother, Henry, dealt with your syndicate, I believe,' he said.

Sir Julius shook his head. 'Henry Redmayne? Don't know the fellow.'

'He holds a position at the Navy Office.'

'Does he?'

'Henry handled the victualling contracts at one point.'

'They were very profitable, in spite of a few ups and downs. So,' said Sir Julius, appraising him afresh. 'You have a brother, do you? Any other siblings?'

'None, I fear.'

'And no family of your own, I'd guess. You have the look of a single man.'

Christopher grinned. 'Is it that obvious, Sir Julius?'

'There's an air of independence about you.'

'Some might call it neglect.'

'Why have you never married? Lack of opportunity?'

'Money is the critical factor,' admitted Christopher. 'I'm still making my way in my profession and have yet to establish a firm enough foundation to my finances. A husband should be able to offer a wife security.'

'Quite so,' agreed the other. 'Romantic impulse is all very well but a full purse is the best guarantee of a happy marriage. That's the one asset my son-in-law does actually possess. Lancelot has little else in his favour.' He gave a nod of approbation. 'You're a practical man, Mr Redmayne. I admire that in you. And after Elijah's recommendation, I have no qualms about your ability as an architect. That brings us to the crucial question.'

'Does it, Sir Julius?'

'Yes, my young friend. What are your politics?'

Christopher gave another shrug. 'I have none.'

'None at all?'

'Not when I'm working for a client.'

'You have no views, no opinions on the state of the nation?'

'Only on the state of its architecture, Sir Julius.'

'Every sane man takes a stand on politics.'

'Then I'm the exception to the rule,' said Christopher with a disarming smile, 'for I find politics a divisive issue. Why look for a reason to fall out, Sir Julius? If we can come to composition over the design of a new house, that is all that matters. My politics are immaterial. You'd be employing me as an architect, not appointing me as the next Lord Chancellor.'

Sir Julius was so taken aback by the rejoinder that he goggled for a full minute. Surprise then gave way to amusement and he emitted a peal of laughter that filled the room. It was at that precise moment that his daughter entered. Susan Cheever was clearly unaccustomed to seeing her father shake with mirth. She blinked in astonishment at him. Christopher rose swiftly from his seat, partly out of politeness but mainly to get a clearer view of the beautiful young woman who had just sailed in through the door. Susan Cheever was a revelation. A slim, shapely creature of medium height, she had none of her father's salient features. For all his eminence, he was patently a son of the soil, but she seemed to have come from a more ethereal domain. It was the luminous quality of her skin that caught Christopher's eye. It glowed in the bright sunlight that was flooding in through the windows. When she spoke, her voice was soft and melodious.

'I wondered if your guest would be dining with us, Father?' she asked.

'Oh, yes,' he replied firmly. 'Mr Redmayne will not only be gracing our table at dinner, he'll be here for the rest of the day. Mr Redmayne will need a bed for the night as well,' he decided. 'I think I've found the right man at last, Susan. He's just made the most politic remark about politics.'

Sir Julius laughed again but Christopher ignored him. His gaze was fixed on Susan Cheever. Attired in a dress of blue satin whose close-fitting bodice advertised her figure, she looked delightfully incongruous in a rambling farmhouse. Their eyes locked for the briefest moment but it was enough to give him a fleeting surge of excitement. Offering him a token smile, she left the room. Her father's comment carried with it the seal of approval. If he were being invited to stay the night, Christopher must have secured the lucrative commission. He was thrilled. He would not only be designing a house for an interesting client, he would have the pleasure of getting to know Sir Julius Cheever's younger daughter. The long ride to Northamptonshire had been more than worthwhile.

He could still smell the fire. It was almost two years since the fateful night when he had been hauled from his bed to fight the conflagration but Jonathan Bale still had that whiff of smoke in his nostrils. As he walked along the dark street, he could even feel the heat striking up at his feet again from the scorched ground. His clothing became an oven. Sweat began to trickle. Invisible smoke clouded his eyes. He was untroubled. Jonathan was used to being tormented by such memories. When he heard the crackling of the flames and the screams of hysteria, he shook his head to dismiss the familiar sounds. The Great Fire would burn on in his mind for ever. He had learnt to live with it.

'Will it ever be the same again?' he asked.

'What?' grunted his companion.

'Our ward.'

'No, Jonathan. We've seen the last of the real Castle Baynard.'

'Much has been rebuilt, Tom.'

'Yes, but not in the same way. We lost homes, inns, churches, warehouses and the castle itself. How can we ever replace all that?'

'They're doing their best.'

'I preferred it the way it was.'

Tom Warburton was a tall, stringy, humourless man. Jonathan was dour by nature but he appeared almost skittish by comparison with his fellow constable. A middle-aged bachelor with no interests outside his work, Warburton took his duties seriously and discharged them with grim commitment. He was an effective officer of the law but he lacked sensitivity and compassion. Jonathan Bale, by contrast, cared for the inhabitants of his ward and took the trouble to befriend many of them. While he was firm yet fair with offenders, Warburton was merciless. Given the choice, the petty criminals of the area would always prefer to be arrested by Jonathan. The bruises did not last quite so long.

It was late. Their patrol took them through the darkest parts of the district. Candles burnt in an occasional window and a passing link boy brought a sudden blaze of light but they were, for the most part, making their way along familiar streets by instinct. Warburton was not a talkative man. He liked to keep his ears pricked for the sound of danger. It was Jonathan who always initiated conversation.

'A quiet night,' he noted.

'Too quiet.'

'Most people are abed.'

'But not all of them with their lawful wives and husbands,' said Warburton sourly. 'The leaping houses will be as full as ever.'

'We can't close them all down, Tom. As soon as we raid one place, another opens up elsewhere. And no matter how big the fine, they always have money to pay it. Vice, alas, is a rewarding trade.'

'I'd like to reward every whore with a long term behind bars.'

'It's not only the women who are to blame,' said Jonathan. 'Many are driven to sell their bodies by poverty or desperation. I could never condone what they do but I am bound to feel sorry for them. It's their clients who are the real culprits. Midnight lechers, buying their pleasures at will. If there were no demand, the brothels would not exist. And if there were no brothels,' he added darkly, 'there'd be a lot less drunkenness and affray. In the company of such women, men are always given to excess.'

Warburton said nothing. His ears had picked up the noise of a distant altercation. Voices were raised in anger, then a fight seemed to develop. The two men quickened their pace. By the time they reached Great Carter Lane, however, the argument had resolved itself. One of the disputants had been knocked to the ground outside an inn and the other had rolled off cursing into the night. Before the constables could reach him, the downed man dragged himself to his feet and scuttled away down an alley. Violence was a regular event inside the Blue Dolphin. This particular row had spilt out into the street to be settled with bare fists. All that Jonathan and Warburton could do was exchange a sigh of resignation and continue on their way. There would be plenty of other brawls in their ward before the night was done.

They were walking down Bennet's Hill when Jonathan felt something brush against his leg. It was Warburton's dog, a busy little terrier that always accompanied its master on his rounds. Sam was an unusual animal. He never barked. During a patrol such as this, he would disappear for long periods then materialise out of thin air when least expected. Warburton treated the dog with a mute affection. It was both his scout and his bodyguard. If his master were attacked, Sam would come to his aid at once. More than one vicious criminal had been put to flight by those sharp teeth. Having returned for a moment, the dog scampered off down the hill and merged with the shadows. Jonathan knew where he was going. Their walk would take them down to Paul's Wharf and there were always vermin to catch beside the river. Sam would be in his element. When they saw him next, he would be holding a dead rat in his jaws.

Rebuilding had begun in earnest. Since the Great Fire, twelve hundred houses had already sprung up along with inns, warehouses and other buildings. Churches had yet to be replaced. Almost ninety had been destroyed by the blaze, including the church of St Benet Paul's Wharf. As they went past its charred remains, Jonathan recalled how he had fought in vain alongside others to save it from the flames. The loss of its churches was a bitter blow to the ward. While religion slept, Jonathan believed, sinfulness came in to take its place. He was still musing on the impact of the fire when they finally reached the wharf. Sam was waiting for them. They could pick him out in the moonlight. As they got closer, they saw that he held something between his teeth.

Jonathan assumed it would be another victim from the rat population but he was wrong. When the dog trotted across to his master and laid his trophy at Warburton's feet, it was no dead animal this time. What the constable picked up was a man's shoe with a silver buckle on it. It was too dark to examine the item properly but he could tell from the feel of it that it was the work of an expensive shoemaker. He handed it to Jonathan who came to the same conclusion. Tongue out and panting quietly, Sam knew exactly what to do. He swung round and loped away, leading them to the place where he had found the discarded shoe. Jonathan and Warburton followed him down to a warehouse not far from the water's edge. The Thames was lapping noisily at the wharf, giving off its distinctive odour. A faint breeze was blowing. Sam went along the side of the warehouse, then stopped to sniff at something in a dark corner. Jonathan was the first to reach him. The dog had led them to the other shoe, but it was different from the first. It was still worn by its owner, who lay hunched up on the ground. Jonathan bent down to carry out a cursory inspection of the man, but he had already sensed what he would find. His voice took on urgency.

'Fetch some light, Tom,' he ordered. 'I think he's dead.'

CHAPTER TWO

Christopher Redmayne was delighted that he was leaving with a new commission under his belt but sorry that he had not had the opportunity to become more closely acquainted with his client's younger daughter. Susan Cheever had made a deep impression upon him, and though he told himself that someone that attractive must have a whole bevy of male admirers in pursuit of her, perhaps even a potential husband in view, it did not prevent him from thinking about her obsessively when he was alone. The problem was that he was very rarely on his own to luxuriate in his thoughts. Sir Julius Cheever was a possessive man who hardly let his guest out of his sight. Susan had joined them for dinner on the previous day but said little and left well before the meal was finished. Her appetite simply could not accommodate the fricassee of rabbits and chicken, the leg of mutton, the three carps in a dish, the roasted pigeons, the lamprey pie and the dish of anchovies that were served. Long before the sweetmeats arrived, she had made a polite excuse and withdrawn from the table.

Dinner had continued well into the afternoon. Sir Julius ate heartily and drank deeply from the successive bottles of wine. Christopher simply could not keep pace with him. Besides, he wished to keep his head clear for their business discussion and that ruled out too much alcohol. The huge meal eventually told on his host and he fell asleep in the middle of a long diatribe for all of ten minutes, waking up with a start to complete the very sentence he had abandoned and clearly unaware that there had been any hiatus. Sir Julius knew exactly what he wanted in the way of a town house. His specifications were admirably clear and Christopher was duly grateful. Previous clients had not always been so decisive. Sir Julius brought a military precision to it all, tackling the project with the controlled eagerness of a commander issuing orders to his army on the eve of battle. When the long oak table in the dining room had been cleared, he stood over the young architect while the latter made some preliminary sketches.

It had been a long but productive day. Susan joined them again for a light supper and Christopher gained more insight into her relationship with her father. She chided him softly for keeping his guest up too late yet showed real concern when he complained about pain from an old war wound in his leg. As the night had worn on, Sir Julius came to look more tired, more lonely and, for the first time, more vulnerable. He turned to maudlin reminiscences of his deceased wife. Susan interrupted him, soothing and censuring him at the same time, bathing him in sympathy while insisting that it was unwise for him to stay up so late. It was almost as if she had taken on the role of her mother. Christopher was touched by the unquestioning affection she displayed towards Sir Julius and impressed by the way she handled him. His only regret was that the closeness between father and daughter obviated any chance of time alone with Susan. Retiring to his bed, an ancient four-poster with a lumpy mattress, he slept fitfully.

After breakfast next morning, on the point of departure, he finally had a brief conversation alone with her. Sir Julius went off to berate a tardy servant and the two of them were left at the table. Christopher had rehearsed a dozen things to say to her in private but it was Susan Cheever who spoke first.

'I must apologise for my father, Mr Redmayne,' she said with a wan smile. 'His manner is a trifle abrupt at times.'

'Not at all, Miss Cheever.'

'When you get to know him, you'll see that he has a gentler side to him as well.'

'I see it embodied in you,' said Christopher with an admiring smile. 'Apologies are unnecessary. I find Sir Julius a most amenable client. It will be a pleasure to work for him.' He fished gently for information. 'Your father mentioned a second daughter with a house in Richmond.'

'Yes, Mr Redmayne,' she said. 'My sister, Brilliana.'

'I understand that he'll be staying there in due course.'

'Until the new house is built.'

'That will be done with all haste.'

'I'm glad to hear it.'

'Will you be travelling to London with your father, Miss Cheever?' he asked, raising a hopeful eyebrow.

'Occasionally,' she replied. 'Why do you ask?'

'Because Sir Julius is a different man with you beside him.'

'In what way?'

Christopher was tactful. 'He seems to mellow.'

'It's largely exhaustion.'

'I marvel at the way you look after him so well.'

'Someone has to, Mr Redmayne,' she sighed. 'Since my mother died, he's been very restless. It's one of the reasons he wishes to take up a political career. It will keep him occupied. Father pretends to hate London yet he wants be at the centre of events.'

'What about you, Miss Cheever?' he said, keen to learn more about her.

'Me, sir?'

'Do you relish the idea of being at the centre of events?'

'Oh, no,' she said solemnly. 'I have no love for big cities. To be honest, they rather frighten me. I was born and brought up in this beautiful countryside. Why surrender that for the noise and filth of London?'

'London has its own attractions.'

'I know. My sister Brilliana never ceases to talk about them in her letters. She and her husband frequently take the coach into the city. Brilliana seems to keep at least three dressmakers in business.'

'Is her husband engaged in politics?'

'Lancelot?' She gave a little laugh. 'Heavens, no! Lancelot is no politician. He's far too nice a man to entertain the notion of entering Parliament. My brother-in-law is a gentleman of leisure. Running his estate and pampering Brilliana take up all his time.'

'Talking of estates,' said Christopher, glancing towards the window, 'you must have a sizeable one here in Northamptonshire.'

'Almost a thousand acres.'

'Sir Julius is obviously a highly successful farmer.'

'He inherited the land from my grandfather and extended it over the years.'

'It's a pity that he has nobody else to carry on the good work. Farming runs in families. Sons take over from fathers. But since you have no brother the Cheever name may have to make way for someone else.' Susan turned away in mild embarrassment. Christopher was immediately contrite. 'Have I said something to offend you?' he asked. 'I do apologise. It was not intentional, I promise you. In any case, Miss Cheever, it's none of my business. Please forgive me. I'd not upset you for the world.'

She met his gaze. 'There's nothing to forgive.'

'I made a crass remark and I'm truly sorry.'

'How were you to know, Mr Redmayne?' she said, getting to her feet. 'You touched unwittingly on a delicate subject. I do have a brother, as it happens, but Gabriel is not interested in taking on the estate. He has...' She searched for the appropriate words. 'He has other priorities, I fear.'

'Your father made no mention of a son.'

'Nor will he,' she warned. 'And I beg you to make no reference to Gabriel. It would cause Father the deepest pain. To all intents and purposes, he has no son.'

'Yet I suspect that you still have a brother?' he said quietly. Susan Cheever coloured slightly and bit her lip. She took a deep breath. 'I think that it's time for you to go, Mr Redmayne.'

Sarah Bale was a woman of bustling energy. Rising shortly after dawn, she cleaned the downstairs rooms, roused her children from their beds, gave them breakfast, took them off to their petty school and, since the weather was fine, returned to make a start on the washing that she took in to supplement the family income. By the time her husband came into the kitchen, she was humming contentedly to herself, her arms deep in a tub of soapy water. Suppressing a yawn, Jonathan crossed to give her a perfunctory kiss of greeting on the forehead.

'Awake at last, are you?' she teased.

'I was late getting back last night, my love.'

'I know.'

'Did I wake you?'

'Only for a moment.'

'I tried not to, Sarah.'

'You're not the quietest man when you move around the house,' she said, drying her hands on a piece of cloth so that she could turn to him. 'Your breakfast is all ready, Jonathan. Sit down. You look as if you need it.'

Lowering himself on to a chair, he gave a nod of agreement. The events of the night had turned a routine patrol into a harrowing experience and left him drained. When he climbed into bed, he had fallen instantly asleep. Now, after barely three or four hours, he was up to face a new day. Bread and cheese lay on the platter before him. Sarah put a solicitous hand on his shoulder as she poured him a cup of whey.

'Did you hear the children?'

'No, my love.'

'Then you must have been very tired. They made so much noise this morning, especially Oliver. I had to be very stern with him.'

'What was the problem?'

'The usual one,' she said, putting the jug on the table and sitting opposite him. 'He didn't want to go to school. And because Oliver complained, Richard joined in.'

'School is important. They must learn to read and write.'

'That's what I told them.'

'They don't understand how lucky they are to be able to have proper schooling. I didn't at their age, Sarah. My parents couldn't afford it.' He took a first bite of bread. 'I had to pick things up as I went along. My father was a shipwright for thirty years and never learnt to read properly. When I took up the trade, none of the apprentices could even write his own name.'

'*You* could, Jonathan. And you'd taught yourself to read the Bible.'

He took a swig of whey. 'I wanted to be able to read the names of the ships I was helping to build. Knowledge gives you power. You don't have to rely on others. The boys must realise what an advantage they'll have in life by being able to read, write and add up properly.'

'I keep saying that.'

'Let me have a word with them.'

'I'd be grateful.'

He addressed himself to his meal and munched away in silence. Pouring herself a cup of whey, his wife sipped it and watched him. Jonathan was gloomy and preoccupied. Sarah could see that something was troubling him but she knew better than to question him too closely about his work. It was a difficult and often dangerous job and he tried to leave it behind whenever he stepped over the threshold. Home was his sanctuary, free from the worries of the outside world. It was a place where he could relax and recover from the strains of his occupation. When he chose to confide in her, Sarah was always willing to listen but she did not prompt him.

She waited patiently until he had cleared his platter. 'More bread?' she offered.

'No, thank you.'

'I have a fresh loaf.'

'I can't stay, my love,' he said, getting to his feet. 'I have to pay an early call.'

'When will I expect you back?'

'For dinner, I hope. I'll speak to the boys then.'

'Good. They listen to you.'

He was about to leave the kitchen when he noticed the quiet concern in her eyes. Feeling that he owed her some kind of explanation, he crossed over to help her up from the table. He pursed his lips as he pondered.

'I was with Tom Warburton last night,' he said at length.

'How is he?'

'As melancholy as ever.'

'I wondered where you'd got that grim look on your face.'

Jonathan smiled. 'Tom is not the most cheerful soul at the best of times. But then,' he continued, his expression hardening, 'there was little to be cheerful about. We found a dead body.'

'Oh dear!'

'To be truthful, it was Sam who actually found it. Tom's little dog. He was sniffing around a warehouse near Paul's Wharf. Just as well, in a way. We'd have walked right past the place and not known the poor devil was there.'

'Who was he?'

'I've no idea, Sarah. That's why I'm going to the morgue this morning. To see what I can find out about the man. One thing is certain,' he said, gritting his teeth. 'He did not die a natural death.' He became proprietorial. 'I don't like murder in my ward. We have enough ugly messes to wipe up around here without finding corpses as well. This crime needs to be solved quickly. I'll make sure of that.'

'Be careful,' she said, reaching out to squeeze his arm.

'I always am.'

'You're too brave for your own good sometimes.'

He gave a weary smile. 'The bravest thing I ever did was to ask you to marry me, Sarah, and you were foolish enough to accept. That shows how lucky I am.'

'Lucky and much loved,' she said, kissing him. 'Remember that.'

'How could I ever forget?'

He gave her a warm hug, then left the room. A minute later, he was leaving the house in Addle Hill to begin the long walk to the morgue. All trace of fatigue was shaken off now. An officer of the law involved in a murder investigation, Jonathan Bale was as alert and zealous as ever.

* * *

Forsaking the safety of travelling companions and anxious to get back to London as soon as possible, Christopher Redmayne rode south at a steady canter. He reproached himself bitterly for causing Susan Cheever dismay with a tactless remark and believed that he had destroyed all hope of a closer acquaintance with her. At the same time, he had elicited an intriguing piece of information about the family. Sir Julius Cheever had three children, one of whom had been his male heir. What provoked him to disown and, presumably, to disinherit his son, Christopher did not know, but it had to be something serious. Susan, by contrast, had not discarded her brother and he was bound to wonder if the two of them were still in contact. Clearly, it was a source of dispute between father and daughter. He came to understand Sir Julius's suppressed anger a little more. The death of his wife and the estrangement of his son were personal sorrows to be added to the profound distaste he felt for the Restoration and its consequences. The sense of loss was unendurable. It soured him. Sir Julius would be a fiery and malcontented Member of Parliament.

He might also be a cantankerous client. Christopher accepted that. There were consolations. Not only had the young architect secured a valuable commission to design a house in London, Sir Julius had insisted on giving him a generous down-payment in cash to encourage him. The money was safely stowed away in Christopher's satchel along with the preliminary drawings he had made. There was an additional feature that brought him particular pleasure. This was the first major project he had won entirely on his own merit. His brother, Henry, had been instrumental in finding him his first three clients and, though one of the houses was never actually built, the two mansions that were completed served as a lasting tribute to his talent. By comparison with these undertakings, the design of a new bookshop for Elijah Pembridge was a relatively simple affair that had brought in much-needed money but would hardly enhance his reputation. For that reason, he did not list it among his achievements. Henry Redmayne had been indirectly responsible for that commission as well but he had no connection whatsoever with Sir Julius. Much as he loved his brother, Christopher was grateful to be striking out on his own at last.

Susan Cheever had been right. Northamptonshire was a beautiful county. In the hectic dash north, Christopher had not taken the trouble to admire the scenery on the way. Now, with two days of hard riding ahead of him, he determined to repair that omission. Heavily wooded in some areas, Northamptonshire was given over almost exclusively to agriculture. The soil was rich but less than ideal for ploughing and grain production, so there was a predominance of dairy farming and sheep-rearing. Herds of cattle and flocks of sheep seemed to be everywhere. Christopher passed the occasional windmill as well. What he noticed was the absence of any major rivers. Since it was largely denied direct access to the sea by means of navigable water, Northamptonshire was curiously isolated. The lack of a major road through the heart of the county was another element that set it apart from its neighbours. On the first stretch of his journey, Christopher was travelling along a small, winding, rutted track. It was only when he crossed the border into Bedfordshire that he found a wider and more purposeful road.

Not long after noon, he stopped at an inn for refreshment. The Jolly Shepherd was a welcoming hostelry that offered good food and strong drink to its customers. A large party of travellers, all men, occupied three of the tables. Christopher found a seat in the corner and sampled the game pie, washing it down with a tankard of beer. A tall, bearded, well-dressed man in his thirties sauntered across to him with an easy smile.

'May I share your table, my friend?' he asked.

'Be my guest,' said Christopher pleasantly.

'I'm much obliged, sir.' The man sat opposite him and set his own tankard down. 'It's rather quieter at this end of the room. Our fellow travellers are in raucous mood.'

Even as he spoke, a jesting remark set the entire party roaring in appreciation. Judging by the amount of food and drink in front of them, they would be there for some time. They were patently making the most of their stop.

'Where are you heading?' asked the man.

'London,' said Christopher.

'So are our noisy neighbours. Fall in with them and you'll have a safer journey.'

'I'll make better speed on my own, I think.'

'Do you have a good horse?'

'An excellent one.'

'Then I'll bear you company part of the way, if I may,' offered the other. 'My home is near Hertford. Could you tolerate me alongside you until then?'

'I believe so.'

The man beamed. 'That settles it.' He extended a hand. 'Zachary Mills at your service.'

'Pleased to make your acquaintance, sir,' said Christopher, shaking his hand. 'My name is Christopher Redmayne.'

'Have you ridden far?'

'I had business in Northamptonshire.'

'Ah, so did I, Mr Redmayne. Sad business, as it happens. I was visiting my sick mother in Daventry. She is desperately ill but I like to think that I helped to sustain her while I was there. The doctor holds out little hope.'

'I'm sorry to hear that.'

'It comes to us all,' said Mills resignedly. He brightened at once. 'But I'll not burden you with my family problems. I'm so relieved to spend some time on the road with a gentleman. Some of these fellows,' he added, nodding in the direction of the three full tables, 'have yet to learn proper manners.' Another roar went up as a more uncouth jest was passed around. 'Do you take my point?'

'I do, Mr Mills.'

'I could see that you would.'

Zachary Mills was a pleasing companion, urbane, well-spoken and attentive. When he had ordered his own meal, he insisted on buying Christopher a second tankard of beer. The conversation was confined to neutral subjects and Mills made no attempt to pry into Christopher's personal affairs. The latter was grateful for that and glad that he would have someone to share the next stage of the journey. In the event of attack from highwaymen two swords were better than one, and Mills had the air of a man who knew how to use his blade. As time passed, however, the rowdiness increased among the other travellers and the two men left by tacit consent. They strolled towards the stables, talking amiably about the advantages of living in London, a city that Mills seemed to know extremely well. He had a sophistication that had been notably lacking among the other guests at the inn. Christopher warmed to him even more.

When they entered the stables, however, Mills's manner changed at once. Putting a hand in the small of Christopher's back, he pushed him so firmly that the latter stumbled to the ground. Christopher was on his feet at once, swinging round to face the other man and ready to demand the reason for the unwarranted shove. He found himself staring down the barrel of a pistol and his question was answered. The plausible friend was a cunning robber. Mills gave him a broad grin.

'You should have stayed with the others, Mr Redmayne. Safety in numbers.'

'I took you for a gentleman.'

'Why, so I am, good sir.'

'Indeed?'

'I extend every courtesy to the people I rob.'

Christopher was sarcastic. 'What would your sick mother say?'

'She's in no position to say anything, alas. She died several years ago.'

'Out of a sense of shame at her son, no doubt.'

'Do not vex me, Mr Redmayne,' cautioned the other. 'This pistol is loaded. All you have to do is remove that satchel and hand it over with your purse. I'll then be obliged to bind and gag you while I make good my escape. By the time that drunken crowd stumble out here and find you, I'll be well clear.'

'How will you tie me up?'

'I have rope in the saddlebags directly behind you.'

Christopher glanced over his shoulder. 'I see that you planned this very carefully, Mr Mills,' he said with grudging respect.

'I leave nothing to chance.'

'That remains to be seen.'

'I'd advise against any futile heroics.'

'I'll remember that,' said Christopher, weighing up the possibilities of escape. They were severely limited. 'May I ask why you singled me out?'

'The satchel gave you away, I'm afraid.'

'Did it?'

'Yes, my friend. In all the time we were at the table, you never once took it from round your neck. That means it contains something valuable.'

'It does. Something that I'll not part with easily.'

'Gold?'

'Drawings.'

Mills was sceptical. 'Drawings?'

'Correct, sir.'

'I've no time to play games, Mr Redmayne.'

'It's the truth. I'm an architect by profession and I've been visiting a client who wishes me to design a new house for him.' He patted his satchel. 'The preliminary sketches are in here. They'd be worthless to you and it's vital that I keep them.'

'That satchel contains more than a few drawings,' said

Mills, levelling the pistol at him. 'Hand it over or I'll be forced to take it from your dead body.'

Christopher shrugged. 'If you insist.'

'I do.'

'Then first let me prove that I'm a man of my word – unlike you, I may say.' Christopher opened the satchel to take out a piece of folded parchment. 'Here, see for yourself. A town house in the Dutch style, commissioned by Sir Julius Cheever.'

Mills took the parchment and flicked it open to glance at the various drawings. They were neat and explicit but he was still unconvinced. The pistol was turned in the direction of the satchel.

'I'll wager there's something else in there, Mr Redmayne, or you'd not have been nursing it like a baby throughout dinner. I'm wondering if this illustrious client of yours might not have given you some money on account. Is *that* what's in the satchel?'

'Alas no!' sighed Christopher. 'But have it, if you must.'

He slipped an arm through it and lifted the strap over his head. Mills glanced down at the drawings in his hand. It was a fatal mistake. Christopher moved at lightning speed, hurling the satchel into his face and diving straight at him, knocking him against one of the stalls with such force that the pistol dropped from his hand. It was no time for social niceties. Grabbing his adversary by the throat, Christopher pounded his head against the stout timber. Mills cursed, struggled and kicked but he was up against someone stronger and more determined. Christopher was annoyed at himself for being duped and that gave him extra power. When Mills tried to pull out his dagger, Christopher hurled him to the ground and stamped on his wrist until the weapon slid uselessly away. The commotion had upset the horses and they neighed in alarm, shifting in their stalls as the two men grappled together on the straw-covered floor.

It was when Mills's flailing body squirmed on to the drawings that Christopher really lost his temper. They were only early sketches but they represented something very important in his life and he was not going to have them treated with disrespect. With a burst of manic energy, he sat astride his opponent and subdued him with a relay of punches to the face, ignoring the pain in his knuckles until Mills lapsed into unconsciousness. Breathing heavily and with bruises of his own from the fight, he hauled himself to his feet. His first priority was to secure and silence the other man. When he found the rope in the saddlebags he used it to bind Zachary Mills to a solid oak post, then took out the latter's own handkerchief to use as a gag. Though his first instinct was to deliver the man up to the local constable, he saw the drawbacks. It would mean an interminable delay as he tried to explain what had happened and Mills would assuredly contest his version of events. Pain and humiliation would be the highwayman's punishment. Trussed up tightly and covered in blood, he would have time to repent of his folly in choosing the wrong victim. It might be hours before he was discovered and released by the departing travellers. Christopher would be in the next county by then.

Slipping the satchel over his shoulder, he recovered the pistol and dropped it in with the money from Sir Julius. He then picked up the parchment with the drawings on it and smoothed it out reverently. When Mills opened a bloodshot eye, Christopher showed no sympathy for him. He held up the parchment.

'You shouldn't have creased this,' he said. 'My drawings mean everything to me.'

CHAPTER THREE

Dead bodies held no fears for Jonathan Bale. He had looked on too many of them to be either shocked or revolted. Those dragged out of the River Thames were the worst, grotesque parodies of human beings, bloated out of all recognition and, when first hauled from the dark water, giving off a fearsome stink. The corpse that lay on the stone slab in the morgue was neither grossly misshapen nor especially malodorous. Wounds were minimal and the herbs liberally scattered in the cold chamber helped to smother the stench of death. Jonathan watched over the shoulder of the surgeon as he examined the body that had been found at Paul's Wharf on the previous night. He was struck by how peaceful the face of the deceased looked, less like that of a murder victim than someone who had passed gently away in his own bed.

'Interesting,' said the surgeon, peering at the cadaver's neck.

'What have you found, sir?' asked Jonathan.

'I'm not sure.'

'He's so young to die.'

'Still in his twenties, I'd say. Young, healthy and well muscled.'

Jonathan nodded. 'What a cruel waste of a life!'

Ecclestone continued his detailed inspection by the light of the candles. He was a small, thin, agitated man in his fifties with colourless eyes and a skin so pale that he might have climbed off one of the slabs in the morgue. A chamber of death was his natural milieu and he had divined most of its secrets. While the surgeon shifted his attention to the naked chest, Jonathan made his own appraisal. The young man had been undeniably handsome in life, the long brown hair well groomed and the carefully trimmed beard hinting at vanity. Smooth hands and clean fingernails confirmed that he was a stranger to any manual labour. There was an ugly red weal around his neck and bruising beneath his left ear. What looked like more bruises showed on the chest and stomach. Only one puncture wound was visible, close to the heart. The man's head lolled to one side. His cheeks had a ruddy complexion.

After a thorough examination, Ecclestone stood back and clicked his tongue.

'Well?' said Jonathan.

'He was strangled to death, Mr Bale.'

'I thought he was stabbed through the heart.'

'He was,' agreed Ecclestone, 'but only after he was dead. That's why there was so little blood. When death occurs, the circulation of the blood ceases.'

'Why stab a dead man?'

'To make absolutely sure that he was dead, I imagine.'

'The murderer took no chances,' noted Jonathan gruffly. 'He not only strangled and stabbed the poor fellow, he beat him about the body for good measure.'

'What makes you think that, Mr Bale?'

'Look at those bruises, sir.'

'That's exactly what I have done.' He squinted up at the constable. 'You were one of the men who found him, I understand.'

'That is so.'

'Then I'll warrant he was face down at the time.'

Jonathan was impressed. 'Why, so he was.'

'And had been for a little while, if my guess is correct.' He pointed a stick-like finger. 'Those are not bruises you can see, Mr Bale. When the blood stops being pumped around by the heart, it gradually sinks to the blood vessels in the lowest part of the torso. In this case, to the chest and stomach, which have a livid hue. After a certain amount of time, the purplish stains become fixed and take on the appearance of large bruises. I've seen it happen so often. No,' decided Ecclestone, gazing down at the corpse once more, 'I suspect that death was swift, if brutal. Someone took him unawares and strangled him from behind, putting a knee into the small of his back as he did so. If you turned him over, as I did before you came in, you'd see the genuine bruise that's been left there.'

'I take your word for it, sir.'

Ecclestone was brisk. 'So, the cause of death has been established. My work is done. It's up to others to discover the motive behind the murder.'

43

'It could hardly be gain,' argued Jonathan. 'There were valuable rings on his fingers and money in his purse.'

'It was fortunate that you came along before anyone else found him.'

'I know.'

'Do you have any notion who he might be?'

'None, sir. There was no means of identification on him.'

'Hardly an *habitué* of Paul's Wharf, that's for sure.'

'Quite,' said Jonathan. 'You won't find a suit of clothes as costly as that being worn in a warehouse. He's a gentleman of sorts with a family and friends who'll miss him before long. Someone may soon come forward.'

'And if they don't?'

'Then we'll have to track his identity down by other means.'

'Do you have any witnesses?'

'Not so far, sir. My colleague, Tom Warburton, is making enquiries near the murder scene this morning. When I spoke to him on my way here, he had had no success. It was late when we found the body. The wharf was deserted at that time of night. We are unlikely to find witnesses.'

'What was a man like this *doing* in such a place?'

'I don't think that he went there of his own accord, sir,' said Jonathan solemnly. 'I begin to wonder if he was killed elsewhere then dumped near that warehouse.'

'Why do you say that?'

'Because of the state of his apparel. When we found him last night, the back of his coat was covered in dirt, as if he'd been dragged along the ground by someone. There were a few stones caught up in the garment.' He took them from his pocket to show them to the surgeon. 'Do you see how small and bright they are, sir? You won't find any stones like this in the vicinity of the warehouse.'

'You've a sharp eye, Mr Bale.'

Jonathan put the stones away again. 'These may turn out to be useful clues.'

'I hope so. Well,' said Ecclestone, pulling the shroud over the corpse, 'I've told you what I've seen. A young man cut down in his prime by a sly assailant. A powerful one, too. The deceased would have fought for his life. Even with the element of surprise in his favour, only a strong attacker could have got the better of him.'

'Unless he was groggy with drink.'

'I detected no smell of alcohol in his mouth.'

'Oh.'

'You can rule that out.' The surgeon turned and walked out of the morgue. Jonathan followed him, glad to quit the dank and depressing chamber. When they stepped out into the fresh air, he took several deep breaths. Ecclestone paused to stare up at him.

'Is there anything else that I can tell you, Mr Bale?' he asked.

'No thank you, sir. You've been very helpful.'

'This was no random murder.'

'What do you mean?'

'It did not happen by accident on the spur of the moment. If you or I wished to strangle someone, we'd never do it as quickly and efficiently as that. Do you hear what I'm saying, Mr Bale?'

'I believe so. It was not the work of an amateur.'

'Exactly. This man has killed before. Often, probably.'

'A hired assassin?'

'Certainly not a person to turn your back on.' He licked his lips and closed one eye. 'You said earlier that you'd have to find out the victim's identity by other means.'

'The search will begin this very morning, sir.'

'Where?'

'Among the most exclusive shoemakers in the city.'

'Shoemakers?'

'Yes,' said Jonathan, producing the shoe that had been picked up at the wharf by an inquisitive dog. 'I want to find out who sold him this.'

'What happened to you, Mr Redmayne?' said Jacob in alarm. 'Your face is bruised and your coat is torn. Is that blood on your sleeve?'

'Yes, Jacob,' said Christopher, putting his satchel down and removing his coat, 'but you'll be pleased to know that it's not mine. A highwayman made the mistake of trying to rob me and had to be put in his place.' He flexed both hands. 'My knuckles still hurt from the fight.'

The servant blenched. 'A highwayman?'

'Don't worry. I learnt my lesson. On the following day, I put safety before valour and joined a party of travellers on their way to London. It slowed me right down but gave me an opportunity to nurse my wounds. I spent the second night at an inn with my companions. And here I am,' he announced, spreading his arms. 'Home again, with no harm done.'

'I wouldn't say that,' argued Jacob, inspecting his

master's coat. 'How on earth did you get involved with a highwayman in the first place?'

'Because I was reckless.'

'That's a kind word for it, sir.'

'I'm in the mood for kind words. Remember that.'

Christopher sat down at the table, and Jacob disappeared into the kitchen with the coat. When he came back, he brought a glass of brandy on a tray. Giving him a nod of gratitude, Christopher took the glass and sipped its contents.

'You sensed my needs exactly, Jacob,' he said.

'That's what I'm here for, sir.'

Jacob Vout was the only servant at the house in Fetter Lane. As a result, the old man had to combine the duties of cook, butler, valet and ostler, volunteering, for no extra payment, to assume a paternal role as well from time to time. Devoted to Christopher as a master, he occasionally treated him like an erring son and spoke with a candour that blurred the social divisions between them. Christopher tolerated it all with good humour. He knew that Jacob watched over him with a mingled sense of duty and affection, and he was reminded of the way that Susan Cheever treated her father, though he liked to think that he had none of the truculence of Sir Julius.

'I dare not ask if the visit was a success,' said Jacob tentatively. 'If you were set on by a villainous highwayman, it obviously was not.'

'A minor irritation, Jacob, that's all. It's out of my mind already. I've far more pleasant things to contemplate,' he said as he thought of Susan Cheever again. He manufactured a frown and rolled his eyes. 'But you're quite correct, Jacob.

The visit to Northamptonshire cannot, I fear, be construed as a success.'

'Oh. I'm disappointed to hear that.'

Christopher grinned. 'It was an absolute triumph!'

'Was it?'

'Without question.'

'Congratulations, sir!' said Jacob, rising to a smile.

'I've been commissioned to design a town house for Sir Julius Cheever,' he explained, taking the parchment from his satchel. 'Here are some early sketches I made for him. They're very rough but they give me a basis from which to work. More to the point, Jacob,' he added, shaking the satchel, 'my client insisted on giving me an advance payment. You'll be able to fill the larder and stock the wine cellar to your heart's content. We are solvent once more.'

'That's very heartening, Mr Redmayne.'

'Indeed, if everything goes to plan, this commission could make me a man of moderate wealth. That will be a welcome change. Most of the money I've earned so far as an architect went to paying off old debts. I may now actually be able to *save* a portion of what I earn. What a novelty that will be!'

'Indeed, sir.'

'This commission could be a turning point of my career.'

'As long as you stay clear of highwaymen.'

'Oh, I will, Jacob. I give you my word. For the first time in my life, I'll actually have something worth stealing.' He looked at the drawings. 'Apart from my talent, that is. But it's so good to be back,' he continued, draining the glass of brandy. 'Sir Julius was very hospitable but this is the only place where I can work properly. I can't wait to make a start on the design for his house.'

'You may have to delay that pleasure for a little while, sir.'

'Why?'

'Because there's an urgent request from your brother.'

'Henry? What does he want?'

'He wouldn't tell me,' said Jacob, exploring an ear with his finger, 'but, from his manner, I think that I can guess what brought him here.'

'Was he in a pit of misery or a state of elation?'

'Neither, sir.'

'Strange. Henry seems to shuttle continually between the two extremes.'

'Mr Redmayne had a hunted look. More a case of desperation than misery.'

'Oh dear! That suggests only one thing.'

'Exactly, sir. He came to borrow money.'

'He must have lost heavily at cards again,' said Christopher ruefully. 'Why does he play games at which he has such consistent ill luck? Henry has a good income from the Navy Office and a generous allowance from our father, yet he will fritter it away at a card table.' He glanced up. 'Did he ask where I was?'

'Repeatedly.'

'What did you tell him?'

'Very little, sir. As instructed.'

'Good man!'

'I merely said that you were visiting friends in the country.'

'No mention of Sir Julius Cheever, I hope?' Jacob shook his head. 'Excellent. I didn't want Henry getting wind of this latest commission until it was in the bag. It's bound to upset him. My brother seems to think that my career will only blossom if he has a controlling interest in it and, grateful as I am for the introductions he gave me to earlier clients, he must learn that I can act independently.'

'Mr Redmayne left a message for you.'

'Call on him immediately, no doubt.'

'Yes, sir.'

'At his home?'

'He'll be either there or at the Navy Office. He was most persistent.'

'Henry likes to keep me at his beck and call.'

'He drank three glasses of brandy while he was here.'

Christopher was surprised. 'Only three? That's abstemious by his standards. He must be out of sorts. Does he know when I was due back in London?'

Jacob smirked. 'I was remarkably hazy on that point.'

'That would have pleased him,' said Christopher with a chuckle. 'Well, Henry can stew in his own juice for a while. I have more important matters to consider than my brother's gambling debts. I have to design a wonderful new house. Clear the table, Jacob,' he said, getting to his feet and rubbing his hands with glee. 'I intend to start immediately.' His eye fell on the satchel. 'Oh, yes. And put that money in my strongbox, please, just in case my brother drops in unexpectedly.'

To the astonishment of his colleagues, Henry Redmayne arrived early and stayed late at the Navy Office, throwing himself into his work with unaccustomed enthusiasm. It was rare that he treated his sinecure as a full-time commitment and even rarer that he lost track of time while he was sifting his way through documents and writing a series of letters. It was mid-evening when he finally came out into Seething Lane. There was another unusual development. An ostentatious man by nature, he always dressed for effect in the latest fashion, but he was now attired in what for him was remarkably sober garb. He had even dispensed with his periwig, hiding his balding pate beneath a wide-brimmed hat. The acknowledged peacock of the Navy Office was now a rather subdued blackbird with ruffled feathers, barely able to take wing. Mounting his horse, he nudged the animal into a steady trot.

On any other evening, Henry would have been looking forward to carousing with his friends, playing cards, drinking heavily, then rolling from one house of resort to another. Dedicated to pleasure, his appetite was insatiable and his stamina legendary, but neither would be on display that night. As he rode towards home, a mask of concentration replaced his normal haughty expression and a furtive look was in his eyes. More than once during the journey, he glanced over his shoulder as if afraid that he was being followed. When he came out through Ludgate, he kicked the horse into a gentle canter, anxious to get back to the relative safety of his home. Like his brother, he was a tall, well-featured man with hair of a reddish hue, but the signs of dissipation set him completely apart from his sibling. Nor did he have anything of Christopher's affability and even temper. Henry Redmayne was a born sybarite, proud, arrogant, self-indulgent and, though capable of acts of true kindness, a confirmed egotist. None of those qualities were in evidence now. The overweening confidence had fled. He was a worried man, skulking home with terror in his heart.

Fleet Street merged into The Strand and he breathed a sigh of relief. He would be there in a mere minute or so. He longed to be able to close his front door behind him and shut out a world that had suddenly become hostile. He needed time in which to think and a refuge that was inviolable. Swinging right into Bedford Street, he caught sight of his house, but the further comfort it afforded was illusory. As he got closer, he saw two figures emerging from the door to stroll towards a waiting coach. Arthur Lunn and Peter Wickens were the last people he hoped to encounter, but a meeting was unavoidable now. The two men had seen him and hailed him aloud.

Henry reined in his horse and exchanged greetings with his two friends.

''Sdeath!' exclaimed Lunn. 'Where have you been, man? A funeral?'

'No, Arthur,' said Henry.

'Then why dress in those appalling clothes? Had I not recognised your face, I'd have taken you for a parson or a haberdasher.'

'Or a devilish pawnbroker,' suggested Wickens.

'I've been working at the Navy Office,' explained Henry over their brittle laughter. 'It's been a most tiring day so I beg you both to excuse me.'

Wickens was stunned. 'Do I hear aright? Henry Redmayne pleading fatigue?'

'It's never happened before,' said Lunn with a roguish grin. 'The ladies still speak of you with awe, Henry. I wish I had your reputation.'

'It's more than a reputation *you* need, Arthur,' warned Wickens.

Arthur Lunn chuckled at the coarse innuendo. He was a short, swarthy, pop-eyed man in his forties with flamboyant attire that accentuated rather than hid his portly frame. Ten years younger, Peter Wickens was slim, sharp-featured and decidedly elegant. Debauchery had left its mark indelibly on both of them. They were fit companions for the Henry Redmayne of old but they had picked the wrong day on which to call.

'We expected to see you at the King's House this afternoon,' said Wickens. 'They played *The Old Trooper* by John Lacy and it was a sight to see.'

'Yes,' agreed Lunn. 'You missed a treat, Henry. Young Nell took the part of Doll Troop and all but milked my epididymis with those wicked eyes of hers. She's the most impudent creature in London, I'll warrant.'

'I've heard others express the same view,' said Henry.

'You should have been there with us.'

'My presence was required elsewhere, Arthur.'

'Elsewhere?'

'Commitments at the Navy Office.'

'What sort of commitments?' asked Wickens peevishly. 'Since when have you put work before a visit to the theatre, Henry? It's so uncivil of you. We had a box all waiting. No matter,' he went on, flicking a wrist. 'You can make amends tonight. We plan to visit Mrs Curtis and her sirens.'

Henry lifted a hand. 'Then you must do so without me, Peter.'

'Nonsense, man!'

'I must regretfully decline your company tonight.'

'This is some jest, surely,' said Lunn irritably. 'I refuse to believe that I am hearing Henry Redmayne spurning an opportunity for endless hours of pleasure.'

'Nevertheless, you are,' insisted Henry.

'On what grounds?'

'Exhaustion and ill health.'

'You have a malady?'

'A headache that's afflicted me all day,' pretended Henry, touching his forehead with the back of his hand. 'It will pass in time if I lie down.'

'There's no better place for that than with Mrs Curtis,' observed Wickens with an oily smirk. 'Lie down there and one of her ladies will tease away your headache with long fingers. A night in the arms of Betty or Patience or the divine Hannah Marklew will cure you of any ailments.'

Lunn sniggered. 'Though they may give you another disease in return.'

Henry shook his head. 'I'll forego that delight, gentlemen.'

'Deny your closest friends?'

'I fear so, Arthur.'

They continued to try to persuade him to join them for a night of revelry but Henry was adamant. Nothing would make him stir outside the walls of his house. Lunn and Wickens were mystified. When they finally adjourned to their coach, they asked each other what could possibly be wrong with their friend. Rejection of their company was akin to an act of betrayal. They were hurt as well as baffled.

Henry, meanwhile, did not linger in the street. A servant was waiting to stable his horse. Storming into the house, Henry tore off his hat, slapped it down on the table in the hall then glowered at the man who came shuffling out to greet him.

'Well?' snapped Henry. 'Any word from my brother Christopher?'

'None, sir,' said the man.

'Damnation!' cried his master, stamping a foot. 'Where the devil can he be?'

Tom Warburton was slow but methodical. He questioned everyone who lived or worked in the vicinity of Paul's Wharf and, when his enquiries proved fruitless, widened his search to streets and taverns a little further away. It was all to no avail. Three days after the discovery of the dead body, he had made no progress whatsoever. Jonathan Bale found his colleague in Sermon Lane with his dog trotting obediently at his heels.

'Good morrow, Tom.'

Warburton gave him a nod of greeting. Sam slipped away to do some foraging.

'Any luck?'

'None, Jonathan.'

'Where have you been?'

'Everywhere. Nobody can help.'

'It's understandable, I suppose,' said Jonathan. 'Anyone abroad at that time of night would have been too drunk to notice anything or too frightened to come forward. I hold to my earlier judgement. The poor wretch was killed elsewhere then brought to Paul's Wharf to be hidden behind that warehouse.'

'Why not dump him in the river?'

'Who knows? Perhaps they wanted him to be found. Or perhaps they intended to throw him into the water but saw someone by the wharf and simply abandoned the body.'

'They?'

'It would have taken more than one man to drag him, Tom. Unless he was slung over the back of a horse or brought in a cart.'

'Nobody mentioned a cart.'

'It would have made a lot of noise, rattling down Bennet's Hill. Someone would have heard it. No,' said Jonathan, 'my guess is that the murder took place somewhere else in the ward and the body was lugged to the wharf by a person or persons unknown who had decided exactly where to hide it. Even in daylight, it would not have been found easily. We have Sam to thank for that.'

The little terrier suddenly reappeared to collect his due share of the praise.

'What shall I do?' said Warburton.

'Widen the search still further, Tom.'

'I've other things on my plate as well.'

'I know,' said Jonathan, 'and so have I. A constable's work is never done. I've already spent an hour at the magistrates' court and taken two offenders off to gaol. Then there were half a dozen other chores before I could come and find you.' He pulled the shoe from his pocket.

'I've finally got some time to continue the search for the man who made this. It's handsome footwear, the work of a craftsman. This wasn't made to walk through the filth of London. It's worthy of being worn at Court.'

'How do you know it's the work of a shoemaker in the city?'

'I don't, Tom.'

Warburton was a pessimist. 'You could be wasting your time.'

'I'll give it one more day. I've already called on most of the cordwainers.' He gave a chuckle. 'If I do much more walking, I'll need a new pair of shoes myself.'

'And if you fail?'

'Then I'll put the shoe aside and ask the coroner for a loan of that coat we found on the corpse. I'll not rest. I'll badger every tailor in London until I find the one who made it. But a shoe is easier to carry,' he said, putting it back into his pocket. 'And I haven't given up hope yet.'

'We could be on a wild-goose chase.'

Jonathan smiled. 'I like the taste of wild goose,' he said. 'Well cooked, that is.'

Bidding farewell to his gloomy colleague, Jonathan set off on his long walk. Tradesmen tended to congregate in certain areas of the city and, though their premises had been destroyed during the Great Fire, most had drifted back to their traditional habitats as soon as they were able. The cordwainers, who made the city's shoes, were concentrated largely in the region of Cripplegate in the north-west of the capital, but some were scattered more widely. Having exhausted the possibilities near Cripplegate, it was these more independent souls whom Jonathan now sought out.

Since it stood in the gardens of St Paul's Cathedral, the Cordwainers' Hall had been consumed by fire along with over forty other livery halls, but Jonathan found a helpful clerk from the guild who furnished him with the relevant addresses. He started to work his way systematically through the list.

It was a daunting task. Not only were the various shops set far apart from each other, but many of the shoemakers he questioned were less than obliging. Some sneered at the shoe and claimed that they would never make anything so inferior, others were openly envious of its quality and detained the constable unnecessarily while they inspected the handiwork, and others again were little short of obstructive. Jonathan had to reprimand more than one awkward cobbler. After several hours, however, he eventually stumbled on a reliable signpost. It was in a shop just off Cheapside.

'It's a fine shoe, sir,' said the man, turning it over in his hands.

'Did you make it?' asked Jonathan.

'I wish I had but it's beyond my mean abilities.'

'Do you have any idea who might have made it?'

'Oh, yes,' said the other. 'I can tell you that.'

'Who is he?'

'Nahum Gibbins, sir. Without question.'

'How can you be so sure?'

'Because I was apprenticed to him at one time. He could mould Cordoba leather to any shape he wanted. Mr Gibbins is expensive but his customers always get more than their money's worth. Let me show you,' he said, angling the shoe so that Jonathan could see the tiny star that was stamped inside it. 'That's his mark, sir. I'd know it anywhere. Where did you find it?'

'Beside a dead body, my friend. That's why I'm so anxious to trace the maker. We need to identify the deceased and that shoe may help us to do so.'

'Of course,' said the man, handing it back to him.

'Where might I speak to this Nahum Gibbins?'

'At his shop in Wood Street.'

'Thank you.'

'The south end, close to the White Hart. Give him my regards,' said the man, anxious to help. 'Tell him that Simon Ryde sent you.'

'I will, Mr Ryde. I'm most grateful.'

Jonathan set off with renewed hope, tiredness leaving him as he got within reach of his destination. He found the little shop with ease. Harness, bottles and all manner of leather goods were made there, but it was his shoes that brought Nahum Gibbins the bulk of his income. He was a tall, spare man, bent almost double by long years at his trade. His bald head had taken on a leathery quality itself and his face had the sheen of goatskin. When the constable explained the purpose of his visit, Gibbins took the shoe from him.

'Simon Ryde, did you say?'

'Yes, Mr Gibbins. He sends his regards.'

'Well might he do so,' said the old man with a cackle. 'He was the most wayward apprentice I ever had. If I hadn't boxed his ears and stood over him, he'd never have learnt the mysteries of working leather. Is he well?'

'As far as I can judge,' replied Jonathan, wanting a firm identification of the shoe. 'Mr Ryde was certain that this was your work.'

Gibbins nodded. 'He was right.'

'But you haven't looked at it.'

'I don't need to, Mr Bale. I can *feel* my handiwork.'

'Can you tell me who bought the shoe from you?'

'I could but I'd be breaking a confidence. Why do you wish to know?' When Jonathan explained the circumstances in which the shoe was found, the old man's manner changed at once. 'In that case, I'll do my best to help.'

'Give me his name.'

Gibbins raised a palm. 'Hold there, Mr Bale. It's not as simple as that. I've made several pairs of shoes of this design. I can't tell at a glance who would have worn this one. The size is one clue, of course,' he explained, scrutinising the length of the shoe before turning it over to expose the sole, 'and the state of wear. That will give me some idea how old it might be.' He rubbed his hand slowly over the leather before coming to a decision. 'Follow me, sir.'

He led Jonathan into the rear of the shop where his two assistants were working away. Gibbins picked up a battered ledger from the table and thumbed through the pages.

'I think I made that shoe six months ago for a young gentleman, sir. He paid me in full and that's most unusual among people of his sort. Credit is always their cry.' He came to the page he wanted. 'His name should be at the top of this list.'

'What is it?' asked Jonathan.

'Bless me, sir! I can't remember everyone who comes into

my shop. And since I can't read a single word, I'm unable to tell you who he is. Numbers are what I mastered. It's far more important to know how much someone owes me than how they spell their name. But I keep a record,' he said proudly. 'I always ask customers to put their signatures in my ledger.' He offered the open book to Jonathan then pointed at a neat scrawl. 'Here you are, Mr Bale. I fancy that this is the man you're after.'

CHAPTER FOUR

The creative impulse is oblivious to the passage of time. Christopher Redmayne was impelled by such a fierce urge to work on his drawings that all else was blocked out. Having spent the greater part of the day amending, improving and refining his design, he continued on into the night with the help of a circle of tallow candles. The simple joy of artistic creation kept fatigue at bay. Aching joints that would have sent most people to their beds hours earlier were blithely ignored. Hunger was disregarded. An occasional glass of wine was all that he allowed himself as he set one piece of parchment aside to start immediately on a new one. Occupying a site that ran to half an acre, Sir Julius Cheever's house would be somewhat smaller than the three mansions Christopher had already designed for clients but it would be just as much of a challenge for architect and builder. As he worked on the front elevation of the house, he took especial care over the way he drew the tall Dutch gables with their sweeping curved sides. He was just crowning the last of them with a triangular pediment when Jacob came into the room.

'Dear God!' exclaimed the servant. 'Up already, sir?'

'No, Jacob,' said Christopher without looking at him. 'I never went to bed.'

'But it's almost dawn.'

'Is it?'

'You need your sleep, sir.'

'Mind and body are telling me otherwise.'

'Then they are deceiving you,' said the old man. 'Why push yourself like this? You'll pay dearly for it, Mr Redmayne.'

'I'm rather hoping that it's my client who will be paying,' replied Christopher, standing back to admire his work. 'Come and look, Jacob.' Still in his nightshirt, the servant moved across to him. 'There now! What do you think of that?'

Jacob peered at the neat lines. 'It's a fine-looking house, sir.'

'Well worth losing a night's sleep over.'

'I don't agree.'

'You're not an architect.'

'That's why I'll live much longer than you, Mr Redmayne. Learn from your brother's example. Burn the candle at both ends and you'll suffer as a result.'

'Yes,' conceded Christopher, 'long nights have certainly left muddy footprints all over Henry's face, but I have something to show for my endeavour. These.' He pointed at the pile of drawings. 'I still have a long way to go but I now have an exact image in my mind of how the building will look.'

'I'm surprised that you can still keep your eyes open, sir.'

'I could work for a week without sleep on this project.'

'Where shall we bury your body?' asked Jacob drily.

Christopher laughed then gave a first involuntary yawn. Aches and pains began to afflict him at last. The fingers of his right hand were stiff. His mouth felt dry, his stomach hollow. He put down his stick of charcoal and shrugged his shoulders. 'Enough is enough.'

Jacob was solicitous. 'I'll fetch a cordial then you can retire to bed.'

'Only for a few hours.'

'You'll need half a day to recover from this folly.'

'That may be, Jacob, but I'll have to take it at a later stage. Now that I've made such valuable progress,' he said as another yawn burst forth, 'I can think of someone apart from myself. I must pay a visit to my brother. Much as I hate the idea of being asked for money by Henry, there are familial obligations. The least I can do is to hear his tale of woe. Apart from anything else, if I go to Bedford Street, it will stop him coming here to interrupt my work.'

'Why not simply send a message?' suggested Jacob. 'I'll gladly take it.'

'Henry would never be fobbed off by a letter.'

'So what will you do?'

'Snatch three or four hours' sleep,' said Christopher, stretching himself and hearing the bones crack slightly. 'Wake me up then and I'll visit my brother. There's no point in going any earlier. Henry never rises before mid-morning.'

* * *

Wearing a thick dressing gown and an expression of utter despair, Henry Redmayne sat at the table in his dining room over a breakfast that remained untouched. His servants were amazed to see him up so early and they had the wisdom to keep well out of his way. Irascible at the best of times, their master was in a most choleric mood. The barber who would arrive to shave him at ten would be in for an especially testing time. Nobody envied him. Sagging in his chair, arms on the table, Henry was staring glassy-eyed at potential catastrophe. He could not remember when he had felt so oppressed. It was a numbing experience. He was so caught up in his predicament that he did not hear the front door bell ringing. Henry was floating helplessly on a sea of self-pity.

There was a tap on the door and a nervous servant popped his head in. 'You have a visitor, sir.'

'Send him away!' snarled Henry.

'Is that altogether wise?'

'Do as I say, you imbecile. Get rid of that baboon-faced barber. I'll not be shaved by him today. I'm likely to tear the razor from his grasp and cut my own throat.'

'But it's not the barber who's here, Mr Redmayne.'

'Turn every visitor away. I'll see no one.'

'Not even your brother, sir?'

Henry jumped to his feet. 'Christopher?' he yelled. 'Why didn't you tell me, you idiot? Show him in straight away and make sure that we're not disturbed for any reason. Do you understand?'

The servant nodded and backed gratefully out. Seconds later, Christopher came into the room, hiding his weariness behind a warm smile. Henry bore down on him.

'Where've you *been*, man!' he demanded.

'Furthering my career, Henry.'

'I needed you here.'

'Why? Do you wish to commission a new house from me?'

'No,' moaned his brother. 'I'm more likely to lose the one I have than be able to afford a new one.' He crossed to the door, snatched it open to make sure that there was nobody in the hall, then slammed it shut again. 'We must talk, Christopher.'

'I came as soon as I could.'

'Did Jacob tell you how urgent it was?'

'Yes, Henry. He also guessed the reason for that urgency.'

'I doubt that.'

'Come now,' said Christopher, putting a consoling hand on his arm. 'Everyone knows your weakness. You will play card games for which you are singularly ill-equipped. What little skill you possess is vitiated by an endless run of bad fortune.' He shook his head sadly. 'How much do you owe this time?'

'If it was only a gambling debt!'

'You mean that it isn't?'

'No, Christopher,' admitted Henry, crossing to drop into his chair. 'It's worse than that. Far, far worse. I'd hardly summon you here for help in clearing a debt incurred at the card table. That would be a mere trifle.'

Christopher was sympathetic. 'So what is the problem?'

'I can hardly bring myself to tell you.'

'Dismissal from the Navy Office? Serious illness?'

'Both would be preferable to the situation in which I find myself.'

'What situation?' said his younger brother, sitting beside him. 'I can see that you're in earnest. Tell me all.'

'In a moment.' A resentful note sounded. 'Where on earth did you go?'

'Northamptonshire.'

'Whatever for?'

'In pursuit of a commission.'

'A commission? Your brother is facing disaster and your only response is to run off to Northamptonshire in pursuit of a paltry commission.'

'It's far from paltry, I assure you.'

'It's meaningless beside the agony that I'm suffering.'

'Is it?'

'Yes,' said Henry, grabbing his shoulder. 'You must help me, Christopher.'

'That's why I'm here.'

'God knows how, though! There seems to be no way out.'

'Out of what, Henry?'

His brother sat back in his chair and ran a hand through his thinning hair. Like Christopher, he had had a sleepless night, but his had been entirely unproductive. Fear had kept him awake through the dark hours. Pale, haggard and unshaven, he looked ten years older than his real age. It took him some time to summon up the courage to speak. When he finally did, his eyes were darting with apprehension.

'First, I must extract a promise from you,' he said.

'Promise?'

'Nothing of what I say – *nothing*, Christopher – must ever find its way to the ears of our father. He preaches enough sermons at me as it is. If the old gentleman knew the position I find myself in now, he'd excommunicate me on the spot and, worst of all, terminate the allowance that he so reluctantly sends me.'

Christopher was frank. 'Father's allowance would be less reluctant if he felt that it was being spent wisely, Henry. He's the Dean of Gloucester. He expects you to behave like the son of a senior churchman.'

'What am I supposed to do? Sing hymns at the card table?'

'Moderate your way of life.'

'Not while I have blood in my veins.'

'I, too, have blood in my veins,' said Christopher defensively, 'but I do not expend my time and money in so reckless a manner.' He checked himself and gave an apologetic smile. 'I'm sorry, Henry. I don't mean to sound like our dear father. And, of course, I'll not breathe a syllable of what you tell me to him. You can trust me.'

'I *have* to trust you. There's nobody else I can turn to.'

'For what?'

'Compassion and understanding.'

'I give those freely.'

'You may not do so when you hear the ugly truth.' He thrust a hand into his pocket and took out a letter. 'This arrived out of the blue two nights ago. It came like a musket ball between the eyes.'

'Why?'

'It's a demand for money, Christopher. A missive that I

incautiously sent to a certain lady has fallen into the wrong hands. It's very explicit. If I don't pay handsomely for its return,' he said, handing the letter to his brother, 'then it will be passed to the lady's husband. You can see how fatal that would be.'

Christopher read the name. 'Lord Ulvercombe?'

'A duel would be unavoidable. He's already accounted for two adversaries.'

'His wife will surely deny all allegations.'

'She did that on both previous occasions but it did not stop her vengeful husband from issuing challenges. No man likes to be cuckolded but Ulvercombe takes resentment to unreasonable lengths.'

'How did your letter go astray?'

'I've no idea. The little minx swore that she'd destroy it.'

'Does the lady know of this attempt at blackmail?'

'No. Nor must she. I don't wish to drag her into it at all.'

'But she might be able to tell you who stole the letter from her. If you can unmask the rogue who sent you this,' said Christopher, holding up the letter, 'you can confront him and demand your private correspondence back.'

'We're not merely talking about my *billet-doux*, alas.'

'No?'

'Read it to the end.'

Christopher did and sat up with a start. When he shot a glance at his brother, Henry was hiding his face in both hands.

Christopher could understand his shame as well as his horror. He put the letter down in front of him.

70

'This looks bad, Henry,' he whispered.

'It's a calamity!'

'How many of those things are true?'

There was a long pause. 'Most of them,' confessed Henry.

'Most or all?'

'Does it matter?'

'I think so.'

Henry lowered his hands. 'I expected you to be on my side.'

'I *am* on your side,' said Christopher, 'and I'll do everything I can to help, but I must know the truth. How many of these allegations have any substance to them?'

'All of them.'

'Could anyone prove that these things actually happened?'

'If they had reliable witnesses.'

Christopher raised a censorious eyebrow. 'How could you be so careless?'

'Step down from the pulpit. You're sounding like father again.'

'That's the last thing I wish to do. You need assistance, not condemnation.'

'At this moment,' wailed his brother, 'I feel in need of the services of an undertaker. This has ruined me. To all intents and purposes, Henry Redmayne is dead. I'll never be able to hold up my head again.'

'Yes, you will,' Christopher assured him.

'How?'

'By nipping this blackmail in the bud.'

'And how am I supposed to do that?'

'I've told you. By learning the identity of the man who wrote this and taking any incriminating documents away from him.' He glanced at the letter. 'The fellow seems uncannily well informed about your movements. He must be someone from your inner circle. There are detailed descriptions of your peccadilloes here.'

'An invasion of my privacy.'

'You should have been more discreet.'

'I was. Most of the time, anyway. Heavens!' Henry protested, snatching the letter back. 'How can any of us remember to look over our shoulders when the wine is rich and the company enticing? A man is entitled to his pleasures without being spied on by some evil little blackmailer.' He thrust the letter back into his pocket and looked more dejected than ever. 'What am I to *do*?'

Christopher took pity on him. Some of the revelations in the letter had shocked him even though he was aware of Henry's love of revelry. The affair with Lady Amelia Ulvercombe was both foolhardy and dangerous, and she was not the only married woman with whom his brother's name was linked. Christopher imagined how their father, the moralistic Dean of Gloucester, would react if the information fell into his hands and he vowed to do all he could to prevent that from occurring.

'Make a list of your intimates,' he advised.

'Why?' said Henry. 'No true friend would betray me.'

'Someone did. If I'm to help, I need to be more familiar with your circle, Henry. I know that Arthur Lunn is a crony of yours. Peter Wickens, too, and Gilbert Sparkish, if memory serves me. Who else? Sir Marcus Kemp?'

'Sir Marcus would die to save my reputation.'

'Let me be the judge of that,' said Christopher. 'I'll not badger you now but I must have a list of names so that I can begin my enquiries. Take heart, brother. It may not be as bad as you envisage.'

Henry shuddered. 'Oh, it is. Believe me.'

'Meanwhile, carry on as if nothing had happened.'

'But something *has* happened,' complained Henry, close to hysteria. 'My whole future is in the balance. I can hardly pretend that I'm not concerned about the threat.'

'That's exactly what you must do,' urged Christopher. 'Don't give this rogue the pleasure of seeing you suffer, Henry. Fight back. Put on a brave face and show him that you're not so easily discomfited.'

'But I'm terror-stricken!'

Christopher was moved. Even allowing for his brother's tendency to dramatise and exaggerate, he could see how shaken Henry was. The warning letter had left him thoroughly dazed. If and when the crisis blew over, it was possible that Henry might even start to mend his ways. That was another reason to come to his aid.

'Do as I suggest,' said Christopher, 'then leave the rest to me. I'll not discuss this with anyone so your shame will not be noised abroad. Whatever you do, you must not give in to blackmail. It's a despicable crime and we'll catch the villain behind it.' He patted his brother's shoulder. 'Bear up. We'll come through this somehow.'

'Will we?'

'Of course.'

Henry managed a pale smile of gratitude. Having shared his grim secret, he felt as if his load had been marginally lightened. Christopher was a younger brother who seemed, in many ways, much older than him. Where Henry was impetuous, Christopher was cool and objective. He was also an extremely resolute man. In the circumstances in which Henry now found himself, his brother was the ideal ally. Henry softened.

'Forgive this whining self-concern,' he said with a gesture of apology.

'I heard no whining.'

'You have news of your own and all I can do is bury you up to the neck in my affairs. It's reprehensible on my part. What's this about a new commission?' His interest was genuine. 'In Northamptonshire, you say?'

'Yes, Henry.'

'How did you come by it?'

'I was recommended by Elijah Pembridge.'

'The bookseller?'

'The very same,' said Christopher. 'Thanks to you, I was able to design his new shop and he was sufficiently pleased with it to pass my name on to a friend.'

'Do I know the man?'

'I doubt it. He was a colonel in Cromwell's army. He's been immured in the country for the last six or seven years and is only forcing himself to reside in London because he is looking to become a Member of Parliament.'

'More fool him! What's his name?'

'Sir Julius Cheever.'

Henry was curious. 'Cheever? No relation of Gabriel Cheever, by any chance?'

'Sir Julius could be his father, I suppose,' said Christopher. 'I know that he has a son called Gabriel but I also know that he's disowned him for some reason.'

'Then it *has* to be the Gabriel I know.'

'What makes you say that?'

'No father would approve of such a son.'

'Why not?'

'Because Gabriel Cheever makes me look like the patron saint of chastity,' said Henry with a mirthless laugh. 'He's one of the most notorious rakehells in London.'

'When do you intend to leave?' asked Susan Cheever.

'In a day or so,' said her father. 'I've business in London.'

'Where will you stay?'

Sir Julius pulled a face. 'In Richmond.'

'Lancelot is your son-in-law,' she told him with a note of mild reproach. 'You ought to make more of an effort to like him.'

'I have difficulty liking Brilliana at times, so don't ask me to waste any affection on that blockhead of a husband.'

'It was a good marriage for Brilliana. They're very happy together.'

'How can any woman be happy with Lancelot Serle?' he demanded. 'Be honest, Susan. Would you accept a proposal from a posturing ninny like that?'

She suppressed a smile. 'No, Father.'

'Thank God I have *one* discerning daughter.'

They were just finishing their meal in the dining room. It was a beautiful day and Sir Julius planned to spend the afternoon in the saddle, riding around the estate to see how his tenants were getting on in the hay fields. Though he had delegated most of the management duties to someone else, he liked to keep an eye on progress and knew that it always improved when he put in a personal appearance. Farming was what he knew best and loved most. Sir Julius needed to remind himself of that before he went off to the urban confines of London. He sipped his wine and looked fondly at Susan.

'While we're on the subject,' he began, licking his lips, 'when are you going to follow your sister down the aisle?'

She was dismissive. 'Oh, there's no hurry for that.'

'Answer my question.'

'I've answered it a dozen times already,' she replied. 'The time to get married is when I find someone whom I consider to be a worthy husband.'

'You have plenty of willing suitors.'

'Willing but unsatisfactory.'

'Your standards are too high, Susan.'

'Are you so eager to get rid of me?'

'No,' he said. 'I'll miss you terribly if you go, but it would be wrong of me to stand in your way out of selfishness. Most young ladies of your age have a husband and children. Failing that, they are at least betrothed.'

Susan's face tightened. 'I tried betrothal, Father. It was an ordeal.'

'Only because you chose the wrong man.'

'I seem to recall that he was chosen for me. That was the trouble. I was more or less talked into it by you and Mother. Not that I blame you entirely,' she went on. 'I take some responsibility. I liked Michael immensely but I could never love him and, as it turned out, the feelings he professed to have for me were not as intense as he claimed.'

'Forget him,' said Sir Julius briskly. 'Michael Trenton was a mistake. I freely concede that. But there are dozens of more reliable young men in the county.'

'I want more than reliability, Father.'

'You need someone who can offer you security, Susan. That's the most important factor. We have to accept that I will not be here for ever.'

Susan smiled. 'Then I insist on looking after you while you *are* here.'

'Why not find someone to look after you for a change?'

'I will, Father. One day.'

A maidservant came in to clear the table and brought that phase of the conversation to a natural end. Susan was grateful for the interruption. Questions about her lack of marital plans always made her feel slightly cornered. After one doomed betrothal, she was loath to enter too hastily into another. Suitors were tolerated but never encouraged. She had come round to the view that, if she were to marry, her husband would live well away from the county of Northamptonshire.

'How long will you be in London?' she asked.

'Four or five days,' he said. 'A week at most.'

'It will be very lonely without you.'

'Then why not make the rounds of your many admirers?' he teased.

'I think I would prefer to come with you, Father.'

He was surprised. 'To London? Whatever for?'

'To keep you company, for a start. And to have the

pleasure of seeing Brilliana again. Yes,' she added as she saw him grimace, 'I know that you hate staying with them in Richmond but I enjoy it. Brilliana and I can take the coach into the city.'

'Anything to get away from Lancelot!'

'Stop being so unkind about your son-in-law.'

'The man is insufferable.'

'I promise to keep him well away from you. There,' she announced. 'Isn't that a good enough reason in itself to take me with you?'

'It's a tempting offer, certainly.' He drained his glass of wine. 'I'll consider it.'

'Thank you.' Susan tried to sound casual. 'Father, while you're in London, will you be seeing your architect at some point?'

'Redmayne? Probably.'

'Where does he live?'

'Fetter Lane, I believe.'

'Those sketches of his were remarkable.'

'He's a competent architect, Susan. I have it on good authority.' He leant forward. 'But why this sudden interest in Christopher Redmayne?'

'A passing thought,' she said. 'No more. I can come with you, then?'

He rose to his feet. 'Give me time to think it over.'

'London has so much to offer at this time of year.'

'Yes, Susan. Blistering heat, a dreadful stench and too many people.'

He moved to the door but she got up from her chair to intercept him. Anticipating what she was going to say, Sir

Julius bristled. His daughter was not to be put off.

'Father,' she began.

'Do I really want to hear this?' he warned.

'Someone else lives in London as well.'

'Thousands of people do.'

'This person is rather special.'

'Not to me,' he snapped. 'Not any more.'

'Gabriel is your son,' she argued.

'I *have* no son, Susan.'

'He still looks upon you as his father.'

'Well, he has no right to do so,' said Sir Julius vehemently. 'Gabriel is a disgrace to himself and to his family. Ours is a proud name and he has forfeited any claim on it. I expect a degree of rebellion in a son. It shows spirit. But he went too far, Susan. It broke your mother's heart to see him stalk out of the house the way he did – and for what? A life of idleness in the taverns and gaming houses of London.'

She clutched his arm. 'Gabriel may have changed by now, Father.'

'I have not,' he said firmly.

Detaching her hand, he walked quickly away before he lost his temper.

Jonathan Bale had too full a day to devote much time to the murder investigation and the enquiries he had been able to make on that score had borne no fruit. As he walked back home with Tom Warburton, he confided his frustration.

'I wish I could devote all my time to it, Tom.'

'Leave that to others,' advised Warburton.

'But we found the body. I feel involved.'

'We've done all we can, Jonathan.'

'And where has it got us?' said the other. 'Nowhere. You've knocked on dozens of doors in search of witnesses but found none at all. I've put a name to the dead man but I've no idea who he was or where he lived. Nahum Gibbins gave me an address but they had never heard of him there.' He ran a hand across his chin. 'Why does a customer give his shoemaker a false address?'

'Maybe the name is false as well.'

'I thought of that.'

They plodded on together. As they passed an alley, Warburton's dog came trotting out to take his place at his master's heels but he soon darted off ahead of them. Jonathan watched him pause to sniff at the wall of a tavern.

He was pensive. 'What puzzles me is that nobody's come forward.'

'True.'

'The man is missing. Someone in the ward must be worried by his absence.'

'Only if he came from round here.'

'Where else?'

'Any part of the city.'

'Why drag him all this way to dispose of the body? No, Tom. He must have some link with Baynard's Castle ward. I feel it in my bones. And the killer must know the area as well. He picked a good spot to hide the body. And a good time.'

'When nobody was about.'

'Nobody who remembers seeing anything, that is.'

'Ah.'

'We must try again tomorrow.'

'Yes.'

Jonathan gave him a farewell wave and turned into Addle Hill. With his dog back at his heels, Warburton continued on towards his own house. It had been a disappointing day and Jonathan was glad to be home again. When he entered, Sarah was coming downstairs, having just put the two boys to bed. Smiling a welcome, she gave him a kiss on the cheek.

'I told them you'd be back in time to read to them.'

'In a moment,' he said, going into the kitchen.

'You look exhausted, Jonathan.'

'Annoyed more than anything else.'

'Why?'

'Oh, it's not fair to bring my troubles home,' he said, dredging up a smile. 'The problem will keep until morning then I'll start all over again.'

'Is it to do with that dead body you found?'

'Yes.'

'I thought you found out a name.'

'I did,' he agreed, 'but that's all I found out. The address I was given was false. For some reason, the young man wanted to cover his tracks. All I know is that he wore expensive shoes and dressed like a gentleman. He might even be a courtier. That's not a world I know – or want to know – much about, Sarah.'

'*You've* been to Court,' she said with pride. 'You've spoken to His Majesty.'

He wrinkled his nose. 'Not with any pleasure, my love. When he saw fit to employ me, I had to obey the King but I was never comfortable in his presence. If the dead man was

81

a courtier, I'll leave it to others to find out more about him. I'll not venture down to Westminster again. It's a vile place.'

Sarah said nothing but her mind was working. While her husband went off to read to his sons from the Bible, she prepared his supper. So rarely did he talk about his work at home that she knew this case held a special interest for him. She wanted to help. When he finally came back to the kitchen, she made a suggestion.

'What about that friend of yours, Jonathan?'

'Friend?'

'Mr Redmayne.'

'He's not really a friend, Sarah.'

'Come now,' she said reprovingly. 'You know that you like him. You and he worked well together in the past so don't pretend you have no time for him.'

'What can Mr Redmayne do?'

'See if the dead man really did go to Court.'

'How could he find out? Mr Redmayne is no courtier.'

'No,' she said. 'But his brother Henry is. I've heard you mention him.'

Jonathan pondered. His wife had made a valuable suggestion. It was an idea that would never have crossed his own mind because he had so many reservations about his occasional partnership with Christopher Redmayne. But it was perhaps a way to secure indirect access to Court. When everything else had failed, it might be worth a try. He fought hard to overcome his prejudices.

'Thank you, Sarah,' he said at length. 'I'll go and see Mr Redmayne tomorrow.'

CHAPTER FIVE

Christopher Redmayne was distressed by his visit to Bedford Street and vowed to help his stricken brother in every possible way. At the same time, however, he could not neglect the work in which he was engaged, marking, as it did, a major advance in his career. It was not merely the first commission to come his way as a result of a property he had already designed, it was also the first to allow him a free hand in the choice of builder. Earlier clients had reserved the right to select their own men and this had sometimes created problems. The builder foisted on him by Jasper Hartwell, for example, had been able but obstructive and, though the house he built was substantially the one that Christopher had designed, he had criticised the architect at every stage and made the project an unnecessarily difficult one. It was a relief to know that this time he could engage a builder who would work with him rather than against him. The choice, in fact, had already made itself. Having found a congenial partner during the construction of Elijah Pembridge's new bookshop, Christopher sought out the same man in the hope that he would be available for hire again. Like most reputable builders, Sidney Popejoy was extremely busy, but his admiration for the architect was such that he promised to recruit additional men in order to take on the project.

They adjourned to the site itself to take stock of any potential hazards.

'A tidy piece of land,' observed Popejoy. 'At a tidy price, I dare say.'

'Sir Julius is a wealthy man.'

'He must be if he can afford to build a house that he'll rarely use.'

'Except when Parliament sits,' said Christopher.

Popejoy grinned. 'Sits and sleeps, from what I hear.'

'Not while Sir Julius Cheever is around. His voice would wake the dead.'

'What sort of client will he be, Mr Redmayne?'

'One that expects to get exactly what he pays for.'

'As long as he's not looking over our shoulder every hour of the day.'

'No danger of that, Mr Popejoy,' said Christopher. 'Once my drawings have met with his approval, he'll leave us alone to get on with our work. Sir Julius hates London. It's taking a huge effort of will on his part to move here.'

'But he's not really *in* London,' noted Popejoy. 'Westminster is a city in itself.'

'It's all one to him. An object of scorn and derision. He wanted a house built here so that it was convenient for his visits to Parliament. Our job is to answer his needs.'

Popejoy gave a shrug. 'I foresee no problems there.'

The two men were standing in a tree-lined road that ran north from Tuthill Street. A number of properties had already been built there but the new house would still allow Sir Julius an uninterrupted view of St James's Park. It was a bonus for a man accustomed to look out on appealing landscapes. Popejoy strode slowly around the site, measuring it out and kneeling down to take a closer look at the ground on which he was to build. He was a short, thickset man with black hair and bushy eyebrows that arched so expressively above his bulbous eyes that he seemed to be in a continual state of surprise. Christopher had the highest respect for him. He had seen how Popejoy could bring the best out of his men. When the builder rejoined him, he nodded towards the park.

'Sir Julius will be able to see the King taking his morning walk.'

'That's the last thing he wishes to do, Mr Popejoy,' said Christopher with a smile. 'Left to him, there would be no King. Unless he went by the name of Oliver Cromwell.'

'What a sour-faced ruler *he* turned out to be!'

'Not in the opinion of our client. He more or less worshipped the man. Whatever else you do,' he cautioned, 'make no comment about politics to Sir Julius or it will set him off. He's fanatical in his beliefs. Disparage the Lord Protector and he's likely to tear up your contract to build his house.'

Popejoy nodded. 'I know when to keep my mouth shut, Mr Redmayne. I've been employed by men of every political persuasion and I made sure that I never spoke a word out of place to any of them. I prefer to sweeten a client. They pay better that way.'

'I agree,' said Christopher. 'Well, have you seen enough, Mr Popejoy?'

'I think so.'

'Do you have any questions?'

'Only one of significance. When do we start?'

'As soon as Sir Julius is satisfied with my design. He plans to be in London very soon and will call on me at the earliest opportunity. It is simply a case of standing by.'

'I'm not one to stand by, Mr Redmayne,' said the builder, eyebrows reaching an even higher altitude. 'I've other work to supervise. When the time comes, that's where you'll find me. Keeping an eye on my men.'

'As I would expect.'

They mounted their horses and rode back in the direction of the city, discussing the purchase of materials and the need to safeguard them at night while they were stored on site. After trading farewells, they parted in The Strand. Christopher went on to Fleet Street at a brisk trot and turned his horse into Fetter Lane. When he reached his door, Jacob came hurrying out to take charge of the animal and to pass on some unexpected information.

'Someone has called to see you, Mr Redmayne,' he said.

'My brother?'

'No, sir. Your friend the constable.'

Christopher was astonished. 'Jonathan Bale?'

'He has been here the best part of an hour.'

'Then it must be important,' decided Christopher,

dismounting and handing over the reins. 'He's ill at ease after two minutes under my roof. To endure it any longer is a sign of real urgency.'

He went in through the door, found Jonathan in the parlour, and waved him back to his seat when he tried to rise. The visitor was patently uncomfortable in a house that was so much larger and better furnished than his own. Notwithstanding his friend's ill-concealed prejudices and dour manner, Christopher had grown fond of Jonathan Bale. Chance had thrown them together on more than one occasion and forged a bond that neither would have believed possible. While Christopher was ready to acknowledge that bond with a cordial smile, the constable was less forthcoming.

'I am sorry to disturb you, Mr Redmayne,' he began solemnly.

'Not at all. I'm always glad to see friends.'

'I come on an errand.'

'So I assumed.'

'Thus it stands.' Jonathan did not linger over the social niceties. As soon as his host was seated opposite him, he gave him a brief account of the murder investigation and explained why he had such a personal commitment to it.

'You have a protective instinct,' remarked Christopher.

'Do I?'

'You guard that ward of yours like a mother hen watching over her brood.'

Jonathan was blunt. 'I won't stand for murder on my doorstep.'

'Nor should you, Mr Bale. But how can I help?'

'By speaking to your brother, Mr Redmayne.'

'Henry?'

'He may just have the answers I need.'

'Don't bank on that,' warned Christopher. 'Henry is not at his most approachable at the moment. He's rather preoccupied.'

'All I am asking is that you tell him the name of the deceased. I have a strong suspicion that the man may have been at Court. In which case, your brother might actually know him.'

'That's not impossible. Henry is a gregarious fellow. Inquisitive, too. He likes to keep abreast of all the Court gossip.'

'Will you take me to him, please?'

Christopher hesitated. 'It might be better if I passed on your request to him. My brother is indisposed. I'm the only visitor he'll permit. Will that content you?'

'It must.'

'Tell me name of the murder victim?'

'Gabriel Cheever.'

'Cheever!'

Christopher was stunned. Mouth agape, he sat there with his mind in turmoil. Could the man possibly be the estranged son of Sir Julius Cheever? If so, how would the latter react when he heard the news? But the question that really skewered its way through Christopher's brain was how the lovely Susan Cheever would respond. Her brother might have shaken the dust of Northamptonshire from his feet but she still recognised him as her sibling and, Christopher suspected, cared for him a great deal. She would be devastated by the news and he hoped that he would be able to soften its impact by being the person to break it to her.

'Of course,' said Jonathan on reflection, 'that may turn out to be a false name. He certainly left a false address with his shoemaker. I found that out.'

'He gave his real name,' murmured Christopher.

'What makes you think that?'

'I've heard of Gabriel Cheever and my brother knew him well.'

Jonathan brightened. 'Will he have an address for the man?'

'Perhaps.'

'How soon can you get it for me?'

'I'll walk to Bedford Street this morning, Mr Bale.'

'Are you all right?' asked Jonathan, peering at him with concern. 'You look pale, Mr Redmayne. Have these tidings come as a shock to you?'

'A profound shock,' admitted Christopher. 'When you arrived here, I was inspecting a site with a builder. I've been commissioned to design a house for a client called Sir Julius Cheever.'

'A relation?'

'His father, I believe.'

'The fog is starting to clear at last,' said Jonathan gratefully. 'The father deserves to be informed at once so he can identify the body for certain. Can you tell me how to find him?'

'He is probably on his way to London even as we speak, Mr Bale.'

'Good.'

'Though I can't guarantee that he'll shed too many tears over his son's demise,' said Christopher sadly. 'The two of them had fallen out, apparently. Sir Julius is a man of high principles. He was knighted by the Lord Protector for his services during the war.' Jonathan's eyes ignited with interest. 'You would have much in common with him, Mr Bale, but not, I would guess, with his son. Gabriel Cheever led the kind of existence that appalled his father so much that he virtually disowned him.'

'I see.'

'But grief might well dissolve their differences. I pray that it does. Every son deserves to be mourned.' He became thoughtful. 'Where is the body?'

'At the morgue.'

'Can you make sure that it remains there until the family has been told?'

'Yes, Mr Redmayne.'

'It would be a cruelty if they arrived to find that Gabriel Cheever had been buried in an unmarked grave because nobody came forward to claim the body. Even if Sir Julius himself does not wish to take responsibility, others in the family may do so.'

Jonathan got up. 'I'll return to the morgue at once and leave instructions.'

'Do that, Mr Bale,' said Christopher, rising from his own chair. 'Meanwhile, I'll repair to my brother's house to see what I can learn about the deceased. He and Henry sound as if they might have been birds of the same feather.'

'The thought had crossed my mind,' said Jonathan quietly.

'Let's about our business.' Christopher led the way to the door, arranged to meet his friend later on then sent him on his way. Having stabled the horse, Jacob was returning to the house.

'I have to go out again, Jacob,' Christopher told him.

'On foot?'

'In the first instance.'

'When shall I expect you back, sir?' asked Jacob.

'It's impossible to say. I may be some time. At all events, prepare no food for me. I'll not be dining at home today.'

'But I understood that you were to work on your drawings.'

Christopher winced. 'That project is in abeyance, I fear.'

Buoyed up by his brother's visit on the previous day, Henry Redmayne resolved to adopt a more positive attitude. He would no longer be cowed into submission by the threats of a blackmailer. Courage and forbearance were needed. It was important for him to resume his normal life in order to show his anonymous tormentor that he was not so easily alarmed. Instead of hiding himself away, therefore, he spent his usual daily eternity in front of the mirror, preening himself and adjusting his periwig, then selected a hat for his walk along The Strand. Before he could even reach the front door, however, the bell rang and it shattered his fragile confidence at once, sending him back into the dining room where he skulked in a corner. He heard the door open and, almost immediately, close again. His servant's footsteps approached the dining room. Henry made an effort to compose himself, one hand on the back of a chair and the other on his hip.

When the man entered, he looked down his nose at him.

'Well?' he asked.

'A letter has come for you, Mr Redmayne.'

'Set it down on the table.'

The man did so and went out, shutting the door behind him. Henry's bold front collapsed again. It was a letter that had transformed his life so dramatically and he feared another from the same hand. Should he open it or should he send for Christopher to do so? If he read the missive, he risked inflicting further misery on himself. Yet, if he ignored it, he might imperil himself by disobeying orders. Eyes on the letter, he walked round the table as if skirting a dangerous animal that was liable to attack him. There was, he tried to tell himself, no certainty that it came from the blackmailer. It might be from a friend, a colleague at the Navy Office, or even – the thought depressed him – from his father. One glance at the neat calligraphy eliminated the Dean of Gloucester from the list of potential correspondents. He could not identify the hand at all. It was reassuring. Whoever had written the letter, it was not the man who had issued the dire warnings.

Henry relaxed slightly. Summoning up the vestiges of his resolve, he picked up the missive. Breaking the seal, he unfolded the letter to read it, then reached out desperately for the support of the chair. Only one sentence had been written on the paper but it was as chilling as it was mystifying. Though penned by a different hand from the one responsible for the first letter, the second clearly came from the same source. Henry lowered himself into a chair and suffered an outbreak of prickly heat. He was still transfixed by the single sentence when the front door bell was rung again. It made him sit up guiltily, and he thrust the letter into his pocket.

When there was a knock on the door he expected his servant to enter, but it was Christopher who came surging into the dining room. Henry almost swooned with relief.

'Forgive this intrusion,' said Christopher.

'You are more than welcome, brother!'

'I need your assistance, Henry.'

'Not as much as I need yours,' said the other, pulling the letter from his pocket. 'This came only minutes ago. Quite what it bodes I cannot tell, but it gave me a turn.'

'Why?'

'Read it for yourself.'

Christopher took the letter and unfolded it. The message jumped out at him. *Pay what I ask or suffer the same fate as Gabriel Cheever.*

'What does it mean?' asked Henry. 'How is Gabriel Cheever involved here? Has he been receiving blackmail demands as well?'

'If he did,' said Christopher, 'he refused to give in to them. Gabriel is dead.'

'Dead?'

'His body was found a few nights ago at Paul's Wharf.'

Henry quailed. 'He was *murdered*?'

'Strangled, apparently, then stabbed through the heart. It's the very matter that brought me here this morning, Henry. My friend Jonathan Bale stumbled upon the body with a fellow constable.'

Henry was not interested in the details. The fact that

Gabriel Cheever had been killed was enough to throw him into a panic. Leaping to his feet, he wrung his hands in despair and darted to and fro like a trapped deer waiting for the huntsmen to strike. The letter contained no idle threat. It was not only Henry's reputation that hung in the balance: his life was now at risk. When he had worked himself up into a lather of apprehension, he flung himself at Christopher and grabbed him by the coat.

'He's going to kill me!' he cried.

'Calm down, Henry.'

'How can I be calm when someone is plotting my murder?'

'It could be an empty threat,' argued Christopher. 'If you were to die, he loses all hope of getting any money out of you. Why sacrifice that? No, Henry. I spy a ruse here. It is simply a means of frightening you into complying with his demands.'

'Cheever was murdered,' said Henry, releasing him to circle the room. 'If he can be killed, then so can I. This is no ruse, Christopher. Do you want a constable to find my dead body on Paul's Wharf?'

'Of course not.'

'Then take the letter seriously.'

'I do,' said Christopher, setting it down on the table. 'It's valuable evidence. With your permission, I'd like to show it to Jonathan Bale.'

Henry was outraged. 'Never!'

'But it's relevant to his enquiries.'

'It's much more relevant to my life, Christopher!' shouted his brother. 'I don't want that narrow-minded constable prying into my personal affairs. You swore that you'd divulge my situation to nobody and I hold you to that vow.'

'Circumstances have changed, Henry.'

'Yes, I've been threatened with murder.'

'Come and sit down,' soothed Christopher, taking him by the arm. 'Nothing will be gained by this frenzy. Take a deep breath and sit still while you hear me out.' He lowered Henry on to a chair. 'We have to look at this dispassionately.'

'Someone is after my blood!' howled Henry.

'I doubt that very much. Now, be still. We're in a position to help each other.' He held up a hand to stifle Henry's rejoinder then sat beside him. 'That letter does much more than threaten you,' he said reasonably. 'It gives us a vital clue to the identity of Gabriel Cheever's killer. Don't you see, Henry? Murder and blackmail are the work of the same man.'

Henry was sarcastic. 'Am I supposed to draw comfort from that?'

'No,' replied Christopher. 'You're supposed to realise that, by helping to snare a killer, you will get rid of the menace of blackmail. The two crimes are linked. Solve one and we solve them both. In short, take Jonathan Bale into your confidence.'

'No. I'll not have a Puritan sitting in judgement on me.'

'He's a dedicated officer of the law. Look what he has achieved in the past.'

'Only because you worked beside him.'

Christopher was determined. 'I intend to do so again, Henry,' he insisted. 'The three of us are in this together. You have received threats of blackmail. Jonathan is investigating a murder. And I am employed by a man whose son has been killed in the most brutal fashion.'

Henry shrank back. 'Spare me the details.'

'Let me at least tell you how I was drawn into this.' Christopher gave his brother a succinct account of the constable's visit to his house and stressed the need for further information about Gabriel Cheever. He was gently persuasive. Slowly but surely, he began to break down Henry's resistance. One point was made with particular emphasis.

'I am not suggesting for one moment that you show Jonathan that first letter. The fact of its existence will be enough for him to know. Details of your private life will not be disclosed, Henry. They would, in any case, be superfluous.'

'What do you mean?'

Christopher smiled. 'Jonathan is unlikely to mistake you for an ascetic.'

'The pursuit of pleasure is the aim of every man.'

'Perhaps,' agreed his brother, 'but we do not all derive pleasure from the same things. Mine comes from my work and Jonathan Bale's from doing his duty. Your pleasures are more unashamedly sensual.'

'Why else were we put upon this earth?'

'If you seek a theological dispute, talk to Father.'

'Keep the old gentleman out of this,' begged Henry, clutching at his chest. 'I have had scares enough for one day.'

'Then let us dispose of the first,' said Christopher,

indicating the letter. 'A serious threat has been issued. I believe it to be groundless but I understand that you wish to take no chances. So,' he went on, 'adopt sensible precautions. You're safe enough here with your servants about you and you would hardly be attacked on the street in daylight. This killer works by night. That much we do know.'

'I'll not stir from the house until he is caught.'

'That would be foolish. Go armed and keep your wits about you.'

'Gabriel Cheever was a finer swordsman than me yet he was struck down.'

'Only because he was taken unawares, Henry. You will be more watchful.'

'Even I do not have eyes in the back of my head.'

'Take a servant with you, then. Or walk abroad with a friend. Now,' he said earnestly, 'tell me all you know about Gabriel Cheever. Where does he live?'

Henry looked blank. 'I have no idea.'

'I thought he was an acquaintance of yours.'

'He was. We saw a lot of each other at one time; Gabriel had lodgings in Covent Garden in those days. That was before he disappeared.'

'Disappeared?'

'Yes,' said Henry. 'It was quite strange. Nobody sought pleasure more ardently than Gabriel Cheever. Yet, all of a sudden, he seemed to vanish. He spurned all of his favourite haunts. I remember commenting on it to Arthur Lunn.'

'Why to him?'

'Because he knew Gabriel better than anyone.'

'What did he say?'

'Arthur was as baffled as the rest of us. For some reason, Gabriel quit his lodging and went to ground. Arthur wondered if he had left London altogether.'

'Did nobody see any sign of him?'

'No.' Henry shook his head. 'Sir Marcus Kemp thought he caught a glimpse of him in Knightrider Street but he could easily have been mistaken. Sir Marcus does not have the keenest eyesight.'

'Knightrider Street?' said Christopher. 'That might put him in Jonathan's ward.'

'Sir Marcus would not swear that it was Gabriel.'

'But it could have been?'

'Conceivably.'

'When he was in Covent Garden, did he live alone?'

'His bed was rarely empty,' said Henry enviously, 'but his guests did not usually stay for any length of time. The only woman with whom I saw him on anything like a regular basis was Celia Hemmings and that association broke up some time ago.'

'Might she know the address to which he moved?'

'It would be worth asking her. I can tell you where to find her.'

'Thank you,' said Christopher. 'I'll want to meet anyone who knew Gabriel well.'

Henry smirked. 'Celia knew him as well as his Maker.'

'What manner of man was he, Henry? You told me that he was a rakehell but there must have been other sides to his character. Have you any notion what brought him to London in the first place?'

'Oh, yes. The same thing that brought me here, Christopher.'

'The lure of pleasure?'

'No,' said Henry. 'Fear of a tyrannical father.'

'You must not let him intimidate you so,' said Brilliana, snipping another rose to place in her basket. 'Stand up to him for once.'

'Sir Julius has such a strong personality,' complained her husband.

'At your age, you should not be afraid of the sound of thunder.'

'It's the flashes of lightning that disturb me.'

Lancelot Serle was a tall, thin, nervous man in his thirties with a handsome face stained by a small red birthmark on his cheek that looked like a permanent dribble of strawberry juice from his mouth. He dressed fashionably but his apparel always seemed faintly too big for him. His wife, Brilliana, had no visible defects. A striking woman with a beauty that kept time at bay, she was wearing the plain dress she reserved for any exploits in the garden. While gathering flowers, she did not even spare her husband a glance. Serle hovered ineffectually at her side.

'They could be here as early as tomorrow,' he opined.

'They?'

'Well, I have every hope that Sir Julius will bring your sister with him. Susan is a godsend on such occasions. She knows how to cope with your father.'

'Nobody copes with him better than I do, Lancelot,' said his wife peevishly. 'Susan is too inclined to let him have his own way. I challenge him at every turn.'

'I know, but it does make for a lot of discord, my dear.'

She rounded on him. 'Are you censuring me?'

'Heaven forbid!'

'Father only respects those who argue with him.'

Serle gave a sigh. 'Whenever I try to argue, he beats me down.'

'Offer your opinions with more force, Lancelot.'

'I prefer a quiet life.'

She gave a snort of disgust and resumed her snipping. They were in the formal garden at the rear of their house in Richmond. It was Brilliana's domain. Watched over by their mistress, a large team of gardeners kept the grass cut, the flowerbeds free of weeds, the topiary trimmed to perfection, the paths clear and the ponds uncluttered with extraneous matter. Trees and bushes had been artfully used to create avenues, glades and endless secret places. Statuary was placed to best effect. Running to well over two acres, the garden was a special feature of the fortified manor house that had been in Serle's family for almost two centuries. Brilliana Cheever had coveted it enough to accept its owner's tentative proposal of marriage. Experience had taught her that she had been too headstrong. Instead of being her pride and joy, the garden at Serle Court was now her only consolation.

'What shall we do with him, Brilliana?' wondered Serle.

'Keep him firmly in his place.'

'Sir Julius will be our guest. How will we entertain him?'

'Father is not coming here to be entertained, Lancelot,' she said, cutting the stem of a white rose. 'He is only tolerating our company so that he can venture into London to discuss this new house of his with an architect.'

'When that is built, he will be our neighbour.'

'Hardly.'

'The city is not far away, Brilliana. We shall see much more of him.'

'On the contrary,' she retorted, 'we shall see much less. Why have a house built at all when he could easily stay here while Parliament is sitting? Father likes to order everyone around and he can never do that to me.'

'I sometimes think you are too harsh on him.'

'Would you rather I just grinned obsequiously at him – as you do?'

Serle was hurt. 'I like to be on good terms with my father-in law.'

'A wife should surely take precedence.'

'Of course, Brilliana.'

'Then stop letting me down when he is here,' she snapped. 'Behave more like the master of Serle Court and less like one of its servants.'

'What an unkind remark!' he protested.

'Unkind but not inaccurate,' she said, facing him again. 'Your ancestors fought hard to build up this estate, Lancelot. Prove that you are a worthy successor. When Father comes, do not accede to his every request. Be your own man.'

'That is what I am.'

'Only to a degree.'

Her basket full, she headed back towards the house. Serle fell in beside her. He ducked under some fronds of willow that overhung the path and raised a new topic.

'What is the likelihood of your sister's coming?' he asked.

'Why?'

'We must take care not to neglect Susan.'

'You can leave my sister to me, Lancelot. We will take the coach into the city and visit the shops. Susan will like that,' she said with a patronising smile. 'She is a country mouse, remember. London is a source of continual wonder to her.'

'Susan must envy you so much, Brilliana.' He did not see the sneer that rose to her lips. 'Indeed, it is with that in mind that I have a suggestion to put. For reasons that I fail to understand, my beautiful sister-in-law is neither married nor even betrothed. I know that she has rejected the cream of Northamptonshire's bachelors and wondered if we might not find one more acceptable to her.'

'We?'

'There are plenty of eligible young men we could invite to the house.'

'Why?' she said with contempt. 'So that she may run her eye over them like a farmer at a cattle market? It is not our task to find her a husband.'

'A helping hand is all that I am advocating.'

'Offer that and you'll get little thanks from Susan.'

'Why?'

'My sister has true Cheever spirit. She insists on making her own decisions.'

'Your brother made his own decisions,' he said ruefully, 'and look what happened to him.'

'Lancelot!' she exclaimed.

'Gabriel had rather too much of the Cheever spirit.'

'That's a dreadful thing to say.'

'Yet it contains a measure of truth.'

Brilliana was quivering with anger. 'Gabriel chose his path in life and he must suffer the consequences. We no longer accept him as a member of the family, as you know only too well. Why do you vex me by mentioning his foul name?'

'He is your brother, my dear,' he said weakly.

'He *was*, Lancelot, but I refuse to acknowledge him now. So does Father.'

'I learnt that to my cost.'

'Then why touch on a subject you know will offend me?'

'No offence was intended.'

'As far as I am concerned,' she emphasised, 'Gabriel does not even exist any more. My brother might just as well be dead.'

Instead of returning to Fetter Lane to collect his horse, Christopher decided to make the journey on foot. The long walk to Addle Hill gave him time to reflect. He was puzzled by the second letter sent to his brother, reasoning that it had to come from someone who was party to Gabriel Cheever's murder because nobody else knew about it. Henry had flown into a panic but the death threat did not entirely convince Christopher. A man who was trying to squeeze money from a victim by means of blackmail would not toss away all hope of profit by killing that victim. Yet that was what was implied by the mention of Gabriel Cheever. Had he foolishly resisted blackmail demands? According to Henry, Cheever had been a single-minded young man with a forceful character.

He had clearly inherited some of his father's traits. Unlike Henry Redmayne, he did not sound like a natural target for blackmail. Why choose someone who would surely never cave in to demands for money? And how could anyone blackmail a man who, it transpired, was so careless of his reputation that he gloried in his debauchery? The rakehell described by Henry would have no qualms whatsoever if his *amours* became public knowledge. He was impervious to extortion.

Something else worried Christopher about the second letter. It was not written by the same person as the first one. Accomplices were at work. One of them had the most graceful handwriting. Jonathan Bale had explained that Gabriel Cheever's assassin must have been a powerful man. Was a vicious killer capable of such stylish calligraphy? The more Christopher thought about it, the more persuaded he became that the blackmail emanated from someone within Henry's circle. The problem was that the circle was rather large. His brother had now provided him with a list of over thirty close friends. A supplementary list of acquaintances included the name of Gabriel Cheever. To pick a way through the complex private life of Henry Redmayne was a formidable task.

As Christopher entered the city through Ludgate, his thoughts turned to Susan Cheever. The death of her brother would be a bitter blow to her and she would be agonised when she learnt the nature of that death. How her father and her sister would react, Christopher did not know. His only concern was for the young woman who had made such a deep impression on him during his visit to Northamptonshire. It grieved him that they had parted on such an awkward note. He did not relish passing on the grim tidings. A mere question about her brother had been enough to upset her. News of his murder might destroy her completely. Christopher resolved to choose his words with utmost care. Eager to see Susan Cheever again, he wished that he could meet her in any circumstances but the present ones.

She remained at the forefront of his mind until he turned into Addle Hill.

'Mr Redmayne!'

'Good day to you, Mrs Bale.'

'It is so nice to see you again, sir.'

'The pleasure is mine, I assure you.'

Though she had only met him on a handful of occasions, Sarah Bale was very fond of Christopher. He was always polite, charming and kind to her children. Having heard that he was due to call, she made sure that she answered the door to him. Once she had shown him into the parlour, however, she left him alone with her husband. They had serious business to discuss and she did not wish to hold them up. Christopher was touched that he had been invited to the house. It was a sign of friendship. Whether out of resentment or from feelings of social inferiority, Jonathan Bale had always been unhappy about his earlier visits, but those objections seemed to have disappeared. Christopher was welcomed and shown to a seat. Turning down the offer of refreshment, he plunged straight into the matter in hand.

'I believe that I know who killed Gabriel Cheever,' he began.

Jonathan was delighted. 'You have a name?'

'Not yet, Mr Bale, but I have critical evidence. The person behind the murder is the same man who has been trying to extort money from my brother.'

After swearing the constable to secrecy, Christopher gave him an abbreviated account of the two blackmail letters, tactfully omitting any scurrilous details about his brother's indiscretions. Jonathan listened with fascination. He was especially attentive when given more details about the murder victim. One fact was pounced upon.

'Gabriel Cheever lived in Knightrider Street?' he said.

'Not necessarily,' warned Christopher. 'Someone claims to have *seen* him there, that is all. There's no guarantee that he had lodgings there.'

'On the other hand, it does establish a possible link with this ward.'

'Granted.'

'Knightrider Street is not far from Paul's Wharf.'

'It might be worth knocking on some more doors.'

'Yes,' said Jonathan. 'Tom Warburton can try his luck there.'

'What of your news?'

'I got to the morgue just in time to stop them arranging a burial. The body will be held until a family member can identify and reclaim it. If Gabriel Cheever is a resident of Knightrider Street, he should be buried in the cemetery of the parish church.'

'That is something for his family to decide.'

'I thought that he had broken with them.'

'Not all of them, Mr Bale.'

106

'Oh.'

'Leave the family to me,' said Christopher. 'Sir Julius has a married daughter who lives in Richmond. He gave me her address. I plan to ride there first thing in the morning to break the news to her and to find out when her father is expected.'

'Would you like me to come with you, Mr Redmayne?'

Christopher smiled. 'No, thank you. But it's a kind offer, particularly when it comes from a man who hates riding as much as you do.'

'Nature did not intend me to sit astride a horse.'

'You prefer to keep your feet on the ground, Mr Bale. In every sense.'

'What can I do in the meantime?'

'Speak to some of the people on this list that Henry gave me,' said Christopher, taking it from his pocket. 'Start with Arthur Lunn. He was closer to Gabriel Cheever than anyone. See what he can tell you about the dead man.'

'How will I find the gentleman?'

'At his favourite coffee house. Sir Marcus Kemp may be there as well. He was the man who claimed to have seen Cheever in Knightrider Street. Between the two of them, they should be able to give you much more information about him.'

'And this...other matter?' asked Jonathan discreetly.

Christopher was decisive. 'Make no mention of it, Mr Bale. Keep my brother's name out of it at this stage. It will be enough for them to know that a friend of theirs has been murdered. That will secure their interest.'

'Arthur Lunn and Sir Marcus Kemp.'

'Both amiable fellows but neither destined for sainthood.'

'I had already decided that,' said Jonathan seriously. 'Well, I'll speak to them at their coffee house and see what I can learn. What of you, Mr Redmayne?'

'The person I intend to meet does not appear on this list.'

'Why not?'

'Because she is not one of my brother's inner circle,' explained Christopher. 'But she may be able to tell me things about Gabriel Cheever that nobody else knows.'

'Who is the lady?'

'Miss Celia Hemmings.'

CHAPTER SIX

Sir Julius Cheever set out for London earlier than planned.
Having made the decision to go, he saw no reason for delay
and he took his younger daughter with him for company.
Susan could read his moods with great accuracy. She knew
when to talk, when to listen and, most important of all, when
to do neither. If he drifted off into a reverie, Sir Julius did not
like to be interrupted and she had thoughts of her own in
which to lose herself for long periods. Their coach rocked
its way noisily over a track hardened by the hot sunshine.
Sleep was out of the question but they learnt to adjust their
bodies to the jolting rhythm and that brought some comfort.
They made good speed. Susan judged the moment to break
the silence.

'We should have ridden there,' she said.

'Why sit on two horses when we can be pulled by four?'

'Because we would have travelled more quickly, Father.'

'Only if we had found enough companions to ensure safety on the journey. Besides,' argued Sir Julius with rough-hewn gallantry, 'I could not ask a delicate young lady like yourself to spend two whole days in the saddle.'

Susan was firm. 'I am not delicate and I love riding. Nothing would have pleased me more than to make the entire journey on horseback.'

'And arrive at Serle Court covered in dirt and perspiration?'

'Travel always imposes penalties.'

'Then the sensible thing is to lessen their number, Susan. Take your ease,' he advised. 'As much as this coach allows you to, that is. We've kept up a steady pace so far. When we arrive in Richmond tomorrow, we'll be fresh and unsullied.'

'Apart from the occasional bruise,' she added with a smile.

'You would insist on coming with me.'

'I wanted to see Brilliana.'

Sir Julius snorted. 'You'd hardly be subjecting yourself to this in order to see your brother-in-law. Why, in God's name, did she have to wed that drooling imbecile?'

'Lancelot is an intelligent man,' she said loyally.

'Then he has a wonderful gift for disguising that intelligence.'

'Don't mock him, Father.'

'The fellow is so irredeemably fatuous.'

'Brilliana chose him and, for her sake, we must learn to love him.'

'Love him?' exploded Sir Julius. 'What is there to love?'

Susan was tactful. 'You'll have to ask my sister that.'

'Brilliana long ago abandoned the pretence that she actually loved that booby. She married him for his house and his wealth. Not that I quibble with that,' he said, lifting a palm. 'Those are perfectly sound reasons for a young lady to wed, but not if it means enslaving yourself to a fool like Lancelot Serle.'

'I don't think that anyone would enslave Brilliana,' observed Susan tartly.

'No, she takes after me.'

'We all do, Father.' He shot her a warning glance and she regretted having included her brother in the reference. 'Well, perhaps not all.'

One of the wheels suddenly explored a deep pothole and the whole coach lurched over to the right. The occupants reached out to steady themselves, and Sir Julius thrust his head through the window to berate the driver.

'Watch where you're going, man!'

'I'm sorry, Sir Julius,' replied the other. 'I didn't see it until it was too late.'

'Are you blind?'

'I'll be more careful from now on.'

Sir Julius lapsed back into his seat with a thud. Susan watched him for a moment.

'Father,' she said at length, 'what do you hope to achieve in Parliament?'

'I mean to introduce a measure of sanity.'

'Can one man exert any real influence there?'

'The Lord Protector did,' he said proudly.

'Times have changed since then,' she pointed out.

'More's the pity!'

Susan was worried. 'You will be circumspect?'

'Circumspect?' he repeated with disgust.

'Hot words might land you in trouble, Father.'

'Parliament needs someone to speak his mind and that's what I intend to do. Circumspect, indeed! They'll not gag me, Susan. I fear nobody.'

'That's my chief concern.'

He was reproachful. 'What do you know of politics, anyway?'

'I know that they can mean danger and even death,' she said levelly. 'I was only a girl when the war raged but I remember the damage it did. Northamptonshire saw more than its fair share of suffering. It taught me to be fearful of politics.'

'Your mother was the same. Neither of you understood what it was all about.'

'Be careful, Father. That is all I ask.'

'I'm a soldier,' he said with a proud chuckle. 'You achieve little on a battlefield if you simply exercise care. To strike a decisive blow you have to go boldly to the heart of the action. That is where I long to be. On my feet in the Commons, demanding justice.'

'For whom?'

'The people of this country, Susan. Taxes are bleeding us dry. And where does all the money go?' he asked, wagging a finger. 'To the King. So that he can fight his wars abroad and keep his mistresses in style. Someone must speak out against him.'

Susan said nothing. There was no point in stirring him up even more. Sir Julius was still fighting battles that had already been won and lost many years earlier. Rooted in the past, he wanted a say in the future, but his language was hortatory rather than persuasive. His fellow Members of Parliament would soon become familiar with the sound of his ranting. Susan let her mind drift to something else. When her father had calmed down enough to permit a civilised conversation, she put her thoughts into words.

'Are you pleased with the design of the new house, Father?'

'I should be. I more or less drew up the plans for it myself.'

'With the help of Mr Redmayne,' she reminded him.

'Well, yes,' he agreed. 'Redmayne actually did the drawings but they were based on ideas that were entirely my own. If I must have a house in London, it must conform exactly to my specifications. Redmayne appreciates that.'

'He seems a most obliging young man.'

'Obliging and capable.'

'Have you seen anything that he designed?'

'Only that bookshop of his,' said Sir Julius. 'It may be small but it's the finest building in Paternoster Row. Elijah Pembridge was thrilled with it and rightly so. He could not speak too highly of Christopher Redmayne.'

'What else has he designed?' asked Susan.

'A couple of houses in London, both far larger than the one I've commissioned.'

'Where exactly are they?'

'Why do you ask?'

'I thought it might be amusing to take a look at them when I go into the city with Brilliana,' said Susan, trying to hide her curiosity. 'Mr Redmayne talked so fervently about his work that he aroused my interest.'

'When was this? You hardly spoke to the man.'

'I heard his voice through the door.'

Sir Julius grinned. 'Eavesdropping, were you?'

'Not at all,' she said without conviction. 'I just happened to be passing when the two of you were discussing the new house. It was impossible not to catch what he was saying about his work. Evidently, it's a labour of love.'

'That's why I chose him. Redmayne has passion.'

'Could you find out where these other houses are?'

'Oh, I think you should do that for yourself, Susan.'

'What do you mean?'

'I may be old,' he said with a paternal smile, 'but I've not lost all my faculties yet. Talk to the fellow in person. Why pretend to be interested in architecture when your real interest is in the architect himself?'

Christopher arrived just in time. Celia Hemmings was on the point of leaving her house in Bow Street when he presented himself at her door. She was a slim woman of medium height, impeccably attired in a low-necked, full-sleeved dress of pink satin with a billowing skirt that opened at the front to reveal an underskirt of a darker hue. Her face was heart-shaped, her lips red and her eyes sparkling. Christopher could see what had attracted Gabriel Cheever to her. After introducing himself, he asked her to give him a few minutes alone in private.

She was cautious. 'I am not in the habit of inviting strangers into my house.'

'The news I carry ought not to be divulged on a doorstep,' he explained.

'Why not, sir?'

'I fear that it is of too heavy a nature.'

'What does it concern?' she said.

'A friend of yours – Gabriel Cheever.'

She tensed. 'You have bad tidings of Gabriel?'

'The worst, alas.'

Celia Hemmings was alarmed. She invited him into the house and took him into the parlour. Christopher suggested that she sat down before he broke the news. Still wearing her wide-brimmed hat, she perched on the edge of a chair and waited with trepidation. Christopher lowered his voice.

'Gabriel Cheever has passed away, I fear.'

'Never!' she cried, hands moving involuntarily to her throat.

'It happened a few days ago, Miss Hemmings.'

'But Gabriel was so strong and healthy.'

Christopher tried to be gentle. 'He did not die a natural death.'

'He was *murdered*?'

'I'm afraid so.'

The woman was so shaken that he thought she was about to keel over, and he reached out a steadying hand. Seizing a handkerchief from her sleeve, she buried her face in it and sobbed uncontrollably. Christopher was unable to console her. It was minutes before she dabbed at her eyes and looked up at him.

'Forgive me, Mr Redmayne,' she said. 'Gabriel was a dear friend of mine.'

'That is why I felt you had a right to know.'

'What brought you to me?'

'I came at my brother's suggestion. I believe you know Henry.'

'Henry Redmayne?' she muttered. 'Yes, of course. I have met him on occasion.' She got up from the chair. 'But who committed this terrible crime? And why? Gabriel was the sweetest man in the world. Nobody could want to kill him. Has anyone been arrested? Tell me all.'

Christopher gave her nothing but the details he had rehearsed on his way there, stressing the need for her help if the killer was to be brought to justice. Eyes still moist, she nodded her consent. The self-possessed young woman he had met at the door now looked weak and vulnerable. He persuaded her to resume her seat, and she removed her hat.

'When did you last see Gabriel?' he asked.

'Some months ago. We reached the parting of the ways.'

'So I understand.'

'It was not a sad event, Mr Redmayne,' she said. 'Gabriel Cheever was unlike any other man I know. There were no violent arguments or bitter recriminations. Thanks to him, it was almost painless. We parted on the most amicable terms.'

'Did you keep in touch with him?'

'Only through mutual friends. Then that suddenly stopped.'

'Why?'

'Gabriel was nowhere to be seen. He seemed to disappear completely. I wondered if he had gone back home to Northamptonshire,' she said wistfully. 'He always talked about being reconciled with his father one day.'

'I know Sir Julius Cheever.'

'Then you will understand why he disapproved of his son.' She gave a wan smile. 'He would certainly have disapproved of me as well, but that does not worry me. I loved Gabriel. When we were together, I'd gladly accept anyone's condemnation.'

'Did he have any enemies, Miss Hemmings?'

'None that I knew of.'

'He must have had rivals.'

'Dozens of them, but they sought to gain advantage over him at a card table, not in some dark alley. That was where he blossomed, Mr Redmayne. In a gaming house.'

'So my brother tells me.'

'Gabriel had the most uncommon skill at cards.'

'Henry described it as damnable luck.'

'It was much more than that, believe me,' said Celia loyally. 'Gabriel had expensive tastes. Since his father had cut him off without a penny, he had to find an income from somewhere. The card table was the making of him.'

'It's been the ruin of my brother.'

'Perhaps he should drink less and concentrate more.'

'How true!' sighed Christopher. 'Henry will over-indulge. But coming back to Gabriel's family, I know that he and Sir Julius were not on speaking terms, but what about his relationship with his sisters?'

'The elder one, Brilliana, was as stubborn as her father.'

'And his other sister, Susan?'

'He always spoke with such affection of her.'

'I can imagine that,' said Christopher, conjuring up her face in his mind. 'Did he ever correspond with her?'

'From time to time.'

'How did he contrive that?'

'His letters were sent to a neighbour and Susan retrieved them from there. It would have been far too dangerous to send them directly to the house. Had her father discovered the truth, Susan would have been in serious trouble. She's very brave.'

'Did you ever meet her?'

'Alas, no,' she said, 'but Gabriel managed to see her when she came to London. She gave her sister the slip one afternoon and spent an hour with him. It meant so much to Gabriel,' she remembered, 'though I suspect that Susan would have been given a stern reprimand for wandering away. Gabriel told me that Brilliana has a vicious tongue.'

Once started, Celia Hemmings was willing to produce many fond recollections of her former lover and Christopher was able to build up a clearer picture of the man in his mind. Much of what she said accorded with Henry Redmayne's description, but she added an important new dimension to the portrait.

'Gabriel hated farming,' she went on. 'He thought there should be more to life than running an estate in Northamptonshire. But that was not the only reason that he and his father fell out. Gabriel had ambitions that could only be fulfilled in London.'

'It sounds to me as if he fulfilled them with zest.'

'No, Mr Redmayne. You misjudge him. He was a much more serious person than anyone realised. The gaming houses may have provided him with his money but it was never frittered away. Gabriel saved it for a purpose.'

'And what was that?'

'To buy himself time.'

'Time?'

'Yes. In order to pursue his real interest.'

'What was that, Miss Hemmings?'

'Poetry,' she said. 'Gabriel wanted above all else to become a poet. He showed me some of his work. He had real talent. When we were together, he was also writing a play. In fact,' she confessed, 'that's what I thought he might be doing when he vanished. Turning his back on us all so that he could write all the things that were bursting to come out of him. That was the true Gabriel Cheever,' she asserted. 'He was not just another unprincipled rake in search of pleasure but a conscientious author who would get back to his lodgings in the early hours of the morning and take up his pen. That's the man I shall remember.'

Jonathan Bale was not looking forward to his assignment. He headed for Holborn without enthusiasm. The constable was much more accustomed to breaking up brawls in rowdy taverns than to venturing into the privileged world of a coffee house. When he found the place, he hesitated at the door, reluctant to enter an establishment where men with whom he would not normally consort were consuming a liquid that he disdained to touch. The smell of tobacco smoke was another deterrent to him but he forced himself to go on. The coffee house was large and well appointed. It buzzed with conversation. Smoking pipes and dispensing gossip, fashionably dressed men lounged at their tables over cups of coffee. Jonathan, patently, did not belong. He collected several disapproving stares and a few unflattering comments, but he was in luck. When he spoke to the owner, he learnt that Arthur Lunn was actually there. Seated alone at a table, the man was sipping a cup of coffee while he waited for a friend. When Lunn was pointed out to him, Jonathan went over to introduce himself.

'Whatever's brought you here?' asked Lunn cheerily. 'Am I under arrest?'

'No, sir, but I'm hoping that you may be able to give me information that may in time lead to an arrest. Mr Henry Redmayne said that I might find you here.'

Lunn was surprised. 'You're a friend of Henry's?'

'Not exactly,' said Jonathan. 'I know his brother.'

'Ah, the aspiring young architect.'

'He thought that you might be able to help me.'

'Very well,' said Lunn offhandedly, 'but at least sit down. You're attracting far too much attention, Mr Bale, and I hate it when someone looms over me like that.'

Jonathan lowered himself uneasily into the seat and glanced around. He was an outsider and the other customers were letting him know it in all manner of subtle ways. He turned back to Lunn.

'I believe that you knew Gabriel Cheever,' he said.

'Yes. A wonderful fellow. Why do you ask?' Lunn chuckled. 'Has the law finally caught up with Gabriel? I knew that it would one day.'

'Mr Cheever has been murdered.'

'What?' Lunn was startled. 'Can you be serious?'

'I was there when the body was found, sir.'

'When was this?'

'Earlier in the week.'

'Where?'

'Paul's Wharf.'

'What on earth was Gabriel doing there?'

'We have no idea as yet, Mr Lunn. Can you offer any opinion?'

'No,' said the other, still dazed by the news. 'To be frank, I rather lost sight of Gabriel. It must be months since we last met. He was living in Covent Garden then but he quit his lodgings one day without telling anyone where he was going.'

'How well did you know him, sir?'

'Extremely well. We were good friends. In the circumstances, that was a miracle.'

'A miracle?'

'Yes, Mr Bale. Gabriel Cheever was the king of the card table. I must have lost a small fortune to him over the years but I never resented it somehow. Gabriel had such charm. He made you feel that it was a kind of honour to lose to him.'

'Is that how he made his money?' said Jonathan with a note of censure. 'By playing games of chance?'

'There was no chance when Gabriel was at the table.'

Arthur Lunn launched into some rambling reminiscences. Jonathan was torn between curiosity and revulsion. Valuable facts about the murder victim were emerging but the world in which he had moved was anathema to the constable. He schooled himself to memorise the information without making any moral judgement. Whatever kind of existence he had led, Gabriel Cheever deserved to have his killer caught and punished. Lunn was in full flow. Most of his revelations were shocking to the ears of a Puritan but he did not even notice the effect he was having, and surged on regardless. As other names surfaced, Jonathan tried to make a mental note of them in case one or two were not on the list that Christopher Redmayne had acquired. Every tiny scrap of information needed to be hoarded. It might all be relevant. By the time Lunn stopped, his voice was maudlin. His affection for the dead man was apparent. Jonathan seized on the name that had been repeated most often.

'You mentioned Sir Marcus Kemp, sir.'

'He and I spent much time in Gabriel's company.'

'I would value a word with him.'

'Sir Marcus will be horrified when he hears the news.'

'Is he here at the moment?' asked Jonathan, looking around.

'No, Mr Bale,' said Lunn. 'It's far too early for him to be up and about. Sir Marcus carouses until dawn as a rule. My guess is that he's still asleep in his bed.'

Sir Marcus Kemp ignored the bell and pounded on the door with his fist. He was a tall, stooping, lean individual in his thirties with a long, sallow face and large, mournful brown eyes. With his periwig resting on his shoulders like huge hairy ears, he had the appearance of an oversized spaniel suffering from distemper. When the door did not open immediately, he attacked it with more vigour. It swung back on its hinges. Pushing the servant aside, he stormed into the hall.

'Where is Henry?' he demanded.

'Mr Redmayne is not receiving visitors today, Sir Marcus,' said the servant.

'He'll receive me.'

'I have instructions to let nobody in.'

'Damn it, man! Do I have to search the house myself?' The servant weakened. 'Let me speak to him, Sir Marcus.'

'Just tell me where he is.'

'Mr Redmayne is dining at home, but—'

Sir Marcus Kemp cut him off in mid-sentence by thrusting him aside for the second time. He strode to door of the dining room and flung it open. Seated at the table, Henry was picking at the meal set out before him. He looked up in surprise as his visitor descended on him. The hapless servant appeared in the doorway to signal his apologies.

'There you are, Henry!' said the newcomer. 'Thank heaven!'

'This is an inopportune moment, Marcus,' said Henry.

'I do not care two hoots for that, man. I am in despair.'

He sank into a chair. Henry waved his servant away and the man closed the door behind him. Seeing the look of terror in his friend's face, Henry poured him a glass of wine and passed it across to him. The visitor downed it in one eager gulp.

'What is the matter?' asked Henry.

'I'm staring death in the face.'

'In what way?'

'The worst possible way, Henry,' said the other. 'Do you recall a night we spent some months ago, enjoying the hospitality of Mrs Curtis?'

'We spent many such nights together.'

'This one was rather special. Two young ladies obliged us in the most wonderful fashion. All four of us shared such harmless delight in that bed.' His voice darkened. 'But it was not as harmless as I thought, Henry,' he said, extracting a letter from his pocket. 'This came for me this morning.

It's a demand for money. Among other things, that glorious night we all spent together in the same bed is described in frightening detail.'

'Do not remind me,' said Henry. 'I have seen that particular description.'

'I'm being blackmailed!'

'You are not alone, Marcus.'

'What do you mean?'

Henry heaved a sigh. 'Have some more wine.'

The ride to Richmond on the following morning gave Christopher Redmayne the chance to review the situation in depth. Events had moved fast. Having returned to London with a prized commission in his pocket, he was now faced with the task of breaking news of a family tragedy to the very person who employed him. The death of Gabriel Cheever was unlikely to stop the new house from being built in Westminster but he did not relish his role as a messenger. Sir Julius was a proud and implacable man. Christopher anticipated trouble both from him and from his elder daughter. The tidings that he carried might well meet with a frosty reception at Serle Court. Gabriel Cheever only had one remaining friend in his family and she was the person Christopher was most anxious not to upset. Yet that was unavoidable. As he thought of Susan Cheever, he was not sure if he wanted her to be at Serle Court or not. Any pleasure that her presence might give him would be offset by the pain he inflicted on her.

The information garnered from Celia Hemmings had been invaluable. She had confirmed that Susan had maintained contact with her brother, albeit under difficult conditions.

It only served to increase Christopher's respect for the beguiling young lady he had met in Northamptonshire. Celia Hemmings had also revealed things about her former lover that nobody else had even suspected, and he had been forced to adjust his view of the dead man. Life on a country estate was not the ideal milieu for someone with ambitions to publish his poetry and write plays for the theatre. Nor would Sir Julius Cheever have looked kindly on activities that had a Cavalier tinge to them. He had willingly supported the closure of all theatres during the Commonwealth. That his only son rejected him and his principles so totally must have rankled with the old man. To a lesser extent, it was a situation replicated in Christopher's own family and he was very conscious of the fact. Henry Redmayne's private life was an act of defiance against the Dean of Gloucester but he was careful to hide it from his father. If sordid details of his sybaritic existence were made public, as threatened, there would be severe repercussions inside one of England's most stately cathedrals.

Christopher was still sceptical about the suggested motive for the murder. Everything he had heard about Gabriel Cheever indicated a young man who would meet blackmail demands with contempt. What could possibly be disclosed that he would find at all embarrassing? The irony was that the only things he kept secret were his literary aspirations and they would hardly be a source of blackmail. Christopher decided to keep an open mind about the reasons that prompted someone to kill him. What had altered the situation slightly was the intelligence, confided by his brother on the previous day, that Sir Marcus Kemp was also a victim of attempted extortion, with one significant difference. In the latter case, no death threat had been received. Why had Henry Redmayne been singled out for additional pressure, if, indeed, that is what had happened? Christopher could not exclude the possibility that others might also have been the target for blackmail and, perhaps, for a secondary threat. One thing seemed incontrovertible. The man behind the letters was an insider. He was part of the social circle that embraced Henry Redmayne, Sir Marcus Kemp and Gabriel Cheever. It was not a world in which Jonathan Bale would be able to operate with any ease. Christopher knew that he would have to take much of the investigative burden on himself.

Following the Thames south as it snaked through the verdant acres of Surrey, he travelled without incident and kept up a steady pace. There was an incidental bonus. His journey took him past Richmond Palace and he paused to enjoy the architectural refinements of a building that dated, for the most part, back to the reign of the first Tudor monarch. Though he had seen it several times before, he feasted his gaze on its sheer splendour. Particular interest was reserved for Trumpeters' House. It was situated off the Green behind Old Palace Yard and Christopher admired its elegant lines for a long while, knowing that he would never be able to design a royal residence but wishing that he might one day be able to put his name to a house as fine as the one before him. The vain thought was soon dismissed. Chiding himself for being deflected from his purpose, he swung his horse round and kicked it into a canter.

Serle Court was little more than a mile away. Set on a

rise in rolling countryside, it was an imposing sight from a distance. Closer inspection revealed its shortcomings. Its turrets looked faintly ridiculous, its battlements ugly and the tiled areas of roof at war with the larger expanse of thatch. Its scale was its chief recommendation. Christopher wished that he could strip away the fortifications to let the manor house stand on its own merits again. Everything else about the estate was impressive. The grounds of the house were well kept, the landscape offered pleasing prospects on all sides and the fountain in the forecourt was a positive delight. What gave him a sudden thrill of recognition was the sight of the coach that was being taken round to the stable yard. Christopher was certain that he had seen it once before in Northamptonshire.

Dismounting from his horse, he handed the reins to an ostler who came running towards him, then presented himself at the front door. He was invited in and asked to wait in the hall. News of his arrival provoked an immediate response. Sir Julius came strutting out to offer him a gruff welcome and to demand what he was doing there.

'I was hoping that you might be here, Sir Julius,' explained Christopher.

'Yes,' said the other, 'but not to discuss business, man. That is best done at your own house in London. This is a family visit. I resent any intrusion.'

'It was forced upon me, I fear.'

'Oh?'

'I have sad tidings to impart.'

The old man started. 'Are you trying to wriggle out of our contract?'

'No, Sir Julius,' said Christopher. 'This has nothing to do with your new house. It's a personal matter.' There was a long pause. 'It concerns a member of your family.'

'What on earth are you talking about?'

'Your son, Gabriel.'

Sir Julius turned puce. He was on the point of issuing a stinging rejoinder when he was interrupted by a voice behind him. Susan Cheever was standing in the doorway of the parlour, composed yet apprehensive.

'Good day to you, Mr Redmayne!' she said politely.

'And to you, Miss Cheever,' he returned.

'Did I hear you mention my brother?'

'Yes, you did.'

'I'll not hear a word about him,' warned Sir Julius angrily. 'If you bring a message from him, Mr Redmayne, you are wasting your breath.'

'What is going on?' said Brilliana, sweeping into the hall past her sister. 'Why is Father shouting like that?' She glared at Christopher. 'Who might you be, sir?'

'My architect,' snapped Sir Julius. 'At least, he was,' he added with a warning glance. 'Whatever blandishments you have brought, you may take them away at once. And you may tell the.person who sent you that I never wish to see him again.'

Lancelot Serle now joined the group in the hall, standing beside his wife with his usual expression of bafflement. Sir Julius was exuding hostility. Brilliana had turned to ice. Susan was clutching her hands together. Christopher was left with no alternative to blurting out his news.

'Your son is dead, Sir Julius.'

The effect on his hearers varied. Sir Julius turned away in disgust, Brilliana stared accusingly at the visitor, Serle dithered helplessly and Susan was so shocked that she had to support herself on the door frame. Wanting to rush across to her, Christopher had to restrain himself and wait for the opportunity to deliver an even more crushing blow. It was Brilliana who first found a voice.

'I can hardly say that I am surprised,' she said without sympathy.

'Brilliana!' cried her sister.

'Those who follow such a despicable life must suffer its consequences.'

Susan was trembling. 'That's a horrible thing to say.'

'It has a degree of truth in it,' ventured Serle, eager to support his wife.

'I would dispute that, sir,' said Christopher defensively. 'Gabriel Cheever did not die in the way that is implied. He was murdered in cold blood.'

The announcement set off another series of reactions. Sir Julius turned back with incredulity on his face, Serle began to gibber wildly and his wife had the grace to look saddened by the news. Christopher was not interested in them. His attention was fixed on Susan Cheever, who took a few uncertain steps towards him then collapsed in a dead faint. He ran across to kneel beside her, slipping a hand under her head. The emergency seemed to bring out the best in the other members of the family. Sir Julius suggested that she be carried into the parlour, Serle helped Christopher to lift the limp body and Brilliana summoned a servant and gave crisp orders. By the time she began to recover, Susan was lying on a couch while her sister held a cup of brandy to her lips. Christopher had been relegated to a position at the rear of the group clustered around her but it was his eyes she sought. Aided by her father, she sat up and waved the brandy away.

'I do not want that,' she said.

'Let me send for a doctor,' said Brilliana.

'There's no need.'

'I am sorry that I gave you such a shock, Miss Cheever,' said Christopher.

'It was not your fault, Mr Redmayne.'

'Would you rather I withdrew?'

'That might be a sensible notion,' decided Brilliana.

'No,' said Susan, raising a hand. 'I am recovered now. Do not leave us, Mr Redmayne. I want to hear what happened.'

'And I wish to know how you came by this gruesome intelligence,' said Sir Julius, clearly shaken.

Lancelot Serle made his first useful contribution by inviting them all to take a seat. Christopher found himself in a chair at the centre of the room. He looked around the expectant faces. Susan was tearful, Brilliana watchful and her husband solemn. Sir Julius was trying to appear detached but his eyes betrayed him. Christopher was tactful. Eliminating the most distressing details and making no reference to his brother's predicament, he explained how Gabriel Cheever's body had been found and why he had been drawn into the investigation. After admitting that no suspects had yet been arrested, he made an attempt to end on a positive note.

'In a sense, it was a blessing that the constable turned to me for help.'

'Blessing?' echoed Sir Julius in a hollow voice.

'Had the body not been identified,' Christopher argued, 'it would have been buried in an unmarked grave with nobody to mourn over it. That would have been very sad.'

'Where is it being held?'

'At the city morgue, Sir Julius. Awaiting the decision of the family.'

That decision, he saw, would not be easy to make. Sir Julius was caught up in a welter of emotions, Brilliana was wrestling with her own feelings and her husband was awaiting her cue so that he could agree with her. Only Susan Cheever knew what she wanted and she feared that her wishes might be overruled.

Christopher rose to his feet. 'I'll trespass no longer on your grief,' he said. 'All that I can do is offer you my profound condolences. If there is anything further that I may do – anything at all – please do not hesitate to call on me.'

'Thank you, Mr Redmayne,' whispered Susan.

'Yes, thank you,' said Sir Julius awkwardly. 'I am sorry to give you so uncivil a welcome. It was good of you to ride all this way with such dreadful tidings. I do appreciate that. Needless to say, this may alter my plans somewhat.'

'Of course, Sir Julius,' said Christopher. 'Our business can wait. Do excuse me.'

He gave a farewell nod and headed for the door. Serle followed him into the hall to add his personal thanks and to wave him off. Christopher departed reluctantly. He wanted to offer some consolation to Susan Cheever but that was impossible while she was surrounded by the others. All that he could do was slip quietly away. When the front door was closed behind him, he looked up at the house and regretted that he had brought such unhappiness to it. He walked slowly to the stables to find his horse, and was about to mount up when a figure suddenly appeared in front of him. Susan Cheever was breathless from her dash to find him.

'Thank goodness I caught you!' she said between gasps.

'Get your breath back before you speak further,' he advised. 'I cannot tell you how grieved I am to be the bearer of such tragic news, but I felt that you should hear it as soon as was conceivably possible.'

'That was very considerate of you, Mr Redmayne.'

'I wish that you could have been spared the shock.'

Susan took a moment to regain her composure then gave a little smile. 'You deserve my thanks,' she said.

'For what?'

'Omitting something from your account of Gabriel's death.'

'I thought it a kindness to do so.'

'I'm not talking about details that might have upset us, Mr Redmayne. You were discreet in another way. I'm grateful to you.'

'It's not for me to pry into your family affairs.'

'You knew,' she said quietly, 'yet you did not expose me.'

'All I know is that you loved your brother as a sister should, Miss Cheever.'

Susan heaved a sigh. 'Father would disagree.'

'Sir Julius may one day come to admit that he did have a son.'

'Gabriel's name will always fester in his memory.'

'And in that of your sister, I fancy,' he observed sadly.

'Brilliana and Gabriel were never close,' recalled Susan. 'When he left home, she spurned him as readily as Father. I could never do that.'

'So I've learnt.' Alarm came into her eyes. 'Have no fear,' he soothed. 'I'll not betray you, Miss Cheever. I applaud your courage. You've done what any true sister would have done.'

Susan looked at him with mingled doubt and affection. She searched his face to see if she could trust him. Christopher was calm beneath her scrutiny. Even at such a difficult time, it was a joy to be close to her again. When she made up her mind, Susan checked to see that nobody could overhear them then stepped closer to him.

'There's something I must tell you, Mr Redmayne,' she began. 'Something which has to be kept from the rest of the family.'

'With good reason, I suspect.'

'It may help with your enquiries.'

'Anything that does that is welcome, Miss Cheever.'

She lowered her head. 'Though it will mean more pain and distress.'

'For whom?'

'Someone I have never even met.'

'You are being very mysterious.'

'How much have you found out about Gabriel?' she asked, looking up.

'Precious little,' he confessed. 'I know that he spent most of his time in the gaming houses and enjoyed an astonishing run of luck at cards. But I also know that he was no mere pleasure-seeker. Your brother had serious literary ambitions.'

'He did. Writing was his first love.'

'I am told that he had exceptional talent.'

'What else were you told?' she wondered. 'Do you know where he lived?'

'No, Miss Cheever. That has been a stumbling block to us. We have no address for him. He lodged in Covent Garden at one time but disappeared from there without warning some months ago. None of his friends had any idea where to find him.'

'I did, Mr Redmayne.'

'Was he still in London?'

'Oh, yes. Gabriel had no urge to leave.'

'Where did he go to ground?'

'At a house in Knightrider Street. I can furnish you with the number. But there is something you must know before I do so.'

'Indeed?'

'Gabriel was not living alone,' she said quietly. 'He was enjoying true happiness for the first time in his life. I dare say that you can guess why.'

Christopher was taken aback. 'He was *married*?'

'Her name is Lucy. Be gentle with her when you break the news.'

CHAPTER SEVEN

Jonathan Bale had a laborious day. He worked excessively hard but had little to show for his efforts. As well as attending to the routine duties of a constable, he interviewed two more people whose names appeared on Henry Redmayne's list, spoke at length to the coroner about the murder investigation, scoured Paul's Wharf afresh for any clues that might lead to the identification of a suspect and kept his eyes peeled, wherever he went, for any stones resembling those taken from the dead man's coat. He also joined his colleague in the tedious process of visiting every house in Knightrider Street. By mid-afternoon, they had almost completed the task. Tom Warburton was more morose than ever.

'Waste of time,' he decided.

'Only one more house to go.'

'I know the people who live there, Jonathan.'

'Do they have a lodger?'

'No.'

'We might as well try while we are here.'

'Why bother?'

'Leave it to me,' said Jonathan.

He knocked on the door and a hulking man in a leather apron soon appeared. Jonathan recognised him as the assistant to a blacksmith in Great Carter Lane. The man was surly and resentful. With five children, a wife and a mother-in-law in the house, he pointed out, a man had no room for a lodger. Nor did he know of a young man called Gabriel Cheever. He went back into the house and closed the door firmly in their faces. Jonathan was left to face his gloomy colleague.

'I told you so,' grunted Warburton.

'It was worth a try.'

'Mr Cheever is not here.'

'He may have moved in recently, Tom.'

'Where? We knocked on every door.'

Jonathan looked down the length of the street and gave a resigned nod. It had been a forlorn exercise. All that they had to go on was a possible sighting of Gabriel Cheever in Knightrider Street by a man who was not entirely certain of what he saw. Even if the fleeting glimpse had been of Cheever, there was no proof that he resided in the area. He might have simply been visiting the ward. The constables were tired. Even the normally ebullient Sam was jaded. It was time to seek refreshment. Jonathan decided to take one last look at Paul's Wharf before going home, but Warburton had other chores to deal with and went off in the opposite direction. Glad to see his master moving with more purpose, the dog scampered after him with something of its old enthusiasm.

When he reached the wharf, Jonathan went to the place beside the warehouse where the body had been found. He kept thinking about the stones caught up in the man's coat. If they had not come from the immediate vicinity, where had they been picked up? He had seen nothing like them on his rounds and he could hardly search every street, lane and alley in London to find a match. Jonathan was irritated at his own lack of progress. Had it not been for his wife's suggestion he would never have thought of calling on Christopher Redmayne, yet the architect's help had been crucial. But for that, the case would have remained insoluble. Cheever's murder had been used as a warning. Given his stern moral code, Jonathan had scant sympathy for the plight of Henry Redmayne, though he wanted the man responsible for the blackmail to be caught and convicted. What pleased him was that he and Christopher were engaged in solving crimes that were linked in some way. It meant that they could team up once more and pool their resources. It also meant that he could renew a friendship that was unlikely but curiously satisfying. He would never have believed that he could like a man of such Cavalier associations. Unlike his brother, Christopher did not patronise the constable. He appreciated Jonathan's virtues and treated him as an equal.

The constable was still examining the patch of ground beside the warehouse when he heard a horse approaching at a brisk trot, and he looked up to see a familiar figure coming towards him. Greeting him with a wave, Christopher reined in his horse.

'Mr Warburton said that I might find you here.'

'I was just taking one last look at the place where we found the body.'

'Have you discovered anything new?'

'Not yet.'

'Well, I have,' said Christopher, dismounting. 'I've been to Richmond and back today. Sir Julius Cheever was there with the rest of the family. I was able to pass on the bad tidings. I left them to make their own decision about the burial.'

'The body cannot stay in the morgue for much longer.'

'They understand that, Mr Bale. But I was very glad that I made the journey.'

'Why?'

'Because I was given Gabriel Cheever's address.'

Jonathan's spirits rose. 'Where does he live?'

'Knightrider Street.'

'Oh.'

'I mean to visit the house immediately.'

'You were misinformed,' said the other with a sigh of disappointment. 'Tom Warburton and I have been to every house and nobody has heard of a Mr Cheever.'

'Then someone was lying to you. Follow me.'

'Where are we going?'

'To meet his wife.'

Jonathan gaped. 'Gabriel Cheever was *married*?'

'So it seems.'

Christopher led his horse by the reins and Jonathan fell in beside him. On the walk back to Knightrider Street, the architect told him about his visit in more detail, though he said nothing about Susan Cheever's clandestine assistance. The long ride back had been sweetened by fond memories of their brief time alone together. Drawn even more to her, he had been given additional reason to track down her brother's killer. Jonathan responded with a terse account of his own day, ruing the fact that so little had been accomplished. Christopher assured him that Knightrider Street might yet yield something of real value to them.

The house was in the middle of a neat row of dwellings close to Sermon Lane that had replaced the tenements destroyed in the Great Fire. Jonathan remembered calling there earlier and being sent on his way by a plump maidservant. When Christopher knocked, the same woman came to the door. Short, round and flat-faced, she had the look of someone who would obey her employer's wishes to the letter.

'Good afternoon,' said Christopher, touching the brim of his hat. 'I wonder if I might see Mrs Lucy Cheever.'

'There's nobody of that name here,' said the woman. 'I told the constable that.'

'Then I think you must be mistaken.'

'No, sir. I know who my mistress is.'

'Is she at home at the moment?'

'Not to unexpected visitors, sir.'

'But I come as a friend,' explained Christopher. 'I must speak to her as a matter of urgency. I have news about her husband, Gabriel Cheever.'

'You must have confused this address with another one, sir.'

Christopher looked her in the eye. 'Are you not interested in what happened to your master?' he challenged. 'You must surely have missed him by now.'

The woman's lids flickered but she held her ground. Jonathan intervened.

'We need to report an accident,' he said.

'What sort of accident, sir?' she asked.

'A serious one.'

The maidservant was in a quandary. Ordered to keep everyone at bay, she wanted to know more details. She hesitated for a full minute. Eventually, she opted to obey her instructions. Deciding to send them on their way, she was on the point of closing the door with a token apology when someone came down the staircase behind her. It was a young woman in a pretty green dress that rustled as she moved.

'Did I hear mention of an accident?' she asked.

'Yes, Mrs Cheever,' said Christopher.

She blushed slightly. 'My name is Henley, sir.'

'Lucy Henley was your maiden name, I suspect. I am looking at Lucy Cheever now. Why deny it?' he went on before she could protest. 'There is no shame. We are here with important news of your husband. It was your sister-in-law, Susan, who gave me this address. You can surely trust her. I think that you should let us in, Mrs Cheever.'

Christopher's soft voice and considerate manner persuaded her. Nodding to the servant to let them in, Lucy Cheever led the way into the parlour. It was a small but cosy room with evidence of money and taste in the choice of furnishings. Christopher noted the small crucifix on the wall. The maidservant lingered protectively in the doorway but her mistress dismissed her with a glance. When Christopher had performed introductions, all three of them sat down. Lucy Cheever was a short, slender woman with a face of porcelain beauty. She looked so small, young and innocent that it was difficult to believe that she was actually married. There was a fragility about her that disturbed both men. Neither of them relished the notion of passing on the news about her husband, fearing that she would be unable to cope with it.

'We thought that you might have come forward,' said Jonathan quietly.

'Why?' she asked.

'To report that your husband was missing.'

'But I was not aware that Gabriel *was* missing, Mr Bale. I've been away for almost a week. I only returned to the house today.'

'Should your husband have been here?'

'Yes,' she said, 'but I assumed he had gone out somewhere.'

'Where was your servant?'

'Anna travelled with me.'

'So you did not realise that your husband had gone astray?'

'No, Mr Bale. I fully expect him to come back some time today.'

Jonathan exchanged a glance with Christopher then let him take over.

'I have some sad news, I fear,' said the latter. 'Your husband will not be returning to his home. Gabriel Cheever was found dead some nights ago.'

'Dead?' Lucy's face contorted with pain and her fists tightened. 'Gabriel is dead?'

'Mr Bale was there when the body was found.'

'Where?'

'The full details may distress you.'

'You spoke earlier of an accident.'

'It was no accident, Mrs Cheever,' he said gently.

Lucy recoiled as if from a blow to the face and Christopher feared that she might topple over, but she made a supreme effort to control herself. Holding back tears, she turned to Jonathan and spoke in a clear voice.

'Tell me what happened, Mr Bale.'

'It will not make pleasant listening,' he warned.

'I want to know,' she insisted.

'Mrs Cheever—'

'I'm his wife,' she said, interrupting him. 'If Gabriel has been killed, I want to know how. Tell me, Mr Bale. I'm not as frail as I may look, I promise you.'

Jonathan swallowed hard then launched into his tale. Christopher was impressed with how tactful he was, giving a clear account of the discovery of Cheever's body without dwelling overmuch on how he was murdered. The constable obviously had long experience of breaking dreadful news to bereaved families. There was a sensitivity about him that Christopher had never noticed before. Lucy Cheever heard it all without a flicker, though her face was drawn and her hands remained bunched in her lap. When the account was over, she looked across at the crucifix before closing her eyes in a prayer. Christopher was struck by her composure. For a woman who looked so delicate, Lucy Cheever had the most remarkable strength of will. When she opened her eyes again, they could see the grief swirling in them.

'Would you like us to leave?' asked Christopher softly.

'No, Mr Redmayne.'

'Shall I call your servant?'

'I can do that for myself when I feel the need.'

'You're very brave, Mrs Cheever.'

'I want to know all that you can tell me,' she murmured.

'There is not much more to tell,' said Jonathan. 'A search is under way for the man responsible but we have so far unearthed no suspects.'

'Where is my husband's body?'

'Being held at the morgue until it can be reclaimed by his family.'

'I am Gabriel's family,' she said with sudden anger. 'Everyone else turned their back on him. Gabriel was a complete outcast.'

'Not to his younger sister,' Christopher reminded her.

She calmed instantly. 'No, that's true. Susan stood by him.'

'She took grave risks for his sake.'

'I know, Mr Redmayne, and I'm deeply grateful to her. I only hope that I will one day have the opportunity of thanking her in person.' She lifted her head and thrust out her chin. 'I should be consulted about the burial of my husband.'

'You have a legal and a moral right,' agreed Christopher. 'But, apart from Susan Cheever, the family are not even aware of your existence.'

'I know.'

'Your marriage was kept secret from them.'

'And from my own family,' she confessed, biting her lip. 'That is why I retained my maiden name. We have only been in Knightrider Street a short while. The few neighbours we have met think of us as Mr and Mrs Henley.'

'That explains why nobody in the street had heard of you,' observed Jonathan.

'Why the need for such deception?' asked Christopher.

She lowered her gaze. 'That's a private matter.'

'Your husband's family will have to be told the truth.'

'I accept that.'

'You are bound to meet them at the funeral.'

'Yes,' she sighed, looking up. 'But nothing would keep me away.'

The effort of holding in her grief was telling on Lucy Cheever. Her body was tense, her cheeks hollow, her eyes whirlpools of anguish. Wanting to ask her so many questions, Christopher felt that it was not the moment to do so.

'Perhaps we should leave now, Mrs Cheever,' he volunteered.

'Not yet,' she said.

'We have no wish to intrude.'

'I am still bearing up,' she said, brushing a first tear from her cheek. 'And while I still can, I would like to help if it is at all possible.'

'It is,' he said. 'You knew your husband better than anyone.'

'I did, Mr Redmayne. I knew about his vices as well as his virtues. But I loved him nonetheless. Gabriel was everything to me. No woman could have had a kinder or more tender husband.'

'Did he ever talk about his past?'

'Nothing was hidden from me, Mr Redmayne. He was very honest.'

'Did he mention the names of any enemies?'

'Not that I can recall.'

'So you know of nobody who might have wanted to kill him?'

'Gabriel talked of wild threats made against him by people who lost heavily at cards but they were words spoken in the heat of the moment. He took no notice of them.'

'And he forsook that life completely?'

'Yes,' she said firmly. 'That was a condition of our marriage.'

Lucy Cheever had none of the sophisticated charms of Celia Hemmings, still less anything of her social poise and worldliness. Yet she had qualities that the other could never possess. Lucy had an integrity that shone out of her and a loveliness that was all the more fetching because she was so unaware of it. She could no more be Gabriel Cheever's mistress than Celia Hemmings could be his wife. The two women represented different sides of his character. Christopher understood the choice he had finally made.

'You told us that you had been away,' he said.

'I was visiting my mother, Mr Redmayne.'

'Was your husband left here alone?'

'Yes,' she confirmed. 'Anna came with me. Gabriel encouraged that he wanted to work on a play he was writing and felt that he could do it best when he had no distractions.'

'I understand that he wrote poetry as well?'

A smile touched her lips. 'Oh, yes. He wrote wonderful poems.'

'So,' continued Christopher, 'while you were away, your husband would have spent most of his time here?'

'All of it, probably. Unless he went out to dine.'

'No friends were likely to call?'

Her voice sharpened. 'He left that world behind him, Mr Redmayne.'

'Of course. I'm sorry.'

'When you returned here,' said Jonathan, sitting forward, 'did you see any signs of a struggle having taken place in the house?'

'None, Mr Bale,' she said.

'Everything was in its place?'

'Yes.'

'No hint of forced entry?'

'None at all.' She paused. 'Although...'

'Yes?' he prompted.

'It was odd,' she recalled. 'Very odd. When we got back today, I felt that something had been stolen from the house. Anna sensed it as well. But we must have been mistaken,' she said with a shrug. 'We could not find that anything was missing.'

Jonathan looked at Christopher before turning back to her again.

'How hard did you search?' he asked.

The wrangling went on throughout much of the day. Sir Julius Cheever felt that he was being torn apart. Stuck with a son-in-law he despised in a house that he loathed, he was

146

forced to acknowledge a son who had betrayed everything for which he stood. Part of him wanted to turn away from the whole depressing business but another part of him urged a degree of reconciliation. When all was said and done, Gabriel was his own flesh and blood. As he struggled to make up his mind, he was not aided by the comments of his elder daughter.

'There is no need for you to go, Father,' Brilliana told him.

'Somebody must,' he said.

'Let me send Lancelot. He can identify the body.'

'Me?' said her husband uneasily. 'Well, yes, my dear. If you wish.'

'I do wish.'

'Sir Julius?'

'No,' said the old man contemptuously. 'The last person who should do this is you, Lancelot. You hardly knew Gabriel. It's a ludicrous suggestion.'

Brilliana bridled. 'I was only trying to spare you, Father.'

'Perhaps I should go *with* you, Sir Julius,' offered Serle.

'Out of the question,' said Sir Julius hastily. 'Whatever else happens, you will not be involved. This is a family matter.'

'Lancelot is part of the family now,' argued Brilliana.

'He's not a Cheever,' said Susan reasonably. 'It's unfair to force this upon him.'

'I'm not forcing anything on anybody.'

'You are, Brilliana.'

'Well, someone has to make a decision,' retorted her sister, taking a more aggressive stance. 'Nobody else seems capable of doing so.'

'I think that we should leave it to Sir Julius, my dear,' said her husband.

'We'll be here until Doomsday if we do that.'

'Brilliana!' Susan rebuked her.

'And I won't hear any criticism from you, Susan,' warned Brilliana. 'All that you've done is sit there and mope.'

'For heaven's sake – our brother is dead!'

'I'm well aware of that.'

'Then try to show some pity,' urged Susan.

'I need no lessons in behaviour from you,' snapped her sister.

Serle touched her arm. 'There's no reason to get upset about it, Brilliana.'

'Leave me alone.'

'We must discuss this calmly, my dear.'

She rounded on him. 'Oh, be quiet, Lancelot!'

'Yes,' said Sir Julius vehemently. 'That's the one thing Brilliana has said that I fully endorse. You've no useful comment to make in this debate, Lancelot, so I beg of you to make none at all.'

Serle was wounded. 'If you say so, Sir Julius.'

'I do. This bickering is driving me mad. I need peace and quiet.'

They were still seated round the table in the dining room. The meal had long since been over but they stayed in the room, locked in argument and unwilling to move. Susan Cheever tried to say as little as possible but some of her sister's comments could not go unchallenged. Anxious to help, Serle only managed to add further confusion. Sir Julius shuttled between a brooding silence and bursts of anger.

The situation had exposed the deep divisions within the family and that made him squirm. He was uncomfortably reminded of his wife's more tolerant attitude towards their son. She had died after Gabriel left home for good but she usually took his side in his disputes with his father. Sir Julius knew what she would advise in the circumstances, and her counsel weighed heavily with him.

Susan took the initiative. 'Father should go,' she said, 'and I'll go with him.'

Brilliana was scornful. 'You, Susan?'

'Gabriel was my brother.'

'He was my brother as well, but that does not mean to say I wish to see him laid out on a slab.' She gave a shiver. 'The very notion is revolting.'

'Nobody will subject you to that, my dear,' promised Serle.

'I should hope not.'

'Father will need company on the journey,' said Susan.

'Lancelot can provide it.'

'He might prefer me alongside him.'

'I'd prefer anyone but Lancelot,' said Sir Julius with asperity. 'But not you, Susan. You stay here. This is not woman's work. I appreciate your offer but this is something that falls to me and I'll not shirk it. Besides,' he added, hauling himself to his feet, 'it's not merely a question of identifying Gabriel. I want to know who killed him and why. Since I have to go into the city, I'll call on Redmayne.'

'What business is this of his?' asked Brilliana.

'He put himself out to bring us the news.'

'That may be so, Father, but we do not want him poking his nose into our affairs.'

'Mr Redmayne has gone to great lengths to help us,' said Susan with a fervour that took her sister by surprise. 'You heard what he said. He is taking part in the search for Gabriel's killer. In other words, he is putting himself in danger on our behalf. If you cannot be grateful to him, at least do not be so critical.'

Brilliana was effectively silenced for once. Her father savoured the moment.

'I've changed my mind, Susan,' he said at length. 'Perhaps you should come with me, after all.'

Henry Redmayne was so stunned by the news that he flopped back down into a chair. 'Gabriel Cheever had a *wife?*' he said incredulously.

'An extremely attractive one, Henry.'

'This must be some kind of jest.'

'It is not,' said Christopher. 'I can assure you.'

'Gabriel married? Never,' insisted Henry. 'I'd sooner believe that the King had taken a vow of chastity or that our own father shares his bed with two naked women and a long-tailed monkey. It's completely against his nature.'

'Perhaps that is why he kept it so secret.'

'But what could have led to such folly?'

'It was no folly. He somehow met the young lady who is now his widow. Lucy Cheever is the kind of person who would inspire any man to change for the better.'

'Why bother with a wife when he could have had almost any woman he wanted?'

Christopher smiled. 'One day you may learn the answer to that question yourself.

'Pah!'

They were in the hall at the house in Bedford Street. Christopher had arrived as his brother was about to venture out. He was pleased that Henry had plucked up enough courage to resume his social life. It signalled a welcome return of his confidence. Henry was still apprehensive, but the fact that Sir Marcus Kemp was also a victim of blackmail had somehow rallied him. His was now a shared pain and that made it easier to bear.

'Say nothing of this to your friends,' suggested Christopher.

'They would not believe me if I did.'

'I agreed to protect Lucy Cheever's secret. She has reasons of her own why the truth should not spread far and wide. We must respect her wishes.'

'Gabriel was a deeper man than I suspected.'

'Did you know he had literary aspirations?'

'No, Christopher.'

'Miss Hemmings confided as much to me. His wife says that he was a talented poet with ambitions to write plays as well. She said that he was a dedicated author.'

Henry shook his head in wonder. 'Getting married? Scribbling away in secret? Forsaking his old friends and haunts? No,' he said, getting up, 'this is not the Gabriel Cheever that the rest of us knew.'

'I fancy there may be more surprises yet before we finish.'

'I hope not, Christopher. I've had rather too many surprises already.'

'Where are you going now?'

'To call on Sir Marcus Kemp. He was as terrified as I

was at first, especially when he heard that Gabriel had been murdered. He wanted to barricade himself in his house. But I put some steel into him,' said Henry, adopting a pose. 'I told him that we must stick together and defy the blackmail threats.'

'You may soon have company.'

'Company?'

'Yes,' said Christopher. 'A person or persons capable of murder will be ruthless in extorting money from their victims. Compromising material may well exist about others in your circle, Henry. They, too, may receive anonymous demands.

'Poor devils!'

'See what you can find out.'

Henry was petulant. 'That will not be easy, you know. I can hardly go up to every one of my friends and ask them to their faces if they have had any unsavoury correspondence lately. It would be in the worst possible taste,' he said haughtily. 'They are bound to ask me why I frame such a question and I have no wish to expose my own wounds to the world.'

'Your friends may come to you. Sir Marcus Kemp did.'

'Only because one of the incidents mentioned involved the two of us.'

'The four of you,' corrected Christopher.

'One of those damnable women betrayed us.'

'Unless Mrs Curtis was listening at the door.'

'I would not put that past her, Christopher. She likes to make sure that her charges are giving satisfaction. I dare say that Mrs Curtis is no stranger to eavesdropping or to peeping through keyholes.' A thought struck him. 'Could she be party to this blackmail?'

'You would be in a better position than me to discover that, Henry.'

'Oh, no!' moaned his brother. 'I'll not go near her or any other woman again until this villain is caught. Sir Marcus and I both agreed on that.'

'Then you are aping Gabriel Cheever.'

'In what way?'

'You are a repentant rake.'

'I repent nothing!' declared Henry.

'Not even your flagrant indiscretions?'

'No, Christopher. Repentance takes the edge off pleasure. I'll have none of it.'

Christopher was glad to find his brother in more buoyant spirits but saddened that his predicament had not forced Henry to view his past actions with at least a modicum of shame. The first letter had contained lubricious details about his private life and he was embarrassed that Christopher had to see them, but he would make no effort to reform. When the crisis was over, Henry would become an impenitent voluptuary once more. That fact did not lessen his brother's urge to help him.

'I'll to the morgue,' said Christopher.

'Whatever for?' asked Henry with distaste.

'To see if Sir Julius has been there to identify the body.'

'Gabriel's wife could have done that, surely?'

'No,' said Christopher. 'It would be far too harrowing for her.'

'What if Sir Julius refuses to acknowledge his son?'

'Oh, he will.'

'You sound very certain of that,' Henry remarked.

'My guess is that even his flinty old heart will melt,' said Christopher. 'Besides, if he refuses to go to the mortuary, someone else will go in his place.'

'Someone else?'

'His younger daughter, Susan.'

Though the circumstances might have dictated a more sedate pace, Sir Julius Cheever insisted that the coachman keep his team of horses moving at speed. Not for him a funereal approach to the city. When they left Richmond, they almost tore through the countryside. It made for an uncomfortable journey. Susan Cheever and her father were jostled so violently that leisured conversation was well nigh impossible. They did not object to that. Sir Julius wanted to wrestle with his ambivalent feelings in silence and Susan was content to let fonder memories of her brother preoccupy her. When the city eventually rose up before them, however, they found their tongues again.

'Where will we stay, Father?' asked Susan.

'Anywhere but Serle Court. We go from one morgue to another.'

'That's unkind. Brilliana and Lancelot did everything to make us feel welcome.'

'Then why am I so relieved to quit the place?' said Sir Julius sourly. 'It will be late evening when we finally arrive. That's a wonderful excuse to stay away from Richmond for a night.'

Susan winced. 'I'd not call Gabriel's death a wonderful excuse.'

'Nor I,' he said, immediately contrite. 'Forgive me, Susan. I was trying to find some small glimmer of light in the darkness that has just descended on our family. I am quite lost. Gabriel is *dead*?' he said wonderingly. 'At such a young age? Why? What on earth did he do to deserve such a sorry end?'

'He did not deserve it, Father.'

'Only time will tell that.'

She gazed through the window. 'Do you know a suitable inn?' she said.

'There are dozens at our disposal.'

'So you have nowhere particular in mind?'

'No, Susan.'

'Perhaps Mr Redmayne can recommend somewhere,' she suggested casually, still looking out at the passing fields. 'He lives in London. He will know where we might find some proper accommodation.'

'I'm sure that he would.'

'May we call on him?'

'I meant to do so in any case.'

'Did you?' She turned back to him. 'Where does he live?'

'Fetter Lane.'

'We can visit him when our business is done.'

'Before that,' he decreed.

'Before?'

'With Mr Redmayne's permission, I will leave you there while I go to the morgue to identify the body and make arrangements to have it moved.'

'But I wish to be there with you, Father,' she protested.

'No, Susan.'

'Gabriel is my brother.'

Sir Julius was peremptory. 'He's my son and I must take full responsibility. A morgue is no place for you, Susan. The stink of death would stay in your nostrils for weeks. After all my years as a soldier, I am used to it. You are not. Besides,' he continued as a distant grief finally started to break through, 'I want to be alone with Gabriel. I need to make my peace with him.'

When Christopher finally got back to his house, Jacob was ready to look after him. After unsaddling and stabling his horse, the old servant prepared him some food, explained what had happened during his absence and generally fussed over him. Over an hour had passed before Christopher was able to set out his materials on the bare table and do some more work on the drawings of the new house. His hand moved with intermittent fluency. Dark thoughts kept invading him. What distracted him most was a consideration of how differently people had reacted to the news of Gabriel Cheever's unnatural death. Celia Hemmings had been rocked to the core, moving between anguish and disbelief. Susan Cheever had fainted, her father had turned away, her sister had made a callous remark and Lancelot Serle had been wholly unequal to the situation. Most astonishing, however, had been Lucy Cheever's response. She was a defenceless young woman who had made immense sacrifices to marry the man she loved and might have been expected to collapse totally when she heard that he was lost to her for ever. Yet she had shown a resilience that was extraordinary.

Jonathan Bale had been impressed by it as well. The two

men had no doubt that, when they left the house in Knightrider Street, the sorrow would be too much for her to bear and she would feel the full weight of her loss. While they were there, however, Lucy had borne up remarkably. There was an inner strength that sustained her and it must have been one of the qualities that attracted her husband to her in the first place. As he reflected on the character of the three women closest to the deceased, Christopher could see that Gabriel Cheever must have been a young man of unusual charm. His wife and his former mistress had almost nothing in common yet both loved him devotedly. Though his elder sister had rejected him, Susan patently adored him, providing, as far as she was able, the familial love that the others denied him. Three disparate characters each found something irresistible about Gabriel. They were now united by a shared pain.

Christopher forced himself to concentrate on the work in hand. It was, after all, the means by which he had been introduced to the Cheever family. Having visited Serle Court, he could see why Sir Julius was so anxious to have a house of his own. Brilliana would be a spiky hostess at the best of times. In the situation thrust upon them, her coldness and selfishness had come to the fore. Well intentioned as he was, Serle himself had hardly distinguished himself in the emergency. It was not a happy place to be. Sir Julius only went there out of a sense of family duty. Christopher was confident that he would insist that plans went ahead for the London abode. It would be his place of refuge from an unfeeling daughter and an irritating son-in-law. The architect applied himself to his task. A more refined version of the house began to appear slowly on the parchment before him.

Lost in creation, he did not hear the coach pulling up outside in the street or even the ringing of the doorbell. Joseph scurried out to see who was calling. The voice of Sir Julius Cheever boomed out. Christopher felt as if he had been shaken forcibly awake. Jacob invited the visitors into the parlour. When Christopher joined them, his surprise at seeing his client was matched by his delight in observing that he had brought his younger daughter with him. For her part, Susan Cheever was at once pleased and discomfited, curious to see inside Christopher's house but embarrassed that they had descended on him without warning. He brushed aside all apologies.

'Do take a seat,' he said. 'Jacob will bring refreshment.'

'I cannot stay, Mr Redmayne,' warned Sir Julius. 'I must visit the morgue. Susan was kind enough to travel with me from Richmond but I'll not put her through the ordeal. You have already shown your consideration. May I be so bold as to trespass on your kindness again and ask if my daughter might remain here while I am away?'

Christopher was quietly thrilled. 'The request is unnecessary, Sir Julius. Please take my hospitality for granted. Miss Cheever is most welcome in my home.'

'Thank you,' she said.

'I will return for her in due course,' announced her father, moving to the door.

'Do not hurry,' said Christopher. 'Your daughter will be safe here.'

'I'm most obliged.'

Sir Julius swept out and Jacob went after him to close the front door in his wake. The coach was heard trundling away. Susan refused the offer of food but was grateful to sit on a comfortable chair after her bumpy journey. Jacob withdrew discreetly to leave them alone. Christopher was nervous. Sitting opposite his guest, he saw how pale and strained she looked. He cleared his throat.

'It pains me to see you in such distress,' he said.

'Father was wrong to foist me on you like this, Mr Redmayne.'

'Not at all, Miss Cheever. I regard it as a stroke of good fortune.'

Her face clouded. 'I'd hardly call it that.'

'The words were ill-chosen,' he confessed quickly, 'and I withdraw them at once. What I meant was that I'm glad of the opportunity to confide something that would have been impossible to tell you in your father's presence.'

'You've seen Gabriel's wife?' she said, interest lighting up her features.

'This afternoon.'

'How did she receive the news?'

'With great stoicism,' he told her, remembering the way that Lucy had borne up. 'Your sister-in-law is an unusual young lady, Miss Cheever. She looks delicate but she is very brave.'

'That was how Gabriel described her in his letters to me,' she said.

'They were obviously happy together.'

Christopher gave her a full account of the visit that he and Jonathan Bale had made to the house. Susan was grateful for each new detail. It irked her that she had been unable to meet the young woman who had brought such joy and stability into her brother's life. Everything that she heard about Lucy Cheever accorded with the information that the fond husband had given in his letters to his sister. There was, however, one thing that her brother had not explained.

'Why did they keep the marriage secret?' she asked.

'I think that your brother wished to make a fresh start, Miss Cheever. That meant cutting himself off completely from his former friends. My brother, Henry, was among them,' admitted Christopher, 'and he was astounded to hear that Gabriel had a young bride. Others would have mocked him unmercifully.'

'There must be more to it than that.'

'I agree. The real answer may lie with your sister-in-law.'

'In what way, Mr Redmayne?'

'I am not sure,' said Christopher, 'but she clearly has good reasons of her own to keep the marriage secret. She was not even using your brother's name.'

'How strange!'

'She is concealing the truth from her own family.'

'Why should she need to do that?'

'Lucy – Mrs Cheever, that is – did not tell us. She bore up well but the strain on her was starting to tell. Jonathan Bale and I left her to mourn in private.' He lowered his voice. 'The facts will have to come out now.'

'I understand that.'

'She will want to attend the funeral as his wife. Sir Julius will have to be told that he has a daughter-in-law he did not know existed. However,' he added tactfully, 'your own part in all this is perhaps better suppressed.'

Susan was defiant. 'I'm not ashamed of what I did.'

'I know,' he said, 'and I admire you for it. But it might be unwise to let your father know that you deceived him all this while. You have to live with him, Miss Cheever. It might cause unnecessary strife if he were to learn that you exchanged letters with your brother. I'll not breathe a word on the subject.'

'That's very considerate of you.'

'What you have told me in confidence will remain sacrosanct.'

Their eyes locked for a second and he saw the first sign of her affection for him. An answering glint in his own eyes seemed to unsettle her. She looked away guiltily.

'It was wrong of us to impose on you, Mr Redmayne.'

'There is no imposition, I promise you.'

'You were simply engaged to design a house,' she said, shifting her gaze back to him, 'not to become embroiled in our family affairs.'

'That was unavoidable, Miss Cheever. I make no complaint.'

Christopher did not want to discuss his brother's problems with her nor reveal that he was involved in a parallel investigation to hunt a blackmailer. It was enough for her to know that he was committed to helping in the search for her brother's killer. It sparked off a sudden show of concern.

'You will be careful,' she warned.

'Of course.'

'I would hate you to put yourself at risk on our account.'

Christopher smiled. 'I am well able to look after myself.'

'The man you are after is a vicious killer.'

'I have an advantage that your brother lacked,' he pointed out. 'Jonathan Bale will be watching my back. He has done that before and I trust him implicitly.'

She relaxed slightly. 'Good. That reassures me somewhat.'

'I'm touched that you are worried on my account,' he said. Another flicker of affection appeared in her eyes. 'Thank you, Miss Cheever.'

There was a long silence. He left it to Susan to break it.

'You told me that Lucy knew all about Gabriel's past,' she resumed.

'That is what she claimed.'

'Did she mention what he had written?'

'Of course,' said Christopher. 'She thought his poetry was wonderful. I suspect that some of it was dedicated to her. It's a small consolation, I know, but she will still have those poems to remember him by. Lucy also talked about the play he was working on.'

'Did she refer to anything else?'

'Not that I recall.'

'No memoirs that he was writing?'

'Memoirs?'

'Yes, Mr Redmayne,' she explained, 'Gabriel had a conscience. Though he enjoyed the life that he led in London, he did so at a price. His conscience tormented him. He was never really comfortable in that world and he found a way to deal with it.'

'What was that?' asked Christopher.

'He kept a diary. A detailed memoir of everything that

happened during those long nights at the card tables and…'
her voice faltered '…and in the other places he visited.
Gabriel did not spare himself,' she went on. 'He listed all
his vices and named all of his friends. That diary was a form
of confession. He was trying to purge himself.' She leant
forward. 'Do you think that Lucy is aware of that diary?'

'Yes,' said Christopher, mind racing. 'I suspect that she
is.'

'If she is not, it would be painful for her to stumble on it
unawares.'

'There is no possibility of that, Miss Cheever,' he said,
thinking of the blackmail threats. 'The diary is no longer at
the house.'

CHAPTER EIGHT

When he had read a passage from the Bible to his two sons, Jonathan Bale said prayers with them, gave them a kiss then came downstairs to join his wife in the kitchen. Sarah was neatly folding one of the sheets that she had washed earlier in the day.

'Are you still working?' he complained.

'I'm almost done, Jonathan,' she said, putting one sheet aside and taking up another. 'The washing dries so quickly in this weather. I could take in much more.'

'You do enough as it is, Sarah.'

'I like to keep busy.'

'Too busy.'

'Would you rather that I sat around and did nothing all day long?'

'No, my love,' he said, brushing her forehead with a kiss. 'You would die of boredom in a week. Whatever else people say about Sarah Bale, they will never be able to accuse you of laziness.'

'While I have health and strength to work, I will.' She noticed a small tear in the sheet she was folding. 'Ah, that will need a stitch or two.'

'Let the person who brought it here do that, Sarah. They only pay you to wash their bed linen, not to repair it.'

She smiled tolerantly. 'This load is from old Mrs Lilley in Thames Street,' she said. 'The poor woman has rheumatism. She can barely move her fingers, let alone sew with them. It will not take me long, Jonathan.'

'I did not realise that it was an act of Christian kindness.'

'Mrs Lilley needs all the help that she can get.'

'Of course. Well,' he said, moving away, 'you carry on. I have to go out again.'

'So late in the evening?'

'I'll not be long, Sarah.'

'But you are not supposed to be on duty tonight.'

'No,' he agreed, 'but I want to knock on a few more doors.'

'I would have thought you'd had enough of that for one day.'

He grinned. 'Yes, my knuckles are a bit raw. Tom Warburton and I spent hours on the doorsteps in Knightrider Street and all to no avail. I'm going back there now.'

'Why?'

'To make amends, my love.'

'For what?'

'I let myself down,' he explained. 'I like to keep an eye on everyone who comes and goes in my ward. After all this time, I know most people by sight and many by name, especially in Knightrider Street. But a man and his wife slipped past me.'

'Have you found them now?'

'Only because of Mr Redmayne. It irks me, Sarah. I have to rely on someone who does not even live here to tell me what's going on under my nose.'

'You should be grateful to Mr Redmayne.'

'Oh, I am,' he said. 'I just wish that I could have ferreted out the truth myself. When we called at the house earlier, the maidservant fobbed us off with a lie. I should have known she was hiding something.'

'Are you going back there?'

'No, it's a house of mourning. It would be cruel to intrude. What I want to do is to speak to the neighbours about the two young people who lived there. They may have seen something of value.'

'Is this to do with the murder?' she asked.

'Yes, Sarah.'

'Did the dead man live in Knightrider Street?'

'Briefly.'

'Where?'

'Close to Sermon Lane.'

'Then you ought to speak to Mrs Runciman,' she suggested.

'Who?'

'She lives on the corner of Sermon Lane, near the house you're talking about. I take in washing from Mrs Runciman quite often. Please remember me to her.'

'I will.'

'The Buswell family live opposite and Mrs Gately is somewhere close.'

Jonathan laughed. 'Do you take in washing from the whole street?'

'No. The only person I work for is Mrs Runciman but she always invites me into the house. I've met Mrs Buswell and Mrs Gately there. You'll get little help from them, I'm afraid. Mrs Buswell is almost blind and Mrs Gately is a little slow-witted. Go to Mrs Runciman first,' she advised. 'She has a sharp eye. If anyone can help you, it will probably be her.'

'Thank you!' he said, kissing her again.

'You should have spoken to me earlier.'

'I can see that now, my love.'

'If you took in washing, you'd be surprised how much useful gossip you could pick up.'

'I think I'll hold on to my present job.'

'Are you afraid of hard work?' she teased.

'No, Sarah,' he replied. 'I thrive on it. Nobody works harder than shipwrights and I was in that trade for several years. But being a constable helps me to look after people. I feel that I can do some good. That pleases me more than I can tell you.'

'There's no need to tell me. I can see it in your face.'

'Not at the moment.'

'No,' she said, giving him a sympathetic hug. 'This case has upset you badly.'

'The murder has caused a deep wound in Baynard's Castle ward.'

'I feel the same about a bad tear in some linen. I want to sew it up again quickly.'

Jonathan was solemn. 'The tear that I have to mend is in a shroud.'

* * *

Sir Julius Cheever needed a few moments to collect himself. During his many walks across battlefields, he had seen death and mutilation hundreds of times and become inured to the sight, but this was very different. His own son lay on the slab beneath the shroud. Gabriel had been young, strong and brimming with energy the last time they had met. The hot words that Sir Julius had flung on that occasion came back to haunt him. They seemed so hollow and pointless now. Anger had taken hold and gnawed away at him for years. At last it was spent. All differences between father and son vanished in death. What remained was remorse and self-recrimination. Gritting his teeth, he peeled back the shroud to look down at the body. The weal round the neck was more livid than ever. He closed his eyes in agony and covered the face up again.

'That's my son,' he said quietly. 'That is Gabriel Cheever.'

Henry Redmayne had taken the sensible precautions advised by his brother. He left the house armed and kept his wits about him. Even when he was among friends in a gaming house, he kept his back to a wall so that nobody could come up unseen behind him. His companion, Sir Marcus Kemp, sat at a table nearby, keeping fear at bay by immersing himself in a game of cards. Glad to be back in one of his favourite haunts, Henry felt curiously uninvolved. It was as if he were seeing the place properly for the first time, albeit through a fug of tobacco smoke. Drink was flowing. Voices were raised. There was an air of sophisticated merriment. All seats were taken at the table where Sir Marcus Kemp was playing but Henry sensed an empty chair. In the past, Gabriel Cheever had always occupied a place at that particular table, winning in style and taking money from the purses of Henry, Sir Marcus and almost everyone else who pitted their skills against his. He had been a popular and respected man in the card-playing fraternity. Only those inflamed by drink had ever accused him of cheating or threatened him with violence.

'I spy a stranger!' said a voice. 'Henry Redmayne, I declare!'

Henry inclined his head in greeting. 'Well met, Peter.'

'Have you risen from your sick bed at last?'

'The thought of what I was missing was the best physician.'

'We have not seen you for days, Henry. Where have you been hiding?'

'Nowhere, my friend. I am back.'

'And most welcome.'

Peter Wickens gave him an affectionate slap on the back. He looked as suave and elegant as ever. Standing beside Henry, he gazed around the room to see whom he could recognise. Regular denizens were all there. He looked down at the nearest table.

'I see that Sir Marcus is ready to part with more of his fortune,' he remarked.

'He seems to be having some luck at last,' said Henry. 'Not before time.'

'He's too reckless a player.'

'Boldness is essential in cards, Peter.'

'Only when tempered with discretion.'

'That was never his forte.'

'Indeed not. I've seen Sir Marcus lose a hundred guineas through a moment's indiscretion at the card table,' recalled Wickens with a wry smile. 'But that was when he was up against Gabriel Cheever.' His manner changed at once. 'Have you heard the terrible news about Gabriel?'

'Yes,' said Henry. 'It's very sad.'

'I was appalled. Arthur Lunn told me. He had it from some constable who came to see him. What a shock for dear Arthur!' he went on. 'He is enjoying a civilised cup of coffee when he suddenly learns that a friend of his has been murdered.'

'Has word of the crime spread?'

'It's the talk of the town, Henry.'

'Gabriel will be sorely missed.'

'Not by Sir Marcus,' said Wickens, nodding at the man. 'He's actually *smiling* at a card table. He never did that when he was sitting opposite Gabriel Cheever. But how did you hear of this dreadful murder?' he asked, turning to Henry. 'I was shaken to the marrow. Do you know any details?'

'None beyond the fact that the body was found on Paul's Wharf.'

'What possessed Gabriel to go there?'

'We may never know, Peter.'

He grimaced. 'Wharves are such insalubrious places. I keep clear of the river whenever I can. It seems to give off an unholy stench at times. And I've no love for the brutish people who make their living beside the Thames,' he added with a supercilious sneer. 'The lower orders are an affront to decency.'

'I am bound to agree with you there.'

'Arthur tells me this constable was an ugly fellow, blunt and uncouth.'

'Who else would take on such work?'

'We deserve better from our officers of the law,' argued Wickens loftily. 'If this constable wishes to speak to me, I shall tell him to mind his manners. Has he come in search of you yet, Henry?'

'No. Why should he?'

'According to Arthur Lunn, the man wants to speak to anyone who knew Gabriel well. I was not an intimate of his but I did enjoy an occasional game of cards with him.' He gave a chuckle. 'And I shared some other pleasures with Gabriel as well.'

'Most of us did that, Peter. He was ubiquitous.'

'The ladies would use a more vivid word for him than that.'

Henry laughed obligingly but he was not enjoying the conversation. Peter Wickens was a man after his own heart, wealthy, self-indulgent, generous with his friends and addicted to all the pleasures of the town. Henry had lost count of the number of times when he and Arthur Lunn had been driven to their respective houses in the early hours of the day by Peter Wickens's coachman. Yet he felt uneasy beside the man now, fearful that Wickens might probe him about his earlier desertion of his usual haunts. When he was last on these premises, he had been as carefree and affable as his companion. Two anonymous letters had altered that.

Behind his token smile, Henry was a frightened man.

'Are you waiting to take a place at the table?' asked Wickens.

'No. I prefer to watch.'

'You normally like to be in the thick of things.'

'Later, perhaps.'

'Arthur and I thought to visit Mrs Curtis tonight.'

'I have other plans,' said Henry, quailing at the thought. 'Give her my apologies.'

Wickens grinned. 'There's only one way to apologise to a lady, Henry, and it does not involve an exchange of words. Mrs Curtis has been asking after you.'

'I'll not keeping her waiting long.'

Wickens was about to reply when one of the men at the table threw down his cards in disgust and got up. Annoyed at his losses, the man stormed out of the room. Peter Wickens moved swiftly. Before anyone else could take the vacant seat, he lowered himself into it and spread a smile around the other players. Sir Marcus Kemp gave him a nod of welcome then waited for the next round of cards to be dealt. They were soon lost in yet another game. Henry envied his two friends. Peter Wickens had no shadow hanging over him and Sir Marcus had found a way to ignore his problems. Henry could do nothing but stand there and suffer. It was excruciating. While everyone else in the room was enjoying himself immensely, Henry Redmayne was under sentence of death.

Susan Cheever was deeply worried about her father. Since his return from the morgue he had hardly spoken a word.

Seated in a chair at the house in Fetter Lane, he brooded in silence. His face was drained of colour, his body of energy. Sir Julius looked as if he had just been dazed by a violent blow. Christopher set the brandy beside him.

'Drink that, Sir Julius,' he counselled.

His guest did not even hear him. Susan picked up the glass and offered it to her father, putting a hand on his shoulder at the same time. Her voice was a gentle caress.

'Take some of this, Father. It's brandy.' He waved it away. 'It will do you good.'

'I want nothing, Susan.'

'You look ill.'

'Should I call a doctor, Sir Julius?' suggested Christopher.

The old man bristled. 'Whatever for?'

'You seem unwell.'

'There's nothing the matter with me.'

'I'm delighted to hear it.'

'I have much on my mind, that is all.'

'Naturally, Sir Julius.'

Before her father could lapse back into silence, Susan leant forward in her seat. 'Perhaps it is time for us to leave,' she said gently. 'Mr Redmayne has been kindness itself but we have imposed on him far too much already and we need to find accommodation for the night.'

'You have found it, Miss Cheever,' said Christopher, opening his palms. 'If you have nowhere to stay, I insist that you remain as my guests.'

'That would be an abuse of your hospitality.'

'Treat my home as your own.'

'I think it better if Father and I withdraw.'

'Why?' said Christopher persuasively. 'You and Sir Julius can sleep here while your coachman spends the night at an inn in Holborn. We have ample room. There's fresh bed linen and Jacob will happily provide anything else that you require. Do please honour me by staying under my roof, Miss Cheever.'

Susan was clearly tempted by the notion but felt unable to make the decision on her father's behalf. The time she had spent alone with Christopher had been pleasant and restorative. It had helped to lift her out of her sombre mood. She felt completely at ease in his house. However, while wanting to accept the invitation, she had reservations about doing so. Sir Julius swept them aside.

'Thank you, Mr Redmayne,' he murmured. 'If we may, we'll be your guests.'

'For as long as you wish, Sir Julius.'

'One night will be sufficient.'

'I'll make arrangements at once.'

Christopher got up to go into the kitchen, closing the door behind him so that he could have a private conversation with Jacob. The servant was cleaning some silverware by the light of a candle. Christopher could not keep the excitement out of his voice.

'Sir Julius and his daughter are staying the night, Jacob.'

'I know, sir. I took the liberty of preparing rooms for them.'

'You will need to speak to their coachman.'

'I've already done so, sir,' said Jacob complacently. 'We unloaded the luggage together. On my recommendation, he is on his way to the King's Head. He'll find lodging there.' He looked up with a smile. 'I read your mind, sir. I knew that you would offer them hospitality.'

'You were ahead of me as usual.'

'Will the visitors require supper?'

'In time, perhaps. Sir Julius is still recovering from his ordeal.'

Christopher went back to the parlour to be given a smile of gratitude by Susan Cheever. Tired and drawn, she was still more concerned about her father's condition than her own fatigue. Sir Julius had drifted off into another reverie, grinding his teeth. Susan waited until Christopher had resumed his seat before she spoke to her father.

'What happened?' she asked quietly.

'What happened?' repeated Sir Julius. 'I saw the dead body of my son.'

'You should have let me come with you, Father.'

'No, Susan.'

'I could have helped you through it.'

'Nobody could have done that,' he said mournfully. 'Gabriel and I needed to be alone together once more, if only for a brief while. I'm grieved that it took something like this to mend the rift between us. What kind of a father have I been to him?' he said in a rare moment of self-doubt. 'Can I only love a son after he's been murdered?'

'You must not blame yourself, Sir Julius,' said Christopher.

'Yes, I must. I drove Gabriel away.'

'He would have gone, whatever you did,' argued Susan. 'Gabriel was restless. He wanted to strike out on his own.'

'Do not remind me.'

'It no longer matters now.'

'Oh, it does,' he said soulfully. 'It does.'

'Did you make all the arrangements?'

'I tried to, Susan. But there is a problem I never anticipated.'

'A problem?'

'Yes,' he said with a note of disbelief. 'It seems that I was not the first member of the family to identify the body. Someone I did not even know existed went to the morgue before me – a young lady claiming to be Gabriel's wife.'

Susan's face remained impassive but Christopher could guess at her anxiety.

'Mrs Lucy Cheever,' continued the old man. 'That was the name she gave. And she showed the coroner legal proof of her marriage so he could not deny her access. I want the body to be taken back home to be buried in the family vault, but this mystery wife wishes to be at the funeral as well. That's what has shocked me,' he confessed. 'I cared so little about my own son that he could not even tell me he was married. Think what that poor woman must be going through. She is not only denied any contact with his family, she has now lost Gabriel himself. She must be in despair.'

'I hope that she'll be allowed to attend the funeral,' said Christopher.

'It would be cruel to keep her away.'

'Did the coroner give you her address? I'll gladly act as an intermediary.'

Sir Julius was brusque. 'Thank you, Mr Redmayne, but this is family business. I may have spurned my son but I'll not turn my back on my daughter-in-law. The lady lives in Knightrider Street. I'll call on her tomorrow.'

'Let me go with you, Father,' urged Susan.

'Why?'

'I'd like to meet her.'

Sir Julius shot her a look compounded of curiosity, affection and distant anger. 'Did you know that Gabriel had a wife?' he asked.

Susan did not hesitate. 'Yes, Father,' she said. 'I did.'

Alice Runciman had preserved a resolute cheerfulness in the face of adversity. Death had robbed her of her parents, her husband, three of her five children and, during the Great Plague, several members of her wider family but no despair clouded her gaze. She was indomitable. Primed by his wife, Jonathan Bale knew that Mrs Runciman had a sharp eye but he had not been told about the permanent smile on her lips. Short and stout, she had a florid complexion that made her cheeks look like shiny red apples. Jonathan warmed to her at once. The name of Sarah Bale gained him a cordial welcome. They were soon ensconced in the parlour, trading gossip about the ward. The constable had to remind himself that he was there on important business.

'Mrs Runciman,' he said. 'I really came to ask about your neighbours.'

'Oh?' she replied. 'Which ones?'

'They go by the name of Henley.'

'Ah, yes. They only moved in recently.'

'What can you tell me about them?'

'Why?' she wondered, suspecting scandal. 'Have they done something wrong?'

'No, Mrs Runciman. Far from it.'

'Then why come to me? You are the second constable in one day to call here. Another man knocked on my door this afternoon.'

'That was Tom Warburton.'

'He wanted to know if a Mrs Cheever lodged here. I knew nobody of that name.'

'She lives a few doors away,' explained Jonathan. 'When she got married, Lucy Henley became Mrs Gabriel Cheever.'

'Then why call herself by her maiden name?'

'I'm not sure, Mrs Runciman.'

'Good Lord!' said the other with a chortle. 'I live that close to someone and I don't even know their real name. A fine neighbour I am!' Her eyelids narrowed. 'Why are you so interested in them, Mr Bale?'

'Gabriel Cheever was murdered earlier this week.'

'Never!'

'I was there when the body was found on Paul's Wharf.'

'Is that who it was?' she said, oozing with sympathy. 'We wondered who it might be. Mrs Gately was talking about it only this morning. She thought it might be a sailor, killed in a brawl. And you say that it was Mr Henley?'

'Cheever,' he corrected.

'He was the murdered man?'

'I fear so.'

'Heavens! Think of his wife! She's far too young and frail to bear such a tragedy.'

'Mrs Cheever is stronger than she looks.'

'There's hardly anything of her. She's such a pretty little thing. Well, who would have guessed it?' she said with a long sigh. 'Her husband was a proper gentleman. He was always so polite. Yet he was killed? Who could do such a terrible thing?'

'We are still trying to find that out, Mrs Runciman. That's why I came.'

'What can I do?'

'Tell me all you know about your neighbours.'

'That's soon done, Mr Bale,' she said, folding her arms. 'I barely knew them. They were very private people. They hardly stirred out of the house.'

'Did they have many visitors?'

'I never saw any.'

'What of their maidservant?'

'I met her in the market once or twice but she had no tongue in her head either. It was an effort to get a word out of her so I gave up trying. Neighbours should be friends, Mr Bale,' she insisted. 'Life is much easier that way. They thought otherwise.'

'They must have had good reason to keep out of sight.'

'I've no idea what it might be.'

'Did you see anything of them at all, Mrs Runciman?'

'Only on Sundays.'

'Sundays?'

'Yes, Mr Bale. They were regular churchgoers, no question of that.'

'What do you mean?'

'They were out of the house before the bells had even started ringing. I'd see them walking down the street arm in arm. They may have had some strange habits,' she went on, 'but I'll say this for them. They were true Christians.'

Jonathan thought about a crucifix nailed to a wall.

Alone in his dining room, Christopher Redmayne looked back on the day with a sadness that was tinged with pleasure. Breaking the news of her husband's death to Lucy Cheever had been even more harrowing for him than carrying the same tidings to Richmond. While the dead man's father and sister could support each other in their bereavement, his wife was completely on her own. That she somehow visited the morgue to identify the body was a tribute to her courage as well as to her love. Christopher had been moved to hear about it from Sir Julius. Yet it was what Susan Cheever had told him that really occupied his thoughts. Her unexpected arrival had been a source of joy to him and her comments about her brother's work had been a revelation. Christopher wondered if he had finally stumbled on the motive behind the murder.

Eager to stay with her as long as possible, he had sensed that he should withdraw in order to let her talk in private with her father. They had been grateful for his considerate behaviour. There was much for them to discuss and it was over an hour before they called him back into the room. Even though Sir Julius still looked hurt and betrayed, a measure of understanding had clearly been achieved between father and daughter. Christopher prevailed upon them to eat a light supper, then they departed for the night to their separate rooms. When Jacob had cleared everything away, his master sent him off to bed as well, wanting to stay up for a while himself to reflect on events. The very fact that Susan Cheever was sleeping beneath his roof gave him a recurring thrill. Even in such unfortunate circumstances, she was a most welcome guest. Her bedchamber adjoined his own. When he laid his head on his pillow, he realised, he would be less than six feet away from her. Christopher picked up the one remaining candle and headed for the stairs.

A knock on his front door made him pause. He wondered who could be calling at such an hour. When he opened the door, he found himself looking at the last person he expected to find there.

'Mr Bale!'

'I am sorry to disturb you, Mr Redmayne,' said Jonathan, hands gesturing an apology, 'but I have learnt something that may be of interest.'

'Come in, come in.'

'No, sir. It's far too late and I've a home of my own to get to.'

'What is it that you have discovered?'

'I spoke to a Mrs Runciman,' explained Jonathan. 'She lives close to the Cheever house in Knightrider Street. Gabriel Cheever and his wife kept themselves to themselves, it seems, though she always saw them going to church on Sundays. It was as I was leaving Mrs Runciman that I was given the news.'

'What news, Mr Bale?'

'The maidservant must have seen me as I went past the house earlier.'

'Anna? The Cheevers' maidservant?'

'Yes. She was waiting for me in the street. After we left her this afternoon, Mrs Cheever asked the maid to search the house more thoroughly to see if anything was taken. It was, Mr Redmayne.'

'Go on.'

'Some of Mr Cheever's papers were missing.'

'I knew it!' said Christopher.

Jonathan was puzzled. 'You did? How?'

'This is not the time to explain. Suffice it to say that Gabriel Cheever had written something that could be a dangerous weapon in the wrong hands. Thank you, Mr Bale,' he said effusively. 'I'm so grateful that you brought this information.'

'I felt that it might be important.'

'It is crucial.'

'Good,' said Jonathan. 'My visit to Mrs Runciman was worth while.'

He bade farewell and set off down the street with his long stride. Christopher watched him until he was swallowed up by the darkness, then closed the front door and withdrew into the house. Before he could retire to bed, however, he was detained yet again.

The clatter of hooves made him prick up his ears. Someone was riding along Fetter Lane at speed. When he heard the horse being reined in outside his door, he knew that he had another visitor. Christopher opened the door to see his brother dismounting from the saddle. Henry was almost out of breath.

'Thank goodness you are here, Christopher!' he exclaimed.

'Why? What ails you?'

'I'm being followed.'

'By whom?' said Christopher, looking up and down the empty street. 'I see nobody. Your imagination is playing tricks on you, Henry.'

'There *was* someone, I tell you. He has been on my tail every inch of the way.'

'You've shaken him off now.'

'Only because I've found sanctuary,' said Henry, glancing over his shoulder. 'He is probably hiding in the shadows somewhere. Let me come in.'

'At this hour?'

'Please. I must.'

'As you wish. Tether your horse by the stable.'

A minute later, Henry stepped gratefully into the house and shut the door behind him. Christopher took him into the dining room, lit some more candles then passed a bottle of brandy to Henry. His brother poured some into a glass and drank it down.

'I needed that,' he said.

'You're shaking all over.'

'You would shake if you had an assassin stalking you.'

'Is that what you think he was?'

'What else could he be?' asked Henry impatiently. 'I receive a death threat and someone follows me home in the dark. Even you must see a link between those two events, Christopher.'

'A *possible* link,' conceded his brother.

'Possible enough for me. I'll go no further tonight.'

'You must, Henry.'

'I'll stay the night here. Have Jacob prepare a room for me.'

'Jacob is fast asleep in bed.'

'Then rouse him from his dreams at once,' ordered Henry. 'Damn it, man! I'm your brother. My safety surely comes before your servant's comfort.'

'Of course, but I already have guests here. There's no room to spare.'

'Guests?'

'Sir Julius Cheever and his younger daughter.'

Henry was indignant. 'Are *they* being preferred over me as well?'

'It is not a question of preference,' said Christopher soothingly, 'but of expedience. They came to London to identify Gabriel's body. I could hardly turn them away.'

'Why not? You turn me away.'

'That's not what I'm doing. Stay if you must, Henry. I'll even surrender my own bed to you, if it means so much to you. All I am saying is that this is not the most convenient time. You must appreciate that.'

'Why talk of convenience when my life is at stake?' complained Henry.

'Hush!' said Christopher with a finger to his lips. 'You'll wake them. I promise you this. If you're too nervous to continue on home yourself, I'll act as your bodyguard and deliver you safely to Bedford Street.' He patted his brother's arm. 'Now, why not tell me exactly what happened tonight and why you believe that you are being followed?' He indicated the bottle. 'Help yourself to more brandy.'

Henry was slightly mollified. After draining his glass, he poured himself another drink then launched into his tale.

His evening at the gaming house had been extended well into the night by Sir Marcus Kemp, who refused to quit the table while he was winning. Banking on his friend's company, Henry had eventually been forced to ride home alone and found that someone was lurking outside to trail him.

'The villain might have struck at any moment!' he concluded.

'Then why didn't he?'

'He was biding his time.'

'It's more likely that he was thinking twice about attacking you when he saw that you carried a sword. You called him an assassin,' said Christopher reasonably, 'but he could just as easily have been a robber, waiting to pounce on some unwary gentleman who was rolling home alone with too much drink inside him.' He gave a smile. 'Or he might just have been someone travelling harmlessly in the same direction as you.'

'There was nothing harmless about this man, Christopher.'

'How do you know?'

'I could *feel* his menace.'

'Henry, you would feel menaced if a cat followed you home.'

'That's a heartless thing to say!' protested Henry. 'Do you want your brother to be stabbed in the back only yards from his own front door?'

'No,' said Christopher, 'but then, that would never happen. Why wait until you reach Bedford Street before attacking you when you've already ridden past a dozen more suitable places for an ambush? Nobody is trying to kill you, Henry. I am sure of that.'

'You saw that letter.'

'It achieved what it intended. To give you a fright.'

'It certainly did that. I've had enough, Christopher.'

'Enough?'

'I'm inclined to pay the money and have done with the whole thing!'

'That's the last thing you must do.'

'My life is more important to me than five hundred guineas.'

'But that will not buy you peace of mind,' asserted Christopher. 'It's only a first instalment. When he's squeezed one payment out of you, the blackmailer will have you at his mercy. The demands will never cease.'

'The first letter promised that they would.'

'How much faith can you put in the word of a man like that?'

Henry was still trembling. 'It's the only hope I have of staying alive.'

'That death threat was hollow,' said Christopher positively. 'I'm certain of it.'

'Gabriel Cheever was killed because he did not pay what was demanded.'

'No, Henry. There was no attempted blackmail where Gabriel was concerned.'

'How do you know?'

'Because I have learnt something about his literary endeavours,' said Christopher. 'Gabriel came to London to fulfil his ambition of being an author. He was very talented.

As well as writing poems and plays, however, Gabriel kept a diary.'

'A diary?'

'A very explicit diary, I gather.'

'In what sense?'

'It was a form of confession. A detailed account of all the nights he spent in the company of dissolute revellers like Sir Marcus Kemp, Peter Wickens, Arthur Lunn and, of course, Henry Redmayne.'

Henry was aghast. 'He wrote about *me*?'

'My guess is that your name figured quite prominently in the memoir. Do you understand now? All that time that you and your friends got up to your devilish antics, you had a Recording Angel at your shoulder.'

'That's an appalling thing to do to us.'

'Gabriel Cheever paid for it with his life.'

'What do you mean?'

'That's why he was killed, Henry. Not because he refused to give in to any demands. What he wrote from personal guilt,' explained Christopher, 'was a potential source of blackmail. Gabriel was murdered so that someone could steal his diary.'

Lucy Cheever passed a sleepless night in an empty bed. A room that had been filled with so much love and tenderness now seemed bleak and inhospitable. She could not believe that her husband was dead. Even though she had seen his body laid out at the morgue, she entertained the ridiculous hope that he would somehow return to her. That hope finally shrivelled away in the darkness. By the time dawn came, she knew that he had gone for ever. Eyes red with weeping, she lay on the bed in despair. She and Gabriel Cheever had given up so much in order to be together. Now she was left with nothing.

Anna was a caring woman. Though Lucy said that she wanted no breakfast, the maidservant coaxed her into eating a little bread and drinking some whey. She also helped to dress her mistress, fearing that she might otherwise simply stay in bed all day and be overcome with grief. Anna had been very fond of her master and was shocked by his death, but the situation compelled her to keep her own emotions under control.

'They'll find the man responsible for this,' she said.

'I hope so, Anna.'

'Put faith in Mr Bale. He'll not rest until the crime is solved.'

'It's Mr Redmayne that I trust,' said Lucy. 'He was so kind to me when he came here yesterday. He never even knew Gabriel yet he was eager to help in the search for his killer. I put my faith in him.'

'He and Mr Bale will work together.'

'Yes.' An upsurge of sorrow made Lucy burst into tears. 'But they'll not be able to bring Gabriel back to me, Anna. My husband is gone.'

Anna put a consoling arm round her. Lucy dried her tears then detached herself to walk around the bedchamber. It was filled with fond memories. They brought a degree of comfort. She was still grasping at some of them when she heard a noise in the street outside. A coach was rattling along the thoroughfare. Anna crossed to the window.

'It's stopped outside the house,' she announced.

'Here?'

'Someone is getting out, Mrs Cheever.'

'I'm expecting no visitors.'

'It's an elderly gentleman and a young lady.'

'Go and see what they want, Anna.'

'I'll send them away,' said the maidservant firmly. 'You can't receive anyone.'

She went bustling out and descended the stairs. Looking at herself in the mirror, Lucy dabbed at her eyes with a handkerchief and adjusted a curl. When the bell rang below, she heard the door being opened. She moved to the top of the stairs so that she could eavesdrop without being seen.

'I wish to speak to Mrs Lucy Cheever,' said the man's voice.

'My mistress is unable to see anyone today, sir,' replied Anna briskly.

'She may wish to see us.'

'I doubt that.'

'Let her know that Sir Julius Cheever has called with his daughter, Susan. I crave a word about my son. We'll not keep her long.'

Lucy was in a turmoil. Everything that Gabriel had told her about his father made Sir Julius sound like an ogre. Had he come to bully his daughter-in-law in the same way that he had bullied his son? Or was he there to argue about the arrangements for the funeral? Whatever his reason for coming, he could not be ignored. Summoning up all of her strength, Lucy came down the stairs and into the hall. Anna stood back so that her mistress could see the visitors. Lucy looked at her father-in-law with apprehension, but it was ill-founded. He was not the tyrant of report at all. Sir Julius Cheever was a sad old man with moist eyes and a tentative smile of welcome. Standing beside him was a handsome young woman whose resemblance to her brother took Lucy's breath away.

It was Susan who made any introductions unnecessary. Flinging her arms round Lucy, she kissed her on both cheeks then stepped back to look at her through her tears.

'Hello, Lucy,' she said. 'Father and I are so pleased to meet you.'

CHAPTER NINE

The funeral of Gabriel Cheever was held at the parish church of St Andrew in the county of Northamptonshire. Built on the summit of a hill, the church acted as a beacon of hope and inspiration to the surrounding villages from which it drew its congregation. Christopher Redmayne took note of its architectural features, admiring the work of the stonemasons who had constructed the church over two centuries earlier and marvelling at the way they had overcome the problems of erecting the massive conical spire that pointed towards heaven with such reassuring certainty. Though its exterior was bathed in sunshine, the inside of the church was cold and cheerless. It seemed too large for the two dozen people who shuffled into their seats. Sir Julius Cheever wanted the funeral to be a quiet affair and only the closest family friends even knew that it was taking place. The deceased was no prodigal son being welcomed home by a delighted father.

He was a murder victim who had left home after violent arguments. His funeral was also a service of reconciliation.

Like everyone else, Christopher was dressed appropriately in mourning clothes, helping to create a swathe of black across the front of the nave. He sat at the rear of the little congregation, wanting to be present but anxious to keep in the background, an observer as much as a mourner. Seated in the front row were the members of the Cheever family and he ran his eye along their heads. Sir Julius was flanked by his two daughters. Brilliana Serle was weeping copiously as if trying to atone for the hostility she had shown towards her brother. Her husband tried to console her but she was too determined to draw attention to herself to succumb to his soothing touch. Susan Cheever bore herself with more dignity, subordinating her own grief to that of the diminutive figure who sat beside her. Christopher was moved to see that Lucy Cheever had been given pride of place alongside the others, her head bowed in prayer, her hand clutching that of her younger sister-in-law. It was ironic that she had to wait until her husband had been killed before she could be accepted by his family. No members of her own family were there. Two rows back, Anna, her loyal maidservant, was on hand to lend support to her mistress in the event of any collapse.

A minute before the service began, two latecomers slipped into the church. Hearing the latch being lifted and the heavy oak door opened, Christopher looked over his shoulder to see a man and a woman making their way slowly down the nave before sitting in a pew a few rows behind the main party. Both were dressed in black and kept their heads down, but Christopher thought that there was something familiar about the woman. When she glanced across the aisle at him, he caught a glimpse of the white face beneath the elaborate black hat and recognised Celia Hemmings. He was touched that she had made such a long journey in order to pay her last respects to her former lover but relieved that she sat apart from the family and close friends as if acknowledging her position with regard to Gabriel Cheever. Christopher wondered who her companion might be but he had no time to speculate because the funeral service began.

The vicar was a white-haired old man who had ministered to his flock for over thirty years and knew the Cheever family well. He conducted the service with practised solemnity. Having baptised Gabriel and prepared him for confirmation, he was able to talk with authority and affection about the dead man, sounding positive notes in the prevailing sadness and omitting any mention of his departure to London and its tragic consequences. Brilliana contributed some loud sobbing at various points in the sermon and Susan Cheever was also tearful but Lucy showed remarkable restraint, memorising every word said about her husband as if learning entirely new facts about him. In saying farewell to the man she had married, she was somehow discovering him.

The burial itself took place in the crypt, a dank, chill chamber lit by a number of shivering candle flames. The last remains of Gabriel Cheever were laid to rest in a family vault that already contained the bones of his mother and his grandparents. Sir Julius was visibly shaken and Brilliana wept more dramatically than ever until her husband, to his credit, put an arm round her to bury her face in his bosom and stifle the noise. Christopher watched Susan Cheever and mused on a paradox. The one member of the family who had not rejected Gabriel was not allowed to mourn his loss properly because she was too busy offering solace to her father and sister-in-law. Indeed, when Lucy's control finally snapped, it was Susan who caught her before she could fall to the stone-flagged floor. Anna moved in swiftly to help her mistress up the stone steps and out of the crypt. Christopher lent a steadying hand. The full force of her loss had finally hit Lucy Cheever and she was inconsolable. They lowered her gently down in a pew so that she could bury her face in her hands. Amid the sobbing, Christopher could hear prayers being said in Latin. The maidservant took charge. When he saw that he was no longer needed, Christopher drifted away.

After such a long time in the shadowed interior of the church, it was a shock to step out into bright sunlight. The fine weather seemed faintly inappropriate for a funeral but Christopher was grateful to be out in the fresh air again. As other members of the congregation filed out, he took the opportunity to intercept Celia Hemmings and her companion, realising, now that he could see the man clearly, that he knew him. It was Arthur Lunn, one of his brother's friends, so renowned for his ostentation that he was virtually unrecognisable in mourning apparel. Celia was tearful and Lunn subdued. They exchanged muted greetings with Christopher.

'It was very good of you to come,' he said.

'I would not have missed it,' murmured Celia.

'How did you know when the funeral would be held?'

'We made enquiries of the coroner,' explained Lunn, 'so we knew when the body was being brought back to Northamptonshire. In fact, we got here ahead of it.'

Christopher nodded. 'The journey took three days. A coffin has to be transported at a respectful pace. But how did you guess where to come?'

'I knew where Gabriel lived,' said Celia quietly. 'Once we found his home, we came here to the church. Word had already been sent on ahead to the vicar so he was able to give us details of the funeral.'

'We might ask what *you* are doing here, young sir?' said Lunn.

'I'm a friend of the family,' said Christopher. 'I'm designing a house in London for Sir Julius, though that project has had to be set aside for a while.' He saw his client, weighed down with sorrow, coming out of the church porch. 'It may be some time before Sir Julius is ready to take an interest in it again.'

Lunn stepped in closer. 'Is the rumour true?' he asked.

'What rumour?'

'We heard a whisper that Gabriel was married.'

'His widow is here today.'

'Was she the young lady you helped out of the crypt?' said Celia.

'Yes,' replied Christopher. 'This has been a dreadful ordeal for her.'

'I can imagine.'

'It was something of an ordeal for me,' said Lunn with a sly grin. 'I found it difficult to keep my face straight throughout that peculiar sermon. Did you hear the way the vicar described Gabriel? He made him sound like a minor saint.' He gave a chuckle. 'That's not the Gabriel Cheever that I remember. Nor you, I'll warrant, Celia.'

'Those days are long gone, Arthur,' she said reprovingly.

'But old memories must have been stirred.'

'All that I feel is sadness that he's gone and deep sympathy for his family.'

'Well, yes,' blustered Lunn, 'I feel the same. That goes without saying. But I'll not deny that I had some merry times with Gabriel – and with your brother Henry for that matter,' he added, turning to Christopher. 'Henry and I spent many a night at the card table with Gabriel Cheever.' He chuckled again. 'Much to our cost!'

'Such thoughts have no place at a funeral,' said Celia with soft reproach. 'Keep them to yourself, Arthur.'

He gave a bow of mock humility. 'I stand rebuked.'

'Besides, I think it's time for us to steal quietly away.'

'Must you?' said Christopher, eager to talk further with them.

'Yes, Mr Redmayne. You have a place here. We do not.'

'We do,' insisted Lunn. 'We were Gabriel's best friends.'

'But not the kind of whom Sir Julius would entirely approve, Arthur. For his sake – and for the sake of Gabriel's widow – we ought to leave now.'

'Why, Celia?'

'Before there is any embarrassment.'

'Nobody can embarrass me,' said Lunn, eyes popping even further out of their sockets. 'I've consorted with His Majesty. Do you think I'll be discomfited by these country cousins with their rural simplicity?'

Christopher was annoyed. 'That's a gross insult to the Cheever family!' he said sharply. 'Miss Hemmings shows the tact and discretion that you so signally lack, Mr Lunn. It is *you* who might embarrass the family, sir. You belong to a part of Gabriel's life that his family would rather forget.'

'Well, I'll not forget it and neither will your brother Henry.'

'Forgive him, Mr Redmayne,' said Celia. 'Arthur is speaking out of turn.'

'I'm entitled to my opinion,' asserted Lunn.

'I only brought him with me to ensure my safety.'

'How disappointing!' he said with a leer.

She pulled her companion away. 'It was a big mistake,' she admitted.

Christopher watched them make their way along the path that wound between the gravestones. Celia Hemmings improved on acquaintance but Arthur Lunn did not. While he had been impressed by the gracious way in which she had conducted herself, Christopher had been irritated by Lunn's remarks and stung by the reminder that Henry Redmayne spent most of his time in the company of such men. If his brother had been more careful in his choice of friends, he reflected, he would not be in such dire straits now. Theirs was a world that had neither charm nor appeal for Christopher, especially now that Gabriel Cheever was such a blatant victim of it.

'Good day, Mr Redmayne,' said a voice at his elbow.

He turned to see Susan beside him. 'Miss Cheever,' he said.

'Thank you for coming.'

'It was the least I could do.'

'And thank you for helping Lucy when you did. I could support her no longer.'

'She did well to hold up as long as she did, Miss Cheever. Where is she now?'

'The vicar is with her.'

'Do you know what her plans are?'

'Father has invited her to stay with us until she's recovered enough to travel.'

'That's very kind of Sir Julius.'

'It will give us a chance to get to know her better,' she said with a pale smile. 'There is so much to catch up on. But you are also welcome to stay with us, Mr Redmayne. It will give us an opportunity to repay your hospitality in London. Father asked me to pass on the invitation.'

'I appreciate his kindness but I must get back to London.'

'Oh,' she said with evident disappointment.

'Much as I hate to leave,' he explained, reluctance showing in his eyes, 'there is important work that calls me back. Now that your brother has been laid to rest, we must renew our efforts to find his killer.'

She reached out to grasp his arm. 'Do you have hopes on that score?'

'Strong hopes, Miss Cheever.'

'Really?'

'Yes, but do not worry about that,' he advised. 'Your place is here, mourning with the rest of the family and getting acquainted with your sister-in-law.'

'I know,' she said, releasing his arm.

'Please thank Sir Julius for his invitation and explain why I'm unable to accept it.'

'Father will understand.'

'I'm more concerned that *you* do, Miss Cheever.'

The affection in his voice drew another half-smile from her. Both wanted to speak further but they were at the mercy of their circumstances. It was neither the time nor place for conversation. Christopher felt guilty about the pleasure he was deriving from their brief encounter. It seemed wrong. Susan, too, was patently uneasy. Giving her a polite bow of farewell, Christopher took a final look at the bereaved family then made his way out of the churchyard.

When he came into the room, Sir Marcus Kemp looked even more like a giant spaniel whose paws had been inconsiderately trodden upon. Without being invited, he dropped on to the chair opposite Henry Redmayne and rolled his eyes in despair.

'I can take no more of it, Henry,' he said dolefully.

'Then we are two of a kind.'

'I think not. My plight is far worse than yours.'

'I doubt that, Marcus.'

'You are single,' his visitor reminded him, 'whereas I am married.'

'Yes,' conceded Henry, 'but you have not received a death threat.'

'Oh, yes, I have!'

'Another letter?'

'The ultimate threat – publication!'

He handed his friend the piece of paper that was

flapping in his hand. Henry read it with mounting alarm. *A Knight at the Theatre* was beautifully printed in bold type. Sir Marcus Kemp was identified by name and a description so cruelly accurate that it provoked a wild grin from Henry. That grin disappeared instantly when he saw his own name linked with that of an actress at the King's House. Sir Marcus was pilloried unmercifully but Henry was not spared.

'This is disgusting!' he said with righteous indignation.

'Yet horribly true, Henry.'

'That's beside the point. Private pleasure should be sacrosanct.'

'So I thought.'

'In any case, I did *not* relieve myself into the coal bucket. It was a china vase.'

'We are both being pissed upon here.'

Henry read the account again and shuddered. He thrust the page back at Kemp. The two of them were in the dining room of Henry's house. Work that should have been done at the Navy Office was spread out on the table but he had made only sporadic attempts to address himself to it. Fear kept him immured in his home. Sir Marcus Kemp had just intensified that fear.

'Is this the only page that came?' he asked.

'It is more than enough,' cried Kemp. 'It's my death threat, Henry. If that account is ever published, it will spell the death of my marriage, my reputation, my place in society and everything that I hold most dear. My whole inheritance is at risk. Dear God!' he exclaimed. 'What will my children think of their father?'

'They will know him for what he is, Marcus.'

'That's no consolation, you rogue. I came for sympathy, not scorn.'

'Your case is not as desperate as you imagine,' said Henry enviously. 'What will your wife learn that she has not already guessed? You spend so little time with her that she must know you have been out carousing with friends.'

'With friends, perhaps, but not with female company. My wife is easily duped. Whenever I got back late,' he explained, 'I told her that I was talking politics with colleagues from Parliament. The dear lady believed me. Until now.' He looked down at the printed page. 'But how convincing will *that* excuse be when she reads this?'

'The most gullible wife would not be deceived.'

'Then you understand my predicament.'

'I share it, Marcus. I, too, am mentioned in that account. Not that publication would have any power to hurt me,' he said, waving a hand. 'I shall be dead by then.'

'Dead?'

'Cut down by the same hand that murdered Gabriel Cheever.'

'Not if you pay up, Henry,' said Kemp, reaching a decision. 'That's what I intend to do. Hand over a thousand guineas.'

'But the demand was for five hundred.'

'A second letter came with *A Knight at the Theatre*. The price has doubled.'

'That's iniquitous!'

'It will be worth every penny if it stops this ruinous material being printed.'

'Supposing it does not?'

'It must, surely?'

'Where is your guarantee?'

'I have a gentleman's agreement.'

'You can only have that with a gentleman, Marcus, and we are dealing with a callous murderer here. My brother Christopher has warned me against paying anything. If we give in to blackmail once,' stressed Henry, 'we'll be trapped. The villain will go on squeezing money out of us until he has bled the pair of us dry.'

'Will he?'

'You would do the same in his position.'

'I'd never *be* in the same position,' retorted Kemp, hurt at the suggestion. 'Damn it, man, I've seen you and all my other friends in the most compromising situations but I'd never dream of exploiting that knowledge for gain. It's against all decorum.'

'We are not dealing with decorum here,' said Henry grimly.

'I know that.' He snatched up the paper. 'How on earth did he catch wind of all this?' he said in dismay. 'Was he hiding beneath the bed?'

'No, Marcus.'

'Up the chimney, then? It would be less painful, if it were not so hideously well written. Look at it, Henry,' he said, tossing it back on the table. 'We'll be the laughing stock of London if this is ever sold. The villain who penned this knows how to wound with words.'

'Yet that was not his intention.'

'It must have been.'

'No, Marcus,' said Henry. 'My brother explained it

to me. *A Knight at the Theatre* was written for private consumption, not with any thought to publication. It is an extract from a diary kept by Gabriel Cheever.'

'The devil it is!' shrieked the other.

'It appears that he kept a careful record of all his nights of revelry. Someone killed him to get their hands on his diary. I can see why now.'

Kemp blanched. 'You mean, there is *more*?'

'Far more, I suspect, and even more damaging than *A Knight at the Theatre*.'

'Then I might as well run myself through with my sword,' confessed Sir Marcus, putting both hands to his head. 'Gabriel witnessed everything. He was with us at the theatre when we invited those impudent ladies to dance naked for us in private. He watched those wonderful breasts bobbing magically in the candlelight. He saw me fling off my own clothes and sat there while you and Amy Dyson ran to the bed and—'

'Yes, yes!' interrupted Henry. 'There's no need to remind me.'

'Gabriel must have had a hundred such tales to write.'

'They will all be used against us, Marcus, be certain of that. You and I are the first victims but others will soon trail in our wake. Arthur Lunn and Peter Wickens have roistered even more than us. So has Gilbert Sparkish,' said Henry, throwing out the first names that came into his head. 'They, too, will certainly have a place in Gabriel's diary. There'll be others in the same plight as us before long.'

'A thousand guineas from each of us? He'll make a fortune.'

'Only if we are weak enough to pay.'

'I'd hand the money over right now!' declared Kemp.

'What happens when he sends you a second page from the diary?' asked Henry.

Kemp was in torment. After playing anxiously with his wig, he tore it off and flung it down, revealing a bald pate with a defiant tuft of hair at its centre. There was no defiance in the man himself. Shocked and humiliated, he sat back in his chair and looked towards heaven. A thought then nudged him.

'Were you the first to receive a threat?' he said.

'What of it?'

'I seem to recall that a letter was involved.'

'It was,' admitted Henry gloomily. 'A *billet-doux* sent on a foolish impulse.'

'To whom?'

There was an embarrassed pause. 'A married lady, Marcus.'

'Which one?' asked Kemp. 'You sniff around so many.'

'Her name is irrelevant. The point is that the letter fell into the wrong hands.'

'How?'

'I wish I knew!'

'So you're not being blackmailed with an extract from Gabriel's diary?'

'Not yet,' said Henry ruefully. 'That time may yet come.'

Kemp was puzzled. 'Why was your life threatened?'

'I think I've worked that out. The man who strangled Gabriel Cheever has no need to murder me. He simply has to show that letter of mine to a certain husband. He's a vengeful man,' said Henry apprehensively. 'He'll insist on a duel. That's why the blackmailer does not need to kill me, Marcus. An angry husband will do the job for him.'

For two days, Lucy Cheever barely left her room. The funeral had been a severe trial for her and she lay prostrate on her bed for most of the time. Even her maidservant was only allowed limited access to her. Lucy's collapse aroused mixed feelings in the household. Sir Julius was at once sad and relieved, sorry that she was suffering so badly but glad to be left alone to nurse his own woes. Before he learnt more about his daughter-in-law, he wanted to clarify his feelings about his son. Lancelot Serle was sympathetic to the young widow but Brilliana was more critical, unable to accept that a secret marriage entitled Lucy to the attention she was receiving and unwilling to embrace her in the way that Susan had done. Brilliana bickered so much on the subject with her father and sister that Sir Julius was on the point of ordering her out of the house. Serle anticipated him and, in a gesture that earned a rare compliment from his father-in-law, more or less hustled his fractious wife into their coach to take her back to Richmond.

The atmosphere in the house improved markedly. As if sensing the fact, Lucy made her appearance on the third day, apologising profusely for imposing on her hosts and for remaining out of sight. Susan Cheever took her off to her own room so that they could talk in private. While Lucy sat in the chair, she perched on the bed.

'How are you feeling now, Lucy?' she began.

'As if all the life has been drained out of me.'

'We all feel like that.'

'What happened to your sister?'

'Brilliana decided to return to Richmond.'

'I heard her voice a number of times.'

'Yes,' said Susan wearily, 'Brilliana tends to shout, I fear, especially when she's losing an argument. It was best for all of us that her husband took her away when he did. The house seems much quieter all of a sudden.'

'Do you see much of your sister?'

'Enough.'

'She is so unlike you, Susan,' said Lucy. 'Gabriel warned me that she would be.'

'Do you have any brothers or sisters?'

'Not any more. I had one of each but both died during the Plague.'

'What about your parents?'

'My mother is a widow.' She felt a lurch of recognition. 'Just like me.'

'Not quite, Lucy. You were unlucky. Gabriel was taken before his time.'

'I wish that I had been killed alongside him!'

Susan was shocked. 'That's a dreadful thought!' she exclaimed.

'At least we'd still be together.'

'You *are* together, Lucy. As long as you preserve his memory.'

'I'll cherish it for ever.'

Susan felt a pang of regret that she had never seen her brother and his wife together. They must have made a handsome couple, but there was far more to their marriage than a pleasing appearance. Lucy had somehow managed to rescue Gabriel from his former dissolute existence and give him a sense of purpose. In doing so, she had found her own true path through life.

'May I ask how you met?' said Susan.

'By accident.'

'Where? Gabriel said so little about you in his letters, apart from the fact that he loved you to distraction, that is. I can see why,' she added with a smile. 'But he told me nothing about how you met and where you were married.'

'We agreed to keep that secret.'

'Why?'

Lucy was wary. 'I'm not able to tell you that, Susan. It's rather complicated. Gabriel had reasons of his own for secrecy. Nobody was to know where we were.'

'Somebody knew,' noted Susan.

'I was not counting you.'

'Nor was I, Lucy. The man who killed Gabriel must have known where he lived as well. From what you told me, Gabriel hardly ever left the house.'

'He was wedded to his work, Susan. He wrote all the time.'

'That sounds like my brother. Gabriel did nothing by half-measures.'

'I miss him so much.'

Lucy's control snapped again and she burst into tears. Leaping off the bed, Susan knelt down to embrace her, fighting off her own urge to cry. They were entwined for several minutes. When Lucy felt well enough to push Susan gently away, she looked into her eyes.

'You've been so kind to me.'

'I loved Gabriel as well.'

'He doted on you,' said Lucy. 'Gabriel could be harsh at times. He told me that he would not mind if he never saw his father or Brilliana again. They had been hateful to him. But he would never spurn you, Susan. You were his one friend in the family.'

'We grew up together. I could never disown him.'

'Your sister did.'

'That's all behind us. Brilliana will mourn his death in her own way.' Susan stood up and regarded her sister-in-law for a few seconds. 'Did you mind being at the funeral on your own?'

'But I was not on my own. I brought Anna with me.'

'I was thinking about your family.'

Lucy's face darkened. 'There was nobody else I wanted there.'

'Not even your mother?'

'No. In any case, she would be too ill to travel.'

'Will you tell her what's happened?'

Lucy shook her head.

'Why not?'

Lucy reached out to hold her hand. 'I don't know you well enough to tell you that yet, Susan. Perhaps I will one day. Until then, please bear with me.' She got up and crossed to look through the window. 'It's beautiful here. I'm sorry I have to leave.'

'Must you?' said Susan, moving to stand behind her. 'Father would like you to stay as long as you wish. He wants to talk to you.'

'I'm not sure how much we have to say to each other.'

'When were you thinking of going?'

'Tomorrow,' said Lucy, turning to face her. 'I need to go back to London.'

'Why?'

'Because that's where Gabriel's killer is and I want to be there when he's caught.'

'If anyone can track him down,' said Susan fondly, 'it is Christopher Redmayne. He's a fine man. Father and I have so much to thank him for, Lucy.'

'So do I.'

'Do you have his address?'

'Yes, he left it when he called on me in Knightrider Street.'

'Good.'

'Why do you ask?'

'Because I think that you might consider telling him what you are unable to tell me. Let me finish,' she went on, silencing the imminent protest. 'Mr Redmayne is putting his own life at risk on our behalf. We must do everything we can to help him. You must have information about Gabriel that nobody else could have. The most trivial details might be valuable clues to Mr Redmayne. Talk to him, Lucy. You can trust him not to break a confidence.' She held her by the shoulders. 'Tell him the truth.'

'No, Susan. I could never do that.'

'Not even if it might lead to the arrest of Gabriel's killer?'

Lucy fell silent and lowered her head. Letting go of her, Susan stepped back to watch her. She had surprised herself with the degree of affection that came into her voice when she mentioned Christopher Redmayne, but she was not ashamed of her feelings for him. Her admiration for him had steadily grown. When he left her in the churchyard after the funeral, she had been bitterly disappointed. She wished that Lucy had the same faith in him that she did. There was a long wait before Lucy looked up at her. When her question came, it took Susan completely by surprise.

'Will you come back to London with me?' she asked.

Jonathan was putting a man in the stocks when Christopher rode up on his horse. Having secured his prisoner, a ragged individual with a straggly beard, the constable gave his friend a nod of welcome.

'I did not expect you back so soon, Mr Redmayne,' he said.

Christopher dismounted. 'There was nothing to keep me in Northamptonshire.' He thought of Susan Cheever and smiled to himself. 'Well, on reflection, there was, but it was imperative that I got back here. That's why I rode so hard.' He patted his horse's flank. 'You deserve a rest, old friend.'

'It's good to see you.'

'Thank you, Mr Bale. And I'm pleased to see you again.' He indicated the man in the stocks. 'More pleased than this fellow was to see a constable, I know that.'

'Leave him where he is, sir. Those stocks are his second home.'

He collected a jeer from the prisoner then set off down the street. Leading his horse, Christopher walked beside him. He gave Jonathan a terse account of the funeral but included a reference to the two unheralded visitors.

'Mr Lunn was there?' he said. 'I met him. He did not strike me as a caring soul.'

'He was there to accompany Miss Hemmings,' explained Christopher. 'It would have been difficult for her to attend the funeral on her own. With a man beside her, she was almost invisible. Had she been there alone, people would have asked what her relationship had been with Gabriel Cheever.'

'The answer would not have been fit to be heard on hallowed ground.'

'Perhaps not, Mr Bale, but I admire the woman. She loved Gabriel once.'

'From what I hear, that young man seems to have had many similar ladies.'

'Yet he gave them all up to marry Lucy.'

'It may have been the one sensible thing he ever did.'

'Yet it may have cost him his life. Still,' said Christopher, 'tell me your news.'

Jonathan shrugged. 'There's precious little of it, Mr Redmayne.'

Christopher had been away for the best part of a week. During his absence Jonathan had been far from idle, but he had made scant progress. He had been pursuing lines of enquiry for which he did not feel best suited.

'Some of your brother's friends look with disdain on constables,' he recalled. 'They have no respect for the law. Or maybe something about me irritates them. Mr Peter Wickens refused to speak to me, Mr Gilbert Sparkish was rude to my face and Sir Thomas Sheasby threatened to set the dogs on me. I had to speak sternly to him.'

'It sounds to me as if all three of them deserved to have their ears boxed,' said Christopher. 'At what time of day did you seek them out?'

'Late afternoon.'

'That was your mistake, Mr Bale. Catch them after dinner and they'll have drunk too much to give anyone a civil answer. No matter,' he continued. 'I'm back to take over the examination of Henry's cronies. I'm on my way to visit one now but I wanted to talk to you first.'

'Who are you going to see, Mr Redmayne?'

'Sir Marcus Kemp.'

'Is he the other gentleman who received a blackmail demand?'

'He is. Apparently, that demand has been doubled.'

'Why?'

'Because he has been too tardy in paying it, Mr Bale. Before I came in search of you, I called on my brother. It seems that Henry had a visit from Sir Marcus earlier today. He brought something with him that had frightened the daylights out of him.'

'A death threat?'

'An extract from Gabriel Cheever's diary,' said Christopher. 'One that did not exactly show Sir Marcus in a flattering light. In the hands of his wife, it could become a dangerous weapon.'

Jonathan was appalled. 'Sir Marcus is married?'

'Several of Henry's friends are.'

'Yet they still lead such shameful lives? What of their marriage vows?'

'They keep them less well than you, Mr Bale.'

'Such wickedness should not go unpunished.'

'Oh, Sir Marcus Kemp has been punished,' said Christopher wryly. 'According to Henry, his friend has been roasting in the fires of Hell. I hope there's something left of him by the time I get there.'

Sir Marcus Kemp was in a quandary. He did not know whether to pay the money demanded from him or not. It would cost him a thousand guineas to prevent some highly damaging material about him from being published. Rich enough to afford such an amount, he did not, however, have unlimited wealth. If he had to pay indefinite blackmail demands, he would be driven to financial ruin. The alternative course of action was not appealing. He could defy the blackmailer and try to limit the damage by making a full confession to his wife about his indiscretions after a visit to the playhouse. The notion was immediately dismissed. There was no way that he could bring himself to tell a God-fearing woman who had borne him three children that two naked actresses had entertained Henry Redmayne and him in the most beguiling manner one evening, or that his supposed late nights with parliamentary colleagues were invariably spent in the arms of an expensive whore. The two worlds of Sir Marcus Kemp were set to collide. By keeping them apart, he could inhabit each with unrestrained pleasure. Once they met in opposition, a huge explosion would ensue.

Lost in thought, he prowled around the room. A tap on the door startled him.

'Yes?' he snarled.

'You have a visitor, Sir Marcus,' said the servant from the hall.

'Send him on his way. I refuse to see anyone.'

'Mr Redmayne says that it's a matter of urgency.'

'Redmayne?' said his master, unlocking the door. 'Why didn't you tell me that it was Henry who had called? He's the one man in London I will see.' He flung open the door to see Christopher standing before him. 'You are not Henry!' he protested.

'There *is* a family likeness, Sir Marcus. Good day to you.'

'What are you doing here?'

'Representing my brother,' said Christopher. 'I may be able to help you with this unfortunate business in which you have become entangled.'

'Keep your voice down, man!' said Kemp, pulling him into the room and closing the door before locking it again. 'What has Henry been telling you?'

'Something of your problems.'

'He swore to keep those secret.'

'Not from me, Sir Marcus. I am on your side.'

Before his host could object, Christopher explained how he had become involved in the murder investigation and how he had learnt about the theft of Gabriel Cheever's diary. Sir Marcus listened with horrified curiosity. He had met Christopher before and been struck by how much he differed from his brother in appearance and inclinations. His visitor was far too wholesome for his taste. It was unnerving.

'That is why Henry confided in me,' said Christopher. 'So that I could have all the facts at my disposal. If I can find the killer, Sir Marcus, I can put a stop to these blackmail demands.'

'I wish that somebody would.'

'May I see the latest communication?'

'No!' howled Kemp. 'I could not show you that, Mr Redmayne.

I only let Henry peruse it because he, too, is mentioned in the piece.'

'I believe that it is called *A Knight at the Theatre*.'

'Its true title is *The Death of Sir Marcus Kemp*.'

'You exaggerate. Help me to catch the villain and your worries will disappear.'

'How can I do that?'

'By lending me this mischievous page from Gabriel's diary.'

Kemp's face reddened in anger. 'Lending it to you?'

'It is a piece of evidence, Sir Marcus.'

'Yes, Mr Redmayne. Evidence of my folly, evidence of my personal proclivities.'

'I know,' argued Christopher, 'but it's been printed, according to Henry. That means the man who sent it engaged a printer. Give the page to me and I'll visit every printer in London until I find the one who accepted the commission.'

'That's tantamount to publishing it far and wide!'

'No, Sir Marcus. They will not need to read the contents. A glance will suffice to tell them if it is their handiwork. Once we know who paid to have it printed, we can arrest the villain and you can breathe freely once more.'

'That document is not leaving this house.'

'May I at least have a sight of it?'

'Certainly not.'

'But it's in your best interests.' Kemp turned away.

Christopher went after him. 'I understand that it was accompanied by a letter. Could I please look at that, Sir Marcus? I merely wish to establish if it was written by the same hand that penned Henry's death threat. That will not compromise you, surely?'

'I'll show you nothing.'

'Then you must resign yourself to your fate.'

'No,' said Kemp, swinging round to confront him. 'I'm going to buy my way out of this mess. If I had had the sense to do that at the start, I could have saved myself five hundred guineas. I'll pay up and have done with it.'

'It will not get the blackmailer off your back.'

'So you say, but I'm ready to take that chance.'

'What happens if you fail?' An idea suddenly popped into Christopher's mind. 'When the first letter came, Sir Marcus, did it explain how the money was to be paid?'

'Yes.'

'Presumably, it is to be dropped somewhere?'

'At a spot in Covent Garden.'

'By you or by someone else?'

'That was not specified.'

'Do you intend to place the money there in person?'

'Heavens, no! I'd not have the stomach for it.'

'Then let me make a bargain with you, Sir Marcus,' said Christopher. 'There's an element of danger here. The blackmailer is also capable of murder. Remember that. Whoever delivers the money is taking a risk.'

'I can see that.'

'What if I were to act on your behalf and go to the designated spot?'

Kemp was grateful. 'Would you?' he asked, grasping Christopher's arm.

'On one condition.'

'Condition?'

'Yes. If your tormentor is bought off with a thousand guineas, all well and good. But if, as I suspect, he takes the money then sends you a further demand, you let me see everything that he has sent you. Is that fair?'

'No, Mr Redmayne. It would be too embarrassing.'

'What is a little embarrassment if it leads to the capture of a vicious criminal? Come, Sir Marcus,' he urged. 'I am not going to be shocked by anything I read. With a brother like Henry, I have been well educated in the ways of the world.'

Kemp chewed his lip and looked shrewdly at his visitor. Christopher was discreet and sincere. If he could not be trusted, his brother would not have confided in him. Kemp was not attracted to the proposition but it did have one advantage. Someone else would be taking any risks involved in delivering the payment.

'Well, Sir Marcus?' pressed Christopher. 'Do you accept my offer?'

'Yes,' said Kemp, overcoming his reluctance. 'The bargain is sealed.'

CHAPTER TEN

When prayers had been said, the Bale family began their meal. The two boys, Oliver and Richard, fell on their supper with relish, chewing it so noisily and swallowing it so fast that their mother had to issue a warning.

'You must not gobble your food like that,' she said. 'It will do you no good.'

'I'm hungry,' replied Oliver through a mouthful of bread.

'Eat more slowly, Oliver.'

'And wait until you empty your mouth before you speak,' added Jonathan.

'Will you read to us tonight, Father?' asked Richard, the younger of the boys.

'Only if you eat your food properly.'

'I want to know what happened to Joseph and his brothers.'

'You will.'

'Oliver says that he kills them all.'

'I said that he *ought* to kill them,' corrected Oliver, still munching happily.

'No, Oliver,' said his father seriously. 'Murder is a terrible crime.'

'But they deserve it,' argued the boy.

'Nobody deserves to be killed.'

'His brothers treated him cruelly. They wanted to get rid of him because they were jealous of him. They left him down that well.'

'Yes,' said Richard, eager to show his knowledge of the story.

'They took his coat of many colours and dipped it in blood. They told their father that Joseph had been killed by a wild beast.'

'That was because Joseph had disappeared,' Jonathan reminded them. 'It was Reuben, the eldest of the brothers, who persuaded the others to spare him. But when Reuben went to release him, Joseph had gone.'

'Where?' asked Richard.

'Wait and see.'

'I want to know *now*.'

'The words of the Bible tell the story far better than I can.'

'But I can tell you this,' said Sarah, brushing Richard's hair back from his face with a maternal hand. 'Joseph does not kill his brothers.'

'Cain killed *his* brother,' noted Oliver.

'That was a dreadful thing to do. Brothers should love one another.'

'Is it always wrong to kill somebody?'

'Yes,' said Jonathan firmly. 'Always.'

'Was it wrong to chop off the head of the last king?'

'Oliver!' chided his mother.

'Was it?' persisted the boy. 'You named me after Oliver Cromwell yet he was the man who murdered the king. Was that a crime?'

'Was it, Father?' asked Richard. 'Was it a crime or a sin?'

'I think it was both,' decided Oliver.

Jonathan glanced uneasily at his wife. 'Finish your supper, boys,' he advised. 'I can explain it to you when I put you to bed. And you will learn what happened to Joseph as well. But only if you eat your food quietly, as your mother told you.'

The boys were sufficiently mollified to eat on in relative silence. Jonathan was learning that it was not easy to bring up two inquisitive sons. Oliver was eight and his brother was fifteen months younger. They asked questions that were sometimes difficult to answer. On the previous evening, Richard had enquired what a concubine was. It had caused Jonathan some embarrassment to explain but he had been honest. Oliver had giggled while Richard had blushed. Looking at his sons, Jonathan reflected how similar they were in appearance yet how different in character. It led to endless squabbles between them. He wondered how they would get on when they became adults and his mind drifted to another pair of brothers. Christopher and Henry Redmayne could not have been more disparate. They led divergent lives. While he admired one brother, Jonathan had polite contempt for the other. Yet they had been raised in the same way by their parents. What had made Christopher and Henry grow in opposite directions? Why had one embraced work while the other espoused idleness? Jonathan was exercised by the thought of how he could prevent the same thing from happening to his own sons.

'Will you be going out again this evening?' asked Sarah.

'Yes,' said Jonathan.

'Not until you have read to us,' Richard piped up.

Jonathan smiled. 'Of course not. I want to know what happens to Joseph myself.'

'Will you be late?' said Sarah.

'I hope not. I am going to meet Mr Redmayne.'

Sarah was disappointed. 'Is he not coming here?'

'Not this evening, Sarah.'

'Do give him my regards.'

'I will,' said Jonathan. 'I told him how helpful you had been. Without you, I might never have got to know the vigilant Mrs Runciman in Knightrider Street. And it was you who suggested that I got in touch with Mr Redmayne in the first place.'

'You and he work well together, Jonathan.'

'I still wonder why sometimes,' confessed her husband.

'You have so much in common.'

'Hardly, Sarah. Mr Redmayne consorts with the highest in the land while my work makes me rub shoulders with the very lowest. Had it not been for sheer accident, we would never have met.'

'Are you glad that you did?'

'I think so.'

Sarah laughed. 'Oh, Jonathan!' she teased. 'You will hold back so. Be honest for once. You know that you like Mr Redmayne as much as I do but you never admit it. He obviously respects you.'

'Does he?'

'I can see it in his face. He thinks you far too good to be a mere constable.'

'Nobody is too good for such important work, Sarah.'

'Could Tom Warburton do the things that you have achieved?'

'Probably not.'

'He could never work with Mr Redmayne the way that you have. And the pair of you *do* have something in common,' she insisted. 'Both of you are like Tom's little dog. You are real terriers. Once you get your teeth into something, neither of you will let go.'

The headache was so severe that Henry Redmayne took to his bed with a flask of wine for consolation. He was still propped up with pillows when his brother called on him. Christopher's news did nothing to alleviate the throbbing pain in his temples.

'Sir Marcus is going to pay up?' he said in astonishment.

'I made a bargain with him, Henry.'

'But you did everything possible to *stop* me from handing any money over.'

'I tried to prevent Sir Marcus as well,' said Christopher, 'but he was determined. So I decided to make virtue out of necessity.'

'In what way?'

'I volunteered to hand the thousand guineas over on his behalf.'

'Why?'

Christopher grinned. 'If I have to part with that amount of money, I want it to belong to someone else.' He became serious. 'I have to catch this villain, Henry. I owe it to Gabriel's family. Paying up is a means of luring the blackmailer out of hiding. That's not how I presented it to Sir Marcus, of course. He thinks that he is buying peace of mind with his thousand guineas.'

'What is this bargain you mentioned?'

'He refused to show me any of the demands he received. Sir Marcus was angry that I even knew about them. It was hard work to strike a bargain with him,' said Christopher, 'but he agreed in the end. If the money is paid and the demands still continue, he's promised to give me the letters and that extract from Gabriel Cheever's diary.'

'But the demands will stop if you arrest the blackmailer.'

'I hope so, Henry.'

'So why reach this agreement with Sir Marcus?'

'To gain access to vital information in case we fail to catch our man.'

'We?' echoed Henry.

'I'll take Jonathan Bale with me.'

'Why?'

'He's been assisting me from the start,' explained Christopher.

Henry was scornful. 'That flat-footed constable is more hindrance than help.'

'Mr Bale is the ideal person for this kind of work.'

'I beg leave to doubt that, Christopher. When will the money be handed over?'

'Tomorrow.'

'Somewhere in Covent Garden, as I remember.'

'Yes,' confirmed Christopher. 'The details were sent in the first letter to Sir Marcus. Someone will be waiting to take the money from the designated spot. He's been there every day at noon so far. When Sir Marcus failed to pay up, the amount was promptly doubled.'

'And he received that chilling extract from Gabriel's damnable diary. What are you going to do?'

'Hand the money over tomorrow while Mr Bale watches from nearby. It is highly unlikely that the blackmailer will take the money from me in person but the man who does will carry it to him.' He rubbed his hands in anticipation. 'With luck, he'll lead Mr Bale to the villain we are after.'

'The one who threatened to kill me.'

'That was a trick to make you pay up at once.'

'It does not feel like a trick,' moaned Henry, putting a palm to his forehead. 'It has robbed me of sleep every night this past week. The Sword of Damocles hangs over me. Well,' he added grimly, 'the sword of a jealous husband, to be exact. All the rogue has to do is to send that letter to Lord Ulvercombe and I am as good as dead.'

'I still believe that you should get in touch with the lady herself.'

'Fatal.'

'Is it?'

'Her husband stands guard over her day and night. It was only when business called him away that I could get anywhere near her.'

'Lady Ulvercombe deserves to be warned.'

'Not by me, Christopher.'

'Could you not write to her?'

'And have my correspondence intercepted by that mad husband of hers? Oh, no!' asserted Henry. 'I've already written one letter to her that is a possible suicide note. Why tempt Fate with a second?'

'How did your *billet-doux* fall into the wrong hands?' said Christopher. 'That's what puzzles me. Someone must have stolen it from her. Lady Ulvercombe may have some idea who that could be. It's another means of unmasking the blackmailer, Henry. Is there nobody who could act as an intermediary between you and the lady?'

'No, Christopher.'

'There must be a reliable confidant.'

'The liaison was strictly a private affair. Nobody else knew about it – until now, that is. Do not vex me with questions,' he complained as his head pounded. 'My only concern is to stop Lord Ulvercombe from killing me in a duel.'

'I share the same ambition, Henry.'

'Then reclaim my *billet-doux* before anyone else can read it.'

'I'll do my best,' promised Christopher. 'But do be more discreet next time.'

Henry grimaced. 'There will *be* no next time.'

'You always say that.'

'Henceforth, I'll confine myself to unmarried ladies. If I live to do so.'

Christopher smiled confidently. 'Have no qualms on that score, Henry. By this time tomorrow, your worries may all be over and you will be forced to concede what a splendid fellow Jonathan Bale is.'

'If he gets me off this hook, I'll sing his praises like a choir of angels.'

'He would enjoy that.' He turned away. 'I'll leave you to get some rest.'

Henry raised a weary arm. 'One moment, Christopher.'

'Yes?'

'When that first blackmail demand arrived, you urged me not to pay.'

'So?'

'Now you are trying to tempt the villain out into the light of day by handing over some money to him. Why act on behalf of Sir Marcus Kemp when you could have done exactly the same for me?'

Christopher went back to him. 'How much were you asked for, Henry?'

'Five hundred guineas.'

'Do you have that amount in hand?'

'Of course not.'

'Then how did you propose to raise it?'

'From friends,' said Henry airily.

'What about me?'

'I would have started with you, naturally, Christopher. But the bulk of the money would have come from the one man who can afford such a sum without blinking an eye.'

'Sir Marcus Kemp.'

'Precisely.'

'Would you have wanted to go cap in hand to him?'

'It would have been galling.'

'Then I've spared you that as well. Now you see what brothers are for, Henry. I want to help. When I hand over that money tomorrow, you will not have to worry about paying a penny of it back to the man who would have loaned it to you.'

Henry rallied visibly. 'How profoundly true! Whether I pay or he does, it is all one. Sir Marcus Kemp's money is handed over either way. You have done me a favour, Christopher. My headache is easing already.'

'Do not swallow gudgeons ere they're catched.'

'What do you mean?'

'It will not be easy to net this blackmailer,' warned Christopher. 'Even with the redoubtable Mr Bale at my side, we will need good fortune if we are to succeed.'

Sir Julius Cheever had been disappointed that his daughter-in-law wanted to return so soon to London. It cut short the time in which they could develop their acquaintance. He had been even less pleased when Susan announced that she wished to travel back with Lucy, and the old man needed a great deal of persuasion before he consented. Sir Julius himself felt that his place was in the family home, mourning his son in the parish where he was born and brought up. The thought of subjecting himself again to the hospitality of his elder daughter and her husband deprived him of even the slightest urge to travel back to the city. Accordingly, the two young women departed without him, joining a large group of travellers for safety.

The jolting of the coach and the presence of Anna, the maidservant, made any intimate conversation impossible but Susan and Lucy did manage to spend some time together during the two overnight stops that the party made at roadside inns. Over supper on the second of those nights, Susan Cheever felt that she was at last beginning to win her sister-in-law's confidence.

'I cannot thank you enough for this,' said Lucy. 'It would have been so dismal to go back to that empty house on my own.'

'You have Anna.'

'It is not the same, Susan. I need someone to whom I can talk about Gabriel.'

'You can do that as much as you wish.'

'Coming from his wife this may sound strange, but I feel as if I never really knew him properly. All the time we were in Northamptonshire, I kept learning things about him that he never even mentioned.'

'Such as?'

'Angling,' said Lucy. 'It turns out that he had a passion for angling. Sir Julius used to take him fishing when he was a little boy.'

Susan nodded. 'Yes,' she said. 'And they always caught something for the table. I remember how upset Father was when Gabriel became so skilled with a line that he managed to catch more fish than him.'

'Why did Gabriel never talk about angling to me?'

'It belonged to the past that he chose to forget.'

'Yet it was something he *enjoyed*, Susan.'

'Gabriel enjoyed most things. That's what I envied about him. His capacity for sheer enjoyment was remarkable. It's something that I never had.' She pulled a face. 'Nor did Brilliana.'

'She never seems to enjoy anything.'

'That's not entirely true.'

Lucy lowered her voice. 'Why did your sister marry Mr Serle?'

'Because he asked her.'

'But she is so critical of him.'

'Brilliana is critical of all men,' explained Susan, 'which is why so many of them were terrified of getting too close to her. She had suitors from all over the Midlands but they always turned tail in the end. Lancelot Serle did not.'

'Does he still love her?'

'Very much. When Brilliana lets him.'

'Gabriel told me very little about her except that she had rejected him.'

'She never had much time for him, I'm afraid.' Susan looked at her companion over the dancing flames of the candle. They were seated at a table in a quiet corner. The atmosphere was conducive to an exchange of intimacies. 'Talking to you makes me feel that I never knew him all that well either.'

'How could you when you were apart for so long?'

'Whole areas of his life were a closed book to me.'

Lucy gave a half-smile. 'Perhaps that is just as well.'

'Did he tell you everything about his past?'

'Everything that I wished to know.'

'And was there anything that you did not, Lucy?'

'Oh, yes. I thought it best to draw a veil of decency over much of it.'

'You were very wise,' agreed Susan, wondering if it was the right moment to probe a little more deeply. 'Did he tell you that he sent me one of his poems?'

'Yes, he did.'

'It was very sad but so beautiful. I had no idea he had such talent.'

'Gabriel was a wonderful writer.'

'Did you read everything that he wrote?'

'Only what he chose to show me.' Lucy's face lit up. 'Several of the poems were written especially for me. Gabriel always said that they were his best work.'

'He was truly inspired.'

'I never read any of his plays. There was no point, Susan. I've never been to the theatre and have no idea what makes a good play. Besides,' she said with a little shrug, 'I think that Gabriel felt I might not approve.'

'What about his diary?' She saw Lucy's jaw tighten. 'You did know that he kept a diary?'

'Of course.'

'Were you allowed to look at it?'

'Gabriel never tried to stop me from doing anything.'

'So you did read the diary?'

'Bits of it,' admitted Lucy. 'It was like reading about a complete stranger.'

'Were you shocked?'

'To some degree. But I was also very amused.'

'Amused?' echoed Susan in surprise.

'Gabriel had such a wicked sense of fun. Some of the entries in his diary were so comical that I burst out laughing.' A hunted look came into her eye. 'Even that pleasure has been taken from me now. Someone stole the diary from the house.'

'Did they take anything else?'

'No, Susan. They only came for one thing.'

'Would you have read the diary in full if it was still in your possession?'

'Who knows?' said Lucy evasively, resisting the gentle interrogation. 'But let us talk about you, Susan. I am grateful for your company, but you must not feel tied to my apron strings while you are in London. Your sister will doubtless want to see you and there must be other friends you can visit in the city.'

'One perhaps,' said Susan wistfully.

'Mr Christopher Redmayne?' She smiled as her companion blinked. 'I may be in mourning, Susan, but that does not mean I am deaf. Since we left Northamptonshire, that gentleman's name has been on your tongue a dozen times. I think that you are fond of Mr Redmayne.'

'He is a personable young man.'

'He is much more than that to you, I suspect.'

'We are barely acquainted,' denied Susan without conviction.

'No matter,' said the other, touching her arm. 'It is none of my business. I just thought that you might be interested in an odd coincidence.'

'Coincidence?'

'Yes, it came back into my mind when you talked about Gabriel's diary just now. I only read a small portion of it but I do recall one of the names I saw.'

'What was it?'

'Henry Redmayne.'

Susan was startled. 'Redmayne?'

'He was part of Gabriel's circle.'

'I see.'

'He may, of course, be no relation at all of our Mr Redmayne,' said Lucy thoughtfully, 'but it is not all that common a name so there is a possibility. Has he mentioned anyone called Henry to you?'

'No,' murmured Susan, frowning with dismay.

Lucy was alarmed. 'Have I said something to offend you?'

'Not at all.'

'I would hate to do that.'

Susan forced a smile. 'You have done nothing of the sort, Lucy.'

'Are you sure?'

'Quite sure.'

But for a reason that she did not understand, Susan was suddenly disconcerted.

Covent Garden was high on Christopher Redmayne's list of favourite architectural sights in the capital. A great admirer of the work of Inigo Jones, he had studied the area with great interest, noting how the houses in the piazza had front doors that opened on to vaulted arcades in the manner of Sebastiano Selio. Not everyone had approved of the importation of Italian styles to a prime site in the capital and Jones had sustained heavy criticism from some quarters, but Christopher had nothing but praise for Covent Garden. The church of St Paul's dominated one side of the square and looked out on the high terraced houses that extended along the other three sides. The properties had an imposing facade, generous proportions, a pleasant garden and stabling at the rear. When they were first built they attracted rich tenants, but the area was slightly less fashionable now and had yielded the palm to the new developments to the west such as St James's Square. The presence of the market brought more visitors to Covent Garden but deterred potential tenants who did not like the crowds that flocked round the stalls in the square.

Christopher had little time to admire the scene on this occasion. Obeying the instruction in the letter to Sir Marcus Kemp, he made his way to the church of St Paul's just before noon and waited at the specified spot. The market was in full swing and the noise of haggling was carried on the light breeze. Somewhere in the middle of the tumult was Jonathan Bale, concealed from sight, keeping his friend under observation and ready to follow anyone who might relieve Christopher of the large purse he was carrying. As the latter stood in front of the church, he wondered if anyone would approach him when it was seen that he was not Sir Marcus Kemp. Suspecting a ruse, the blackmailer might simply retreat. Noon came and passed but nobody stopped to speak to him, let alone to relieve him of one thousand guineas. Christopher's thoughts turned to the magnificence of the square again. Inigo Jones had begun as an apprentice to a joiner in St Paul's Churchyard. It always seemed incredible to Christopher that a man from such humble origins could rise to the position of the King's Surveyor of Works and be responsible for such buildings as the Banqueting House and the New Exchange.

Caught up in his admiration of a fellow architect,

Christopher did not notice the young boy who came trotting up to him. He was a tall, thin lad with tousled hair. His clothing was shabby and his manner obsequious.

'Are you from Sir Marcus Kemp, sir?' he asked.

'Yes,' said Christopher, seeing him for the first time.

The boy held out his hand. 'I am to take what you have, sir.'

'Who sent you?'

'A gentleman, sir. Give it to me or I get no reward.'

'Which gentleman?'

'In the market.'

'Where? Point him out.'

'Please, sir. He'll not wait.'

'Did he give you a name?'

'No, sir.'

Christopher showed him the purse. 'Point him out and you shall have the money.'

'There, sir,' said the boy, indicating a tall man in the crowd.

'Where?'

'Beside that stall.'

Having distracted Christopher, the boy grabbed the purse and went haring off.

'Wait!'

Christopher's shout was drowned beneath the sea of voices in the square. Though he tried to keep track of the boy, he soon lost him in the mêlée. The lad disappeared into the heart of the market and for a moment Christopher feared that Jonathan Bale might have missed him as well, but he trusted in the constable's vigilance. Whichever way the boy went, the constable would somehow follow him. All that Christopher could do was wait outside the church until his friend returned with information about the whereabouts of the blackmailer. It might even be that an arrest would already have been made. He wondered if he should slip into the church and offer up a prayer for the capture of the man who had caused such grief to so many people. Inevitably, his thoughts settled on Susan Cheever.

He did not have long to wait. As soon as he saw Jonathan Bale emerging from the throng, however, he knew that there were bad tidings. The constable was alone. When he reached Christopher, he lifted his broad shoulders in apology.

'He was too quick for me, Mr Redmayne.'

'That lad could certainly run.'

'Not him, sir,' explained Jonathan. 'The man we're after. He's more cunning than I bargained for. My legs are not that slow. I caught the lad before he got to The Strand. He was eating an apple that he bought with the money he earned.'

'Where was the purse?'

'He was paid to slip it to another boy by one of the stalls.'

'Which stall?'

'He could not remember,' said Jonathan sadly, 'and there was no point in trying to shake the truth out of him. The lad was an innocent pawn in all this. He did not even get a proper look at the man who employed him.'

'It was cleverly done, Mr Bale.'

'I know. He took the purse from you, darted into the crowd, and gave the money to a second boy who then passed it on to the man we want. The villain was taking no chances. He used two boys as his couriers and watched it all from safety.'

'Yes,' sighed Christopher. 'We were outfoxed.'

'Only because we were expected, Mr Redmayne.'

'Expected?'

'The blackmailer realised that a trap was being set for him.'

'How?'

'I have no idea,' said Jonathan, 'but that lad did not pick you out by chance.'

'What do you mean, Mr Bale?'

'It was one thing I did squeeze out of him.'

'Well?'

'He knew your name, Mr Redmayne. Someone recognised you.'

Christopher felt as if he had just been kicked hard in the stomach.

Celia Hemmings was writing a letter when she heard the doorbell ring. Pleased to learn that the visitor was Christopher Redmayne, she asked that he should be shown into the room at once. She gave him a cordial welcome and swept aside his apologies.

'If you are in the area, call at any time,' she said.

'That's most kind of you, Miss Hemmings,' said Christopher, taking the seat that was offered, 'but I would hate to impose on you.'

'From what I hear, Mr Redmayne, you impose on nobody.'

'Who told you that?'

'Your brother. You were mentioned in passing on more than one occasion by Henry. As someone who cheerfully loathed the very notion of work, he simply could not comprehend how you could enjoy it.'

'I luxuriate in it, Miss Hemmings.'

'Quite, sir. So I need hardly fear a daily visit from you.'

'No,' said Christopher pleasantly. 'Once we have solved this murder, I will be spending all of my time on the new house for Sir Julius Cheever.'

'He is not at all as I imagined,' she observed. 'Gabriel had painted him as a monster yet he seemed like a dignified old man when I saw him at the funeral.'

'His son's death mellowed him considerably.'

'Then he really does breathe fire?'

'Not exactly, Miss Hemmings,' replied Christopher with a smile, 'but he can singe your ears if he has a mind to do so.'

'I hope he does not even know of my existence.'

'I am certain that he does not.'

'Good.'

'I must say that I was touched to see you at the funeral. Did you get back safely from Northamptonshire?'

'Eventually,' she said. 'Arthur Lunn took us by the most roundabout route.'

Christopher was critical. 'I did not detect any real sorrow in Mr Lunn.'

'Expressing his emotions is something that Arthur regards as beneath him. I dare say that he had sincere regrets about Gabriel's death but he would never admit to them. He was there to make it possible for me to attend.'

'I appreciate that, Miss Hemmings.'

Christopher was glad that he had succumbed to the impulse to call on her. After the setback he had just suffered in Covent Garden, he was in search of consolation. Since she lived so close to the square, he hoped that he might find it at her house. Wondering why he had come, Celia Hemmings subjected him to a searching gaze. Bereavement left her subdued but there was the faintest hint of flirtatiousness in her eye. She adjusted her position in the chair. Unlike Lucy Cheever, she was very conscious of her charms and knew how to make the most of them. The chasm between the two women was deep and wide. Christopher wondered afresh how Gabriel had bridged it so successfully.

'Did you see what you wanted at the funeral?' he asked quietly.

'I went to see Gabriel being buried, Mr Redmayne,' she said sharply, 'and not to peer at his widow.'

'That's not what I meant.'

'Oh?'

'I assumed that you would be interested to take a look at the house where he had lived and the family he had talked so much about. You must have been curious.'

Her tone softened. 'I was and I'm sorry that I misunderstood you. As it happens, Arthur and I did take the trouble to ride out to the estate. It's a beautiful house but I can see why Gabriel ran away from it. There's nothing to look at but sheep.'

'I don't believe that it was the sheep who drove him away.'

'No, it was his father. You have a troublesome client, Mr Redmayne.'

'I can cope with him, Miss Hemmings.'

'I think that you can cope with anything,' she said with a warm smile.

The glint came into her eye again and it made him slightly uncomfortable. There was a directness about Celia Hemmings that he found both attractive and disturbing. He moved on quickly to the questions that took him there in the first place.

'You and Gabriel were very close,' he began.

'Intermittently,' she said. 'I loved him dearly but we never lived together for any length of time. Gabriel was too shy of commitment.'

'Did he discuss his writing with you?'

'From time to time. He read a few of his poems to me once.'

'What about his diary?'

She looked blank. 'Diary?'

'Were you aware that Gabriel was keeping a diary?'

'No, Mr Redmayne.'

'Did you not see him making entries?'

'This is the first that I've heard about it,' she said. 'What sort of diary was it?'

'A revealing one, by all accounts. He recorded his exploits in full.'

Celia grew angry. 'Are you telling me that *I* am mentioned in this diary? That would be disloyal as well as disgusting. It would be unforgivable. No,' she decided, calming down at once, 'Gabriel would never do that to me. I trust him.'

'So did other people,' he pointed out. 'Henry was one of them. But that did not stop him being mocked in the pages of the diary.'

'Mocked?'

'Along with many others in his circle.'

'Have you seen this diary?'

'No, Miss Hemmings. I did not even know that it existed until it was stolen from his house in Knightrider Street. It's my belief that his diary was responsible for his death. Someone killed him in order to get their hands on it.'

'But why?'

'Because it contains unlimited possibilities of blackmail.'

Celia Hemmings was shocked. Rising to her feet, she walked around the room in thought before coming back to stand close to Christopher. She looked down at him.

'Are you saying that someone may try to blackmail me?'

'I think it highly unlikely.'

'That's a relief!'

'What surprises me is that you had no knowledge of the diary.'

'Gabriel was very secretive about his work, Mr Redmayne. I was only allowed to see what he was prepared to show me. To be candid, it has come as something of a thunderbolt.' She resumed her seat. 'I can imagine the kinds of things that Gabriel put in that diary. He had a malicious pen at times.'

'Is there anyone else who might have known that he was keeping it?'

'Anyone else?'

'Yes, Miss Hemmings,' he said. 'The person who killed

him knew exactly where to find the diary and what it would contain. Gabriel must have told *somebody*.'

'Well, it was not me.'

'Then who might it have been?'

Her brow furrowed. 'I can think of only one person.'

'Who is that?'

'Arthur Lunn,' she said. 'Gabriel lodged at his house when he first came to London. They went everywhere together at first. Arthur is definitely no killer,' she affirmed, 'but I have to admit this. If anyone knew about that diary, it was him.'

Arthur Lunn strode into the room and clapped Henry familiarly on the shoulder.

'Get dressed, Henry,' he announced. 'You are dining at Long's with me.'

'I've no wish to go out.'

'What's wrong with you, man?'

'Until an hour ago, I was twisting and turning on a bed of pain. When I felt better I ventured downstairs, but I gave express instructions that nobody was to disturb me.'

'Instructions do not apply to friends like me.'

Henry groaned inwardly. Attired in a garish silk dressing gown, he was reclining in a chair in his parlour when Lunn descended on him. In his present condition, he did not wish to see anybody, least of all an ebullient crony in all his finery. The mourning clothes worn by Lunn at the funeral had been discarded in favour of apparel that made Henry's dressing gown look dull by comparison. Lunn beamed down at the recluse.

'Where have you *been,* Henry?' he demanded.

'Indisposed.'

'Oh, is that the reason? You've been taking the cure.'

'No, Arthur. This is not a disease of the body.'

'It comes to us all at times, no matter how careful we are in our choice of ladies.'

'I do *not* have the pox!'

'Then what is the problem?'

'I've had…things on my mind,' explained Henry.

'You always have things on your mind,' said Lunn with a chuckle. 'The same things that occupy my waking thoughts. Good wine, rich food and warm women – with a game or two of cards thrown in for good measure. Come, sir,' he insisted, taking hold of Henry's arm. 'Dine with me.'

'I intend to eat at home today.'

'Then I'll come for you this evening instead,' decided Lunn, releasing him. 'We will surrender body and soul to a night of sheer abandon.'

'Go without me, Arthur.'

'Why, man?'

'Because I am not inclined to pleasure.'

Lunn stared quizzically at him. 'Are you telling me that you've grown impotent?'

'No!' yelled Henry indignantly.

'Is that your problem? No more standing of the yard?'

'It is nothing to do with that.'

'Prove it by coming to Mrs Curtis with me.'

'No, Arthur. I am not in the vein.'

'Then at least sit at the card table with me for an hour.'

'An hour there and I am doomed for the whole night.

Listen,' said Henry, rising to his feet, 'I would be delighted to join you at any other time but not tonight, Arthur. As you see, I'm dressed for bed and will retire there after dinner.'

Lunn was scandalised. *'Alone?'*

'Just me and my dark thoughts.'

'What has happened to everybody? Marcus is the same. When I called on him just now, he refused to join me this evening as well. Why?' he wondered, spreading his arms. 'It surely cannot be that you have become sated with pleasure. You and Marcus can keep going all night.'

'And we will again,' predicted Henry. 'Very soon.'

Lunn strutted around the room in consternation, at a loss to understand why two of his closest friends were shunning the delights of the town. When he came back to Henry, he pointed an accusatory finger at him.

'You are to stay in bed all afternoon?'

'All day, I expect,' said Henry.

'Then I have plumbed your secret,' claimed Lunn with a snigger. 'Who is she, Henry? You have someone tucked away in your bedchamber, I'm sure of it. Do I know her? She must be a nimble filly if she can keep you occupied all day.'

'There is nobody else here, Arthur!'

'Do you swear that?'

'On my father's Bible,' vowed Henry, 'and he is the Dean of Gloucester!'

'And you'll not come out with me? Even if I bring a coach to pick you up and promise to drop you off again at your doorstep? Think, man,' he urged. 'What better cure for your illness than a bracing game of cards with friends? You only need stay an hour. What harm can there be in that?'

Henry was tempted. The idea that he would be conveyed to and fro in Lunn's coach was very enticing and his enforced exile was taxing his patience. There was another reason that made him consider the offer favourably. His brother was acting as an intercessor between Sir Marcus Kemp and the blackmailer. It might even be that Christopher had apprehended the man by now. At the very least, he would have handed over a thousand guineas and appeased him. With money from one victim in his pocket, the blackmailer might be less likely to exert pressure on Henry. The cloud above Henry's head lifted somewhat and he did miss his old haunts.

'What do you say, Henry?' pressed Lunn. 'Will you come with me?'

'Yes, Arthur. Pick me up from here this evening.'

Sir Marcus Kemp was frothing with impatience. He was offhand with his wife, sharp with his children and almost vicious with his servants. Everyone else in the house chose to keep out of his way. By the time Christopher Redmayne finally arrived, Kemp was in a foul temper. Pulling him into the dining room, he glared at his visitor.

'Where have you been, man?' he demanded.

'To Covent Garden,' said Christopher.

'It is no more than ten minutes' walk away. Why the appalling delay?'

'I was made to wait outside the church.'

'But he did come in the end?'

'No, Sir Marcus.'

Kemp spluttered. 'No? I am still in danger?'

'I hope not,' said Christopher. 'I did not deal with the blackmailer himself. He sent a boy to relieve me of the purse. As you requested, I handed it over.'

He gave Kemp a shortened version of events, omitting any reference to Jonathan Bale and the failed plan to ensnare the blackmailer. The visit to Celia Hemmings was described as a chance meeting in the square. Kemp slowly relaxed. His fears, he decided, had been groundless. He even rose to a hollow laugh.

'So that is it,' he declared. 'I am free.'

'With luck, Sir Marcus.'

'He has what he wants. It is only fair that I get something in return.'

'You presume too much on the blackmailer's notion of fairness.'

'I feel as if I've been released from a prison!' He looked at Christopher. 'I must thank you for your part in all this, Mr Redmayne. When you first came here I was angry that you even knew about my situation, yet you have been my salvation. *I* would never have dared to hand over that money in Covent Garden,' he confessed, 'and I could hardly send one of my servants. You saved me, Mr Redmayne.'

'I am hoping to save my brother as well, Sir Marcus.'

'Is he going to pay up?'

'No,' said Christopher, 'he is following a different course of action. But while I am here,' he went on, seeing an opportunity to gather information, 'I wonder if you could tell me something about Arthur Lunn.'

'Arthur? Why? Has he had blackmail demands as well?'

'Not that I know of, Sir Marcus.'

'I think it improbable,' said Kemp. 'He was here just over an hour ago, pressing me to join him for dinner. Since I was waiting for your news, I would not stir from the house so I sent him on his way.'

'Is it true that Gabriel Cheever once lodged at his house?'

'Yes, Mr Redmayne. For some months.'

'So Mr Lunn must have known that he was keeping a diary.'

Kemp was taken aback. ''Sdeath! I never thought of that. I suppose he must. Arthur is the most inquisitive soul alive. He pokes his nose into everything.'

'I met him at Gabriel's funeral.'

'What was he doing there?'

'Ostensibly, he was escorting Miss Celia Hemmings,' said Christopher, 'but he may have had his own reasons for making the journey to Northamptonshire.'

'You think that Arthur Lunn was somehow involved in this blackmail?'

'I begin to wonder, Sir Marcus.'

'But he is the most obliging fellow in London.'

'Then why did Gabriel break with him? Mr Lunn was his closest friend. Why did Gabriel go into hiding without even telling him where he was?'

'I've no idea, Mr Redmayne. But I do know that Arthur was very upset.'

'How upset?'

'Deeply, I would imagine. It's difficult to say with a man like that who hides his feelings so well. But Arthur Lunn was hurt badly,' he said. 'He was cut to the quick.'

Christopher speculated on whether or not Lunn was sufficiently wounded to seek revenge. A man who valued his friendships so much would be bruised by the way in which he lost this particular one. It would be worth taking a closer look at Arthur Lunn.

Kemp reached for his purse. 'What do I owe you, Mr Redmayne?'

'Owe me?'

'For the help you gave me today.'

'You owe me nothing, Sir Marcus.'

'Come, come, man. You must have some reward for what you did.'

'If you insist,' said Christopher, 'but I'll not take it in money. All I ask is that you let me see the letters you received. Along with the extract from the diary.'

'But there is no need now.'

'There is every need, Sir Marcus. Where are they?'

'Locked away where nobody will ever find them,' said Kemp. 'I'm sorry, Mr Redmayne. I could not expose myself to ridicule by letting you see them. To be frank, I am tempted to burn them.'

'No!' implored Christopher. 'You must not do that, Sir Marcus.'

'But my ordeal is over. So is Henry's, I dare say. All that the blackmailer wanted was to frighten money out of one of us. A thousand guineas would satisfy any man,' he said confidently. 'We are liberated at last. There will be no more blackmail demands.'

* * *

Henry Redmayne was preening himself in the mirror in the hall when he heard the doorbell ring. Believing that Arthur Lunn had come to collect him, he opened the door himself, but his visitor was no beaming crony about to whisk him off to a gaming house. It was Peter Wickens and he glanced furtively over his shoulder before stepping into the hall. Henry had never seen him in such a state of anxiety. Wickens was usually so poised and urbane yet he was now twitching nervously.

'What is wrong, Peter?' asked Henry.

'Forgive this intrusion,' said Wickens. 'I simply had to come.'

'Why?'

'I need your advice.' He took something from his pocket. 'This arrived today.'

'What is it?'

'Read it, Henry,' he said, handing the letter over. 'I am being blackmailed.'

CHAPTER ELEVEN

When he returned to Fetter Lane that evening, Christopher Redmayne met with a double surprise. Not only was Jonathan Bale waiting for him, an even more welcome visitor was sitting contentedly in his parlour. She looked up at him with a smile. After the ordeal of her brother's funeral, Susan Cheever had regained some of her radiance. She was pleased to see him again and he, in turn, was openly delighted.

'Miss Cheever!' he exclaimed.

'Good evening, Mr Redmayne.'

'What are you doing here?'

'Mr Bale kindly brought me to your house.'

'I thought that you were still in Northamptonshire.'

'Lucy invited me to stay with her for a while in Knightrider Street.'

Christopher was thrilled. 'So close?'

'That was how I came into it,' explained Jonathan,

noting the fond glances that were being exchanged between the two of them. 'Miss Cheever had a message for you. Knowing that I live nearby in Addle Hill, she called to ask if I would deliver it. Since the message has a bearing on the investigation, I thought it best if Miss Cheever gave it to you in person.'

'Thank you, Mr Bale.'

'Did I make the right decision?'

'Without question,' said Christopher.

Realising that he had ignored Jonathan, he greeted him properly and urged him to stay for refreshment, but the constable had other work to do. He rose to his feet, took his leave of Susan then followed Christopher into the hall, where he lowered his voice to ensure that they were not overheard.

'I assured Miss Cheever that you would see that she got back safely.'

'I shall insist on it.'

'I had a feeling that you might, Mr Redmayne,' he said, face impassive. 'But how did you fare when we parted this afternoon?'

'Very well.'

Eager to get back to his guest, Christopher recounted, in only the briefest outline, details of his respective meetings with Celia Hemmings and Sir Marcus Kemp. The constable's eyebrows lifted at the mention of Arthur Lunn.

'He was not a man I could ever admire,' he said.

'You and he are hardly well matched.'

'Do you wish me to speak to him again?'

'No, Mr Bale,' said Christopher, opening the front door.

'I'll take care of Mr Lunn from now on. In fact, I had planned to track him down this very evening.'

'I felt so out of place in that coffee house.'

'You would feel even more out of place in one of his nocturnal haunts. For that's where I am likely to run Arthur Lunn to ground.' He eased Jonathan into the street. 'Leave him to me. I'll call on you tomorrow and report anything that I find out.'

'Thank you, Mr Redmayne.'

Christopher waved him off before closing the door. He was deeply grateful to his friend. Jonathan had not merely brought Susan to his home. He had tactfully left them alone together, knowing that Christopher would elicit far more from his visitor if he were not sitting between them. The thought of accompanying her back to Knightrider Street was a joy in itself. Christopher went back into the room with anticipatory pleasure.

'What can I offer you, Miss Cheever?' he said.

'Nothing, thank you. Jacob has been looking after us.'

'So he should.' He grinned broadly. 'I cannot tell you how happy I am to see you again. Did Sir Julius travel back to London with you?'

'No, Mr Redmayne. Father remained at home. He prefers to mourn there.'

'I can understand that.'

It was a timely reminder that Susan herself was still in mourning, dressed in sober attire and rather subdued. Christopher saw the impropriety of grinning at her. Making an effort to look more serious, he took the seat opposite her.

'Did you tell Mr Bale what this message was?' he asked.

'Yes,' she replied. 'He is assisting you in the inquiry.'

'It's more a case of my assisting him, Miss Cheever. He is the officer of the law, not me. It was Mr Bale, after all, who helped to find the body on Paul's Wharf.'

'I know. I asked him to show me the spot.'

Christopher frowned. 'You went there?'

'Before we set out for Fetter Lane.'

'It's hardly a fit place for a young lady.'

'Nor for my brother, I would have thought. What was Gabriel doing there?'

'That has still to be ascertained.'

'Mr Bale believes he was killed elsewhere and carried to the wharf.'

'I'm sure that the full truth will emerge in time.'

The pleasure of being with her again was making it difficult for Christopher to concentrate. When he parted from Susan at the funeral, he had resigned himself to a wait of several weeks before he chanced to see her again, and that meeting would certainly be in the presence of Sir Julius Cheever. Yet here she was, unencumbered by her father, talking to him alone under his own roof. He had to force himself to keep to the matter in hand.

'What *is* this message, Miss Cheever?'

'Lucy and I have spent a lot of time together,' she explained. 'I think that she is slowly learning to trust me.'

'You are one of the most trustworthy people I have ever met.'

'She is still wary of everyone, Mr Redmayne, and still in a state of shock.'

'Has she told you why her marriage had to be kept secret?'

'Not yet. But she may do so in time.'

'I hope so. It will be relevant to our inquiry.'

'What she has done is given me a few hints.'

'Hints?'

'They were not deliberate,' said Susan, 'but they dropped out in conversation.'

'Go on.'

'She knows something important about the time that Gabriel was killed. Lucy was visiting her ailing mother in St Albans. Her maidservant went with her. Gabriel was left in the house on his own. But he was not there when he was attacked.'

'What makes you say that?'

'I think that he was meant to be somewhere that night,' she said. 'Lucy more or less confirmed it. Gabriel was ambushed on his way to or from this place and murdered. His body was carried to the wharf.'

'He was certainly not killed at the house. There would have been signs of the struggle. Besides, someone as cautious as Gabriel would not have let a stranger in.'

'Mr Bale explained that.'

'Oh?'

'He says that the killer must have stolen Gabriel's key.'

'Quite probably,' said Christopher, thinking it through. 'There was no indication of forced entry. When she got back, your sister-in-law had the feeling that someone had been in the house but everything seemed to be in its place. It was only when she carried out a thorough search that the theft of the diary came to light.'

'Yes,' said Susan under her breath. 'The diary.'

'What do you propose to do, Miss Cheever?'

'Try to break down Lucy's reserve completely so that she tells me the truth.'

'And if that fails?'

'I was hoping that you might speak to her, Mr Redmayne.'

'Gladly. If you think she is up to it.'

'She is,' Susan assured him. 'Lucy has an inner strength.'

'Tell me when to come and I'll be there immediately.'

'Let me try first of all.'

'I will,' agreed Christopher. 'You are in a much better position to win her over. When the rest of your family rejected Gabriel, you stood by him. Lucy knows that. You are probably the only person with whom she can discuss her husband.'

'We've been doing nothing else for the past few days.'

'It must be very lowering for you.'

'Not really, Mr Redmayne. It's been something of a revelation.'

'In what way?'

Susan did not reply. She looked deep into his eyes. He met her gaze, his affection for her shining through, but it sparked off no response. She was looking at him with a curiosity that was tempered with faint disappointment. Christopher felt uncomfortable.

'Is something wrong, Miss Cheever?' he asked.

She appraised him carefully. 'May I ask you a question, please?'

'As many as you wish.'

'Do you know a Henry Redmayne?'

'I should do. He's my brother.'

'And was he one of Gabriel's friends?'

'For a time.'

'Why did you not mention it before, Mr Redmayne?'

Christopher shrugged. 'It did not come up in conversation.'

'Well, it should have,' she said with a note of reproof. 'I had a right to know. It would have saved me some embarrassment when Lucy mentioned his name.'

'Lucy?'

'Yes.'

'But she has never met Henry.'

'It seems that your brother's name appears in Gabriel's diary?'

'So I hear.'

'Yet you did not have the courtesy to pass on the information to me?'

'Miss Cheever—'

'Let me finish,' she went on, anger beginning to show. 'How can you expect me to confide in you when you hold back something as important as this from me? You put me in a very awkward position. Imagine how foolish I felt when Lucy recalled the name of Henry Redmayne and wondered if the two of you were related. Not only that,' she emphasised. 'Your brother's name appears in the very diary that led to Gabriel's murder so he is involved here. You've been deceiving me, Mr Redmayne.'

'Not intentionally.'

'I feel hurt.'

Christopher was contrite. 'I would never willingly hurt you.'

'Then why have you been hiding your brother?'

'For two very good reasons,' he explained. 'The first concerns Sir Julius.'

'Father?'

'He has many virtues but tolerance is not one of them. And what my brother requires most of all from others, I fear, is a tolerant attitude. Henry leads the kind of existence that Gabriel managed to escape.' He sat forward. 'Can you understand what I am saying, Miss Cheever?'

'I think so. You are telling me how keen you were to design the new house.'

'Would Sir Julius be equally keen to retain me if he knew that I had a brother like Henry? He would assume that I, too, was the kind of rakehell that he so despises.'

'Father would not make that mistake. He's a good judge of character.'

'I wanted to be judged for my work and not in terms of my brother.'

'That is still not reason enough to lie to me.'

'I did not lie,' he stressed. 'I simply held back a portion of the truth.'

'You said that there were two reasons.'

'Yes,' said Christopher sadly. 'The second concerns you.'

'Me?'

'In my own blundering way, I sought to protect you.'

'From what?'

'The full horror. Gabriel's murder has been a shattering blow for you, Miss Cheever. I did not want to distress you any further by telling you about its ugly consequences. If you feel that I hid things from you unfairly,' he said, leaning even closer to her, 'then I apologise unreservedly. I promise to tell you all that you wish to hear.'

'Why should I be distressed by it?'

'The details are rather sordid.'

'Nevertheless, I will hear it,' she said. 'Do not think to spare me.'

Christopher took a deep breath. 'If you insist.'

He gave her a clear and comprehensive account of events from the very start, hiding nothing from her and describing in detail the failure of his plan to catch the blackmailer in Covent Garden. Susan Cheever listened to it all without a tremor. The name that caught her attention was that of a woman.

'Miss Celia Hemmings?'

'Yes,' he said. 'Did Gabriel ever mention her in his letters?'

'No, Mr Redmayne.'

'He obviously made a deep impression on her. She was at the funeral.'

'Was she?' asked Susan with mingled surprise and disapproval.

'She left discreetly soon afterwards.'

'I'm glad to hear it.'

'Do not be too harsh on her. She was a good friend to Gabriel.'

'That may be so, Mr Redmayne, but she had no place at a family funeral. Think what pain it would have caused Lucy if she had known of the woman's presence and of her relationship to Gabriel. It was wrong of Miss Hemmings to come.' Susan cocked her head slightly and stared at him. 'Are you ashamed of your brother?'

'Ashamed? No, Miss Cheever.'

'Why not?'

'With all his faults, I love Henry.'

'I loved Gabriel – with all *his* faults.'

'It's not a fair comparison.'

'Why not?'

'Your brother repented,' he argued. 'He turned his back on his days as a rake and tried to lead an honest, sober, blameless life as a married man. That takes courage. Henry's case is very different,' he conceded. 'In spite of all that has happened, he has no thought of repentance and he would no more contemplate marriage than emigration to some uninhabited wilderness in America.'

'Gabriel and your brother were still two of a kind.'

'Up to a point.'

'And so are we, Mr Redmayne.'

'We?'

'Yes,' she said resignedly. 'Each of us found ourselves with wayward brothers. There's no escaping that fact. Neither of them would aspire to canonisation.'

Christopher laughed. 'Henry would feel insulted if it were offered to him.'

'Our brothers drew us into this.'

'Granted.'

'But for them, we would not be sitting here now. In view of that, it is surprising that you chose not to confide in me.'

'Nothing will be hidden from you in future, I swear it.'

'I'll keep you to that,' she warned. 'Gabriel Cheever and Henry Redmayne are both weak men who went astray. We supported them. That gives us a real bond.'

Christopher felt the full strength of that bond and gave a quiet smile.

Sir Marcus Kemp was in his element. Having paid the blackmail demand, he felt that his life could begin again in earnest. He repaired to his favourite gaming house that evening and had a run of good fortune at the card table. He decided that it was an omen. His troubles were completely over. Henry Redmayne watched him from a distance, envying the confidence that his friend exuded and wishing that he had the same air of freedom. Gone was the hunted expression and the feverish manner. Kemp was determined to make up for lost time. Arthur Lunn was also happy. Henry had played a few games of ombre but he had still not mastered the intricacies of the new fad and lost each time. Lunn, by contrast, was slowly amassing a sizeable amount of money from his opponents at the table. Henry wondered if he would be able to drag his friend away.

When Kemp's luck finally changed, he had the sense to quit the game. Seeing Henry in the far corner, he strode across to him with a benign smile on his face.

'Welcome back, Henry!' he said expansively.

'I might say the same to you, Marcus.'

'All's well that ends well!'

'Unfortunately, it has not ended in my case.'

'Then do as I did,' urged Kemp. 'Grit your teeth and pay up. You'll not regret it. Yes,' he added genially, 'and employ that brother of yours to hand the money over. What he is like as an architect I do not know, but Christopher is a sterling fellow.'

'It's a quality that runs in the family.'

'He pulled me out of the pit of despair, Henry.'

'I wish that he could do the same for me.'

'Did your brother not tell you how he delivered the money to Covent Garden?'

'Yes, Marcus,' said Henry. 'When he left you this afternoon, Christopher called on me in Bedford Street but he was not as sanguine as you are about the future. He feels that the extortion is not yet over.'

'It is in my case.'

'That's little comfort to me – or to Peter Wickens.'

'Wickens? How does he come into this?'

'He received a blackmail demand this very day.'

'Never!'

'I saw it with my own eyes, Marcus. Penned by the same hand that wrote one of my letters and both of yours. Peter was utterly desolate,' he said. 'All of his indiscretions were neatly listed. The threat of publication all but deranged him.'

'How much was the demand?'

'Five hundred guineas.'

'Advise him to pay at once or it will be doubled.' He looked around. 'I'll tell him myself. Is Wickens here this evening?'

'No, Marcus. He is skulking at home just as we did.'

'I've no need to do that any more.'

Henry writhed in discomfort. 'Do not rub salt into my wounds.'

'Be not so full of apprehension,' urged the other. 'Bow to the inevitable and pay for your pleasures. Your suffering will then cease. If you need to borrow the money, I'll gladly offer you a loan. Ah!' he said as a figure approached them. 'Chance contrives better than we ourselves. Here is the very man you will need as your intermediary.'

Henry was astonished to see his brother there. Christopher was not interested in trying his luck at the card table and he had resisted all his brother's efforts to lure him to various brothels. Henry sensed that Christopher must have a particular reason for venturing into the gaming house. As soon as the social niceties were over, he wanted to know what it was.

'What brings you here, Christopher?'

'I was looking for you, Henry.'

'He knew where to find you,' remarked Kemp with a chuckle. 'Find a card game and you will soon find Henry Redmayne. Excuse me,' he said, about to move off.

'Before you go, Sir Marcus,' said Christopher, blocking his path, 'I wanted to remind you of the bargain we struck.'

'That's null and void.'

'Not if you receive another blackmail demand.'

'But I will not. I'm in the clear.'

'Wait a while before you celebrate,' advised Christopher. 'All I ask is that you do not destroy the letters or the printed extract. I may need to look at them.'

'Only if I am harried again and that will not happen.'

'Promise me that you will not burn the evidence.'

'I'll do what I please with it, Mr Redmayne,' said Kemp airily.

He went off to speak to some other friends. Henry looked after him.

'Sir Marcus assumes that the problem has been solved,' he commented.

'That's a foolish assumption.' Christopher glanced around. 'Is there somewhere we can talk in private, Henry? I need a word with you.'

Henry nodded and led him to an empty table. Drinks were served, and Henry lit a pipe. Christopher sat back to avoid the smoke, consoling himself with the fact that his brother was unusually sober. At that time on a normal evening, Henry would be incapable of articulate conversation.

'I'm glad that you came, Christopher,' he said. 'I have news.'

'Of what?'

'Another demand.'

'You've had a third letter?' asked Christopher.

'No. Another victim has been singled out.'

'Who is it?'

'Peter Wickens.'

Henry told him about the unexpected visit from Wickens and described the calligraphy and the wording of the letter. Christopher was relieved to hear that his brother had urged his friend not to pay the demand.

'I knew that there would be more victims,' he said.

'He has dozens to choose from,' Henry remarked. 'Peter Wickens has had his wilder moments but there are plenty whose antics are far more outrageous than his. Will they be targets as well, do you think?'

'Most probably. If they appear in Gabriel Cheever's diary.'

'Who will be next?'

'Nobody – if we find the blackmailer.'

'How do we do that?' asked Henry gloomily.

'We are closer than you imagine,' said Christopher earnestly. 'I still believe that he is one of your own circle. He may even be here this evening. That is what brought me here tonight, Henry. I wish to speak to Arthur Lunn.'

'Arthur? You surely do not suspect him?'

'Everyone must be considered.'

'But he's a good friend to me and Sir Marcus.'

'Let me probe the strength of that friendship,' suggested Christopher. 'When time serves, invite him over and leave us to talk alone. Do not tell him why I am here. There is no point in putting him on the defensive at the start.'

Henry shook his head. 'Arthur Lunn? No, I'll not accept it.'

It was a long wait. Lunn was enjoying himself too much to be drawn away from the table. When he eventually did rise from his seat, Henry moved in swiftly to guide him across to Christopher. Lunn raised a cynical eyebrow.

'This is hardly your world, Mr Redmayne,' he observed drily. 'Have you come to gape in disgust at us hardened libertines?'

'No, Mr Lunn. I merely craved a word with you.'

'Speak up, then.'

'Gabriel Cheever once lodged with you, I gather.'

'All the world knows that.'

'Had he started to write at that time?'

'Why, yes,' said Lunn, adjusting his periwig. 'He scribbled away whenever he could. I thought that he was writing letters to his sister but he had literary ambitions.'

'Did he show you any of his work?'

'Bless you, no! Why should he?'

'You were close friends.'

'We drank, played cards and whored together, perhaps.'

'There was more to it than that, Mr Lunn. He lived under your roof.'

'Only until he made enough money to afford lodgings of his own.' Lunn gave a sudden chortle. 'As it happens, most of that money came from me at the card table. Even when he moved out, I was still helping to pay for his accommodation.'

'Did you resent that?' asked Christopher.

'A little, perhaps.'

'Was there anything else you resented about Gabriel?'

'Of course not,' replied the other. 'Why should there be?'

'He did vanish without trace,' Christopher reminded him.

Lunn was rueful. 'That's true. And I admit I was a trifle irritated by that.'

'I suggest that it was rather more than irritation, Mr Lunn.'

'What do you mean?'

'It must have been galling to be abandoned like that,' said Christopher.

'I was not abandoned!' retorted Lunn.

'Then why did Gabriel give no warning of his departure?'

'Who knows?'

'You must have felt badly let down.'

'That's my business,' snapped Lunn, temper starting to show.

'Why did you go to the funeral?' prodded Christopher.

'Celia Hemmings told you that. I was there to act as her escort.'

'I think you may have had a more personal reason, Mr Lunn.'

Lunn flared up. 'It was not for the pleasure of meeting you, Mr Redmayne.'

'Was it remorse that took you to Northamptonshire?' said Christopher. 'Or were you simply there to gloat over the dead body of a friend who deserted you?'

'I was gloating over nobody.'

'Are you pretending that you actually *cared* for Gabriel?'

'What is it to you?'

'I am curious, Mr Lunn. As you so rightly pointed out,' he said, waving a hand to include the whole room, 'this is not my world. But it is yours. A man who likes pleasure as much as you do would need a very strong motive to brave the highways of England for two whole days in order to spend a mere half an hour at a funeral.'

'Why are you pestering me like this?' demanded Lunn.

Christopher was calm. 'I am putting some simple questions to you, that is all.'

'Do not expect any answers from me, sir.'

'Why not? Do you have something to hide?'

'No,' snarled Lunn, jumping to his feet. 'Now leave me be.'

'If you tell me one last thing.'

'I'm rapidly losing my patience with you, Mr Redmayne.'

Christopher stood up. 'How much of Gabriel Cheever's diary did you read?'

Arthur Lunn turned purple and started to bluster. Mastering the urge to lash out at Christopher, he instead turned on his heel and stalked away. Henry sidled over to his brother with a look of alarm on his face.

'You upset him,' he said.

'I know, Henry. That was the intention.'

Lucy Cheever sat motionless in the chair. Her eyes were open but she was quite unaware of the fact that her sister-in-law sat directly opposite her. Susan waited patiently. It was not the first time that Lucy had been in the grip of her memories. A smile occasionally brushed her lips but sadness prevailed. When she finally shook herself awake, she was overcome with guilt at ignoring her guest.

'I am so sorry,' she said, reaching out to touch Susan. 'Do forgive me.'

'There is nothing to forgive.'

'I was daydreaming.'

'It's too late for daydreams, Lucy,' said Susan. 'Night is starting to fall.'

'Heavens! Have I been that long? You should have given me a nudge.'

'Why? You were exactly where you wanted to be.'

'I invited you here so that we could get to know each other better,' said Lucy apologetically. 'And all I do is forget all about you.'

'You need some time alone with your memories.'

'I had that while you went to visit Mr Redmayne.' Interest brought a proper smile to her face. 'Was he pleased to see you, Susan?'

'Very pleased.'

'I thought he would be.'

'Mr Bale is the person to thank. He took me all the way.'

'And who brought you back?'

'Mr Redmayne himself. He insisted that I sit on his horse while he led it along.'

'I told you that he was a gentleman.'

'Every inch,' agreed Susan.

'What did you want to ask him?'

'Oh, there were a number of things, Lucy.'

'Did you find out if he knew a Henry Redmayne?'

'It's his brother, it seems. He leads a somewhat dissolute life, which is how he got into Gabriel's diary. Christopher and Henry Redmayne may be related,' she said, 'but they are different in every way. Like me and Brilliana.'

'Nobody would take you for sisters.'

'There are times when Brilliana denies the connection.'

Lucy gave a little laugh. 'I'm glad I did not invite *her* to stay.'

'She would have made quite an impact on this house, believe me.'

'Brilliana likes to be in charge.'

'Yes, Lucy. Given that urge, I believe that she married the right man.'

'And what about you?'

'Me?'

271

'When will you find the right man?'

'Oh,' said Susan, tossing her head. 'I doubt if I shall ever marry. Father has pushed many suitors in my direction but none of them has been remotely appealing.'

'Perhaps you should look further afield.'

'Young ladies are not supposed to look, Lucy. We take what is offered.'

'Or remain single.'

'Quite,' replied Susan. 'It is an attractive option in many ways.' She sat back and regarded Lucy with curiosity. 'You still have not told me how you met Gabriel. All that you would say was that it was a chance encounter.'

'It was, Susan. In a churchyard.'

'A churchyard? Why there?'

Lucy became nostalgic. 'I happened to be taking a short cut through it when I saw this handsome young man bending down in front of one of the gravestones. At first, I thought he was paying respects to a family member, then I realised what he was doing.'

'And what was that?'

'Copying the inscription,' said Lucy. 'Reading the words that had been carved into the stone. I was so surprised that I stopped to watch him. We began to talk. Gabriel was searching for interesting epitaphs,' she went on, the memory bringing some light into her eyes. 'That was his first commission as a poet, you see. To write epitaphs.' She gave another little laugh. 'Imagine that, Susan. You know the kind of wicked life he was leading yet they paid him to write epitaphs. Gabriel told me that he had not been near a church for months until he got the commission. We talked for ages.'

'What happened?'

'I made sure that I took that short cut whenever I could.' Tears threatened and she bit her lip. 'I met him in one churchyard and bade him farewell in another.' Susan moved over to put an arm round her. 'He always wanted to write his own epitaph, you know.'

'In a sense, he did,' said Susan. 'With that diary of his.'

Lucy turned to her. 'Do they know who killed him, Susan?'

'No, but they are getting closer to him all the time.'

'What did Mr Redmayne say?'

'That he is making steady progress. However,' Susan continued, 'he is still collecting evidence. What he really needs to know is where Gabriel was likely to have been on the night he was killed. Do you have any idea, Lucy?'

'He should have been here.'

'He was somewhere else. Mr Redmayne is certain of it. Where was it?' Lucy shook her head. 'You must do all you can to help. Where did Gabriel go?'

'How would I know?' said Lucy, breaking away to get up. 'He might have gone out for a walk. He worked all day but he was not chained to the house.'

'If you do remember—'

'How can I?'

'If you do,' repeated Susan, 'please tell Mr Redmayne. It could be important.'

Lucy gazed ahead of her. 'Nothing is important any more,' she murmured. 'Not since Gabriel died.' She seemed on the point of drifting off again but she checked herself and turned to Susan. 'What will happen if this case is solved?'

'Gabriel can rest easy in his grave at last.'

'I was thinking about you.'

'All that matters to me is to catch Gabriel's killer.'

'Will you go back to Northamptonshire?'

'Probably.'

'That would make it very difficult for you.'

'Difficult?'

'When I wanted to see Gabriel, I had my short cut through the churchyard.' She put a hand on Susan's shoulder. 'You can hardly find an excuse to visit Fetter Lane if you go back to live with your father. How will you manage?'

Susan was perplexed. It was a question she had already been asking herself.

Henry Redmayne was grateful that his brother had sought him out. The cards were again falling so favourably for Arthur Lunn that it might be hours before he could be prised away from the table. The promise to give Henry a lift back to Bedford Street in his coach was forgotten. Christopher came to his brother's rescue, offering to act as his bodyguard and take him home.

'There is one condition, Henry,' he warned.

'What is that?'

'We first call on Peter Wickens.'

'This late?' said Henry peevishly. 'Why not leave it until the morning?'

'He may have made the wrong decision by then. I want to speak to Mr Wickens before he gives in to the blackmail demand. Come on,' said Christopher. 'I know that he lives quite close to you. It is not much out of our way.'

'Peter may not even let us into the house.'

'He will if he has any sense. Meanwhile, tell me more about Arthur Lunn.'

'Arthur?'

'I want to hear just how close he was to Gabriel Cheever.'

The walk through the dark streets gave Henry plenty of time to reminisce. He talked at length about Lunn, insisting that it would be quite out of character for him to be involved in a murder and in the subsequent blackmail demands.

'If he was threatening to kill me, why take me out in his coach this evening?'

'Mr Lunn could be playing a deep game.'

'He's far too shallow for that,' said Henry dismissively. 'The only games that Arthur will ever play are at the card table or in a lady's bedchamber.'

'Is he rich?'

'Tolerably.'

'Then he is not in need of money?'

'Arthur is always in need of money, Christopher.'

'When we left, he seemed to be doing extremely well.'

'You caught him on a good night. He is not usually so fortunate. He never loses as heavily as Sir Marcus Kemp but I've known him take some severe falls.'

'He would not sneeze at a thousand guineas, then?'

'Offer him that and he would snatch your hand off.'

Christopher was rueful. 'That is effectively what happened.'

The house was in St Martin's Lane and Henry was astonished how quickly they seemed to get there. He was also pleased that he had not once felt uneasy during the journey. Christopher's presence was reassuring. Henry would never have dared to walk home on his own. Fear of attack still haunted him.

'What sort of man is Peter Wickens?' asked Christopher.

'I thought you had met him.'

'Only once or twice. He seemed like the rest of your friends, Henry.'

'Noble and upstanding?'

'Disreputable.'

Henry laughed. 'Peter is as disreputable as the rest of us,' he confessed, 'but that does not mean he has no care of his reputation. He guards it jealously. It is one thing to revel in private, quite another to have your revelry displayed for one and all to see.'

'Is he a weak man?'

'On the contrary.'

'Then he might hold out against the blackmail demands.'

'You will have to ask him about that, Christopher. All I can say is that Peter Wickens is a good friend, a lively companion and a generous host. If he has a fault, it is that he has a serious side to his character.'

'What do you mean?'

'Peter actually goes to the playhouse in order to enjoy the play.'

With a scornful laugh, Henry reached out to ring the doorbell. They were in luck. Wickens was still up and received them at once. Puzzled by their arrival, he ushered them into a small room off the hall. The three of them took seats round the flickering candles in the silver candelabrum.

'To what do I owe this visit, Henry?' asked Wickens.

'I told Christopher about your little problem.'

'Then you had no business to do so,' said the other hotly. 'It's a private matter.'

'Not when it has a bearing on Gabriel Cheever's murder,' said Christopher. 'If we can solve that, you will have to pay no blackmail demand.'

Wickens was sceptical. 'Have you taken it upon yourself to solve the crime?'

'I became involved through my brother, Mr Wickens.'

'Christopher has helped me through the ordeal,' agreed Henry.

'What use is that to me?' said Wickens.

Christopher calmed him down and explained his role in the murder investigation. Wickens slowly shed his reservations. Instead of being annoyed at Christopher's intrusion into his affairs, he began to be interested in what he was hearing. The questions he put were intelligent and searching. Christopher felt that he was winning the man over. Wickens was not like the other blackmail victims he had met. Henry had been gripped by hysteria while Sir Marcus Kemp had ranted and raved. Wickens was much more in control of his anxiety. It was possible to have a sensible dialogue with him.

'When did the letter arrive?' asked Christopher.

'Late this morning.'

'What did you think when you read it?'

'Rational thought was impossible at first,' said Wickens.

'The truth is that I was in turmoil. I do not pretend to be celibate but the notion of having my indiscretions made public was terrifying. My first instinct was to pay the money at once.'

'I am glad you fought against the impulse.'

'I needed advice. Your brother was the obvious person to turn to for counsel.'

Henry smirked. 'I do have flashes of sagacity from time to time.'

'It was only then that I discovered that Henry himself was a victim. It explained why we had seen so little of him recently. Why on earth did you not turn to me, Henry?' he wondered. 'You could have relied on my help.'

'Henry chose me instead, Mr Wickens,' said Christopher. 'Having been a victim yourself, you'll understand the urge to tell as few people as possible.'

'Oh, yes!'

'So what do you intend to do?'

'Sleep on the matter and decide in the morning.'

'Which way do you incline at the moment?'

'Towards complying with the demand.'

'That would be a mistake, Mr Wickens.'

'What else can I do?'

'Ignore the letter.'

'And see myself ridiculed in print?' said Wickens sharply. 'It is not an enticing prospect, sir. Gabriel Cheever is taking revenge on us from beyond the grave. Had I known that he was keeping this scurrilous diary about his closest friends, I would have made him destroy it.'

'I doubt that, Peter,' said Henry. 'He was not the kind of man to take orders.'

'Besides,' added Christopher, 'the diary was not intended for publication.'

Wickens was adamant. 'It must never see the light of day.'

'Then help me to prevent that happening, Mr Wickens.'

'How?'

'First of all, I would like to see the letter you received.' Wickens was about to protest. 'I do not intend to read it,' promised Christopher. 'A cursory glance will be more than enough.'

'Do as he says,' urged Henry.

Wickens hesitated. 'I do not feel that it is necessary.'

'My brother believes it came from the same person who sent one of the letters to him,' explained Christopher. 'I merely wish to confirm that. Nothing more.'

With considerable reluctance, Wickens took the missive from his pocket. The visitors waited while their host wrestled with the problem. At length, he thrust the letter into Christopher's hand with a stern warning.

'Do not read it through, Mr Redmayne.'

'There is no need.' Christopher looked down at the neat handwriting, then he raised the paper to sniff it. He gave it back to Wickens. 'Thank you.'

'Henry tells me that Sir Marcus has also been a target,' said Wickens, pocketing the letter. 'That must have scared the wits out of him. He has a wife to worry about.'

'Not any more,' Henry told him. 'Sir Marcus paid up.'

'Who can blame him?'

'I do, Mr Wickens,' said Christopher. 'It was folly.'

'Yet you went along with it, Christopher,' his brother reminded him.

'Only because I hoped to set a trap.' He turned to Wickens. 'Since he was determined to hand the money over,' he explained, 'I offered to act as his intermediary and had a man concealed in the crowd to watch. We hoped to catch the blackmailer but he was too cunning for us.'

'He seems to hold all the cards,' sighed Wickens.

'Not all of them. We have one or two of our own.'

'You know who he is, then?'

'We will do in time.'

'What happens to us meanwhile?' asked Henry.

'You sit tight and do nothing.'

'But I have a death threat hanging over me.'

'Have you seen the slightest sign of danger?' said Christopher. 'No, of course not. It was simply a device to lever the money out of you.'

'I take the threat more seriously.'

Wickens was concerned. 'So would I in your place, Henry. Take care, my friend.'

'I'm glad that someone has sympathy for me.'

'Henry,' said his brother, bridling at the criticism, 'we have just walked along dark streets that afforded endless possibilities of ambush. Were you attacked? Were you menaced in any way?'

'No, I was not.'

'How many days has it been since that death threat arrived?'

'Several, Christopher.'

'I rest my case.'

'You are too glib, Mr Redmayne,' said Wickens. 'According to your brother, Gabriel was murdered so that someone could get his hands on that diary. We are not just dealing with a blackmailer here. If he has killed once, he may kill again.'

'Or get an irate husband to do it for him,' moaned Henry.

'You know my position, Mr Wickens,' said Christopher. 'The decision is yours.'

'I'll not make it until the morning.'

'Will you let Henry know what you do?'

'If you wish.'

'I do, sir.'

'So do I, Peter,' said Henry. 'It will help me to make up my own mind. The suspense is ruining my health. Sleep has become a complete stranger to me.'

'You will soon be able to sleep as long as you want,' said Christopher.

'In my coffin?' Henry gave a mirthless laugh and brought the conversation to an end. When the visitors took their leave, Wickens seemed to be in two minds. Christopher hoped that his own advice would be followed but he feared that it would not be. Henry, too, was on the verge of paying the demand. He would not hold out much longer.

Walking side by side, they headed for The Strand. Henry was more nervous.

'I wish that I had not remembered that death threat,' he complained.

'The fact that you were able to forget it so easily shows its true worth.'

'Let's walk faster.'

'Why? The streets are empty at this time of night.'

'I feel suddenly afraid.'

'When you have me beside you?' said Christopher, patting him on the back. 'We are both armed. There was a time when you were quite skilled with a sword.'

'I still am.'

'Then walk as if you know it, Henry. Show some confidence. Exhibit fear and you invite assault. Put out your chest,' he encouraged, 'and strut along as if you own the city. That is your usual gait.'

Trying to obey the advice, Henry almost tripped himself up before he reverted to the mincing step he had used since they left Wickens's house. On the journey back to Bedford Street, he was harassed and furtive. Only when they reached his front door did he allow himself to relax.

'Thank you, Christopher,' he said. 'Will you come in?'

'No. Jacob will be waiting for me.'

'High time you had a young woman waiting for you, not a decrepit old servant.'

'Jacob is not decrepit.'

'A woman would give you a sweeter welcome.'

'I'll have to take your word for that, Henry.'

After an exchange of farewells, Christopher set off in the direction of Fetter Lane. The encounters with Arthur Lunn, Sir Marcus Kemp and Peter Wickens had each been instructive but his mind rejected all three of them in favour of Susan Cheever. It was she who would defeat time most pleasantly during his walk. Christopher was glad that she had confronted him about the way he had kept certain things from her. It showed spirit on her part and exposed his mistaken assumption about her. Susan was no weak vessel who had to be shielded from disturbing news. Christopher was sorry that his behaviour had upset her and resolved to be more open with her in the future. He felt that their conversation at his house had strengthened the bond between them. Susan Cheever occupied his thoughts in the most delightful way.

It was not until he reached Fetter Lane that he realised he was being followed.

CHAPTER TWELVE

Christopher Redmayne could hear no footsteps but he was certain that someone was behind him. He had no idea how long he had been followed and he chided himself for his lack of alertness. Fond thoughts of Susan Cheever had taken his mind off the possibility of danger. It now threatened. A tingling sensation went right through him. Quickening his pace, he reached for his dagger. Before he could even take it out of its sheath, however, his hat was knocked off from behind and Christopher felt something being looped swiftly round his neck. The sudden attack took him completely by surprise. It was a moment before he realised what was happening. A rope was chafing his neck and making it difficult for him to breathe. It was being tightened inexorably. Whoever his adversary might be, the man was strong and purposeful. Christopher began to choke. The pain was agonising. When he felt a knee in his back, he was spurred into action. If he did not strike out now, he would be strangled to death.

Pummelling with both elbows, he struck his assailant's chest so hard that the pressure on the rope eased slightly. Christopher got one hand inside it to gain himself more relief. He was panting for breath and the blood was pulsing in his temples but he could not rest. As the man renewed his attack, Christopher twisted sharply to the left and threw him off balance, kicking out with one leg as he did so. It tripped his adversary up. Falling to the ground, he pulled Christopher after him, but he had lost the advantage now. The rope was no longer a murder weapon. Christopher rolled over to deliver a relay of punches with both hands, forcing the man to release the rope altogether. The blows drew grunts of pain and Christopher felt blood spurt over his knuckles when they made contact with a nose. With a yell of rage, the man fought back, punching, biting and scratching at Christopher's face before flinging him aside with an upsurge of energy. He leapt to his feet and snatched out a dagger but Christopher was equally nimble, jumping up and producing his own weapon to ward off his attacker.

While the man circled him, Christopher at last had some idea of whom he was up against. It was too dark to see the other's face clearly but he could make out the solid body and the broad shoulders. The man was young, powerful and experienced in fighting. One mistake would cost Christopher his life. Arms spread wide, he moved round on his toes. When the dagger jabbed at him, he stepped back quickly out of range, using his own weapon to prod the man away when he tried to close in. It was a tense encounter. Christopher was handicapped by the searing pain round his neck. He could still feel the way that a knee had thudded into his spine. This was no random assault. He sensed that he was up against the same assassin who had squeezed the life out of Gabriel Cheever. His sympathy for the dead man increased tenfold. Christopher now had some idea of what his ordeal must have felt like. He had no intention of succumbing to the same fate.

Instead of waiting for the next jab, he went on the attack himself, moving round in search of an opening before feinting a thrust at the chest. When his assailant brought up his dagger to parry the strike, Christopher stabbed him in the arm and drew the loudest cry yet from him. His response was immediate and frenzied. Rushing at Christopher and roaring with anger, he slashed wildly at him, forcing him to dodge and weave. Christopher was elusive but the dagger nevertheless sliced open his sleeve, drew blood from his shoulder and grazed his forehead. The man became even more desperate, cursing, jabbing and kicking out simultaneously. He was losing blood freely. As the wound in his arm began to smart unbearably, he shifted his dagger to the other hand and lunged once more. Christopher was ready for him. Parrying the thrust with his own weapon, he seized the man's wrist and swung him in circle so that he could fling him against the wall of a house. The impact stunned the man momentarily and his dagger clattered to the ground. After kicking it away, Christopher threatened him with the point of his own dagger.

'Who sent you?' he demanded.

'Nobody,' growled the man.

'Was it Arthur Lunn?'

'I'm bleeding to death,' said the other, holding his wounded arm.

'Tell me the truth.'

'I need help.'

'Did you kill Gabriel Cheever?'

'I'm *dying*!'

Nursing his arm, the man bent double. He was obviously in great pain. Christopher relented and let his weapon drop to his side. It was a mistake. Diving straight at him, the man butted him in the stomach and sent him reeling back. It took all the wind out of Christopher. By the time he had recovered himself, it was too late. Abandoning the field, the man had sprinted round the corner and disappeared into the night. Christopher tried to give chase but there was no sign of his attacker. His own injuries now made themselves known. His neck was still painful, his face was scratched, his shoulder gashed. He could feel a trickle of blood down one cheek. Bruises seemed to be everywhere. Retrieving the rope and the dagger discarded by the man, he picked up his hat and trudged slowly back to his house.

When Jacob saw his master by candlelight, he made an instant and accurate appraisal.

'Heavens!' he exclaimed. 'What happened, sir? You look half dead.'

Henry Redmayne had his first complete night's sleep for over a week. It restored his spirits. Awaking refreshed, he felt much more ready to face the trials of the day ahead. He decided that his brother's advice was sound. Defiance was the watchword. He would not give in to the demands of a blackmailer. As soon as he thought of the repercussions, however, his resolve crumbled. Lord Ulvercombe would come after him. The letter to his wife had boiled over with passion. Henry regretted that he had ever sent it but the lady herself had asked for some sign of commitment. He had given it to her and reaped the reward the same night. In retrospect, it had all been a hideous error. Henry blamed her. If the letter had been so important to Lady Ulvercombe, why had she let it go astray? Her carelessness might land her quondam lover in a duel that he was bound to lose.

Sitting up in bed, he bewailed his misfortunes, but he was not permitted to wallow in self-pity for long. There was thunderous knocking on the door before it burst open and Sir Marcus Kemp charged into the bedchamber with two servants plucking at his arms as they tried unsuccessfully to restrain him.

'Whatever is going on?' demanded Henry.

'Get these lackeys off me!' howled Kemp.

'I'm sorry, Mr Redmayne,' said one of the men. 'He forced his way in.'

'Why?' asked Henry.

'Because I need to see you,' said Kemp.

'Could you not at least wait until I had risen, Marcus?'

'No, Henry. This will brook no delay.'

Henry saw the despair in his face. It was the expression of a spaniel that had just been run over by the wheels of one coach and sees another approaching. Snapping his fingers, Henry sent the servants on their way then reached for his wig. Even though he was still in his night attire, he wanted to have a shred of dignity. Kemp stamped across to the bed and glared down at him.

'Did you know about this, Henry?' he asked.

'About what?'

'This brainless scheme of your brother's to catch the blackmailer.'

'Well, no,' lied Henry. 'What is Christopher supposed to have done?'

'He has ruined everything,' said Kemp, holding up a letter. 'Instead of simply handing over my thousand guineas, he and an accomplice set a trap and *I* am the one who has been caught in it.'

'What do you mean, Sir Marcus?'

'This letter came this morning. It's another demand for money.'

'How much?'

'A thousand guineas.'

Henry whistled through his teeth. 'Another thousand!'

'As a punishment, he says. Because I tried to deceive him, I have to pay the amount all over again and this time I have to hand it over in person. Damnation!' protested Kemp, flinging the letter on to the bed. 'I was not responsible for any deception. All that I wanted to do was to buy this rogue off.'

'Christopher did warn you that there would be another demand.'

'Only because of his folly.'

'I disagree, Marcus.'

'If he had obeyed the instructions, everything would have been fine.'

'I doubt that.'

'Take him a message from me!' Kemp ordered.

Henry shrank back into the pillow. 'Could you stand further off and shout less?' he implored. 'All this commotion is giving me a headache.'

'What do you think that letter gave *me*?'

'Permit me to read it and I'll hazard a guess.'

Henry picked the letter up and ran his eye over the contents. He soon blenched. The tone was harsh, the demand peremptory. What startled him was that his brother was mentioned by name. He ran a tongue over lips that had suddenly gone very dry.

'You *knew*,' concluded Kemp, watching his reaction.

'Not exactly, Marcus.'

'You were party to this botched plot.'

'That's not true.'

'Why on earth did you inflict that brainless brother of yours on me?'

'Yesterday, you told me what a sterling fellow he was.'

'A sterling fool, more like. Did he really think that he could get away with it?'

'Christopher was only trying to help you.'

'Help me?' echoed Kemp. 'How does a second demand for money help me? I acted in good faith. It's the Redmayne family that is at fault here.'

'Moderate your passion a little, Marcus.'

'I'll moderate nothing.'

'Then at least exclude me from your rage. I am quite innocent.'

'Are you?' said Kemp sourly. 'Who was it who foisted his brother on to me in the first place? Who was it who broke a confidence and told that idiot sibling of his that I was a victim of blackmail?'

'Christopher is no idiot.'

'He betrayed my trust.'

'My brother tried to catch the villain,' argued Henry. 'Had he done so, you would have got your thousand guineas and your peace of mind back. You should be grateful to Christopher for taking the initiative on your behalf.'

Kemp grabbed the letter. 'This is the result of his initiative.'

'Let me show it to him.'

'No, Henry.'

'He has a right to see it.'

'Keep your brother away from me. All that I want from him is the money.'

'What money?'

'The thousand guineas, of course,' said Kemp, brandishing the letter. 'He got me into this mess so he must buy me out of it.'

'Christopher does not *have* a thousand guineas.'

'Then you can share the cost with him, Henry. I think that you are in this with your brother. He discussed his plan with you beforehand. Did you try to stop him? Did you have the sense to warn me? No!' he asserted. 'You are as guilty as he is. I want five hundred guineas from each of you by this afternoon.'

Henry gurgled. 'Why not ask for five thousand?' he said with heavy sarcasm. 'You are just as likely to get it. This is preposterous, Marcus.' He hopped out of bed to confront his visitor. 'Christopher may have misled you slightly but it was only for your own good. Look at the tone of that letter,' he advised. 'We're dealing with a ruthless man here. Even if you had handed over the money yourself yesterday, I can promise you one thing. You would still have got another demand.'

Kemp's ire slowly drained away and he flopped down on the edge of the bed. 'What am I to do Henry?'

'Take heart, my friend. All is not yet lost.'

'It is if I have to pay out a thousand guineas time and time again.'

'Christopher did say that this would happen,' warned Henry.

Kemp shook with rage. 'Who *is* the callous devil behind it all?'

'Help us to find out, Marcus.'

'How do I do that?'

'Keep to your side of the bargain,' said Henry softly.

'What bargain?' asked Kemp, looking at him.

'The one you struck with my brother,' Henry reminded him. 'If, for whatever reason, you received another blackmail demand, you agreed to show Christopher all the correspondence you have received.'

'I feel as if I want to stuff it down his throat!'

'What would that achieve? Christopher is on our side.'

'Is he?' wondered Kemp.

'Yes,' said Henry reasonably. 'This is not his fight. He need never have got involved. He could have let the pair of us stew in our own juice. But did he? No, Christopher has done everything in his power to help. But for my brother,' he admitted sadly, 'I'd have been driven insane by this whole business.'

Kemp's fury had burnt itself out. Instead of hurling wild

accusations, he was a crumpled figure with barely enough strength to sit upright. He widened his eyes.

'I am done for, Henry,' he murmured. 'I might just as well be dead.'

It was a paradox. In trying to find out more about her sister-in-law, Susan Cheever was instead learning a great deal about herself. She had liked Christopher Redmayne from the start but it had taken Lucy's gentle teasing to make her realise how deep her affection for him had become. Susan was faced with a dilemma. Wanting to see him again, she could not imagine how it could be arranged. Her stay in London was not indefinite. Once Lucy had recovered enough to make decisions about her future, Susan would have to return home. It would be possible for her to visit her sister for a while but Christopher would have no call to travel to Richmond so her chances of meeting him there were slim. To call on him unannounced would be improper yet she was sorely tempted to do that. She tried to manufacture an excuse. Everything depended on Lucy. If Susan could extract some valuable information from her sister-in-law, she would have a legitimate reason to visit Fetter Lane yet again and she was desperate to help in the search for her brother's killer. When breakfast was over, she began to probe.

'How did you sleep, Lucy?' she asked solicitously.

'Fitfully.'

'You need proper rest.'

'I have too much on my mind.'

'Try to catch up on your sleep during the day.'

'If only I could,' sighed Lucy. 'But I cannot sleep properly in that bed. I keep waking up in the hope that I will find Gabriel lying beside me.'

Susan gave her a smile of sympathy. Lucy was pale and tense. She looked smaller and more defenceless than ever. The cumulative effect of her bereavement was telling on her more obviously. She had only eaten a frugal breakfast.

'What will you do?' asked Susan gently. 'Are you going to stay on here alone?'

'No,' said Lucy firmly. 'I could never do that. The house has too many bad memories for me now. It holds some wonderful memories as well, of course, and they have helped me through this dreadful time, but I could never go on living so close to the place where Gabriel was...' Her voice tailed off. 'You understand.'

'Yes,' said Susan. 'Where will you go?'

'I am not sure yet.'

'Back to your mother?'

'Probably. It's my duty to do that. Mother is failing badly and she needs me.'

'Perhaps you need her as well,' suggested Susan. 'When we travelled back from Northampton, I had no idea that your mother lived near St Albans. It could not have been too far out of our way. I remembered how restless you were on the second day of our journey. You kept glancing through the window of the coach. Were you thinking about your mother?'

'Yes,' admitted Lucy. 'I felt guilty that we were passing within a few miles of the house. Mother would have been delighted to see me but, in the circumstances, it was quite impossible.'

'Why?'

'She would have noticed my sadness and asked what caused it.'

'Did she not notice your joy when you last visited her?'

'She would have put that down to something else.'

'What else?'

Lucy shook her head. 'I need time, Susan. I am still dazed by it all. I need time to recover from this blow. I will not make any decisions until I can think properly again. When that happens, I expect I will return to St Albans.'

'What will you tell your mother?'

'That I have come back to nurse her.'

'Will you tell her why?'

'No.'

'Surely, she deserves to know that you were married? You cannot keep it from her for ever. Until she learns the truth, she will not be able to help you.'

'It is Mother who is in need of help.'

'Is she not well enough to cope with the truth?'

Lucy pursed her lips in thought. Her eyes shone with concentration. Susan felt that she was on the verge of learning something important but she waited in vain. At the very moment when Lucy was about to speak, the doorbell rang. The noise made her start. She was annoyed at the interruption; she felt robbed. It would not be easy to bring Lucy to that same point again. The maidservant answered the door and voices were heard in the hall. Susan paid no attention until Anna came into the room.

'You have a visitor, Miss Cheever,' she said. 'His name is Mr Vout.'

Susan was puzzled. 'Vout? I know nobody of that name.'

'He said that he came from Mr Redmayne.'

Susan was on her feet immediately, brushing past Anna to go into the hall. Hat in hand, an old man was waiting deferentially. Susan recognised him at once. She saw the look of concern on his face and became alarmed.

'What is the matter, Jacob?'

Jonathan Bale listened with a mixture of interest and dismay as Christopher Redmayne told him about the events of the previous night. Eager to hear every detail, the constable was upset to see his friend in such a state. The lacerations on Christopher's face were vivid and a bruise discoloured his cheekbone. Through the open neck of his shirt, the bandaging on his shoulder was visible. Christopher's knuckles bore testimony to the ferocity of the fight. One hand was bruised while the other had lost some skin from the backs of the fingers. Jonathan felt guilty that he had not been there to protect him.

'Next time you go out at night, Mr Redmayne, I will come with you.'

Christopher grinned. 'To a gaming house?'

'If need be,' said Jonathan.

'I'll not be caught off guard again, Mr Bale.'

'No, sir. I will be watching your back.'

'It was my own fault,' recalled Christopher. 'My mind was on something else. I should have realised that someone was following me. The irony is that I had just acted as Henry's bodyguard. I deliver him safely to his house in Bedford Street then I'm the one who is attacked.'

'He obviously put up a fight.'

'Yes,' said Christopher modestly, 'but, luckily, he came off far worse.'

'He may try again.'

'Not for some time, Mr Bale. I managed to stab his arm.'

'It must have been the same man who killed Gabriel Cheever.'

Christopher felt his neck. 'He used the same method, I know that. He was a strong fellow. I can see how he overpowered Gabriel.' He saw Jonathan's grim expression. 'Do not look so gloomy. I am not destined for the grave just yet.'

'I hope not, Mr Redmayne. Thank you for sending for me.'

'Jacob insisted on going for you.' He glanced around. 'By the way, where is he?'

'He said that he had somewhere else to go.'

'Where? Jacob should have come back with you. Those were his orders.'

'He is probably on his way now.'

'It's so unlike him to go missing.'

'Forget your servant,' said Jonathan. 'Tell me about your visit to Mr Wickens.'

'He was reluctant to show me his anonymous letter at first. It's understandable, I suppose. No man wants his vices to be put on display like that, though I suspect that Peter Wickens had less to hide than Sir Marcus Kemp. In any case,' said Christopher, 'we persuaded him eventually and he allowed me a glimpse of the letter.'

'Was it written by the person who sent your brother's demand?'

'Yes, Mr Bale. The hand was identical to that which penned the second letter to Henry. A different correspondent wrote the original demand. Someone with a bolder and more looping style.'

'So we are looking for two people.'

'Three, at least,' corrected Christopher. 'You forget my midnight companion. He did not strike me as the kind of man who dashes off a neat letter. His task is to carry out the threats, not to frame them in the first place.'

'How long do you think he was following you?'

'From the time we left that gaming house, probably. Henry and I were too busy talking to notice him and he could hardly make his move while we were together. No,' he said, running a finger round his sore neck, 'my guess is that he lurked outside the house when we called on Peter Wickens. Then he shadowed us all the way back and waited until I was on my own.'

'But why attack you, Mr Redmayne? Your brother received the death threat.'

'I'm the one investigating the murder. Being ambushed like that was not the most pleasant experience,' said Christopher, 'but there is one compensation.'

'You survived.'

'That was an additional bonus. No, Mr Bale, we should take it as a sign that we are making good progress. They know that we are after them and sense that we are closing in. That's why I was attacked,' he concluded. 'They are afraid.'

Before Jonathan could reply, he heard the front door opening and the sound of footsteps in the hall. Jacob had returned. Christopher was about to rebuke his servant when someone else came into the room ahead of him. Susan Cheever made no attempt to hide the affection beneath her anxiety. Hurrying across to his chair, she looked down at Christopher with consternation.

'Jacob tells me that you were attacked, Mr Redmayne,' she said.

Astonished to see her, all that Christopher could manage was a nod. He tried to catch Jacob's eye but the servant slipped off into the kitchen without looking at him. Susan was taking a rapid inventory of his face and neck. She winced when she saw his raw knuckles.

'Are you badly hurt?'

'No,' he said, relishing her proximity. 'I'll live to fight another day. But do sit down, Miss Cheever. You know Mr Bale, of course.'

Susan gave the constable a nod of recognition. When she came into the room, Jonathan had risen to his feet. As she sat down, he resumed his seat. Susan had not come to see him. Her attention was fixed solely on Christopher.

'What happened?' she said. 'Jacob would not give me any details.'

'I do not remember very much,' replied Christopher. 'It was over in a flash.'

'I do not believe you. Tell me the truth.'

He blinked at her directness. 'There is not much to tell.'

'Yes, there is,' she insisted. 'You did not get those injuries in the space of a few seconds. I think that you are trying to fob me off again, Mr Redmayne. Have you so soon forgotten your promise to tell me everything?'

'Mr Bale has heard it all before. It would bore him.'

'Not at all,' said Jonathan. 'I'd be glad to listen again, sir. Some small details may emerge that you forgot the first time. I am used to taking statements and I always make witnesses go over the story at least twice. There is usually something new that comes out and it is often crucial.'

Christopher turned back to Susan. Worried and attentive, she was also determined to hear the full truth. He could not hold things back from her again. Making light of the courage he had shown, he gave her a lucid account of the attack and assured her that his injuries looked far worse than they really were. Susan was not reassured.

'We are to blame for this,' she said guiltily. 'If you had not been trying to help my family, you would have been perfectly safe.'

'I'm acting on behalf of my brother as well, remember.'

'Someone tried to kill you, Mr Redmayne. I feel responsible.'

'Needlessly.'

'You took the most appalling risks to track down the man who murdered Gabriel.'

'He tracked *me* down, Miss Cheever.'

'That's what alarms me.'

Christopher did his best to calm her down and Jonathan repeated his pledge to act as a bodyguard in future. She was only partially mollified. Jacob came into the room and stood beside his master.

'Shall I bring in some refreshments, sir?' he enquired.

'What I need from you,' said Christopher, 'is an explanation.'

The old man beamed. 'Do you have a complaint, sir?'

'No, Jacob, but I want you to follow instructions in future.'

'I felt that Miss Cheever ought to know what had transpired.'

'Thank you,' she said. 'I'm very grateful to you, Jacob.'

Christopher smiled. 'Well, yes,' he said on reflection. 'I suppose that I, too, am grateful. Perhaps you acted wisely, after all.'

Jacob was basking in their approval when there was a loud knock at the door. He hurried out into the hall to see who had called. He returned almost at once and handed a letter to Christopher.

'This is from your brother, sir,' he said. 'His servant awaits your answer.'

Breaking the seal, Christopher read the brief note and got to his feet.

'Tell him that we will come immediately.' While Jacob went off to relay the message to the servant, Christopher turned to Susan. 'Forgive us, Miss Cheever. We will have to leave you for a while. But do please remain here. We may have important news for you when we return.' He smiled at Jonathan. 'Give me a few minutes to get properly dressed and I'll gladly employ your services as a bodyguard.'

Sir Marcus Kemp moved between recrimination and dejection with no intervening stage. One minute, he was berating the Redmayne brothers; the next, he was imploring Henry to come to his aid. His lightning shifts of mood were bewildering. The two men were in the parlour of the house in Bedford Street. Shaved, dressed and wearing his wig,

Henry felt in a better position to cope with his ambivalent visitor. Kemp's plight somehow made his own troubles seem less immediate.

'In your position, I'd refuse to pay the thousand guineas,' he said airily.

'Even if it means public vilification and certain divorce?'

'Play for time, Marcus.'

'The letter insists on immediate payment.'

'Then give this bloodsucker a small amount by way of deposit and tell him that you will pay the rest in instalments. Yes,' said Henry, pleased with the notion, 'that will remove the threat and give you space in which to breathe. It will also give my brother more time to hunt this villain to his lair.'

'As long as he does not offer to hand over my money again,' said Kemp with asperity. 'I can do without any assistance from Christopher Redmayne.'

'But he is only our hope.'

'Then we are truly doomed.'

'Have more faith in him. After all, he is a Redmayne.'

'That means he has the mark of failure on him.'

Henry was offended. 'The Redmayne family is known for its resilience.'

'It has brought me nothing but misery,' insisted the other, lapsing back into deep gloom. 'There is no hope. The net is closing in remorselessly.' The sound of the doorbell injected some rancour back into him. 'That will be your brother now,' he said. 'I'll warm his ears until they burst into flame. Christopher Redmayne is a bungler!'

Taking a stance with his hands on his hips, Kemp was

ready to fire a verbal broadside the moment Christopher entered, but he was taken aback at the sight of the lacerated face and bruised cheekbone. The presence of Jonathan Bale also helped to silence him. After staring in horror,. Henry rushed across to his brother.

'Look at the state of you!' he exclaimed.

'I was attacked on my way home from here last night,' said Christopher.

'Attacked?' repeated Kemp. 'By whom?'

'I will tell you, Sir Marcus. First, let me introduce my friend, Jonathan Bale, the finest constable in London.' He turned to his companion. 'I am sorry you will have to listen to this for the third time, Mr Bale, but it cannot be helped.'

'Pray continue, Mr Redmayne,' said Jonathan, eyeing Kemp with controlled distaste. 'Your brother and his guest ought to know the risk you took on their behalf.'

Christopher's recital abbreviated the facts to the bare essentials. They were more than enough to make both Henry and Kemp shudder with fear. Inevitably, Henry saw the incident entirely from his own point of view.

'It was I who was the real target!' he wailed, clutching his chest. 'That assassin was sent to carry out the death threat against me. Dear God! What a narrow escape I had! If I had been abroad alone last night, Mr Bale would probably have found my corpse by now on Paul's Wharf.'

'It was your brother who was attacked, sir,' Jonathan reminded him.

'Only because I was not available.'

'You were protected, Mr Redmayne. Your brother was not until now.'

'This is insupportable,' said Henry, flinging himself into a chair and hugging himself defensively. 'I shall not set a foot outside the front door.'

'With respect, Henry,' said Christopher, 'the assassin was not after you. I was the target last night because I have been searching for Gabriel Cheever's killer. They *know* that I am on their tail.'

'Exactly,' said Kemp. 'Your name was mentioned in my last letter.'

'That proves it must be someone in your circle, Sir Marcus. Someone who has met me through Henry and recognises me by sight.'

'Dozens of my friends can do that,' observed Henry. 'I gave you that list.'

'Yes, Mr Bale and I have been working through it.'

Kemp scowled. 'Without success, it seems.'

'Only because you refuse to help us, Sir Marcus.'

'You surely cannot point a finger at me.'

'I must,' said Christopher. 'Henry showed me both the letters that he received and even Mr Wickens allowed me a glance at the demand sent to him. But you have rejected every entreaty even though you may have in your possession the one piece of information that will enable us to catch this man.'

'A magistrate will take a poor view of anyone withholding evidence,' added Jonathan seriously. 'Especially where a brutal murder is involved.'

Kemp looked cornered. 'It's an unwarranted invasion of my privacy.'

'Henry's message said you might have changed your mind,' Christopher commented.

'Well, he had no right to tell you that.'

'You *promised,* Marcus,' said Henry.

'I merely said that I would consider it.'

'Show my brother the letters and get it over with.'

'No, Henry. I am still undecided.'

'Then you are impeding this investigation, Sir Marcus,' warned Jonathan.

'I don't need a mere constable to teach me the law,' retorted Kemp waspishly.

'Would you rather this villain remained free to extort more money from you and to make another attempt on Mr Redmayne's life? He must be arrested at once.'

'Mr Bale is right,' said Christopher. 'We must have your help.'

'Those letters are highly personal.'

'Then do not show them to me, Sir Marcus. What I really want to see is the extract from the diary. That will open up a completely new line of enquiry.' He saw the uncertainty in Kemp's eyes. 'If you fear that a printer will read of your misdemeanours, borrow a pen from Henry and scratch out your name.'

'Mine, too, while you're at it!' agreed Henry.

'Nobody need know to whom that page in the diary refers.'

'I know,' said Kemp despondently.

Henry got up. 'I have pen and ink here in the room,' he said, crossing to the table. 'Eliminate yourself, Marcus. Remove me at a stroke.' He held up the quill. 'Strike out our names and we are acquitted of any shame.'

'Do as Mr Redmayne suggests,' urged Jonathan.

'Take the pen,' coaxed Henry.

'Which is it to be, Sir Marcus?' asked Christopher, adding more pressure. 'Will you give us the opportunity to catch this rogue or would you rather go on paying him a thousand guineas every time he chooses to demand it?'

Sir Marcus Kemp resisted for as long as he felt able then capitulated. Tearing the letters and the extract from the diary out of his pocket, he thrust them at Christopher.

'Here, sir!' he said wearily. 'Take the entire correspondence.'

Elijah Pembridge was a slim, angular man of middle years with curling grey locks and wispy facial hair that could not decide if it was a beard or not. There was an element of uncertainty about his clothing as well, as if he could not make up his mind what was the most appropriate dress for a bookseller. Torn between smartness and slovenliness, he ended up looking like an elegant gentleman who had fallen on particularly hard times. About his profession itself, however, there was no hint of wavering. Pembridge loved his books with a passion that excluded all else. The devotion that other men gave to their wives, their sports and their mistresses he reserved for the wonder of the printed page. When the visitors arrived at his shop in Paternoster Row, he was caressing a copy of *De Imitatione Christi* as if he were stroking the head of a favourite child.

'Good morning, Mr Pembridge,' said Christopher.

The bookseller looked up and a smile fought its way out of his hirsute face. 'Mr Redmayne! It is wonderful to see you again.' His pleasure turned to anxiety when he saw Christopher's cuts and bruises. 'What happened to you?'

'I lost my footing and fell into some bramble bushes.'

'You look as if someone hit you.'

'No, no. I banged myself hard on the ground, that is all.'

Christopher introduced Jonathan who was looking around at the shelves of books with curiosity. Huge leather-bound tomes nestled beside piles of chap-books. Volumes on all subjects and in many languages were everywhere, neatly stacked and free from any spectre of dust. The sense of newness was overwhelming. Jonathan was duly impressed by the range of titles.

'You were lucky, Mr Pembridge,' he observed. 'Most book-sellers lost their entire stock in the Great Fire.'

Pembridge sighed. 'That was because they made the mistake of carrying everything to St Paul's,' he recalled. 'I did not. They thought their stock would be safe in there but all they did was feed the fire. Well over a hundred and fifty thousand pounds' worth of precious literature perished in the blaze along, of course, with Stationers' Hall.'

'I remember it, sir. St Faith's burnt like the fires of Hell.'

'My colleague, Joseph Kirton, lost thousands,' continued Pembridge, 'but it was the destruction of *Critici Sancti* that was most lamentable. All nine volumes of it were consumed in the flames at a cost of thirteen thousand pounds to Cornelius Bee and his partners.'

Jonathan was astounded. 'Thirteen thousand pounds for *books*?'

'They can be rare objects, Mr Bale. Take this one, for instance,' he said, holding up the book in his hand. 'It is one of the products of the Imprimerie Royale and is quite priceless. Look,' he invited, turning to the title page, '*De*

Imitatione Christi, published in 1642. As you can see, it is a folio volume set in types based on Garamond. The Imprimerie Royale, also known as Typographia Regia, was established by King Louis XIII at the suggestion of Cardinal Richelieu. I have spent years trying to find a copy.'

'How much does it cost?'

'Oh, I would never part with it,' said Pembridge, hugging the book to him. 'I want the pleasure of owning it for myself. Not that I have any sympathies with the Old Religion, you understand,' he said quickly. 'I value it solely as an example of the printer's art and not because of anything between its covers.'

'Mr Pembridge did not lose a single page in the fire,' explained Christopher. 'He hired a horse and cart to move his entire stock to the safety of Westminster.' He looked around. 'I had the honour of designing this new shop.'

'It has won the admiration of everyone, Mr Redmayne.'

'I'm gratified to hear that.'

'In fact, I took the liberty of passing on your name to a customer of mine. Sir Julius Cheever asked me if I could recommend a good architect and I told him to look no further than Christopher Redmayne.' He scratched his nose. 'Did Sir Julius ever get in touch with you?'

'He did, Mr Pembridge. I am commissioned to design his new house.'

'Congratulations, sir!'

'How do you come to know Sir Julius?'

'The only way that I get to know anybody – by selling them books.'

'He did not strike me as a reading man.'

'Then you underestimate him badly,' said the bookseller. 'Sir Julius knows what he likes. Because he does not come to London often, he orders books by letter and has them collected by his son-in-law, Mr Serle.'

'Yes, I've met Mr Serle.'

'Not a bookish man, alas, but we may win him over in time. So,' he went on, 'you are to design the new house for Sir Julius, are you? An interesting man, is he not? Where is the house to be built and in what style?'

Christopher was fond of Pembridge and had found him a most amenable client. In other circumstances he would have tolerated the man's cheerful garrulity, but priorities forbade it on this occasion. Explanation had to be kept to a minimum. If he told the bookseller what lay behind his visit, he would have to endure a lecture on the dangers of London wharves at night and a history of the crime of blackmail. Pembridge might even have books on both subjects. Christopher made no mention of murder or extortion. One page from an unpublished diary was all that the bookseller would see.

'You must be familiar with every printer in London,' he began.

'All twenty of them,' replied Pembridge.

'Is that all there are?' asked Jonathan.

'Yes, Mr Bale,' explained Pembridge, seizing the opportunity to display his knowledge. 'The number of master printers was limited to twenty in 1662 when the office of Surveyor of the Imprimery and Printing Presses was given to Roger L'Estrange. Severe curbs were placed on the liberty of the press.' He ran a hand through his hair.

'John Twynn was indicted for high treason for publishing a seditious book. Other printers have been fined, pilloried and put in prison for publishing work that Mr L'Estrange considered offensive. Simon Drover was one. Nathan Brooks, the bookbinder, was another who fell foul of the law. As a matter of fact—'

'Mr Pembridge,' said Christopher, cutting him off before he worked his way through the entire list of victims, 'we need your advice. If I were to show you a page from a London printer, would you be able to identify him for me?'

'Possibly.'

'How would you do it?'

'Each man has his own peculiarities, as distinctive as a signature.'

'Ignore what the words say,' suggested Christopher, taking the page from his pocket. 'You might find them offensive. All we need to know is the name of the printer most likely to have produced this.'

Pembridge took the page and clicked his tongue in disapproval when he saw that it was defaced with inky blotches. Names had been crossed out but the remainder of the text was there. Ignoring Christopher's suggestion, he read the words and chortled.

'This is very diverting, Mr Redmayne. Did these things really *happen*?'

'Apparently.'

'What strange urges some men have!'

'Forget the memoir, Mr Pembridge. Just examine the print.'

'Oh, I have. The typeface is Dutch.'

'Are you sure?'

'I know my trade. This typeface was invented by Christoffel van Djick, a goldsmith from Amsterdam, one of the great type founders. It was he who taught Anton Janson.' He burrowed into his stock. 'I have other examples of that typeface here.'

'We'll take your word for it,' said Christopher quickly.

'Simply tell us who could have printed that page,' added Jonathan.

'A name is all that we require.'

Pembridge turned back to them and scrutinised the paper again, rubbing it between his thumb and forefinger. He held the page up to the light then nodded.

'Yes, that would be my guess,' he decided.

'Who printed it?' asked Christopher.

'Miles Henshaw.'

'Henshaw?'

'He's your man, Mr Redmayne. I'll wager money on it.'

'Where will we find him?'

'In Fleet Lane. But have a care when you speak to him.'

'Why?'

'Miles Henshaw is a big man,' said Pembridge. 'With a choleric disposition.'

Left alone in his house, Henry Redmayne grew fearful. The attack on his brother had robbed him of any pretensions to bravery. Certain that he would be the next victim, he ordered his servants to let nobody into the building except Christopher. Wine was his one consolation and he drank it in copious amounts, hoping to subdue his apprehensions. Yet the more he drank, the more menaced he felt. His case, he told himself, was far worse than those of his friends. Peter Wickens had only been asked for five hundred guineas. Sir Marcus Kemp had already paid twice that amount and faced a second demand but neither man's life was in danger. Henry quivered. Why had he been singled out? It was unnerving. He began to wish that he had never confided in his brother at all. Had he appeased the blackmailer when the first demand came, all might now be well. Henry would have come through the crisis and Christopher would have known nothing about it.

It never occurred to him to lay any blame on himself. Self-examination was foreign to his character. When his own actions landed him in trouble, he always sought to place the responsibility on someone else. As he swallowed another mouthful of wine, he decided that the real culprit was the woman with whom he had enjoyed a surreptitious romance. Lady Ulvercombe had been a passionate, if fleeting, lover and Henry had allowed himself to make commitments to her that flew in the face of discretion. Instead of ruing his own folly, he blamed her need for reassurance. Having extracted the fateful letter from him, she promised that she would destroy it before her husband returned to the house. Lady Ulvercombe had broken that promise and the consequences could be disastrous. Henry felt such a sharp pain in his stomach that he almost doubled up. It was as if the vengeful sword of her jealous husband were already penetrating his flesh.

Circling the room, he was sufficiently desperate to offer up a prayer for his own salvation. It was no act of humble supplication. In return for divine intervention, he did not offer to renounce his wickedness henceforth. If God would not help him, he would turn aside from religion altogether. Faced with extortion himself, he was sending a blackmail demand to the Almighty. A heavenly response, it seemed, was instantaneous. No sooner had the prayer ended than the doorbell rang. His hopes soared. Had Christopher returned to say that the blackmailer was now in custody? Had the doughty constable arrested the man who attacked his brother? Were his troubles at last over? Sensing release, Henry let out a cry of elation and vowed to celebrate that night in the haunts he had so cruelly been forced to neglect.

When a servant entered with a letter, Henry snatched it from him and sent the man out. He tore the letter open. A glance at the handwriting was enough to fracture his new-found confidence. He scrunched up the paper and emitted a howl of agony.

'Christopher!' he yelled. 'For God's sake, *help* me!'

As the two men approached the printer's shop in Fleet Lane, they could hear a voice raised in anger. Anticipating trouble, Jonathan Bale straightened his shoulders and led the way into the premises. In a room at the back, Miles Henshaw was admonishing a wayward apprentice. Judging by the boy's pleas for mercy, the printer was reinforcing his words with blows. Jonathan banged the counter to attract attention.

'Mr Henshaw!' he called.

The shouting stopped and the boy's ordeal was temporarily over. Composing his features into the flabby smile he reserved for customers, Henshaw came into the front of the shop. He was a tall, big-boned, corpulent man in his fifties with tiny eyes glinting either side of a hooked nose. When he saw Christopher's facial injuries, he blinked in surprise. Sobbing was heard from the back room. Henshaw gave an explanatory chuckle.

'The lad must learn the hard way,' he said, rubbing his hands together. 'I was an apprentice for eight years and a blow from my master taught me quicker than anything else.' He broadened his smile. 'What can I do for you, gentlemen? If you wish to have something printed, you have come to the right place.'

'We want to discuss your work, Mr Henshaw,' said Christopher.

'Has someone recommended me to you, sir?'

'Not exactly.'

Christopher performed the introductions then took out the page from the diary. Handing it over to Henshaw, he studied the man's reactions. The printer's jaw tightened visibly and his smile congealed. He glared at Christopher.

'Why have you brought this to me?' he said.

'Because we believe that it is your handiwork.'

'There's some mistake. This is not mine.'

'Do you not use that typeface, Mr Henshaw?'

'From time to time,' the printer conceded.

'Then rack your memory,' said Christopher. 'Try to recall when you used it for this particular commission. It's very important.'

Henshaw sniffed. 'I'm sorry,' he said, tossing the page on to the counter. 'I've never seen this before. Nor would I care to, sir. It's not the kind of thing a respectable shop like mine would be interested in touching.'

'How do you know? You did not read it through.'

'I saw enough.'

'Let me speak to your apprentice,' said Christopher.

'Why?'

'I fancy that he may be more alert than his master. He may recollect setting the type for this particular commission. Call the lad through, Mr Henshaw.'

'No, sir.'

'What harm can it do?'

Henshaw was belligerent. 'My apprentice has work to do and so do I. If you are not here to do business, I bid you farewell.' He grabbed the page from the counter and thrust it at Christopher. 'Take this out of my shop.'

'Not until you tell us what we came to find out,' said Jonathan, taking the page from him. 'You recognised this work as soon as you saw it. I dare say that you have printed others from the same source.'

'Go your ways,' snarled Henshaw.

'All in good time.'

'I cannot help you.'

'You mean that you *will* not,' said Jonathan levelly. 'At the moment, that is.'

'Obviously, you require a little persuasion,' said Christopher easily. 'I'm sure that you are familiar with the name of Elijah Pembridge.'

'I know Pembridge and all his pernicious tribe,' sneered Henshaw. 'Booksellers are the bane of my life. They outnumber us completely and enforce terms that take away any profit we might enjoy. The Stationers' Company will be the ruin of us.'

'We did not come here to listen to your woes,' said Jonathan bluntly.

'Then take yourselves off.'

'You have not heard us out yet,' resumed Christopher. 'Mr Pembridge is a friend of mine. When it comes to printing, I respect his judgement. According to him, that page is your work, Mr Henshaw. I'd take his word against yours.'

'So would I,' added Jonathan.

'Pembridge is wrong,' insisted Henshaw.

'Is he?' said Christopher. 'Supposing that Mr Bale and I were to show this to every other printer in the city. What would happen if every one of them denied any knowledge of it? The trail would lead us straight back to you, Mr Henshaw. Why not save us a great deal of time?'

The printer hesitated. Jonathan wearied of his lying. It was time for action.

'You will have to come with us, Mr Henshaw,' he declared.

'Why?' said the printer.

'Because I'm placing you under arrest, sir.'

'On what charge?'

'You are an accessary to blackmail.'

'That is ridiculous!'

'Save your protests for the magistrate, sir,' said Jonathan, going round the counter. 'We have evidence to link you to a conspiracy to extort money by means of blackmail.' He held up the page. 'This is only the first link in the chain.'

'Stay away from me!' said Henshaw, pushing him away.

'Leave him be, Mr Bale,' said Christopher. 'He may yet

be innocently involved here. Let me explain the seriousness of the situation, Mr Henshaw,' he went on, turning to the printer. 'We are not just talking about blackmail. Murder has also occurred.'

'Murder?' gasped Henshaw.

'The killer tried to add me to his list of victims. As you see, I still bear the scars of the encounter. But let me tell you exactly what we are dealing with here.'

Christopher gave him a terse account of the crimes, omitting the names of the blackmail victims but mentioning the amounts of money demanded. Henshaw's face was eloquent. Shock gave way to fear, then quickly changed to self-pity.

'I knew nothing of this, Mr Redmayne!' he protested. 'I swear it!'

'Did you print that page?' asked Christopher.

Henshaw bit his lip. 'Yes,' he admitted.

'Have you printed anything similar?'

'Not yet, sir. But another commission is promised to me.'

Christopher looked around. 'Do you have the diary on the premises?'

'No, sir. The gentleman said he'd bring it in due course.'

'What gentleman?' said Jonathan.

'The one who paid me handsomely for that single page,' replied Henshaw.

'Did he give you a name?' asked Christopher.

The printer nodded. 'Yes, Mr Redmayne. A name and an address.'

'Excellent!' Christopher leant forward with excitement. 'We want them.'

'I'll need to look in my book,' said Henshaw, easing Jonathan back so that he could reach behind the counter. He pulled out a ledger and set it down, beginning to flick through the pages. 'Here it is,' he said at last, finding the correct place.

'Give us the name!' demanded Christopher.

'Gabriel Cheever, sir,' announced Henshaw. 'He lives Knightrider Street.'

Chapter Thirteen

Susan Cheever tried hard to conceal her disappointment but it showed clearly in her eyes. Hoping that they had returned with good news, she was dismayed when Christopher explained what had happened at the printer's shop. What hurt her most was the fact that her brother's name had been used to disguise the identity of someone who was implicated in his murder. It was a detail she intended to keep from her sister-in-law.

'I am sorry that it was all such a waste of time, Mr Redmayne,' she said.

'But it was not,' said Christopher. 'We feel heartened by what we discovered.'

'Heartened?'

'Yes, Miss Cheever. We know who printed that extract from the diary and he assures us that his customer promised to return soon. Mr Bale has left a colleague of his watching the shop. When the man does return,' he said, 'Mr Henshaw will give a signal and an arrest can be made.'

'Are you sure that you can trust this printer?'

'Oh, yes. Thanks to Mr Bale. He frightened the life out of Miles Henshaw.'

'It was the only way to get his help,' said Jonathan with a smile. 'He was a surly fellow who had been sworn to secrecy by his customer. He was very obstructive at first. When I threatened to haul him before a magistrate, he thought better of it.'

'Was he aware that Gabriel's diary was being used for blackmail?'

'No, Miss Cheever. He was simply paid to print that extract.'

'By whom?'

'That is what we've yet to establish,' confessed Christopher, 'but Mr Henshaw gave us a good description of the customer. Apparently, he was a well-built young man with a handsome face but a rough manner. I have a strong feeling that I met the fellow in the dark last night.' He grinned quietly. 'After the way I flattened his nose, he may not be quite so handsome now.'

'You say that he had a rough manner?'

'Mr Henshaw meant that he was uneducated, Miss Cheever. He spoke less like a master than a servant. That may be a valuable clue.'

It was late morning and the three of them were sitting in the parlour of the house in Fetter Lane. Jonathan was anxious to continue their investigation but Christopher felt that they had to report back to Susan first. He had not forgotten the way she had surged into the room to enquire after his health. It was almost worth taking a beating to enjoy the sheer luxury of her concern. Since she had appeared, his injuries no longer caused him the slightest twinge of pain.

'What will you do now, Mr Redmayne?' she asked.

'First, I will tell Jacob to escort you safely home.'

'Must I go?'

'You can remain here if you wish but it may be a long wait. Mr Bale and I have so much more to do. Besides,' said Christopher reasonably, 'your sister-in-law will be wondering what happened to you. It must have been a great shock to her when you suddenly left.'

'It was.'

'Go back and reassure her.'

'What shall I say to her?'

'Tell her that her husband's death will soon be explained.'

'Am I allowed to mention the attack on you, Mr Redmayne?'

'No,' he said. 'It would only upset her needlessly. She has enough things to worry her as it is. Say nothing about me, Miss Cheever. Try to get *her* to do the talking.'

'I will.'

'Are you making any headway on that front?'

'I think so,' she said. 'Lucy is close to confiding in me.'

'Then it is important for you to stay with her.'

'I suppose so.'

'She needs your support.'

Susan gave a nod of agreement. Reluctant to leave, she

accepted that she had to go. She had travelled to London at her sister-in-law's express request and could not desert her for any length of time. The visit to Fetter Lane had served to deepen the unspoken affection between her and Christopher. While she waited for him to come back, she had learnt a great deal more about him simply by sitting in his house and imbibing its atmosphere. It was an interesting place and it reflected his character with accuracy. Jacob had even let her see some of his master's drawings. Marvelling at Christopher's skills, she was grateful that her father had retained him as an architect. It was her one source of consolation. She rose sadly to her feet.

'Yes,' said Christopher, reading the query in her face. 'I promise that we will keep you informed of any progress we make. It's a blessing that Mr Bale's house in Addle Hill is so near to Knightrider Street.'

'I hope that you will find time to come yourself, Mr Redmayne.'

'Of course.'

'I still believe that you may be the one to gain Lucy's confidence.'

'As long as I have yours,' he said.

'You do,' she assured him.

Jacob was summoned and given instructions. All four of them soon left the house together. Pausing in the street, Susan bestowed a valedictory smile on Christopher.

'Where will you go now?' she asked.

'To pay a call on a man who will not be pleased to see us.'

'Who is that, Mr Redmayne?'

'Mr Arthur Lunn.'

'Are we to search the coffee houses for him?' said a worried Jonathan.

'No, Mr Bale,' said Christopher, 'we'll call at his home first. Even if he is not there himself, we may find out something of crucial importance.'

'What is that?' said Susan.

'If he has a servant with a wounded arm and a broken nose.'

Fleet Lane was well outside Tom Warburton's territory but he could not refuse his colleague's request. He had been with Jonathan Bale when the dead body was discovered and he had the same commitment to finding the killer. Choosing a vantage point with care, Warburton kept the printing shop under surveillance. His dog, Sam, seemed to realise the significance of the assignment. Instead of wandering off to forage, he stayed close to his master's feet, curling up and falling asleep. The constable's orders were simple. He was to watch customers going in and out of the shop and await a signal from the printer. Miles Henshaw had given him a description of the wanted man so he knew his salient features.

It was a lengthy wait. Several customers appeared but none of them resembled the person that Warburton was after. He stamped his feet to fight off cramp. Sam opened an eye to see if he was needed then closed it again. A group of people sauntered down the lane towards them. A young man, who had attached himself to the rear of the group, suddenly peeled off and went into the shop. Warburton took close interest. One glimpse of the customer alerted him. Nudging the dog awake, he kept his gaze on the printer's shop. The latest customer was inside for some time. When the man emerged, Miles Henshaw came out with him to trade a few words before waving him off. Warburton moved forward, ready to break into a trot at the printer's signal. Sam emitted a low growl. But it was all to no avail. As soon as the customer had gone a few yards, Henshaw turned to the constable and shook his head vigorously. It was not the wanted man. Warburton drew back and Sam curled up again. The dog was soon fast asleep.

When he opened the front door, the servant was taken aback to see a burly constable standing there with a young man whose face was covered in lacerations. He recovered quickly and looked from one to the other.

'May I help you, gentlemen?' he said.

'We have called to see Mr Lunn,' said Christopher. 'Is he at home?'

'Yes, sir, but Mr Lunn is not receiving visitors today.'

'Tell him it's a matter of some urgency.'

'I will pass that message on to him,' said the man, dismissing them with a cold smile. 'Good day, gentlemen.'

'Wait!' ordered Jonathan. 'Close that door in our faces and you'll answer to me.'

'My master is not available today, sir.'

'Tell him that Mr Redmayne and Mr Bale wish to speak to him.'

'It would make no difference,' said the man with exasperation.

'We'll not be denied,' warned Christopher.

'I never admit strangers.'

'We are both known to Mr Lunn. I was with him at a gaming house last night and Mr Bale here has shared a table with him at a coffee house.'

Jonathan winced at the reminder. 'I come on official business,' he said. 'If you try to turn us away, I'll fetch a warrant to gain entry. What will your master say to that?'

The man's certainty slowly vanished. He could see how determined the visitors were. Leaving them at the door, he risked his master's displeasure and went to report the request. When he returned, he had a hangdog expression.

'You are to come in,' he mumbled, 'but Mr Lunn can spare you very little time.'

'We will not require much,' said Christopher.

They were conducted into a large hall with a high ceiling. The floor was marble and a marble staircase curled its way upwards. Located in St James's Square, the house was bigger and more sumptuous than those of either Sir Marcus Kemp or Peter Wickens. Christopher estimated the number of servants it would take to run such an establishment. Arthur Lunn was in the dining room, seated at the head of a long table with writing materials set out in front of him. He was still in his dressing gown but he wore his periwig. His paunch was accentuated, his swarthy face darkened even more by a scowl. When the visitors entered, he gave them no word of greeting. He stared at Christopher's injuries without comment then glowered at Jonathan.

'What is this nonsense about a warrant?' he demanded.

'It did not prove necessary,' said Jonathan.

'I'll not have you upsetting my servants.'

'How many do you have here, Mr Lunn?' asked Christopher.

'That's none of your damn business, Mr Redmayne.'

'Is one of them nursing a wounded arm?'

Lunn's eyes bulged even more recklessly. 'Wounded arm?' he said. 'Is that why you came here – to discuss the condition of my servants?'

'It may be relevant, sir.'

'To what?'

'Something that happened to me last night. I was attacked.'

'I can see that. But do not expect any sympathy from me.'

'What I would like is an explanation, Mr Lunn,' said Christopher, moving closer. 'When I spoke to you last night, you were very brusque with me. Someone followed me from the gaming house and waited for the moment to strike. Is that not a coincidence?'

Lunn hauled himself up. 'Are you suggesting that I set someone on to you?' he said. 'That's a monstrous allegation.'

'Is it a truthful one?'

'No, of course not!'

'You seemed very annoyed with me.'

'I was, Mr Redmayne, but I'd never let anyone else do something that I would enjoy myself. Had I wanted you beaten, I'd have thrashed you with a horsewhip.'

Christopher met his gaze. 'It would not have stayed long in your hand.'

'Mr Redmayne was not beaten,' said Jonathan solemnly.

'An attempt was made on his life. We have reason to believe that the man responsible has killed already.'

'Why tell me all this?' demanded Lunn.

'We wondered if you might know the fellow, sir.'

'How could I?'

'By employing him to run errands for you,' said Christopher. 'Was he the same person you sent to Miles Henshaw, the printer?' Lunn looked bewildered. 'What is he? A servant? A friend? Or merely a hired assassin?'

'Will somebody tell me what this is all about? I'm baffled.'

'Let me jog your memory. An unknown person has been sending blackmail demands to a number of people,' he said, glancing at the correspondence on the table. 'My brother Henry was the first to receive one, Sir Marcus Kemp came next and the latest victim, as far as we know, is Mr Peter Wickens. There is a clear pattern. Large amounts of money are demanded. The blackmailer has to come from within my brother's circle or he would not be in possession of the sensitive information that he has acquired. Mr Bale and I have been searching for the man.'

Lunn was incredulous. 'Are you accusing me?'

'We merely wish to ask you some questions.'

'Am I supposed to have written these letters?'

'Let us just say that our enquiries have led us to your door, Mr Lunn.'

'Then they can lead you straight back out again,' snapped Lunn. 'Sir Marcus Kemp, Peter Wickens and your brother are all close friends of mine. Why should I want to blackmail them?'

'You have expensive tastes.'

'I can afford them, sir.'

'Even when you lose heavily at cards?' said Christopher. 'That was why you resented Gabriel Cheever. He took a small fortune from your purse and then he discarded your friendship like an empty bottle.' Lunn shuddered at the reminder. 'I suggest to you that you got your revenge on Gabriel and stole his diary so that you could recoup some of the money that you had lost. Is that what happened?' Lunn's head sank to his chest and he sat down again. 'How many blackmail demands have you sent?'

'None.'

'None at all? Then who has been sending them?'

'You tell me, Mr Redmayne,' said Lunn, looking up at him. 'I want to know.'

'We think that you are involved somehow.'

'Oh, it's true. I am involved.'

'To what extent?' said Jonathan.

'I am the latest victim,' he explained, picking up one of the letters from the table. 'If you came in search of proof, here it is. A blackmail demand for five hundred guineas. Even *I* would not be stupid enough to send a letter to myself.'

Christopher suddenly felt very uneasy. He did not dare to look at Jonathan.

'I think that we owe you an apology, Mr Lunn,' he said at length.

Lunn waved the apology away. 'You were only doing what you felt was right,' he said wearily. 'And it's a relief to know that somebody is trying to catch this devil. When I got his letter this morning, I all but collapsed with the shock.'

'Was anything sent with the letter?'

'Not this time.'

'This time?'

'I figure largely in Gabriel's diary, it seems,' confessed Lunn. 'If I do not pay five hundred guineas, an account of my exploits will be printed and distributed throughout London. It's too hideous to contemplate. No man knew my weaknesses better than Gabriel. He was in a position to crucify me.'

'You must accept some of the blame, sir,' Jonathan pointed out.

'Why?'

'You could not be blackmailed over vices you did not have.'

'Save me from the fellow's morality, Mr Redmayne,' said Lunn angrily.

'I was only offering an opinion, sir.'

'This may not be the most appropriate time, Mr Bale,' said Christopher tactfully. 'Mr Lunn,' he continued, 'the other victims were kind enough to let me peruse their letters so that I could compare the handwriting. Would you please extend the same privilege to me?'

'To you, Mr Redmayne,' said Lunn, eyeing Jonathan, 'but not to Mr Bale.'

'Thank you.'

Christopher took the proffered letter and read it quickly. It was couched in the same terse language as the other missives and written by the person who sent the orginal letter to his brother. He gave it back to Lunn.

'I can see why you did not wish to receive visitors today.'

'While this is hanging over me, I'll not show my face in the streets.'

'Do not be cowed by it.'

'Now I understand why Henry was so loath to venture out with me,' said Lunn, 'and why Sir Marcus refused even to let me in. And Peter Wickens is a victim, too?'

'We called on him last night.'

'Is he going to pay up?'

'I advised strongly against it, Mr Lunn.'

'Why?'

'Sir Marcus handed over a thousand guineas,' said Christopher, 'and thought he was free of danger. But a second demand for that amount has now come.'

'Death and damnation!' cried Lunn. 'The villain has us by the throat.'

'I fancy that we have loosened his grip slightly.'

'Is there any hope of catching him?'

'Every hope,' said Christopher, 'especially if you lend your assistance.'

'What can I do?'

'Tell us more about your friendship with Gabriel Cheever. Why did he turn his back on everybody? Why did he renounce the life that he was living? You must have some idea, Mr Lunn,' he suggested. 'What prompted this repentance of his?'

Arriving back in Knightrider Street, Susan Cheever was surprised to learn that Lucy had been out for a walk. Wherever she had been, it had given her a lift. Lucy's cheeks had some colour back in them and she seemed more at peace with herself. It was the first time her eyes were not red-rimmed from crying. When they sat down to dine together, Susan was able to have a proper conversation with her.

'Where did you go, Lucy?' she asked.

'For a walk.'

'In which direction?'

'Oh, up towards the ruins of St Paul's. I took no notice of where we were going,' said Lucy. 'I simply went where Anna led me and enjoyed it.'

'The fresh air was obviously good for you.'

'I needed to get out of the house.' She chewed some food and swallowed it before speaking again. 'But what about you, Susan?' she said. 'You told me there was nothing wrong with Mr Redmayne but, in that case, why did he send his servant for you like that?'

'Jacob came of his own volition.'

'Why?'

'He felt that Mr Redmayne might want to talk to me.'

Lucy smiled. 'I might have told you that.'

'Jacob was sent to summon Mr Bale and, being so close to Knightrider Street, came on here to ask for me.'

'Was Mr Redmayne pleased to see you?'

'I think so.'

'And were you glad to see him?'

'Very glad,' confessed Susan. 'But I did not come to London to visit anyone else, Lucy. I'm here at your invitation and you must call on me whenever you wish. It was pleasant to go to Fetter Lane again but I am back now and at your command.'

'I have no commands, Susan.'

'Then I'll just sit with you and offer comfort.'

'Thank you.'

They ate in silence for a while. Susan was desperate to tell her about the attack on Christopher, partly for the pleasure of talking about him again but mainly in order to impress upon Lucy that he was taking perilous risks on her behalf. Christopher had advised against it lest it upset Lucy and the advice had seemed sound at the time. Watching her sister-in-law now, however, Susan wondered if she might broach the topic. If Lucy had recovered enough to venture out for a walk, she could surely cope with some distressing news, especially as it might engage her sympathies. Susan plunged in.

'There was more to it than that, Lucy,' she said.

'To what?'

'My visit this morning. Mr Redmayne has been injured.'

'Injured?' echoed Lucy. 'How badly?'

Susan described the state he was in when she arrived at his house. When she talked about the attack, she mentioned that both Christopher and Jonathan Bale were convinced that the would be killer was the same man who had murdered Gabriel. It opened fresh wounds for Lucy and she began to sob. At first, Susan thought she had made an error of judgement, but her sister-in-law soon recovered and brushed away her tears. She looked at Susan.

'Why is Mr Redmayne doing this for us?' she said.

'He sees it as a kind of mission, Lucy.'

'Even though his own life is in danger?'

'He is a strong man. He fought off the attacker.'

'Gabriel was strong yet he was unable to do that.'

'Perhaps he had more than one man to fight against.' Susan paused before returning to a familiar request. 'It would help so much if we knew where the murder took place,' she said. 'Gabriel was not killed in this house or there would have been signs of disturbance. He was out somewhere.'

'Yes,' murmured Lucy.

'And you know where he was.'

'I might guess.'

'Where was it, Lucy?'

'Do not ask me.'

'But Mr Redmayne needs to know.'

'Gabriel was killed. That is the only fact that matters to me, Susan.'

'But you want his killer caught, surely?'

'Of course.'

'And you want to save Mr Redmayne from further attack?' She leant in closer. 'What will happen if the assassin strikes again, Lucy? Think how guilty you will feel if Mr Redmayne is murdered.'

'It will not be my fault.'

'I know, but you can at least help to reduce the possibility.'

'How?'

'By telling the truth. Not to me,' she added quickly, 'because I can see that I am not the person in whom you will confide. Tell Mr Redmayne. He is such a kind and understanding man. He will respect any confidences. I have not known him long but I have formed the highest opinion of him.'

'So have I,' said Lucy quietly.

'He needs all the help that he can get. Why are you holding back?'

Lucy shrugged helplessly. 'Because I must, Susan.'

Henry Redmayne pounced on his brother like a hawk swooping down on its prey. 'Where have you been, Christopher?' he said, shaking him vigorously.

'Here, there and everywhere.'

'But I needed you beside me.'

'How can I continue the search if I am trapped here?' asked Christopher. 'You must try to shed this anxiety, Henry. Under your own roof, you are completely safe.'

'That is what I thought.'

'What do you mean?'

'I received another letter.'

'A blackmail demand?'

'Of a kind,' groaned Henry. 'But first tell me your news. Did you find the man who printed that extract from the diary?'

'I did. His name is Miles Henshaw.'

'He deserves to be hanged, drawn and quartered.'

'No, Henry. He was simply printing what he was given. Mr Henshaw had no idea what cruel use his work would be put to by the blackmailer. Let me explain.'

Eager to hear his brother's tidings, Christopher gave him only a shortened account of the visits to Elijah Pembridge and to Miles Henshaw. The call on Arthur Lunn was summed up in a few sentences. Henry sank even further into dejection. He had been hoping for results that had simply not materialised. As far as he was concerned, a dangerous killer was still on the loose and he was the man's next target.

'What about you?' said Christopher, ending his narrative. 'Show me this new letter that you received today.'

'Even you will not be allowed to see that.'

'Why not?'

'Because I've already burnt it.'

'Whatever for, Henry?'

'It is the only safe thing to do with that particular correspondence.'

'Who sent it?'

'Amelia.'

'Lady Ulvercombe?'

'Yes. She has only just discovered that my *billet-doux* is missing. Why has it taken her so long? I thought she had destroyed it, as she vowed she would do, but she clung on to it for sentimental reasons. It was, I have to confess, worded in such a way to excite a lady to the very pitch of delight. But does she read it every day to keep the flame of our romance alive? No, no, no! It takes her well over a week to notice that my deathless prose has been stolen. I am desolate, Christopher. Heavens above! It is insulting. A man is entitled to expect a mistress to drool over his correspondence.'

'At least, Lady Ulvercombe has learnt the worst now.'

'Not before time.'

'What did her letter say?'

'She wants to meet me,' said Henry. 'This very afternoon. How can I venture outside that door when an assassin is lying in wait for me? And why, in any case, should I choose to confront the very woman who landed me in this infernal mess?'

'No, Henry,' said Christopher firmly. 'You landed yourself in this mess.'

'Amelia lost the letter.'

'You wrote it.'

'Only because she pestered me.'

'A moment ago, you were boasting about the way you had worded it.'

'Well, yes,' agreed Henry. 'It was a small masterpiece of its kind. But destined for the eyes of one person only before being consigned to the flames.'

'Is Lady Ulvercombe afraid that her husband will find out?'

'She is terrified. He already has suspicions of me. Were that letter to fall into his hands, he would not hesitate to wreak his revenge. Not that Amelia has any concern for me,' he added. 'Her anxiety is for herself.'

'Go on.'

'She insists on meeting me to discuss the matter. Otherwise – and this is the most drastic form of blackmail – she will make a full confession to the egregious Lord Ulvercombe and beg his forgiveness.' He flung his hands in the air. 'Where will that leave me?'

'Reason with her.'

'Desperate women have no truck with reason.'

'Assure her that the letter will be recovered somehow.'

'It may already be on its way to her husband.'

'I doubt that,' said Christopher. 'Once sent, it loses its power to extract money from you. Lady Ulvercombe must be told how it is being used to blackmail you. It could

338

easily be employed against her in the same way.'

'Amelia would panic and throw herself on the mercy of that brutish husband.'

'You must calm the lady down, Henry.'

'How can I when I dare not leave the house?'

'You must.'

'No, Christopher. It is not simply fear that keeps me immured. The truth is that I do not wish to see Amelia again. She unsettles me.'

'But the two of you were so close at one time.'

'Revulsion is the Janus-face of romance.'

'That's not the remark of a gentleman,' said Christopher reproachfully.

'I'm not talking about my revulsion for *her*,' explained Henry. 'For my sins, I still have a vestigial affection. It was Amelia who turned against me. I have no idea why. I was encouraged, favoured then summarily discarded. That does not make a man wish to have a rendezvous with a woman he once adored.'

'If you do not go, Lady Ulvercombe will tell all to her husband.'

'There's the rub.'

Christopher pondered. 'Where does she ask you to meet her?' he said at length.

'At a secret address.'

'Where is it?

'Less than five minutes from here.'

'Would you meet the lady if I were to accompany you there?'

'No. I could not bear the embarrassment.'

'Then I will go in your stead,' decided Christopher.

'You?'

'Give me the address, Henry. The meeting may prove fruitful.'

While the two men talked, neither took their eyes off the printer's shop owned by Miles Henshaw. Hours had passed since Tom Warburton took up his station nearby. Jonathan Bale was having difficulty replacing him.

'There is no point in both of us staying, Tom,' he said.

'I'll linger awhile.'

'Mr Redmayne asked me to relieve you.'

'Why?'

'He felt that you had been here long enough.'

'I have.'

'Then go back home and have some dinner. Come back later.'

'I might miss him.'

'We have no guarantee that he will come today,' said Jonathan, 'though there is one promising sign. The gentleman we visited this morning has been threatened with publication of shameful details about his private life. Not that he had the grace to be ashamed about them,' he added grimly, 'but we'll let that pass. Those details will need to be printed by Mr Henshaw so that they can be used to cause the gentleman further grief. The commission may come today.'

'Then I'll stay.'

'Leave him to me.'

'You may need help, Jonathan.'

'I can manage.'

'We are in this together.'

'True.'

'You, me – and Sam,' said Warburton, fondling his dog. 'He found the body.'

'I have not forgotten that, Tom.'

Jonathan was pleased at the prospect of company during what might prove to be a long vigil but worried that he might not be able to make the arrest himself. The attack on Christopher Redmayne had upset him deeply. Jonathan felt that he had a personal score to settle on behalf of his friend. If the man posing as Gabriel Cheever did arrive at the printer's, he wanted to be the one to confront him. It was a selfish attitude and he chided himself for it but that did not lessen his desire to be instrumental in the arrest. There was, however, another factor to be taken into account. If the man did reappear, he might not be alone. His accomplice might be with him. That could cause a problem even for Jonathan. His colleague's support might be valuable, after all, and it would be very unfair to exclude the dog.

'Thanks, Tom,' he said with feeling. 'Good to have you with me.'

Sam gave a bark of gratitude. He wanted to be involved in any action.

The unheralded arrival of Sir Julius Cheever took both women by surprise. Lucy was quite overwhelmed when he suddenly appeared on her doorstep and she did not know how to react. Susan was dismayed. Much as she loved him, she felt that he had come at an awkward time. During their long conversations, she and Lucy were drawing ever closer. The presence of Sir Julius in such a limited space made any exchange of confidences quite impossible.

'Why have you come, Father?' she asked.

'I felt that I had to, Susan,' he said. 'I cannot mourn my son properly until his killer has been brought to justice. Instead of sitting in Northamptonshire, I ought to be here, helping in the search.'

'It is good to see you again, Sir Julius,' said Lucy.

'My apologies for coming unannounced.'

'They are unnecessary.'

They were in the house in Knightrider Street. Travel had patently tired Sir Julius. He had lost much of his animation. Lucy felt obliged to offer him accommodation.

'You are most welcome to stay here,' she offered.

'No, no, Lucy,' he said, 'I would not dream of it.'

'Anna can soon prepare the other bedchamber.'

'I have already taken a lodging at the King's Head in Holborn. It is close to Mr Redmayne's house in Fetter Lane. I called there first but his servant told me he was out. He also said that Mr Redmayne had been attacked.' He turned to Susan. 'Is this true?'

'Unhappily, it is.'

'Was he injured?'

'Yes, Father,' she said, 'I saw him myself this morning.'

'Tell me what happened.'

Conscious of Lucy's presence, she chose her words carefully, describing the violence of the attack but making no mention of the fact that Christopher had been out with his brother. While she was able to praise Christopher's bravery, she knew that the plight of Henry Redmayne would provoke only disgust in her father. Susan went on to explain that Christopher and Jonathan Bale were continuing their investigations.

'How can I get in touch with them?' said Sir Julius anxiously.

'Mr Redmayne promised to call here if there was any news to report.'

'When did you last see him?'

'A few hours ago.'

'We have already dined, Sir Julius,' said Lucy sweetly, 'but you are welcome to refreshment after your journey.'

'No, thank you,' he said. 'I seem to have lost my appetite lately.'

'So have I.'

'What I would like to do, with your permission, is to stay here awhile.'

'Please do, Sir Julius.'

'Yes,' said Susan without enthusiasm. 'It will give us an opportunity to catch up on your news. Does Brilliana know that you are back in London?'

'No. Nor must she at this stage.'

'Why not?' asked Lucy innocently.

'My elder daughter behaved very badly after the funeral,' said Sir Julius. 'I will not easily forgive her for that. Fortunately, her husband had the sense to take her back to Richmond. I never thought I'd be grateful to Lancelot Serle but I am. He did the right thing. I'm grateful to the fellow and – dare I admit it? – profoundly sorry for him, being married to someone like Brilliana.'

'He was very kind to me,' recalled Lucy.

'Lancelot is a very considerate man,' said Susan.

'That may be,' agreed Sir Julius gruffly, 'but he is still a dolt and best left down in Richmond until this whole business is settled.' He slapped his knee. 'This inaction will be the death of me. I was not meant to sit around and do nothing. I want to join in the hunt. Where is Mr Redmayne? I want the latest news.'

It was the ideal place for a tryst. Situated in a quiet lane not far from Charing Cross, the house was small, neat and indistinguishable from those either side of it. When he first saw the building, Christopher Redmayne felt a slight flush of guilt. Its very anonymity had recommended the house to his brother as a place in which to further his romance with Lady Ulvercombe. Assignations had taken place there over a brief period. Looking at it now, Christopher wondered yet again why Henry permitted himself to get drawn into such entanglements. They invariably ended in sorrow. This particular relationship might have even more serious consequences. Christopher was mildly embarrassed that he was put in the position of trying to rescue his brother from the ire of a cuckolded husband. He was not looking forward to the task but somebody had to take it on.

When he gave his surname at the door, he was admitted at once. It was only when he stood in the hall and removed his hat that the servant was able to take a close look at him. After flinching at the sight of his injured face, the man became suspicious.

'You are not Mr Henry Redmayne, sir,' he said.

'I am his brother, Christopher.'

'Is Lady Ulvercombe expecting you?'

'Tell her that I have come on Henry's behalf.'

The man's eyes clouded with doubt and he disappeared for a long time. Christopher feared that Lady Ulvercombe would refuse to see him and he would be sent ignominiously on his way. It made him even more self-conscious. He glanced at the staircase, wondering how many times his brother had climbed it with his fleeting conquest. When the servant reappeared, he warned Christopher that he would be seen on sufferance. It was evident from his tone that Lady Ulvercombe was very annoyed that Henry had not come in person. Steeling himself, Christopher went into the parlour.

She was standing beside the window that overlooked the garden, choosing a position where the light fell on her to best advantage. Lady Ulvercombe was a tall, stately woman in her thirties who paid meticulous attention to her appearance. She had the kind of glacial beauty that reminded him of Brilliana Cheever but her immaculate attire marked her superior social status. When she turned to Christopher, she wrinkled her nose at the sight of his face.

'I apologise for my appearance, Lady Ulvercombe,' he said politely, 'but I was attacked in the street last night.'

She was unsympathetic. 'Did you bear any resemblance to your brother *before* that incident?' she said. 'I can discern none whatsoever now. Where is he?'

'Unable to come.'

'Does he not understand the importance of the summons?'

'Only too well, Lady Ulvercombe. He was aware that the letter had gone astray.'

'How?'

'Henry is being blackmailed.'

Her poise wavered. 'Somebody has the letter?' she asked. 'That was my fear.'

'It is causing my brother rather more than fear,' said Christopher. 'If you would care to sit down, I will explain. These injuries you see,' he added, indicating his face, 'are a small part of the explanation.'

'Henry should be here to give it in person.'

'Bear with me, Lady Ulvercombe, and you will understand why he is not.'

She regarded him with a blend of interest and unease. His bearing was impressive and his voice persuasive but she was distressed that he knew about an item of intimate correspondence. If his brother had confided in him, then he had to be trustworthy, she hoped, but she would need reassurance on that score. Crossing to a chair, she lowered herself into it and assumed another pose. Christopher had a vision of Henry and his mistress together, preening themselves in front of each other and attaching far more importance to outward show than to any emotional commitment. He took a seat.

'It is a long story, I fear,' he began.

'Must I hear it all?' she sighed.

'It started with a brutal murder, Lady Ulvercombe.'

She jerked backwards in alarm. Having secured her attention, he did not pause. He described the circumstances of Gabriel Cheever's death and, while refraining from giving any names, told her of the people who were being blackmailed by means of extracts from a secret diary. In showing her that the disappearance of her letter was only one detail in a much larger picture, Christopher expected to shake her self-absorption but he was mistaken. All that concerned her was her own situation.

'I have never met this Gabriel Cheever,' she said haughtily. 'Who was he?'

'A friend of my brother's.'

'His death is unfortunate but irrelevant to me.'

'I would dispute that, Lady Ulvercombe.'

'Is there any reference to me in his scandalous diary?'

'Not as far as I know.'

'Then let us forget it, Mr Redmayne,' she insisted, 'and turn our attention to the missing letter. Did Henry give you any indication as to its contents?'

'He did not need to, Lady Ulvercombe,' said Christopher with gallantry. 'I have only to look at you to understand the nature of the communication. Henry was rightly devoted to you.' His flattery drew a thin smile from her. 'The important thing now is to save your reputation.'

'I could not agree more.'

'To do that, I need to ask some personal questions.'

'Not too personal, I trust,' she warned.

'Where was the letter kept, Lady Ulvercombe?'

'I have a small cabinet in my bedchamber.'

'Is the cabinet locked?'

'Most of the time.'

'Did you ever take the missive out to read it through?'

'Really, sir!' she rebuked. 'What a lady does with her keepsakes is her own affair. If your questioning is to take this turn, I'll hear no more of it.'

'I'm sorry, Lady Ulvercombe,' he said. 'I'm simply trying to establish when it went astray. It was well over a week ago that Henry received the blackmail demand. Think back, if you will. Were you absent from the house for any period of time?'

She pondered. 'As a matter of fact, we were.'

'Oh?'

'My husband and I stayed with friends in Sussex.'

'How long were you away?'

'Several days, Mr Redmayne.'

'And when did this visit take place?'

'A fortnight or so ago,' she recalled. 'Are you suggesting that the letter was stolen from the house while we are away?'

'Unless you took it with you, Lady Ulvercombe.'

She flared up. 'You are starting to irritate me again, sir.'

'There are only two possibilities here,' he said. 'The first is that you had it in your possession and mislaid it. That, I know,' he went on swiftly, 'is well nigh impossible as you would never be so careless.'

'Or so foolish.'

'Then we have to accept the second possibility. It was stolen from you.'

'Why?'

'In order to blackmail Henry and embarrass you.'

'But nothing else was taken,' she argued, 'and I have a whole drawer of keepsakes. The house is well guarded while we are away. There were no reports of a burglary when we returned.'

'Then we must look elsewhere, Lady Ulvercombe.'

'Elsewhere?'

'At your servants.'

Her eyes flashed again. 'I refuse even to countenance that suggestion. Each and every one of them is above reproach, Mr Redmayne. They have been with us for years.' She remembered something. 'With one exception, that is.'

'Who might that be?'

'A chambermaid we took on six months ago.'

'I see.'

'But I would exempt her from any suspicion,' said Lady Ulvercombe. 'She came to us with the highest recommendation. The girl was formerly in the employ of one of your brother's friends, as it happens.'

'A friend of Henry's?' said Christopher, his curiosity aroused.

'I mentioned that my steward was looking to engage a new chambermaid.'

'And Henry found one for you?'

'The girl was looking for a new post.'

'Who was this friend of his?'

'Miss Hemmings,' she said. 'Celia Hemmings.'

The afternoon sun beat down on Fleet Lane and made their protracted vigil even more uncomfortable. Both men were sweating profusely. Jonathan Bale was hungry, Tom Warburton was bored and the dog had grown restless. There were several hours to go before the printer's shop closed and they would have to resume their position early next morning if they were to be there when Miles Henshaw opened for business. Warburton was fractious.

'We could be here for days, Jonathan.'

'If that is what it takes, I do not mind waiting.'

'You are not even sure he will come.'

'No, Tom. I am following my instinct.'

'I would rather follow my belly.'

Jonathan smiled. 'So would I, but someone has to keep watch. Leave me here on my own. You and Sam have done your share. The pair of you deserve some solid food.'

'Shall we bring something back for you?'

'No, Tom. But you might give a message to Sarah.'

'Her husband is starving?'

'Just tell her that I may be late back.'

'I will.'

Having elected to go, Warburton nevertheless loitered for a while, torn between a sense of duty and the need to eat. Eventually, he decided to make his move. The dog jumped eagerly to his feet. Before they could leave, however, Jonathan motioned in the direction of the printer's shop. A young man was approaching on a horse. They were too far away to see his face beneath the broad-brimmed hat but they saw how gingerly he carried his right arm. Looped round his neck was the strap of a leather satchel. The man dismounted, tethered his horse, took off the satchel and went into the shop. Neither Warburton nor Sam wanted to go now. They waited as patiently as Jonathan.

A quarter of an hour passed before the customer reappeared. Miles Henshaw came out with him, ostensibly to wave him off but really in order to give a signal to the watching constables. Jonathan anticipated it. Before Warburton could move, Jonathan came out of hiding and strode purposefully towards the shop. Henshaw saw him coming and squandered the element of surprise. When he saw the expression on the printer's face, the customer became suspicious and glanced over his shoulder to see a constable bearing down on him. Pushing the printer away, the man rushed to mount his horse, using his left hand to help himself up into the saddle.

'This is him!' yelled Henshaw.

'Hold there, sir!' cried Jonathan. 'I want a word with you.'

'He brought more pages of the diary.'

The rider kicked his horse forward but Jonathan managed to grab the reins. The animal neighed loudly as it described a rapid circle. Jonathan held on firmly. He looked up at the man and saw the ugly swelling around his nose. Identification was confirmed.

'You are under arrest, sir,' he declared.

'Stand off!' warned the man.

Taking a pistol from his belt, he pointed it at Jonathan, shifting it to cover Warburton as well when the other constable lumbered towards him. Jonathan was uncertain what to do. The man could not shoot both of them. Still holding the reins, he took a step closer, but it brought him within range. The man slipped a foot from his stirrup and kicked out to send Jonathan sprawling. The bridle was now free and escape possible. Pistol in hand, the man urged his horse on with a sharp dig of his heels and it lunged forward. The ride was short-lived. Before it reached the end of the lane, the horse was confronted by a small terrier. Yapping noisily, Sam showed no fear of the flashing hooves. It was the horse that took fright. Sliding to a halt, it reared up so abruptly on its hind legs that its rider was thrown from the saddle, knocking his head on the ground with an audible thud. Warburton did his best to control the horse while Jonathan got up to run across to the fallen man. The rider was unconscious, blood trickling from a gash in his skull to disfigure his face even more.

Having done his work, the dog went off to lift his leg against the wall of a house.

'There,' said Warburton proudly. 'I thought you might need us, Jonathan.'

Christopher Redmayne rode down Knightrider Street at a canter until he reached the house. Before he could even dismount, he was given a welcome. Flinging open the front door, Sir Julius came bursting out to him. His daughter was close behind.

'Where have you been, Mr Redmayne?' said Sir Julius. 'Is there any news?'

'A great deal,' replied Christopher, 'but I did not think to find you back in London, Sir Julius.'

'Father arrived this afternoon,' explained Susan, delighted to see Christopher again and annoyed that her father was monopolsing him. 'Let Mr Redmayne come in, Father. We can hardly talk out here in the street.'

'Why not?' said Sir Julius. 'I've waited long enough. I've been watching through that window for you this past hour or so, Mr Redmayne.' He peered up at him. 'Look at those scratches. You *have* been in the wars, I see. Susan told us how well you fought. You merit our congratulations.'

'It is Mr Bale who has earned the congratulations.'

'How?'

'The news from him is good,' said Christopher, dismounting to tether his horse. 'But there is so much of it to tell that it might be better if we were all sitting down.'

Susan led the way into the house and, once she had recovered from the shock of seeing his lacerations, Lucy added her own welcome. Christopher had hoped to speak to Susan alone first in order to savour the joy of her response, but he had to settle for a general announcement. His face lit up with a smile.

'We have caught him,' he said.

Sir Julius let out a yell of triumph, Susan felt a surge of relief and Lucy was so overcome that she burst into tears. Christopher waited until she had recovered enough to let him go on. Sir Julius was impatient.

'Who is the rogue?' he asked.

'He will not give his name, Sir Julius.'

'But you have him in custody?'

'Mr Bale is with him now,' said Christopher, 'though he denies any claim to heroism during the actual arrest. He gives the credit to Sam.'

'Sam?' repeated Susan.

'A dog belonging to Mr Warburton, another constable. I suppose it was only fitting that Sam should help to catch the killer,' he decided. 'It was he who found Gabriel's body on Paul's Wharf that night.'

'Tell us about the arrest,' urged Sir Julius.

'I can only give you Mr Bale's account. I have just left him.'

Christopher did not mention that he had first visited his brother, interviewed Henry's former mistress, repaired

353

to Bedford Street again to confirm what Lady Ulvercombe had told him about her chambermaid then called in at his own house. Jacob had passed on the urgent message left there by Jonathan Bale. Christopher had ridden hard to the gaol to see the captive for himself. Without even referring to the diary, he gave his listeners an account of how a trap had been set outside a printer's shop in Fleet Lane. Two constables and a dog had caught the man who murdered Gabriel Cheever. The prisoner was also responsible for the attack on Christopher and was unrepentant about it when his victim confronted him.

'He admits the attack, then?' said Sir Julius.

'He almost gloried in it.'

'Wait until I get my hands on the villain!'

'Let the law take its course, Sir Julius.'

'I'll tear him limb from limb.'

'I think it best if you keep away from him until the trial,' said Christopher. 'Mr Bale is with him now, trying to get more information out of him. But he'll yield up neither his name, his address nor the identities of his accomplices.'

'How many of them were there?' asked Susan.

'Two at least.'

'Oh,' she said with disappointment. 'So it is not all over yet?'

'Not yet, Miss Cheever, but our main task has been accomplished. The killer is behind bars. He was the most dangerous of them. It is only a matter of time before we track down the others,' he said confidently. 'We are all but there.'

'You and Mr Bale have done wonders.'

'Yes,' agreed Sir Julius. 'I'd like to meet this brave constable of yours.'

'You may already have done so, Sir Julius.'

'Oh?'

'Mr Bale would never tell me this himself,' said Christopher, 'but his wife has confided in me that her husband bore arms at the Battle of Worcester.'

Sir Julius was cautious. 'On which side?'

'The winning side.'

'Then I insist on meeting the fellow!'

'He was very young at the time, Sir Julius, but he's a born fighter. I've learnt that on more than one occasion. You might wish to meet Mr Warburton as well. He assisted in the arrest.'

'I would like to meet the dog,' said Lucy quietly.

'You will meet them all in time,' said Christopher.

'What about the accomplices?' asked Lucy. 'Do you have any idea who they are?'

'I believe that I know the name of one of them.'

'Tell me who he is,' demanded Sir Julius, 'and I'll help in the arrest myself.'

'More evidence is needed before we can move to that stage, Sir Julius. As it happens I will need some help in obtaining it.'

'Count on me, Mr Redmayne.'

'Actually, I was hoping that your daughter might be able to assist.'

'Me?' said Susan in astonishment.

'Yes, Miss Cheever.'

'What can Susan do?' said Sir Julius with mild scorn.

'Make use of my experience here. I am skilled in the art of interrogation. Tell me who the man is and I promise to get the truth out of him in no time at all.'

'I still think that your daughter would be more suitable.'

'Why?' asked Susan.

Sir Julius was hurt. 'Are you spurning my offer?'

'I have to,' said Christopher. 'The suspect I have in mind is a woman.'

Celia Hemmings was scolding her dressmaker when the letter arrived at her house in Covent Garden. Having paid so much for it, she expected every detail to be exactly as she had prescribed, but her new dress fell short of perfection in several ways. With a final burst of vituperation, she packed the dressmaker off to make the necessary alterations before she snatched the letter from her servant's hands and gave it a casual glance. It was only when she returned to her bedchamber that she thought to open it. The letter was short, polite and written in the most elegant hand. What made her blink was the name of the sender. Celia read the letter through once more.

'Susan Cheever?' she said to herself. 'Why does she wish to meet *me*?'

The prison cell was small, dark and fetid. The hot weather served to intensify the stink. Manacled to an iron ring in the wall, the man crouched in the corner. He was wearing only shirt, breeches and shoes now. When Christopher arrived, Jonathan Bale was still trying without success to elicit the truth from the prisoner. It was arduous work.

'What has he told you?' asked Christopher.

'Nothing at all, Mr Redmayne.'

'Were there no clues on him as to his identity?'

'None,' said Jonathan. 'All that he was carrying when he went into the printer's shop was a leather satchel. It contained two more extracts from the diary.'

Christopher turned to the man. 'Where is the rest of the diary?' he said.

'Search for it up my arse!' sneered the other, offering his buttocks.

'Show some respect!' ordered Jonathan.

'I respect nobody.'

'You'll respect the hangman, I dare say,' observed Christopher. The man spat into the filthy straw that covered the floor and glared at him with open defiance. Christopher was interested to take a longer look at him. The prisoner was exactly as Henshaw had described him. He was young, dark, brawny and, until his nose had been broken, passably handsome. His manner was uncouth. Even though he was chained to the wall, he still possessed an air of menace. There was great strength in the broad shoulders and long arms. Having fought with the man himself, Christopher could see how Gabriel Cheever had been overpowered by him.

'Someone helped you to kill Gabriel,' he said.

'Did they?' replied the man with mock surprise.

'Who was he?'

'I've been asking him that repeatedly,' said Jonathan.

'You strangled him,' said Christopher, moving close to the man, 'but someone else ran him through with a sword. Is that right? Were there two of you?'

The man gave a broad grin. 'I like to kill on my own.'

'Those days are over,' said Jonathan.

'Not if one of you comes close enough.'

'Watch him, Mr Redmayne.'

'Oh, I'm safe enough,' said Christopher, only a foot away from the prisoner. 'He never attacks from the front, do you, my friend? That would be a fair fight. He prefers to sneak up on someone in the dark and take him unawares.'

'Only cowards do that,' remarked Jonathan.

'I'm no coward!' asserted the man.

'Yes, you are.'

'I agree, Mr Bale,' said Christopher, trying to provoke the man. 'That's the reason he'll not name his accomplices. He's afraid of them. He's a coward.'

'No!' yelled the prisoner. 'What I did takes nerve.'

'What you did was pure wickedness,' said Jonathan with contempt, 'and you'll pay for it on the scaffold with your accomplices alongside you.'

'There was nobody else.'

'Yes, there was.'

'Somebody set you on,' said Christopher. 'You may be clever enough to kill someone who is not looking but all that you are fit for, apart from that, is to fetch and carry. They *used* you, my friend. They made you do all the work while they sat back and give orders. And where has it got you? Chained to a wall in this sewer.'

'With two rats like you for company,' retorted the man.

'Guard your tongue!' warned Jonathan, moving in.

'Who's the coward now?' jeered the other. 'You'd only dare to take me on when I've got these manacles on my wrists. Set me free and we'll see who is the strongest.'

'I wish I was allowed to do just that.'

'Ignore him, Mr Bale,' advised Christopher. 'He is baiting you. Let's leave him to lie in his own ordure for a night or two. He might be more amenable to persuasion by then. We'll get nothing more out of the rogue today.'

They went out of the cell and Jonathan turned to close the door.

'Wait!' begged the man, weakening at last. 'I'll strike a bargain with you.'

'What sort of bargain?' said Jonathan.

'Do you have any influence with the gaoler?'

'I might have.'

'Get him to bring me some decent food.'

'In my opinion, you've no right to eat anything at all.'

'Hear him out, Mr Bale,' suggested Christopher. 'Supposing we could arrange some better food for you,' he said to the prisoner, 'what would you tell us?'

'The name you want.'

'Is he the man who is behind the blackmail demands?'

'Yes,' said the other, lowering his head.

'Who is he?'

'Promise you'll get me the food first.'

'Mr Bale will do what he can.'

'I need more than that. Give me a firm promise.'

'Very well,' said Jonathan. 'I'll speak to a friend here. I give you my word.'

'Now tell us the name,' said Christopher.

'I will,' consented the other solemnly.

'Well?'

'Sir Julius Cheever!'

The man went off into a peal of derisive laughter. Annoyed that they had been taken in by the deception, Jonathan slammed the door shut and locked it. They could still hear the wild laughter as they left the building.

CHAPTER FOURTEEN

Jonathan Bale guessed at once who the visitor might be. When he opened his front door, he was suddenly facing the commanding figure of Sir Julius Cheever, stern, watchful and full of purpose. Though Jonathan had only seen Gabriel Cheever's face on a slab at the mortuary, he discerned a clear resemblance between father and son.

'Mr Bale?' asked Sir Julius.

'Yes, sir.'

'My name is Sir Julius Cheever.'

'I know that,' said Jonathan respectfully.

'Then you will understand why I want to shake your hand,' said Sir Julius, offering a firm grip and pumping his arm. 'We owe you a great debt, Mr Bale.'

'It was not all my doing, Sir Julius.'

'Come now.' He released his hand. 'Let us have no false modesty here. Mr Redmayne has told us how you were instrumental in the arrest of the villain and you have been a model of fortitude throughout the investigation.'

'Tom Warburton must take some credit,' said Jonathan.

'So I am told.'

'He's my fellow constable.'

'With a rather special dog, I gather.'

Jonathan gave a smile. 'Sam is worth his weight in gold.'

He was astounded to see Sir Julius on his doorstep. Christopher Redmayne had told him of the old man's return to London but Jonathan had never expected to meet him properly, let alone be sought out for congratulation. Simultaneously embarrassed and flattered that Sir Julius had walked the short distance from Knightrider Street to the house in Addle Hill to meet him, he was lost for words. Sir Julius was studying him carefully.

'You did well, Mr Bale.'

'Thank you, Sir Julius.'

'I'm a generous man. You'll be rewarded.'

'Arresting the killer was the only reward I wanted,' said Jonathan quickly. 'I never accept money. All I did was my duty as a constable. I helped to wipe an ugly stain off the face of my ward and that gives me great satisfaction.'

'So it should.'

'There are accomplices still to be tracked down.'

'You caught the villain who murdered my son,' said Sir Julius seriously, 'and that is the main thing. Mr Redmayne tells me that he is proving stubborn.'

'At the moment.'

'Let me have access to him.'

'That will not be possible, Sir Julius.'

'But I am Gabriel's father.'

'It might distress you too much to meet the man,' said Jonathan. 'He has a vile tongue and is quite unrepentant about his crime.'

'I'll make the devil repent soon enough!'

'No, Sir Julius.'

'Give me five minutes alone with him, that's all I ask.'

'It would not be up to me to sanction that.'

'Then take me to someone who can.'

'I'm sorry, Sir Julius,' said Jonathan. 'There are strict rules. Access to prisoners is controlled, especially when they are dangerous felons like this man.'

'He'll find out what danger means if I get my hands on him!' vowed Sir Julius.

'Leave him to us.'

'But you have got nothing out of him so far.'

'We will, Sir Julius. In time.'

The old man was frustrated. 'Is there *no* way that I can get to see the prisoner?'

'None, I fear.'

'Even if I make it worth the sergeant's while?'

'He is not supposed to accept any bribes.'

'Prisons are run on bribery, man,' said Sir Julius irritably, 'we all know that. The more the wretches can pay, the better their accommodation in those foul places. Introduce me to the prison sergeant. I'll soon buy my way into the cell with that killer.'

Jonathan stood firm. 'It will not be allowed, Sir Julius. I understand your anger at the man but justice must be allowed to take its course. We'll get the truth out of him soon.'

Sir Julius gave up. Having failed to persuade Christopher to take him along to the prison, he had thought that he would have more chance with a humble constable, but he was mistaken. Jonathan was even more resistant to his offer. Sir Julius heaved a sigh then looked over his shoulder.

'They have packed me off, Mr Bale.'

'Packed you off?'

'In the politest way,' said Sir Julius with a fond smile. 'My daughter, Susan, wanted me out of the house so that she could talk alone with Mr Redmayne. There is a possibility, it seems, that he may be able to win the confidence of my daughter-in-law, who could have useful information that is being held back.'

'So Mr Redmayne told me.'

Sir Julius brightened. 'What he told me is that you fought at Worcester.'

'Yes,' said Jonathan quietly, 'but I was very young at the time.'

'War seasons a man. What are your memories of the battle?'

'I try to put them out of my mind, Sir Julius.'

'Why?'

'Those days are long gone.'

'Yet you keep them alive in the names of your sons, I gather.'

Jonathan was unsettled. 'Mr Redmayne had no call to mention that fact.'

'He had every call. I wanted to know as much about you as possible. You have done my family an immense favour. You caught my son's killer.'

'With help from others.'

'Yes, yes, of course. I accept that. But it troubles me that you turn your back on a time when you bore arms in a noble cause.'

'It may be more sensible to forget it, Sir Julius.'

'Nonsense, Mr Bale!' said the other. 'You should treasure those memories, especially now when we are afflicted with this prancing lecher of a King and his corrupt court. Remember a time when virtue was triumphant and the nation was cleansed. Well,' he said briskly. 'Will you not invite me in?'

'Into my house?' said Jonathan, rather flustered.

'Do you have any objection?'

'No, no, Sir Julius.'

'Then stand aside, man. I do not wish to converse on the doorstep like an old woman passing on gossip. Let's sit down together,' he said, stepping into the house as Jonathan made way for him. 'We have much to discuss.'

Alone with her at last, Christopher Redmayne was able to look at her properly for the first time since he had returned to the house in Knightrider Street. Susan Cheever had changed. The news that her brother's killer had been apprehended had brought the most enormous joy and relief. It showed in her face, her movements and her manner. She and Christopher were sitting in the parlour while Lucy was in her bedchamber. Though they were talking about a serious matter, their eyes carried on a more light-hearted dialogue.

'I do admire how you did it, Miss Cheever,' he said.

'Did what?'

'Eased your father out of the house. You managed Sir Julius superbly.'

'Father was in the way.'

'He realised that eventually.'

'Only after I had dropped enough hints, Mr Redmayne. This is the perfect time to draw Lucy out. She is thrilled that Gabriel's killer has been caught, and overcome with gratitude. If the two of you can be left alone for a little while,' she said softly, 'I'm sure that you could find out what you need to know.'

'I hope so. The man himself will tell us nothing. He is positively defiant. We need every bit of help we can get to track down his accomplices.'

'Lucy may provide some of that help.'

'In what way?' he asked. 'Has she given you any inkling at all?'

'Not really. She grows fearful when I touch on the subject. For some reason, she will not confide in me. You may have more luck.'

'I will certainly try.' He glanced upward. 'How long will she be?'

'Not long.'

'Did she retire in order to sleep?'

'No, Mr Redmayne,' said Susan. 'Lucy wanted to be alone with her thoughts. That is only natural. But she was also keen to give us some time together.'

Christopher grinned. 'That was very obliging of her.'

'She knew that we would have a lot to talk about.'

'We certainly do.' The intensity in his voice made her smile. 'It is a great pity that you may have to return to Northamptonshire.'

'I am very reluctant to do so,' she admitted.

'You could be so helpful to me here.'

'Helpful?'

'Yes, Miss Cheever,' he explained. 'Once the accomplices have been caught, my work is over and I can turn to the project that brought us together in the first place. Sir Julius will want to keep me under scrutiny while his new house is being built. He will watch over my shoulder and that could be uncomfortable. I lack your skill in handling him,' he finished. 'Your presence would be invaluable.'

'Is that all I am?' she teased. 'Someone who knows how to control Father?'

'Oh, no, you are much more than that to me!'

The ardour of his declaration surprised both of them and they were at first perplexed. Christopher reminded himself that Susan was still in mourning and any display of emotion on his part was untimely. On her side, Susan was very pleased but equally confused, basking in the warmth of his affection but wondering whether or not she should encourage it at such an unpropitious time. Uncertain how to proceed, they abandoned the conversation by tacit consent and simply gazed at each other in silence. Their pleasure was foreshortened. The sound of footsteps on the stairs told them that Lucy was coming. Their expressions became more solemn.

'Oh!' said Lucy entering the room. 'Am I interrupting something?'

'Not at all,' said Christopher, getting up to welcome her. 'You could never interrupt anyone in your own house, Mrs Cheever. We are the guests, not you.'

Lucy sat down and indicated that he should follow suit. Susan's hopes were raised. Her sister-in-law was calm and poised. After a period of reflection, she might have decided to speak more openly about certain matters. The important thing was to leave her alone with Christopher. Susan bided her time.

'I cannot thank you enough, Mr Redmayne,' said Lucy.

'Wait until the whole business is over before you thank anyone,' said Christopher. 'We caught the most vicious of them but others are still at large, including the man who set up the murder. I want to find out *why* your husband was killed.'

'So do I.'

'And where,' he stressed.

'Yes,' she murmured, tossing a glance at Susan.

'Do you have any idea, Mrs Cheever?'

Lucy lowered her head and gazed at the floor. There was a long pause. Susan took the opportunity to make an excuse and withdraw to the next room, closing the door firmly behind her. Christopher knew that he might never again get such a good chance of winning Lucy's confidence. He tried to be as gentle as he could.

'Mrs Cheever,' he began, 'I think I know why you are holding back.'

'Do you?' she said, looking up at him with alarm.

'Let me say at once that I respect your rights of conscience.'

'Not everyone takes that view, alas.'

'I do,' he assured her. 'I admire anybody who is true to her beliefs.'

'Even if those beliefs are forbidden?'

'Especially then.'

Lucy was uneasy. 'When did you guess, Mr Redmayne?'

'When Mr Bale spoke to one of your neighbours. She told him how devout you and your husband were. I remembered seeing the crucifix on the wall.'

'There is no harm in that,' she said defensively.

'As far as I am concerned, there is no harm in anything you do, Mrs Cheever. Though I do appreciate your desire to keep it from the rest of the family. Your sister-in-law would be very understanding,' he said, looking towards the dining room, 'but I could not promise the same of Sir Julius or of his elder daughter. It should be kept from them.'

'That is why we were so secretive.'

'Did your husband embrace the Old Religion as well?'

'Gabriel was taking instruction.'

'A case of true repentance, then.'

'Very much so, Mr Redmayne,' she said softly. 'I was brought up in the Roman Catholic religion. My parents were devout, my uncle was a Jesuit priest who had to flee abroad. These are dangerous times for people like myself. The King has a Catholic wife yet we are still cruelly persecuted.'

'How did your husband come to share you views?'

'It was a slow process. At first, Gabriel was very cynical about religion in general. His faith had never helped him, he said. But he came to see just how important it is to have a spiritual side to your life.'

'Apart from anything else, it was the only way that he could be close to you.'

'Yes, Mr Redmayne.'

'Love came first and commitment followed.'

'Only after long arguments.'

'You must have been a powerful advocate.'

'No,' she said. 'I was simply someone who believed so strongly in my faith that I would not compromise it to be with the man I loved.' A painful memory made her wince. 'And yet I did compromise. I've been tormented by guilt ever since.'

'Guilt?'

'I was forced to make a choice, Mr Redmayne.'

'Between what?'

'Gabriel and my family.'

'Was there no possibility of reconciling the two?'

'None whatsoever,' she explained. 'Mother could never have accepted a man with Gabriel's past. She would have forbidden the marriage just as forcefully as Sir Julius would have done, had he known about it.'

'Who performed the ceremony?'

There was another pause. 'Someone we could trust.'

'In other words, a Catholic priest.'

'I would never marry under any other conditions,' she affirmed. 'Gabriel knew that and he accepted it. Eventually, that is.'

'Those long arguments must have been quite acrimonious at times.'

'They were punishing for both of us.'

'But you achieved harmony in the end.'

'Yes,' said Lucy, her features lighting up for an instant. 'When we were together we were so happy. Gabriel told me that I had saved his life.' Her face clouded. 'Yet, in another sense, I was responsible for his death.'

'That is absurd,' he told her.

'If he had not met me, he would still be alive.'

'Not necessarily.'

'He only turned his back on his friends because of me,' she argued. 'In that world, he was safe, popular and successful. Gabriel had a name.'

'But not one of which he could be altogether proud,' said Christopher. 'His was an ugly world, Mrs Cheever, full of cruelty, deception and licentiousness. I know, believe me. I've had to wade through that swamp myself. What you did,' he went on, 'was to take him away from it all. You not only gave him a new life, you saved his soul.'

Tears welled up in her eyes. 'That's what I try to tell myself, Mr Redmayne.'

'It's the truth.'

'Thank you.'

'Where was he on the night of his murder?'

'I am not sure,' she said, biting her lip. 'I know where he was supposed to be.'

'And where was that?'

Lucy hesitated. 'I cannot give you a name.'

'I accept that.'

'If it were known that he was living there, it could be fatal for him.'

'Nobody will be told a thing, Mrs Cheever. On my word of honour.'

'What about Mr Bale?' she asked suspiciously. 'He is bound to ask why you are going there. Mr Bale is a good man but he is no friend to the Old Religion. His duty is to suppress it. What will you tell him?'

Christopher was explicit. 'No more than he needs to know.'

Lucy closed her eyes and-agonised for minutes before making a decision. 'Gabriel was going to take instruction that night,' she said at length. 'It was somewhere in Warwick Lane.'

'Warwick Lane?'

'Near the junction of Newgate Street. Do not ask me to tell you which house,' she said forlornly, 'because I have sworn never to divulge its exact whereabouts. But that is where Gabriel would have been, Mr Redmayne. My husband may well have been murdered somewhere in that vicinity.'

'Thank you,' he said with feeling. 'We will go there at once.'

'You will search for him, will you?'

'No, Mrs Cheever. All that we will hunt for are some stones.'

'Stones?'

'Yes, Mr Bale tells me there were some small stones caught up in Gabriel's coat. He's kept them as evidence. If we can find out where they came from, we'll know where he was struck down.'

'I see.'

'At least we now have some idea where to look,' he said, getting up.

She held his arm. 'As for the other things I told you...'

'Nobody will ever know anything about them from me.'

'Thank you.'

'But what about your mother?' he said. 'Will you tell her the truth now?' She shook her head. 'It might be a way to bring you closer together.'

'Mother is too ill to cope with terrible news. If she heard that I had betrayed her by going behind her back, she would never forgive me. She might even say that Gabriel's death was a judgement on me. In a way,' she confessed, 'I suppose it is.'

'No, Mrs Cheever. Your were unlucky, that's all. It was a quirk of fate.'

'Catch them, Mr Redmayne,' she urged. 'Catch them all.'

'We will.'

After giving her more assurances, he went into the dining room to tell Susan that he was leaving. Sorry to see him go, she could tell from his expression that Lucy had confided in him. When she accompanied him to the door to wave him off, something was troubling her.

'Mr Redmayne?'

'Yes?'

'Earlier today, you dictated a letter for me to write.'

'Yes – to Miss Celia Hemmings.'

'Why did you ask me to send it?'

'There's a simple answer to that.'

'Is there?'

'Yes,' he said with a grin. 'I want to read her reply.'

Celia Hemmings took time to make up her mind. She was tempted to accept the invitation, if only to gain more insight into the family from which Gabriel Cheever sprang. But she could see the perils implicit in the situation as well. A meeting with a bereaved sister could be embarrassing for both of them. After mulling it over, she came round to the view that nothing was to be gained by a meeting with a woman she did not know and had no desire to befriend. Reaching for a sheet of paper, she dashed off a quick note.

Five minutes later, it was being carried towards Knightrider Street.

'Why are we going to Warwick Lane?' asked Jonathan Bale, walking beside him.

'That's where Gabriel went on the night of the murder,' said Christopher.

'Why?'

'To see a friend.'

'Is that what his wife told you?'

'Yes, Mr Bale.'

'Why had she kept the information back until now?'

'Who knows?' said Christopher evasively. 'Bereavement has strange effects.'

They turned into Creed Lane and headed north, wondering if they were following the route that Gabriel Cheever had taken on the night he was murdered.

'Warwick Lane is not far,' noted Jonathan. 'It's in Faringdon Ward Within. Not an impossible distance from Paul's Wharf. They might have killed him there and brought his body to Baynard's Castle Ward.'

'That's only supposition.'

'I agree.'

'He could have been brought to the wharf by boat.'

'That, too, is possible. I just have the feeling that the murder did not occur in my ward. If I could prove that,' he confessed, 'it would make me feel better.'

Christopher smiled. 'To prove that your ward was innocent?'

'Oh, there's nothing innocent about it, Mr Redmayne. You should walk through its streets at night. All sorts of crimes take place there under the cover of darkness.'

'I dare say.'

'We have our share of murders, alas.'

'It was how we first met, Mr Bale. When one of my clients was killed.'

'I am not likely to forget.'

'Nor me,' said Christopher. 'It was my first commission. I spent all that time working on the drawings but the house was never built. At least, this latest commission will not be abandoned because of a murder,' he went on happily. 'Sir Julius insists that he still wants his new house.'

'Yes, Mr Redmayne, he mentioned that to me.'

Christopher was surprised. 'You've met Sir Julius?'

'He called on me earlier,' said Jonathan. 'When you came to fetch me, Sir Julius had only just left. He wanted to thank me for my part in the arrest.'

'Quite rightly.'

'Then he more or less ordered me to invite him in.'

'That sounds like Sir Julius Cheever.'

'We talked for a long time.'

'I knew that the two of you would get on.'

'You should not have told him about the Battle of Worcester,' said Jonathan, turning to him. 'It's something I never speak about.'

'Why not? Are you ashamed of your part in it?'

'Quite the opposite.'

'Then you must have enjoyed meeting one of your colonels in that battle.'

'I did, Mr Redmayne. Sir Julius is an interesting man.'

'And an unpredictable one.'

They crossed Ludgate Street and continued along Ave Maria Lane. Though they were chatting easily, both of them kept their eyes peeled for any lanes or alleys that might have been used in the ambush of Gabriel Cheever. At the next junction, they crossed into Warwick Lane itself and carried on until they almost got to Newgate Street. Jonathan spotted an alleyway to the left and decided to explore it, studying the ground with care as he did so. Unable to find what he was after, he gave up the search and went back to Warwick Lane to discover that Christopher had vanished. Assuming that his friend had turned into Newgate Street, he walked in that direction but a call brought him to an abrupt halt.

'Mr Bale!' shouted Christopher.

'Where are you?' asking Jonathan, looking around.

'Down here!'

Another narrow alleyway ran off to the left and bent sharply. Christopher's voice was coming from round the corner. Jonathan lengthened his stride and went down the alleyway. When he came round the bend, he saw that his friend was kneeling down.

'Take a look at these, Mr Bale,' said Christopher.

'Stones?'

'Hundreds of them.'

Jonathan joined him and bent down to scoop up a handful of small white stones. Holding them on the palm of one hand, he used the other to reach in his pocket. When he brought out the stones that had been caught up in the dead man's coat, he placed them beside the others. Christopher scrutinised them.

'A perfect match!' he observed.

'I've never seen stones like this anywhere in my ward,' said Jonathan, feeling their texture. 'They're like chippings from a statue. There must be a stonemason nearby.'

'Then he deserves our thanks,' said Christopher with a grin. 'I think we may have stumbled on the scene of the crime, Mr Bale. And all because you kept a few stones in your pocket.'

Jonathan looked around. A number of houses backed on to the alleyway. Some had doors to their gardens. Even in daylight, it was a fairly private place. At night, it would make an ideal venue in which someone could lurk.

'Who was this friend that Mr Cheever was visiting?' wondered Jonathan.

'His wife refused to tell me.'

'Her husband was killed here. I'm certain of it. They must have taken him to Paul's Wharf across the back of a horse.' He scratched his head. 'Why kill him when they could have stolen the diary while he was out of the house? And if they did have reason to murder Gabriel Cheever, why move him? Why not leave the body here?'

'They had to go to his house, remember,' said Christopher.

'My guess is that they were fearful of being discovered so they threw his body across a horse, took Gabriel with them, used his key to steal what they wanted then went down to the river to find a hiding place for the corpse.'

'Paul's Wharf. They dumped the body beside the warehouse,' recalled Jonathan. 'It had far less chance of being discovered there than in this alley.'

'They reckoned without Mr Warburton's dog.'

Jonathan tossed all the stones away. 'We need to search for witnesses,' he said. 'It may just be that someone heard or saw something suspicious that night. I'll start with the houses that back on to the alley.'

'You'll have to do that on your own, I fear,' said Christopher.

'It's not my job, Mr Redmayne. I want to help you to hunt down those accomplices. I know two of the constables in this ward. They can knock on doors in my stead. I'll go and speak to them. But thank you for bringing me here,' he said solemnly. 'Now we know where he was killed. That's put my mind at rest.'

'Good. I'll get back to Knightrider Street to continue the search.'

'For what?'

'Somebody with neat handwriting, Mr Bale.'

'Stay as long as you wish, Sir Julius,' said Lucy Cheever. 'You're very welcome.'

'I'll inconvenience you no longer than is necessary,' he said. 'But I would like to wait until Mr Redmayne gets back. Where has he gone, Susan?'

'For a walk with Mr Bale,' said his daughter.

'I met the worthy constable when you turned me out into the street.'

'I did *not* turn you out, Father.'

He gave a chuckle. 'You told me how close Mr Bale lived because you knew that I'd want to speak to the fellow. We had a long talk. Did you know he was a shipwright?'

'No,' she said.

'He spoke very highly of Mr Redmayne.'

'I can understand that.'

'So can I,' said Lucy. 'Mr Redmayne has been so good to me. Whenever I look at that face of his, I remember that he got those scars fighting for his life against Gabriel's killer.'

They were in the parlour at the house in Knightrider Street. Sir Julius was anxious for the latest news. One man might be in custody but there were accomplices still at liberty. He was very disappointed not to be able to confront his son's killer. It made him even more eager to take part in the hunt for the others.

'How long will they be?' he said impatiently.

'I have no idea, Father.'

'But they will come back here?'

'Mr Redmayne promised that he would.'

'They have not gone all that far,' volunteered Lucy.

'I wish I'd been here when they left,' said Sir Julius, tapping his foot. 'I could have gone with them. They obviously went in search of more evidence.'

'It might be best if you did not interfere,' suggested his daughter.

'Interfere? It was my son who was murdered, Susan.'

'His killer is now in prison. Thanks to Mr Redmayne and Mr Bale. They can manage very well on their own, Father, without having you under their feet.'

'I'm under nobody's feet.'

'No, Sir Julius,' said Lucy. 'Of course not. But Susan makes a sound point. They have worked so well on their own, it might be easier if they continue that way.'

'What am I supposed to do – sit on my hands and wait?'

'Yes,' said Susan firmly.

'It's foreign to my nature.'

She laughed. 'You need hardly tell me that.'

'I want to be involved in the *action*!' he declared.

Sir Julius pulled himself to his feet and crossed to the window. Susan gestured an apology at Lucy who responded with a tolerant smile. Both women were relieved when he saw something that made him hurry out of the room to open the front door. Hoping that Christopher had returned, Susan went out after him. Lucy waited with trepidation, unsure whether or not Christopher had kept his promise. She had entrusted him with a secret that could be dangerous in the wrong hands. As soon as he came into the room with the others, however, she knew that he had not betrayed her. His greeting was warm, his smile full of gratitude.

'Where have you been?' demanded Sir Julius.

'Father!' scolded Susan. 'Let Mr Redmayne catch his breath.'

'I want to know.'

'We were looking for the scene of the crime, Sir Julius,' said Christopher. 'Acting on information from an anonymous source, we went to Warwick Lane and found what we have been after for some time.'

His version of events was succinct and carefully edited. Lucy was relieved that he made no reference to her, though she was distressed to think that her husband had been murdered in one place then transported through the streets to the wharf. Susan was delighted to have Christopher back in the house and signalled with a glance that she had something for him. Sir Julius kept pressing for details that Christopher did not give.

'Where did this information come from?' he asked.

'That's immaterial,' said Christopher. 'The point is that we now know who killed your son and where the crime occurred. All that is left to establish is motive.'

'How will you do that?'

'By gathering evidence.'

'Let me help you.'

'No, Sir Julius. This is work for Mr Bale and me.'

'Three men are better than two.'

'Not in this case. We know what to look for and where to find it.'

Sir Julius was hurt. 'Am I to be excluded altogether from the hunt?'

'Yes, Father,' said Susan. 'I told you not to impede Mr Redmayne.'

'That's not what he's doing, Miss Cheever,' said Christopher. 'I have great sympathy with your father and I'm grateful for his offer of assistance. But it is not what we need at this point. We have to move stealthily.'

'Is there no role at all for me?' asked Sir Julius.

'Wait until we get back, Sir Julius. Here or at the King's Head.'

'The King's Head it will be,' said the other disconsolately. 'I've no wish to intrude here any longer. Where will you go, Mr Redmayne?'

'I have to see someone in Bedford Street.'

'Another of your anonymous informants?' said Sir Julius sceptically.

'Oh, no. This gentleman is far from anonymous. I wonder if you would excuse us if I ask for a moment alone with your daughter, Sir Julius?' asked Christopher, moving to the door. 'I will not keep her a minute.'

Susan did not wait for her father's permission. She followed Christopher into the hall and closed the door behind them. They spoke in whispers.

'You had a reply?' he said.

'Yes, Mr Redmayne,' she said, handing over the letter that she pulled from her sleeve. 'It arrived just before Father did.'

'What does she say?'

'Miss Hemmings declines my invitation.'

Christopher looked at the distinctive handwriting and felt a surge of triumph. 'It is just as well,' he said. 'For she will be quite unable to meet you now.'

Unaware of developments elsewhere, Henry Redmayne was still suffering the torments of the damned. He writhed in unremitting pain. A blackmail demand had been issued and a death threat made. All that he needed to compound his misery was an unexpected visit from his censorious father. If the Dean of Gloucester were to arrive on the heels of Lord Ulvercombe, he thought, he would at least be on hand to identify his son's dead body. He rebuked himself yet again for his folly in writing so passionately to his mistress. It had earned him a night of ecstasy but the memory of that was of little practical use to him; indeed, he now looked back on it with dread. Lady Ulvercombe had been a spirited lover but an indiscreet one. At least, he consoled himself, he would never have to see her again.

The sound of the doorbell made him jump from his chair in the dining room. When his brother was shown in, he clasped him like a drowning man about to go under the water for the last time.

'Praise God!' he exclaimed with unaccustomed sincerity. 'You're back.'

'And I bring glad tidings, Henry,' said Christopher.

'You found my letter?'

'No, but I've brought one that may turn out to be far more important. The crisis is past,' he announced. 'You can breathe freely again.'

'What do you mean?'

'The killer has been arrested. He's languishing in a prison cell. In addition to that, we've stopped any further extracts from the diary being printed.'

Henry was not reassured. 'How does that help me?'

'The death threat has vanished.'

'Not if my *billet-doux* finds its way to Lord Ulvercombe.'

'I doubt if that will happen, Henry,' said his brother. 'The man who has it will be too busy trying to make his escape when he learns that his accomplice is behind bars.'

'And who is this man?'

'We are still not quite certain,' admitted Christopher.

'Then why come rushing in here to announce a false dawn?'

'Are you not pleased that we have captured a vicious killer?'

'Of course,' said Henry petulantly. 'The only thing that would make me more pleased would be to hear that Lady Ulvercombe was locked up in the same cell with him. I hear no relief in what you tell me. Whoever has that letter holds the whiphand over me.'

'Not for much longer.'

'You do not even know who he is.'

'I'm fairly certain who his accomplice is. Arrest her and we will get to him.'

'Her?' said Henry. 'A woman is involved?'

'That calligraphy was too neat for a man's hand,' explained Christopher. 'When I sniffed the letter sent to Peter Wickens, I caught a faint whiff of perfume.' He clicked his fingers. 'Where are the blackmail demands sent to you, Henry?'

'Why?'

'I need the second one now.'

'I carry both of them with me,' said Henry, rummaging in his pocket. 'As a penance.' He found the letters and handed them over. 'Take them.'

Christopher found the second of the two demands and set it on the table, placing the letter to Susan Cheever beside it. There was no possibility of error. The same hand had written both letters. Over his shoulder, Henry noticed a signature.

'Celia Hemmings!'

'She got hold of your *billet-doux.*'

'How?'

'By accident, probably,' said Christopher. 'Do you remember putting Lady Ulvercombe in touch with her regarding a chambermaid?'

'Vaguely.'

'The girl had worked for Miss Hemmings and her first loyalty was to her. My guess is that she stumbled upon your letter, sensed its potential and gave it to her former mistress. That's putting the kindest construction on it,' he conceded. 'It's just as likely that Miss Hemmings instructed her to look for compromising material. She is clearly well versed in the art of blackmail.'

'I'll throttle her!' yelled Henry.

'You'll do nothing of the kind.'

'Celia Hemmings is a witch!'

'She's a very cunning woman,' said Christopher with a hint of admiration. 'She took me in completely at first. But you can stay here, Henry. Having finally unmasked her, I insist on being the one to confront Miss Hemmings. Jonathan Bale can have the pleasure of making the actual arrest.'

'I want to be there, Christopher!'

'No.'

'I need to repossess that letter before anyone else sees it.'

'I'll take care of all your correspondence,' said Christopher, putting all three letters into his pocket. 'Besides, Miss Hemmings may not have Lady Ulvercombe's letter. It may well be kept by her accomplice. I suggest that you stay here and toast your release. Send for the best wine in your cellar, Henry.'

'I drank it all during my ordeal.'

'Then send out for more. You can afford it now that you will not have to pay five hundred guineas. Enjoy your freedom.'

'What I want to enjoy is the sight of Celia Hemmings being apprehended.'

'Leave that to Mr Bale and me.'

'Why do you need him? Take me instead.'

'He's earned the right, Henry. He's also made a new friend in Sir Julius Cheever.'

'A friend?'

'Yes,' said Christopher, 'they both fought with Cromwell at Worcester. Jonathan Bale has been sharing memories of the battle with him.'

'I hope they remembered that the wrong side won,' said Henry sourly. 'Warn your bellicose constable not to compare memories of that undeserved victory with Arthur Lunn or he may stir up a nest of hornets.'

'Why?'

'Arthur was captured at the battle and imprisoned in Worcester Cathedral. He's still very bitter about it. So is Peter Wickens, I seem to recall. He lost his only brother in that battle. Mr Bale had better not boast about his military record to them.'

'Mr Bale boasts about nothing.'

'You'll not show my letter to *him*,' said Henry with sudden panic.

'No, Henry. He would blush to read it.'

'Let me come with you to make sure.'

'Stay here and celebrate. This is a wonderful moment for you.'

'It is at that,' said his brother as the implications began to sink in. 'I feel that I have been reborn. All that I need is to have Celia Hemmings roasting on a spit and my joy would be complete.' He gave a cackle. 'I have just had a wicked thought. Arthur Lunn was so lucky to have been imprisoned in Worcester Cathedral. Had he been incarcerated in Gloucester, our dear father would have bored him to death with his interminable sermons.'

Jonathan Bale waited at the designated place and hoped that their second visit to Covent Garden would be more profitable than the first. Having set two constables the task of searching for witnesses in Faringdon Ward Within, he had returned to Addle Hill to find that Christopher had left a message for him. Responding to its request, he hurried straight off to Covent Garden and took up his position. The meeting with Sir Julius Cheever had left him feeling oddly satisfied. Though the old man lacked his Puritan restraint, they had much in common. Jonathan had been intrigued to hear how Sir Julius had marshalled his men at Worcester and at some of the battles preceding it. He could understand only too well how a man with such high moral standards would refuse to acknowledge a rakehell like Gabriel Cheever as his son. Jonathan imagined how he would feel if one of his own boys grew up to cast aside every precept he had been taught.

Christopher Redmayne did not keep him waiting for

long. Arriving on his horse, he dismounted to explain to his friend what had happened in his absence. They now had clear proof that Celia Hemmings was involved in the blackmail. When Christopher pointed out her house, Jonathan had some misgivings.

'Let me wait outside,' he said, shifting his feet. 'I am never happy in such places.'

'I was going to suggest that you go round to the back of the house, Mr Bale. We are dealing with a slippery lady. If she tries to bolt, my guess is that it will be through the rear entrance of the house.'

Jonathan gave a grim smile. 'I'll be waiting for her, Mr Redmayne.'

'Do not be too gentle. The lady is an accessary to murder.'

'I've arrested lots of women before. They sometimes fight harder than the men.'

Christopher tethered his horse and gave the constable time to get to the back of the house. When he rang the doorbell and gave his name, he was invited into the hall at once. Hearing of his arrival, Celia Hemmings had him shown in and gave him a cordial welcome until she saw his face. She recoiled slightly at the sight of the cuts and bruises but recovered to offer her hand. Christopher took it with gallantry and brushed her fingers with a kiss.

'This is an unlooked for pleasure, Mr Redmayne,' she said.

'That remains to be seen, Miss Hemmings.'

'What happened to your face?'

'Do you really need to ask that?'

'You look as if you've been in a brawl.'

'I survived.'

'I'm delighted to hear that. What exactly happened?'

'Forget about my injuries,' he said, producing a letter from his pocket and showing it to her. 'I believe that you wrote this. It was sent to Miss Susan Cheever.'

'Yes,' she replied warily. 'She invited me to meet her.'

'No, Miss Hemmings. I dictated that letter to her. Miss Cheever only agreed to write it on the understanding that she would never have to come face to face with you.'

Celia was angered. 'You *dictated* the letter, Mr Redmayne?'

'It was the only way to get a sample of your handwriting,' he explained, taking out another missive. 'I wanted to compare it with the hand on this death threat to my brother. They show a remarkable similarity.'

'A mere coincidence.'

'I think we shall find many more coincidences before we have finished. Like the fact that you once used a strange phrase about Gabriel Cheever to me. You said that his rivals sought to defeat him at the card table, not in a dark alley.' He gave her a smile. 'We found that alley today just off Warwick Lane. How did you know that Gabriel was killed in a place like that?'

'It was just a wild guess.'

'Tell that to the judge.'

'You have no evidence on which to charge me,' she said defiantly.

'We have these two letters and the others you wrote to your victims,' he argued. 'We have the fact that your former

389

chambermaid stole something very compromising from Lady Ulvercombe. And we now know that you went to Gabriel's funeral to gloat.'

'I loved him.'

'Yes, Miss Hemmings. But that love turned sour when he left you.'

'That's not how it happened.'

'I've heard your version,' he reminded her. 'How you bore him no malice when he dropped you like a stone and vanished from sight. That was a blatant lie. In fact, you were furious. I've seen the limits to which that fury pushed you.'

'Have a care, Mr Redmayne,' she warned. 'You're in dangerous waters.'

'They are far less dangerous since my good friend, Mr Bale, took your man-of-war out of the fleet. Do not look for him to come to your aid. Gabriel's killer is locked up safely in prison.'

She leapt to her feet. 'That's impossible!'

'He was taken outside a printer's shop in Fleet Lane. Mr Henshaw kindly pointed him out when he came there earlier today.' A hunted look came in her eyes. 'Who else was in on the conspiracy, Miss Hemmings? Who wrote the first letter to my brother, and the one to Arthur Lunn?'

'Nobody.'

'There must have been.'

'No, Mr Redmayne.'

'I've *seen* that foul-mouthed rogue you employed to do your killing,' he said. 'I even fought him in the dark. You and he are scarcely natural bedfellows. There has to be someone else with the wit to set this whole scheme up. Admit it.'

'I admit nothing.'

'That former chambermaid of yours may be more willing to speak up.'

'Leave Hetty out of this.'

'But she played such a crucial part. Oh, and by the way,' he remembered, 'could I please have my brother's letter back? It has caused more than enough anguish to Henry.'

'Good!'

'Why did you pick on him? Henry has his vices but he's essentially harmless.'

'Your brother is an idiot.'

'No,' said Christopher defensively. 'He's a flawed man who has occasional moments of idiocy. Just like the rest of us. That includes you, Miss Hemmings. After all, you were idiotic enough to imagine that you could get away with this. Gabriel Cheever was killed to assuage your hatred of him. It's only fitting that it was his sister who helped to expose you.' He put the letters back in his pocket. 'You overreached yourself. You wrote one letter too many.'

'What do you want?' she said icily.

'The name of your accomplice or accomplices.'

'There were none.'

'Why prevaricate? You've been caught in your own trap.'

Thinking hard, she moved in closer. 'Did you come on your own, Mr Redmayne?'

'I did not imagine that I would need an army.'

'Who else knows what you've just told me?'

'That's irrelevant, *I* know, Miss Hemmings.'

'How much would it cost to make you forget it for a while?'

'Are you trying to bribe me?' he said, insulted at the very notion.

'All you have to do is look the other way.'

'No!'

'Not even for a hundred guineas?'

'A thousand guineas would not afflict me with temporary blindness,' he asserted. 'Fetch my brother's unfortunate letter to a certain lady, then I'll take you to be charged.'

Celia sagged and nodded in defeat. 'Very well. Let me call my servant,' she said. 'He knows where I keep everything.' She opened the door. 'David! Come here, please.'

The servant who had let Christopher into the house now reappeared. He was a stolid man in his thirties with dark eyes set into a craggy face. His deferential manner suggested someone who was devoted to his mistress.

'Yes, Miss Hemmings?' he enquired.

Her tone changed. 'Mr Redmayne's behaviour is highly offensive to me,' she said harshly. 'Please show him off the premises.'

'At once.' He turned to Christopher. 'This way, sir.'

'Miss Hemmings and I are leaving together,' said Christopher.

'I think not, sir.'

The servant took a firm grip on his arm to march him out. Explanations were pointless. He would not listen to anything Christopher said. His job was simply to obey orders. Wrenching his arm free, Christopher swung round and saw that Celia had already quit the room by means of another door. When he tried to open it, he found that it was locked. He also had the problem of a strong man grabbing his shoulders from behind. Violent action was required. He had no quarrel with the servant but David was now trying to force him across the room. Christopher resisted, trod hard on the man's toe then pushed him over when he hopped in agony on one foot. Before the servant could recover, Christopher caught him on the jaw with a solid punch and dazed him sufficiently to make good his escape. Dashing into the hall, he went out towards the rear of the house until he found a way into the garden. He ran down the path and let himself out through the door in the garden wall.

Jonathan Bale was waiting for him with a squirming Celia Hemmings in his arms.

Christopher grinned. 'I forgot to mention that Mr Bale was with me,' he said.

Henry Redmayne was a self-appointed angel of mercy. Having been given the wondrous news, he wanted to share it with his fellow victims so that they, too, could celebrate their escape from the horror of blackmail. The home of Arthur Lunn was his first port of call and his friend embraced him warmly when he heard the good tidings. Sir Marcus Kemp was even more relieved, bursting into tears and hugging Henry so tightly that he feared for the safety of his coat buttons. When he rode off to visit Peter Wickens, there was still a damp patch on his shoulder from the unmanly display of weeping. Two victims had been delighted with his news.

Henry expected a similar reception from Peter Wickens. Shown in to see his friend, he struck a pose and beamed inanely.

'How are you, Peter?' he asked.

'Worried,' said Wickens. 'Deeply worried.'

'Have you paid the blackmail demand yet?'

'No, but I intend to do so.'

'There is no need, my friend. I'm here to save you five hundred guineas.'

'How?'

'By giving you the glad tidings that the plot against us has foundered,' said Henry. 'My brother called on me not an hour ago. One of the villains is already in prison and Christopher was on his way with a constable to arrest his accomplice.'

Wickens was taken aback. 'His accomplice?'

'Yes, Peter. Prepare yourself for a shock.'

'Why?'

'It was Celia Hemmings. Actually,' said Henry airily, 'I suspected her all the time. Celia was the only woman who stayed with Gabriel long enough to have access to that diary of this. She knew exactly how profitable it might be.'

'On what evidence was she arrested?' pressed Wickens.

'My brother used a simple ruse. He asked Gabriel's sister to write to Celia and suggest that they met. Celia refused but those few lines that she dashed off in reply sealed her doom. The handwriting matches exactly that on the second letter sent to me.'

'That was clever of your brother.'

'He takes after me.'

'What about this man who was taken?'

'Christopher set a trap for him outside a printer's shop in Fleet Lane,' said Henry. 'When the man turned up to get some more extracts from the diary printed, he was ambushed by two constables.'

'I see,' said Wickens thoughtfully. 'Did the man name his accomplices?'

'No, he was a surly beggar. Christopher could get nothing out of him.'

'Then how did he track down Celia Hemmings?'

'Ask him yourself, Peter. The point is that you, Arthur, Sir Marcus and I have been set free at last. Look more cheerful, man,' he urged. 'Are you not pleased?'

'Delighted,' said Wickens, forcing a smile.

'You see now how wise I was to argue against paying any money to them.'

'I thought that was your brother's counsel.'

'Mine, too,' boasted Henry. 'I held firm against the blackguards. Like you, I did not give them a single penny.' He emitted a high laugh. 'But poor Sir Marcus parted with a thousand guineas. I left him wondering if he would ever get it back.'

Stroking his chin, Wickens moved aside for a moment, deep in meditation. When he turned back to Henry, he manufactured a broad grin and patted his friend on the arm.

'Thank you for telling me, Henry. It was kind of you to come.'

'We must all celebrate tonight with Mrs Curtis and her girls.'

'Yes, yes,' said Wickens without enthusiasm. 'A capital notion.'

'By that time,' said Henry, 'everyone involved in the plot will be locked up behind bars. Christopher will soon get the truth out of Celia Hemmings. I doubt if she'll enjoy the stink of a prison cell. They are not too fastidious in Newgate.'

'Quite so.'

'Sir Julius Cheever was overjoyed when they caught the man who killed Gabriel. Wait until he and his accomplices are hanged,' said Henry. 'I'll wager that Sir Julius will be at the front of the crowd.'

Wickens was interested. 'Is he in London at the moment?'

'Apparently. My brother met him at the house in Knightrider Street where Gabriel used to live with his wife. She'll be relieved by the turn of events as well.'

'Yes, Henry.'

'It's a golden day for all of us.'

'So it seems.'

Henry rubbed his hands. 'Shall we join Arthur and Sir Marcus?'

'You go on ahead,' said Wickens, easing him towards the door. 'I'll join the three of you later. I have some business to attend to first then I'll carouse with you until dawn.'

'We can raise a glass in memory of Gabriel.'

'We will indeed.'

'The repentant rake.'

Celia Hemmings proved to be an unhelpful prisoner. Confronted with irrefutable evidence of her guilt, she responded with angry denials and refused to name any accomplices. Christopher was disappointed. Someone involved in the plot was still at large and he was no nearer identifying that person or, in point of fact, the man who was already in custody. There was one compensation from the visit to Covent Garden. He now had his brother's *billet-doux* in his pocket. Jonathan Bale's presence had deterred the servant from any further heroics on behalf of his mistress and the visitors had been able to enter the house to retrieve Henry's letter. What worried Christopher was that there was no sign of Gabriel's diary. He decided that it must still be in the hands of an unknown accomplice and might yet be a source of danger to those whose misdeeds the nascent author had chronicled in such detail.

While Jonathan took charge of the prisoner, Christopher went back to Knightrider Street to report the latest success. He was in luck. Susan Cheever not only answered the door, she explained that her sister-in-law had retired early to bed. She and Christopher were alone again. Her affection for him was more obvious than ever and his fondness for her kept a permanent smile on his face. Christopher explained how Celia Hemmings had been caught and thanked her for her part in the ruse.

'I did very little,' she said.

'You did a great deal,' he told her. 'You were the one person who could have coaxed a letter out of Miss Hemmings. Had I written to her, she would have suspected a trick. You appeared to hold no threat for her. Your innocence exposed her guilt.'

'What will happen to her, Mr Redmayne?'

'She will stand trial with the others and suffer the same fate.'

Susan gulped. 'A horrible way for a woman to die.'

'Miss Hemmings brought it on herself,' said Christopher with a sigh. 'There was no hint of remorse from her. She despised your brother for the way he cast her aside and vowed to get her revenge. At least, we now have her where she belongs. I must pass on the good news to Sir Julius. Did he go back to Holborn?'

'Yes, Mr Redmayne.'

'Then I had better call on him now,' he said, reluctant to go.

'Will you come back here afterwards?' she asked hopefully.

'Oh, yes. If you wish.'

'I will count the minutes while you are gone.'

It was the closest she had ever come to a declaration and it gave him the confidence to reach out to take her hands. Susan did not resist. Words were abandoned. They stood there for several minutes without moving. Her hands were warm. Her smile of contentment matched his own. It was Susan who broke the spell.

'You may get to Holborn in time to meet Father's other visitor,' she said.

'Other visitor?'

'Yes, Mr Redmayne. He left here not long before you arrived. He said that he was an old friend of Father's and was anxious to meet him again.'

'Did he give his name?'

'Mr Peter Wickens.'

Christopher was startled. 'Peter Wickens came *here*?'

'Do you know the gentleman?'

'Only through my brother,' said Christopher, his mind grappling with the news. 'How on earth did Mr Wickens realise that your father was back in London? And what brought him to this address?' he added. 'Nobody knew that Gabriel lived here.' He took her by the shoulders. 'Did you tell him where Sir Julius was staying?'

'Yes. I saw no harm in it. Mr Wickens was very polite.'

'I know. He has great charm when he wishes to use it.'

'He went straight off to the King's Head.'

'Was he on foot?'

'No, Mr Redmayne. He came on his horse.'

'Then I had better get after him at once,' decided Christopher, moving swiftly to the front door. 'Whatever else he is, Peter Wickens is no old friend of your father's, Miss Cheever. I believe that Sir Julius may be in danger.'

Alone in his room, Sir Julius sat on the edge of the bed, drumming his fingers impatiently on his knee. He was not used to waiting on the actions of others. Throughout his life, he had always taken the initiative and forced himself to the centre of events. His capacity for leadership and for making prompt decisions had helped his military career to take wing. Promotion had come early and he had gone on to distinguish himself repeatedly in the field. Yet he was now forced to sit in a room at the King's Head, isolated from the action, wondering what was going on and obliged to leave everything to others. His son had come back into his life in the most distressing way. As he reflected on their estrangement, he had to admit that Gabriel was not entirely to blame. It was not simply a case of youthful rebellion that took him to London. Had he shown his son more understanding, Sir Julius could have retained the friendship that had been so important to him in earlier days. He could see that he had been too intractable.

A sharp knock on the door got him to his feet. He was cautious.

'Who is it?' he called.

'My name is Peter Wickens,' came the reply. 'Mr Redmayne sent me.'

'You have a message for me?'

'Yes, Sir Julius.'

Unbolting the door, Sir Julius flung it open in the hope of hearing good news. Instead of that, he had a pistol held against his forehead. Wickens pushed him back into the room and closed the door behind him. He guided his captive to a chair. When Sir Julius sat down, Wickens took a step back to appraise him, keeping the pistol aimed at his head. Sir Julius was more curious than afraid.

'Who are you?' he demanded.

'I was a friend of your son, Gabriel,' said Wickens. 'In my view, he was the only good thing to come out of the Cheever family, but we had to kill him none the less.'

Sir Julius was horrified. 'You killed my son?'

'Not exactly but I was there when it happened. Just to make sure that he was dead, I ran him through with my sword.' He gave a mocking smile. 'He died quite peacefully.'

'You devil!' said Sir Julius, trying to get up. When the pistol was placed against his skull again, he lowered himself back into his seat. 'What do you want, Mr Wickens?'

'It's called revenge.'

'Against me?'

'Against you and your family, Sir Julius,' said Wickens,

stepping back again. 'I came to like Gabriel or I would have killed him much sooner. He bore a name that I've been taught to hate. Then he told me how much he loathed the famous Colonel Cheever and I gave him the benefit of the doubt. I spared him until I heard that his father had ambitions to enter Parliament.'

'It's a foregone conclusion.'

'Not any more. I could not have you moving to London and living under my nose. The stench would offend my nostrils.'

'Do you always talk with a pistol in your hand, Mr Wickens?' said Julius, icily calm. 'Put it aside and we can have a proper conversation.'

Wickens gave a sneer. 'You once had a proper conversation with my brother.'

'Did I?'

'His name was Michael Wickens,' said the other. 'Not a name that you would recall, I dare say, because he was only one of many people you killed on the battlefield. Witnesses told me that Michael was shot from close range by a Colonel Cheever. Do you remember the carnage at the Battle of Worcester?'

'That war is over and done with, sir.'

'Not as far as I'm concerned.'

'I fought hard for my side just as your brother must have fought nobly for his.'

'But you are still alive,' said Wickens darkly. 'Michael is not.' He held the pistol within a foot of his captive's head. 'I felt it only right that you should know why I arranged to have your son murdered and why you must follow him to the grave. Say your prayers, Sir Julius. You are going to join your Maker.'

Sir Julius closed his eyes and heard the other's soft laughter. He could not believe that he was being called to account for an unremembered incident in the heat of a battle that took place many years before. Evidently, it was remembered only too well by Peter Wickens.

'You chose an appropriate place, Sir Julius.'

Sir Julius opened his eyes. 'What do you mean?'

'The King's Head. Where better for a traitor who helped to remove a king's head to lose his own life? Farewell, Sir Julius. Go off to join the Lord Protector in Hell.'

He levelled the pistol and took careful aim. Before he could pull the trigger, however, the door burst open and Christopher Redmayne came hurtling into the room. Wickens was momentarily distracted. Seeing his chance, Sir Julius swung an arm to knock the barrel of the pistol away from him and the weapon went off, firing its ball harmlessly into the ceiling. Wickens was enraged. He used the pistol to club Sir Julius, opening a deep gash in his head. Christopher was on him at once, diving recklessly at Wickens and knocking him to the ground. The ride from Knightrider Street had given him time to work out that he would be dealing with the very accomplice whose name Celia Hemmings had refused to divulge. Wickens was ruthless. He would not scruple to kill again. Christopher grabbed the wrist holding the weapon and twisted it sharply until his opponent was forced to leave go. Sir Julius had staggered back to the chair, holding the wound on his head as he tried to stem the blood, unable to do anything but look on.

Wickens was a determined adversary. Deprived of his weapon, he used his hands to punch, push and claw at Christopher. They grappled, rolled, knocked over a low table then struggled fiercely to get the upper hand. Wickens was spurred on by a combination of revenge and sheer fury but Christopher's will was even stronger. Certain members of the Cheever family helped to fuel his resolve. He was fighting on behalf of a young husband who was murdered in a dark alley. He was representing a helpless widow who saw her happiness cruelly snatched away from her. In Sir Julius himself, he was striving to save a man whom he admired and a client whom he needed. But, most of all, he was there to rescue Susan Cheever from further distress. As Wickens sat astride him and got both hands to his neck, Christopher summoned up extra reserves of energy. He pulled the hands away, threw his man off then hurled himself on top of him. Urged on by Sir Julius, he punched until resistance slowly began to fade.

Covered in blood and close to exhaustion, Wickens gave up. Christopher pinned him to the floor. The landlord had been roused by the shot and the commotion. He came bustling into the room to see what was happening, and blinked in amazement at the scene.

'What is going on, sirs?' he asked querulously.

'Summon a constable,' said Christopher.

Henry Redmayne was mortified. It was bad enough to be hauled out of his bed by a visitor at that time of morning. After a night of merriment, he had intended to sleep until dinner. When he heard what Jonathan Bale had to say, his misery was compounded. His cheeks were crimson with embarrassment.

'It was *my* fault?' he said, swallowing hard.

'So it appears, sir,' said Jonathan sternly. 'You were the person who told Mr Wickens what had happened. He went charging off in search of Sir Julius Cheever.'

'How was I to know that Peter Wickens was party to this whole plot?'

'You acted too thoughtlessly.'

'I believed that he was a victim like me. Hell's teeth, man!' he exclaimed. 'Peter came here and showed me the letter he had received.'

'That was to throw us off the scent, Mr Redmayne. Did you never ask yourself why he came to you and not to one of his other friends?'

'No, Mr Bale.'

'It was because he wanted us to *know.* Realising that your brother was hunting for the blackmailers, he showed that letter to you because you were sure to mention it to your brother. Mr Wickens was never a true victim,' he went on. 'Miss Hemmings wrote that letter for him so that he could hide behind it.'

'Very effectively,' conceded Henry. 'I'm shocked to learn that Peter was behind the whole thing. We've shared such jolly times together.'

'There was nothing jolly about the way that Gabriel Cheever was murdered,' said Jonathan. 'Thanks to you, his father was almost killed as well.'

'Dear God!' said Henry, contrite for once. 'What did I do?'

'Your brother will call later, sir. He asked me to explain

what occurred yesterday. Mr Redmayne did call here last night but he was told that you were celebrating with friends.' He drew himself up. 'I think that those celebrations were premature.'

Henry nodded in agreement. 'I was too impulsive.'

'Think more clearly next time, sir.'

'I will.'

They were standing in the hall and Henry was feeling profoundly guilty. While he and his friends were carousing the previous night, Christopher was engaged in a desperate fight with Peter Wickens, having saved Sir Julius from certain death. The fact that he had unwittingly alerted Wickens made Henry squirm inwardly. He looked at his visitor.

'Did you find out the name of the assassin?' he asked.

'Reresby, sir,' said Jonathan. 'Caleb Reresby. A discharged soldier.'

'Who hired him? Peter or Celia Hemmings?'

'Mr Wickens. All three will stand trial together.'

'They deserve no less. They put me through an ordeal.' Sensing Jonathan's disapproval, he reined in his self-concern. 'Not that my woes compare with those of Gabriel's widow, of course,' he said, sounding a compassionate note. 'I am free to carry on as before while the Cheever family remains in mourning.'

'Yes, sir.'

Henry could see why his brother had sent Jonathan Bale to break the news to him. The constable was like a figure of doom. His presence was unnerving in a house that was an indictment of all the principles for which he stood. Christopher knew that his friend would make Henry feel at least partially remorseful. In asking Jonathan to visit his brother, Christopher had been playing a joke on him for a serious purpose. Henry was cowed and ashamed. It was only when his visitor was about to take his leave that he remembered something.

'Did Christopher say anything about a letter of mine?' he said anxiously.

'No, Mr Redmayne.'

'Ah.'

'Though he did take one away from the house in Covent Garden,' recalled Jonathan. 'I believe that it had something to do with you, sir.'

'It had *everything* to do with me!' said Henry under his breath. 'Where is it?'

'Your brother talked about returning it to the person to whom it belonged.'

'That would be cruel!' howled Henry.

'Discuss it with him when he comes, sir.' He opened the front door and bells were heard chiming nearby. 'You may not know this, Mr Redmayne,' he said, noting Henry's dazed expression, 'but it happens to be Sunday.'

Henry blinked in surprise. 'Is it really?'

'Church is the best place for repentance, sir. Goodbye.'

Work began on the new house a few days later. Christopher Redmayne's face was no longer quite so battle-scarred and the wound on Sir Julius Cheever's head was starting to heal. Wearing hats to conceal their injuries, both men were in Westminster to watch the foundations being dug under the vigilant gaze of Sidney Popejoy.

'At last!' declared Sir Julius with a smile of satisfaction.

'I'm sorry for the unfortunate delay,' said Christopher.

'It was not your fault, Mr Redmayne. But for you, there'd be no house at all. If Wickens had had his way, you'd now be attending my funeral.'

'I try to hang on to my clients.'

'This one is deeply grateful to you.' The old man's face clouded. 'I still don't understand why Wickens had to kill Gabriel. His hatred of me is easy to comprehend. In the heat of battle, I did shoot his brother, I can't deny that. But why did Wickens have to go after my son as well?'

'The answer is simple,' explained Christopher. 'He bore your name. It's ironic, Sir Julius. The one thing that Gabriel did not leave behind when he left home was the family name. He carried it with pride and it proved to be his downfall.'

'Yet he and Peter Wickens were friends for a time.'

'That was until you appeared on the scene yourself,' said Christopher. 'His friendship with Gabriel had already turned sour and the news of your imminent return to London only intensified the situation. When Sir Marcus Kemp mentioned that he'd seen Gabriel in Knightrider Street, Wickens was determined to kill him. And as we discovered,' he sighed, 'he had an accomplice to strengthen his resolve.'

'Miss Celia Hemmings.'

'Yes, Sir Julius. She had her own reasons to hate Gabriel,' he said, tactfully omitting any details of their earlier relationship. 'When she stumbled upon something of his that could be used for the purposes of blackmail, she and Peter Wickens joined forces against your son. They were a formidable team.'

'So were you and Mr Bale.' A spasm of pain shot through him. He gritted his teeth. 'In a sense, I'm to blame,' he said guiltily. 'My return to London prompted Gabriel's death. If I had not conceived the ambition to enter Parliament, my son might still be alive.'

Christopher shook his head. 'I think that unlikely. With enemies like Peter Wickens and Celia Hemmings, your son's life was always under threat. They went to great pains to track him down when he turned his back on them,' he pointed out. 'They were ruthless. They wanted revenge. Don't blame yourself, Sir Julius.'

'I'm bound to, Mr Redmayne.' He saw the builder approaching and brightened. 'Here comes Popejoy. You might have found me someone with a different name,' he said with a chuckle. 'Popejoy, indeed! Why saddle a confirmed Protestant like me with a builder called that? I take no joy from any Pope.'

'You'll find him an excellent man.'

'I'm sure.' He glanced across at the nearby coach. 'I need to speak to him alone, Mr Redmayne,' he said with a twinkle in his eye. 'This might be the moment for you to bid farewell to my daughter.'

Christopher needed no more encouragement. He hurried across to the coach. Susan had been watching them through the window but she now leant back in her seat. Christopher removed his hat to speak to her.

'I hope that you're not going to stand out there, Mr Redmayne,' she said.

'Well, no, I suppose not.'

'Step inside, sir. We're entitled to a little privacy.'

'Of course,' he said, getting into the coach. 'I was about to suggest that.' He sat opposite her and felt a surge of pleasure. 'I'll miss you,' he confessed.

'Will you?'

'Northamptonshire is such a long way away.'

'But that's not where I'm going, Mr Redmayne.'

'Oh?'

'Father is taking me to Richmond so that I can stay with my sister and her husband,' she announced. 'He'll then go back home on his own.' His delighted reaction made her giggle slightly. 'You seem pleased by the news.'

'I'm overwhelmed with joy,' said Christopher.

'I could hardly stay in the city,' she went on. 'Not now that Lucy has decided to go back to her mother. London holds too many bitter memories for her.'

'I know,' he said sadly. 'It was sensible of her to agree to the destruction of that diary. I had immense satisfaction from burning it. In the wrong hands, your brother's memoirs did untold damage.' He moved to the edge of his seat and searched her eyes. 'Why did you choose to go to Richmond?'

Susan gave a shrug. 'The thought of being stuck in the house with Father was not altogether enticing,' she explained. 'I elected to stay with Brilliana instead.'

'May I call on you there?'

'I'm relying on it, Mr Redmayne. I'll need some diversion.'

Christopher pulled a face. 'Is that all I am to you? A mere diversion?'

'What else are you?' she teased.

'I'll be happy to show you.'

He leant forward to kiss her on the cheek and she squeezed his arm fondly.

'I fancy that my sister and I will be doing a lot of shopping in London,' she said artlessly. 'Of course, there will be times when Brilliana will be too busy to accompany me. I may have to come here alone, Mr Redmayne.'

Christopher beamed. 'You'll have no cause to repent that decision,' he promised.

Their laughter sealed the bond.

The Restoration series

'Consummate story-telling, a love of period and astute
characterisation and plotting'
The Guardian

The young and ambitious architect Christopher Redmayne
is never short of work; following the Great Fire of London
a few years previously, much of the capital city is in need
of restoration or rebuilding, and Christopher is keen to
make his mark on London's developing landscape. But a
bustling city in latter half of the seventeenth century is a
hotbed of crime, and Christopher cannot stand by when
he witnesses an injustice. Along with his good friend the
Puritan constable Jonathan Bale and Christopher's dissolute
brother Henry, Christopher seeks to right wrongs and
provide justice for the victims. Searching for the truth whilst
rebuilding the pride of a city destroyed would be a taxing
task for any man, but it is one Christopher Redmayne is
happy to undertake.

The King's Evil
The Amorous Nightingale
The Repentant Rake
The Frost Fair
The Parliament House
The Painted Lady

The Railway Detective series

'A detective story with a difference ... a cracking cops-and-robbers tale with a dimension of crackling suspense'
Good Book Guide

London, 1850s. With the development of the railways comes a new breed of criminal, one who chooses train travel as the fastest means of escape, or who takes exception to the mounting interest in the engineering triumphs of the advancing rail network and attacks the cargo, carriages or – worse – the people on board. But to tackle these criminals there is a new type of policeman: the Railway Detective. The dapper Detective Inspector Robert Colbeck and his good friend Sergeant Victor Leeming are the front line against all crimes involving the railway. Travelling across the country, they witness firsthand the changes wrought by the progress of technology – and not all of it is for the good...

The Railway Detective
The Excursion Train
The Railway Viaduct
The Iron Horse
Murder on the Brighton Express
The Silver Locomotive Mystery
Railway to the Grave
Blood on the Line

The Captain Rawson series

Introducing Captain Daniel Rawson –
soldier, spy, charmer …

It is 1704 and Europe is at war. The dashing young captain is called upon to undertake many dangerous missions in the course of his duty, including leading his men into battle against the French enemy and travelling in disguise. He must succeed at all costs – the future of England is at stake. But no adventure is too big for Daniel, and as he and his soldiers march across the Continent, Daniel is delighted to find distraction in the various ladies he meets along the way…

'This author is at his best writing about amiable heroes and hissable villains having some good-humoured adventures in an entertaining plot.'
Historical Novels Review

Soldier of Fortune
Drums of War
Fire and Sword
Under Siege

a&b

WWW.ALLISONANDBUSBY.COM

For more information and to place an order, visit our website where you'll also find free tasters, exclusive discounts, competitions and giveaways. Be sure to sign up to our monthly newsletter to keep up-to-date on our latest releases, news and upcoming events.

Alternatively, call us on
020 7580 1080
to place your order.